Mavis Cheek was born and educated in Wimbledon and until recently lived her entire life in London. Now happily ensconced in the English countryside she is writing her eleventh novel. Her short stories and travel articles have appeared in various publications and her first book *Pause Between Acts* won the SHE/John Menzies First Novel Prize. The *Mail on Sunday* wrote on publication of her most recent novel *Mrs Fytton's* Country Life, 'Cheek's writing is infused with terrific comic energy and she possesses the wickedly sharp eye of a born satirist.'

D1321973

MAVIS CHEEK

Parlour Games

faber and faber

First published in 1989
by Bodley Head
This paperback edition first published in 2002
by Faber and Faber Limited
3 Queen Square London WC1N 3AU

Typeset by RefineCatch Limited, Bungay, Suffolk
Printed in England by Mackays of Chatham plc, Chatham, Kent

A CIP record for this book
is available from the British Library

ISBN 0–571–21512–2

2 4 6 8 10 9 7 5 3 1

For Audrey Watson, my tutor, who opened many doors

This they all with a joyful mind
Bear through life like a torch in flame,
And falling, fling to the host behind –
'Play up! Play up! and play the game!'

Henry Newbolt *Vitai Lampada*

PART ONE

Let us first begin with the place in which Celia lived, and the house within which Celia lived within the place.

Celia lived in a nice part of London called Chiswick and in an even nicer part of Chiswick called Bedford Park. In Bedford Park the residents are justified in shaking their heads over televised reports on inner-city decay and saying, 'Well, well – nothing like that ever happens here – surely the media has exaggerated it a little?' And so it must seem, for Bedford Park streets show no signs of negligence save for the passing nuisance of dog turds hidden in the thickly scattered blossom of spring or under the dry rustling leaves of autumn.

The same trees which decorate the pavements with their droppings from time to time bear plaques upon their proud trunks, announcing, 'This is a Neighbourhood Watch Area'. Prospective felons would do well to note this. The signs mean what they say. The men of Bedford Park are good at organising and the Neighbourhood Watch is no idle boast. Understandably, since there is much to protect. The scheme has been adopted with amicable consensus among the wide range of professions represented locally. Accountants, lawyers, and businessmen have structured the committee with interior designers, journalists, and even the esoteric fringe of painters and actors – not usually known for their ability to deal with the harsh realities of life – has rallied round to make the Watch work. The organisation has left the local police feeling slightly frayed by its zeal. In the first few weeks of its implementation they were besieged by calls from alert neighbours and, among many minor confusions, officers were called out to arrest a visiting granny in Priory Avenue and a slightly tipsy semi-retired judge who had, perfectly reasonably, decided to snooze it off in the back garden when he could not quite manage the front-door key. However, such things are comfortably excused as teething problems and the neighbours go on watching all the same. As a group the Bedford Parkers present, with some few exceptions, a liberal face to the world. They have a strong sense of community, a democratic Residents' Association and enough foreigners from EEC countries to make them feel cosmopolitan. Mid-life incomes are high as is professional attainment and serious financial difficulties are represented in the main by the complications of tax returns.

There are no garden gnomes in Bedford Park and while walking its streets you could be forgiven for thinking that no dark secrets abide behind its tasteful and well-maintained walls.

Bedford Park wives tend not to go out to work while their children are young. The few who do employ nannies or *au pairs* whose moderately punkish appearance and streetwise fashion give the pavements a pleasingly *avant garde* look as they wheel their charges around. Those wives who *do* have some kind of paid employment are generally tagged 'Consultants' or 'Freelance' which means they can stay at home when the nanny walks out or when the children *and* the *au pair* get mumps. Some form of domestic help is commonplace: Bedford Park wives (as should *all* wives, they agree) gave up their jobs to be mothers, not housewives. What is the point, in their economic situation, of wrestling with vacuum cleaners and Windolene when there are people crying out for jobs?

As a group these women are a good example of the scientific law that says there are no natural vacuums: whatever time they have, they fill. They are energetic, intelligent, articulate. They play tennis, go to the gym or attend pottery and foreign language classes. When they are not doing this they are in each other's houses drinking tea or wine while their pre-playgroup offspring socialise on their own level around their ankles. At the end of the day these women may justifiably say to their late-returning spouses that they, too, are tired; that they, too, have been on the go all day, and that – despite what their husbands

4

might think – there is no grape peeling and lying back on silken cushions for them either. On the whole they will not admit to enjoying life at home but since its only real justification in this liberated part of the world is because small children make any other choice impossible, some of these women will go on to have a third and a fourth child just to continue it. These additional offspring are generally called 'accidents'.

Bedford Park was designed in 1875 for private tenants of the wealthy classes to live in exemplary fashion in a perfectly planned environment. Norman Shaw, its revered and influential architect, would be proud of the long-term survival of his original tenets. He was a Good Man: intelligent, sensitive, second-wave Renaissance (or possibly it just took that long for England to catch up) and what he designed is as relevant today as it was in his time. A strictly structured suburb with strong, solid, no-frills houses; all the breadth and none of the clutter of Victorian bourgeois pomposity: firmly practical houses for a firmly practical future untarnished by overdecoration and indulgent excess. Houses that present a clean, family image. Respecting, respectable and cultivated. Tabloid newspapers are not taken in such homes.

And Celia lives in one of these.

It has a high, delicately railed wooden fence to its small front garden: a chunky, brick-piered front bay, a little overhanging balcony to the first floor and a nicely pitched roof under which the attics (now converted) sit comfortably. The dark ruddy brickwork makes a pleasant contrast against the white paint of the doors and windows and most of the neighbouring houses maintain this pattern of colour. Good taste abounds (or rather sits discreetly) around here.

Celia's road, like the rest, is tree-lined and well endowed with the second cars of the resident wives. These are small, nippy affairs recognisable by their internal disarray of toys and crisp packets and baby seats. It is a peculiar piece of inappropriateness that the first cars of the families, the husbands' cars, tend to be large, fast, rather status-conscious mobiles – usually of foreign origin – whereas the daily run of school, shopping, and jaunts to the swimming baths is crammed into little Metros or Pandas which you can sometimes see bouncing along with five or more children tucked inside. Volvos, BMWs and the larger-engined Peugeots are husband material and the wives say it is just as well because those monsters are so difficult to park. On the whole Bedford Park residents never buy Fords.

A few streets away from Celia's home is a small corner of shops where such items as avocado pears, kiwi fruit, Normandy pâté and taramasalata may be purchased without recourse to the supermarket which is driving distance away. This parade of interesting shops is very handy. Nowadays they are almost all run by Asians who are deferential, quick to understand what their customers require and remind the shopper of what it used to be like before British shopkeepers became so cavalier with service. The new owners are pleased to be offering their tartrazine-free goods and stone-ground bread in an area which is liberal enough to accept their origins without referring to their existence beyond the occasionally overheard, 'What would we do without them?' This is the general consensus. There is certainly no Paki-bashing in Bedford Park.

Behind Celia's house is a garden of about fifty by thirty feet. Since she has lived here for twelve years, and has a flair for that sort of thing, the garden is very pleasant. Its size and shape reflect all the other gardens surrounding it – Norman Shaw's plan was firmly mathematical – but Celia likes to think it has the stamp of originality, which it has, without destroying the harmonious uniformity of the designer's concept. Or upsetting the ever watchful Residents' Committee. Bedford Park holds within its perimeters the parameters of its being. It is a designated Conservation Area and only the trees, mature, defiantly rampant and protected from human attack, are permitted to break the skyline. One of these, a tall, majestic conifer, takes all the sun from Celia's garden by four o'clock in the afternoon, but she doesn't complain. What is the loss of sunlight compared to the benefits of living in a locale which cares so passionately for

Nature? She did complain when she first moved here – but then, she also voted for the Labour Party in those far-off days. Some things must change in order that others may stay as they are.

In her garden are shrubs, flower beds and a small, tasteful shed which is beautifully hidden by a Russian Vine. Large terracotta and blue and white pots (brought back from a Spanish holiday some years since and quite an innovation then though they have since been copied) are full of trailing lobelia, petunias, scented stocks and other summer delights, reflecting the romantic side of Celia's nature. There is a barbecue area, of course, and a small conservatory built on to the house in which both plants and children thrive on wet days when the pocket-handkerchief lawn is out of bounds. She used to enjoy propagating her own plants in here, tucking up the new seedlings into their compost beds, but now time doesn't allow it and each spring sees another trip to the local garden centre for re-stocking.

Even the washing line is in keeping. Norman Shaw's grand plan seems not to have taken account of washing days but Celia has overcome this by erecting a folding appliance, discreetly hidden by the morello cherry tree near the bottom of the garden, which becomes a pollard of wire and plastic when not in use. Its distance from the house is a nuisance when a sudden shower means wet feet in the haste of collecting in the washing but it is a small price to pay. Neighbours' gardens are similarly colourful and cared for but Celia has resisted the newest idea, prevalent in some, of setting a patch of wild garden to flourish within the domestic one. Followers of Bellamy and 'Gardeners' Question Time' hope to attract a little wildlife into their outdoor plots by letting dandelions and nettles and other such kidney grow free: they have spent a small fortune in purchasing wildflower mixtures from conservation-conscious seed producers and enriching the ground with organic manure so that these pieces of rampant nature may survive. On the whole these ecological paradises are sited at the bottom of the garden and are less seen than talked about at the various social gatherings that are a regular feature of Bedford Park Life.

Yes, the neighbourhood is pleasingly social. During the day there is lots of to-ing and fro-ing between the women, and at weekends there is the more formally organised socialising of drinks, barbecues and dinner parties. The wide range of professions represented in the neighbourhood makes these occasions varied and enjoyable: one does not have to look far for stimulating, entertaining company. An actor will sit down with a surgeon, a journalist with an opera singer, and all well within walking distance if the weather is fine. All that is necessary to conviviality is there within the tiny radius of Bedford Park. Normally Celia would scarcely need to look further when planning the guests for a dinner party. Despite her twelve years' domain the Bedford Park set is not exhausted – people come and people go but the mix remains much the same. But for tonight, since the occasion is a particular one, the mould will be broken. If we move away from the exterior of Celia's home and come inside we shall find that she is, at this very moment, on this sunny June morning, thraping away in her kitchen to prepare for just such a mould-breaking occasion.

There she stands among the well-planned units and the volcanic noise of both dishwasher and washing machine, effectively drowning out the phone-in on Radio Four which this week is devoted to healthy eating. But the noise level scarcely bothers her, for her mind is already immersed in thoughts of preparation. She is surrounded by equipment: food processor which will soon add its busy whine to the cacophony of its electrical companions, *bain-marie*, saucepans and her sharp French knives bought from the enticing kitchen shop in Covent Garden. The bowls and dishes that fill her work-surfaces come from the same source, which is one of her irresistible paradises: it works its magic on her as once, in far-off days, Biba's shop did, though now it is scarlet colanders rather than feather boas that she brings home.

And in amongst all this equipment, bursting and spilling over the kitchen like some lavish still-life, is food. Wonderful, fresh ingredients – coriander, basil, parsley – heaped in careless swathes; lemons nestling close to pink-fleshed salmon trout; summer fruits in scarlet and crimson cascades. And in the centre, place of honour, a perfectly symmetrical piece of veal, supplied by her local butcher after detailed consultation – for here in Bedford Park the exhortation to Consult Your Butcher has real meaning. Something low in cholesterol, she had said, and something low in cholesterol she got. Perhaps it is more expensive than buying from the supermarket, but then, the things that are good for you never come cheap. She surveys the other delectable comestibles, their rich textures and colours like some opulent Dutch painting: interesting salad ingredients – fennel, chicory, nasturtium flowers, the maroon-veined hearts of lettuces – lie heaped beside the tenderest snap beans imported from Kenya and the tiny, perfectly round potatoes from Egypt that look like little waxen marbles when cooked. Celia cracks one of the beans between her fingers and feels the snap of it with satisfaction. Finally there are the requisites for the puddings, of which she will make two: a raspberry sorbet (for which she is renowned) and a chocolate mousse with a wicked lacing of rum. This last, according to the cookery books, may be made well in advance and frozen but Celia will make them fresh for tonight as is her pleasure. The vacuum will always be filled.

So, here she stands – contemplating now – happy in her life and with no more to worry her than the scheduling of preparation. Pushing the flat of a French knife against her pursed lips as she makes her appraisal and asks herself the enjoyable question: where to begin? Probably, she considers, it would be best to cook the fish first so that it can cool properly before she skins and fillets it. The watercress can be sorted later. She pops it into a jug of water where it sits like a bloomless posy. She will deal with the first course first. Her brow clears and her lips cease to pucker on the blade. She swivels the dial to Radio One to get herself in the mood. Now she can start.

Celia is forty years old today. No, no, she smiles to herself, not quite. Not until one minute past midnight will she truly reach the prime of life. Until then, she smiles again, she is only

9

thirty-nine. Well, well, whatever the minutiae of it – forty or not – she is to be congratulated, for Celia is undoubtedly looking good. Very good indeed. She has put on some make-up and is wearing a shocking-pink jump suit in softly clinging velour that shows her figure to be more womanly than girlish nowadays, which is fair enough. Perhaps she has taken a little more trouble with her appearance this morning but she is never less than well turned-out. Dressing casually in Bedford Park is not a licence to slob. No stretched tee-shirts and greasy hair for these women-at-home. Birthday or not, Celia would never be embarrassed to open her door to a surprise visitor, though she sincerely hopes there will not be one of those today. She is looking forward to an undisturbed orgy of culinary activity broken only, half-way through the morning, by a coffee break with her cleaner, Mrs Green. That, she hopes, will be the only disturbance – and that, she thinks, is more than enough.

Mrs Green is currently hoovering away upstairs. It must be said that she is also casting her non-Bedford Park eye around Celia's bedroom in an effort to discover some hint of sexual activity there. She did once: a condom (in the days before such things entered either the polite vocabulary or vagina) with attachments, stuffed under a pillow, called Dirty Harry by its manufacturers though Mrs Green, of course, did not know that. Ever since this exciting find Mrs Green has been keen to know more, feeling in a mysterious way that such discoveries give her ascendancy over her employer. At fifty-nine Mrs Green still has to make do with the launderette and Celia's home is a veritable Aladdin's Cave of consumer durables: it eases the disparity to have discovered the human frailty of Dirty Harry. So far, today, she has found nothing. She hoovers on, looking forward to the coffee break when they sit together, sipping their drinks, making what conversation they can. Mrs Green knows that Celia would prefer to leaf through a magazine during this hiatus, which makes the coffee break an even sweeter occasion for her.

Celia sings the chorus of the current number-one hit as she sets about the fishkettle. The song has been reverberating in her

10

head since yesterday's visit to the hairdresser whose salon is next to the Pakistani delicatessen. Adrian makes no concession to age in his business: tapes of Queen, U2, and Sting pound the walls and buzz around the hairdryers. His own hair is lime-green and spiky and he speaks with a peculiarly camp lisp though, as he winks into the mirror at his female clients, there is nothing unisex about him. He knows his clientéle and constantly produces *avant garde* ideas for his ladies: for the gentlemen he is more circumspect since many of them must go among the unenlightened of the business world. It is thanks to Adrian that Celia is today wearing a peacock-blue highlight in her dark hair. As her reflection in the chrome bowl of her food processor tells her, it has done exactly what he said it would and enhances the green of her eyes. She wears modest make-up: a little eye-shadow, a little mascara, and on her pale skin, which is creamy rather than washed-out, she has put a hint of blusher to enhance her cheekbones, which are, as *Vogue* might say, good. Some of her lipstick has adhered to the blade of the knife but there is enough left to define a generous, shapely mouth. Birthday bravado has placed a pink bow in her hair, which looks very dashing and matches exactly the pink of her jump suit. Only such as Mrs Green would find this undignified. Mutton dressed as lamb is not a phrase much used in this neighbour-hood, where crow's feet are laughter lines and the ills that flesh is heir to are not readily entertained. Besides, most of Celia's contemporaries dress with similar youthful vigour.

In Victorian times, indeed, when this very house was built, there was no such thing as puberty. One day, if female, you were a little girl – tea in the nursery and trotted out for parental appraisal just before bedtime – and then, suddenly, the next your hair was put up, your skirts were let down and bingo (or should it be mah-jongg?) you were a young lady. Similarly nowadays in Bedford Park there is no such thing as middle age. You are still a young woman shopping in trendy shops until suddenly, one day, you have a fall in Chelsea Girl and need a hip operation. Youth to old age in one move.

The few women of Celia's acquaintance who do not fit into this pattern are usually of the green wellie brigade and go hacking off to their country cottages at weekends. On the whole Celia tends to be on nodding terms only with them, finding their manners and their minds too rigid for her taste. She prefers the more free and easy variety of Bedford Park wife, such as her best neighbourhood friend Hazel.

Celia met Hazel at somebody's drinks party ten years ago. They were both just pregnant and sat side by side on a settee with a peanut-sized progeny in their respective wombs and glasses of orange juice in their hands. Celia cast a covert look at Hazel and saw a large-boned, fair-haired woman with the fresh complexion often associated with well-bred girls from the Home Counties. The sort of woman whom Celia would normally have avoided. But circumstances change attitudes. Celia also recognised, from the slightly drooping mouth and watery eyes, that this was someone who, like herself, was not feeling too good. So she spoke. And so bound up in her newly discovered state of fertilisation was she that her first words were, 'Hallo, I'm pregnant,' instead of, 'Hallo, I'm Celia.'

This had caused the two of them much queasy laughter, the amusement continuing when they discovered that their *accouchements* were to be within days of each other.

'That means,' Celia had said, 'that we were both At It somewhere in Bedford Park at about the same time . . .'

'I don't think I shall ever feel like doing it again . . .' Hazel said. '. . . Do you?'

Their close friendship, forged and bonded by the uncharted waters of new experience, has stayed supreme. And though others have joined the coterie since, there is no one quite as close to Celia and Hazel as they are to each other. From each other these two have no secrets. They talk about their anxieties regarding their children, they discuss their bodies freely, and in exceptional circumstances they will speak about the emotional hummocks that occur between man and wife in any Bedford Park family. Such exchanges are very therapeutic and help maintain the balance nicely. On the whole they do not talk about their lives Before Children, which are less secrets than irrelevancies and another country to them now. They very seldom talk about BC – for it has little relevancy to their daily lives. Occasionally there is a fusion of the past and the present but it is seldom intimate. Pre-Bedford Park life is an island somewhere offshore. Celia and her neighbours are all settled on the mainland which is a far more sedate community.

But tonight, because it is Celia's very special fortieth-birthday dinner, she has decided to mix it a little. She has invited six guests in all, a small number by Bedford Park standards. Usually Celia is a gregarious creature but on this most intimate and personal of shibboleths she has decided to spend it simply, with those three couples who know her best and who straddle the old and the new of her life. This then is what Celia prepares for. A celebration of her past and her present. Forty years down and another forty to go. She has no role to play tonight, she has merely to be herself. She can, metaphorically, put her feet up. She can relax. She has to prove nothing to these guests who all know her so well. Even – and perish the thought – the food can go wrong and it will not matter. She is safe in the bosom of their knowing her, rather as Cromwell would have liked it, with warts and all. Not that there are many warts on this cheerful, untroubled woman, but the few there are need not be disguised. It is a very happy thought.

Now the air is redolent of gently steaming fish. The kitchen suddenly, miraculously, becomes silent as both machines in perfect accord finish their cycles. Celia turns towards the eggs and the beater and the good-quality Lucca oil (first pressing, cold) and begins. She is in a state close to rapture for not only is she cooking (which she loves) but the Golden Oldie slot on Radio One is playing Hits from a year familiar to her youth. She would not tell Adrian but sometimes she wishes he would play a few of these as well as current bands. Probably, she thinks, the other wives who use his salon wish the same – but like Celia they never say anything either. Adrian can make you feel very old if you speak out of line. It is a sign of a splendidly misspent youth that she knows all the words to the songs: Beatles, Stones, Manfred Mann – how wonderful it was to be alive then.

She lets the oil trickle into the bowl of yolks slowly, singing away as she does so. And how good it is to be alive now. She can honestly say that she is perfectly happy and content with the way her life is moving on. She will be able to say this tonight, wholeheartedly and unashamedly. She will be able to say to her guests that in her own way, and not to make too much of it, she has been blessed in the past forty years, and that she expects to be blessed just the same in the next.

As she meticulously completes the beating process, unhurriedly – for none but a careless cook would rush mayonnaise – Celia savours a warm rush of pleasure and an incontrovertible sense of being at one with humanity. She thinks about her guests. Her elder sister Isabel, naturally, with her husband Dave. Her oldest friend from schooldays, Susannah, and her husband Tom. And, of course, Hazel and John. What a very good mixture that will be. Oh yes, oh yes. Life is good. Even Mrs Green, stooping and sniffing about her business of emptying first the washing machine and then the dishwasher, cannot deflate the warm bubble of happiness that surrounds Celia as she makes her preparations and thinks her pleasing thoughts. No, not even Mrs Green can dispel all *that*.

'A beautiful drying day,' says Celia.

Mrs Green pulls her porridge-coloured cardigan around her thin shoulders as comment, and goes out into the garden.

It is good that it is a beautiful drying day, since Celia does not want washing hanging around tonight. She has learned in her forty years (nearly, nearly) to bless the little joys as well as the big ones in her life. To seek for silver linings. For out of small things, big things grow. Do they not?

She begins the final sensual trickling of best-quality Lucca into the bowl of yolks.

Mrs Green comes in.

'Hazel is having the children for tea today, Mrs Green. Isn't that nice of her?'

'Indeed.' The lady sniffs. 'You'd have thought she'd have enough to do looking after her own.'

'That's just what I said,' says Celia happily.

Mrs Green sniffs again, remembering that she had two children and none of this in and out of each other's houses nonsense. She forgets that her mother lived in the same street. She begins to remove what seems to her an outrageous amount of cutlery from the machine.

'Do you want this in the dining room?' she asks grimly.

'No thanks. You can put it away. We'll be using the posh stuff tonight.' Reluctantly Celia lets the warm bubble disperse. Mrs Green's sniffing has reached orchestral proportions. 'Have you got a cold?'

'No,' says the lady, dropping each piece into its appropriate slot in the cutlery drawer, counting it under her breath, wishing as she does so that she *had* found some intimate appliance upstairs. Nobody should have this much cutlery.

Percussion over and drawer closed as noisily as its well-made John Lewis runners will permit, Mrs Green says, 'I'll put the kettle on, shall I?'

Celia indicates the mayonnaise which is nearly done, and says, as usual, 'No, no. You go and sit down. I'll do that.' She moves the dish of albumen out of the way and as she does so she smirks, for the thought has come to her, out of nowhere really, that a bowl of raw egg-white looks rather like a giant puddle of semen. Her cleaner would have a fit if she could know the thought, she thinks. Quite right. Mrs Green would love to squirrel away that dirty notion. She has counted over fifty pieces of cutlery. No wonder we lost our powers of ESP at around the same time we lost the use of our appendix or Celia would be much disturbed by her cleaner's thoughts. Nature is a sensible matron – sometimes.

'Good old Hazel,' she says out loud. 'It really is the best of birthday presents: a whole day to myself. Not that I don't love my children, Mrs Green – but it's so nice to be free of them once in a while and to do something purely for me . . .'

Sniff, sniff.

Children – ah yes. In Bedford Park there are quite a lot of these. It is a wonderful area for bringing up a family. There are plenty of parks and open spaces in which they can mix with their peers. The primary schools are excellent as befits the institutions of a Conservation Area: people used to fighting for their environment make a strong lobby in other matters. Here the teachers are keen, the children motivated and bright (a few have 'learning problems', but are fortunately never designated 'thick'). The premises are well-kept and any short-fall in resources is soon made up by the tireless fundraising of the Parents' Association. Indeed, it has done this so well over the years that the local authority relies on it now and relevant governmental departments have been heard to say that if this little corner of London can do it for their schools why cannot other little corners like Tooting and Tower Hamlets? 'Well, well, nothing like that ever happens here . . .' may be extended to the national problems of state education. In Bedford Park only a snob would send their child to a private primary school: in Bedford Park the state system is a success and Celia's and Hazel's children use it. Well – while they are younger, anyway . . .

Henry is nine, Rebecca is six. These are Celia's. Hazel has two, also, of the same age but of opposing sexes. Verity and Caspar. On the whole they are good children except that Rebecca, being bright (rather than difficult) tends not to sleep much at night – and Hazel's Caspar still fouls his pants. They both agree that their respective children will grow out of these traits – after all, Rebecca is a sensible child, and as for Caspar, well, no one has yet met a racing driver who cannot control his bowels and that is what Caspar wants to be. He may well achieve this for he already walks upon opportunity's carpet as a Bedford Park boy.

Unfortunately, this cohesive similarity in their children will soon be at an end. For while the primary schools are excellent, the state secondary education simply will not do. And since the two women have not matched up the sexes of their offspring (or rather, as they ruefully riposte, their husbands did not for it is, of course, the male who determines gender) these happy days of swapping around and sharing school runs must terminate. Older children are educated privately and the girls are separated from the boys. Celia's Henry will begin this expensive business next year. This has not been an easy decision for her. Indeed, in truth, it was not her decision at all for it was taken by her husband, Alex, to whom it was scarcely a matter for conjecture. It was the natural way. If Celia had the faintest sense of conscience, the residue, perhaps, from her Labour Party days, Alex had none. To him it was merely the way of things and his decision as both father and husband. Private secondary education is quite normal in Bedford Park and Celia accepts this. On the whole she tends to accept most of the local tenets and, largely, agrees more and more with Alex's point of view. As her husband says, if they can afford it why shouldn't they have it?

Well, *quite.*

Ah, yes – husbands. In this house in Bedford Park in which Celia is even now listening for the kettle to boil, there dwells one of these. Alex. Well, just at this particular moment, of course, he does not dwell there because he is somewhere else doing his job. In fact, what with coming back at eight or eight-thirty, often being away for two nights in the week and accounting for seven hours' sleep a night, Alex spends only about sixty waking hours in his home in each seven days. Not surprising then that he and Celia have a good marriage. On the whole you are either striving to maintain a good one, endeavouring to reclaim a bad one, or going for gold, hereabouts. Marriage is very much In and sanctified. And husbands tend to be rational and reasonable, as Alex is.

He is a nice man. He has thinning, sandy-coloured hair, pale-blue eyes, a tall, spare body with a little paunch which, at forty-three, is not surprising. He is a business lawyer and has done very well out of the Big Bang. He works hard and enjoys his job and votes Liberal as he always did. This sets him apart from many of his colleagues but still, he doesn't mind, he is brilliant enough to carry the eccentricity – rather enjoys it – and anyway, that is where his social conscience lies. He may live like a Tory, he says, but that does not mean he has to vote like one. Both he and Celia agree that they are lucky to have what they have and that it is not, necessarily, the fault of the deprived that they are deprived. The diplomacy of his job spills over into his private life. Alex appears to get on well with everyone – it is only to his wife that he speaks the truth. This makes life much easier for Celia and Hazel since he and John rub along together very well. John is a designer, partner in a firm of building developers, and a hail-fellow-well-met jolly type; Alex is more introverted but on the common ground of their wives' relationship they do well enough. It would be awful, the women agree, if they did not. Alex does respect John's skills (applied art is good art) and his professionalism. This latter counts for much. Professionalism makes the world run smoothly, emotionalism merely clogs the wheels.

When Celia and Alex were planning the various restructurings of their home (the few allowed under the conservationist's charter) very wisely they did not consult John professionally. The heads that rolled afterwards in the usual disappointed aftermath of design and building did not include John's. He could only commiserate with them when the second bathroom's plumbing proved faulty and the handmade windows for the back extension were half an inch out all round and the slope on the patio at the back caused a small flood indoors during the first thunderstorm after completion.

Alex, being a professional man, understands other professional men. He would not dream of asking John casually about anything to do with the design of his house, just as John would never dream of asking Alex anything about business law in a casual manner. It would be like asking the butcher for a free sausage or requesting an extra dollop of ice cream without paying for it. In less salubrious neighbourhoods this is practised

– it is known as the black economy – but here it is certainly not embraced by Alex or John or their likes. They have no need of it.

Sometimes Celia gets a bit cross with Alex over this. Once, when a friend of hers wanted to know what the difference between employment and consultancy meant in broad terms (she had just been offered the latter by a publisher and as her children were older than Celia's she thought she might be able to fit such work in), Celia had asked Alex on her behalf. 'It would only take two sentences,' Celia said lightly to her husband. But no. Two sentences, one free sausage. It is all the same. This caused, however, no friction with the friend who was married to an osteopath. After all, she had said, her husband never did soft-tissue on a Bedford Park jogger for nothing and she understood Alex's point of view. The friend went on to take up the consultancy work anyway which paid for the part-time nanny, weekends away, children's music lessons and better quality soft furnishings, so she was quite happy.

And Celia's embarrassment over Alex soon faded into no more than a fleeting envy for her friend's new activity. But she counselled herself that there were years and years ahead before the children would be old enough for her to find time on her hands. She need not envy the little extras that the money bought, since she and Alex were quite comfortable. She vaguely envied her friend's independent earning capacity and rather hated her, briefly, when she came round all flushed for a cup of tea and flapping a cheque for three hundred and fifty pounds made out to her and her alone – but that was all. And that soon died in Celia when she thought what she could do, given the current circumstances, which was very little. For she had no intention of going back to being a high-titled, low-esteemed dogsbody in a Bond Street art gallery, which was what she had done before the marriage and the children. Try making that seem important, she had said grimly to the mincing attachment of her Mouli as soon after this she made the children's shepherd's pie, when you've negotiated the minefield of marriage, the rearing of offspring, and the total coordination of people's lives. Getting the year of a painting on a catalogue wrong would be a gnat bite after that.

But still, on sullen February mornings, Celia has been known to feel herself approaching the black pit of uselessness, which is generally wiped away by organising lunch for five under-threes and their mothers. Coordinating something like that soon makes you feel a power house again. Besides, on days like today Celia can be very easily put off the worry of the Future. Her friend doing the consultancy work might be earning, but she could never stand in her kitchen on her fortieth birthday, as Celia now does, and plan a whole day of cutting radishes prettily into roses, making mayonnaise or crushing these delectable raspberries. She has earned her right to these homebound enjoyments for she is a good mother and a faithful, supportive wife. It would be puritanical sour grapes to suggest anything else.

Alex's father died over twenty years ago and his mother lives down on the South Coast in a distinguished little development of bungalows where she plays bridge, gardens fussily, and boasts about her grandchildren. When they married, Celia and Alex inherited all the furniture that had been put in store after the bungalow move and so their house is a comfortable mixture of good-quality Edwardian furniture and their own purchases from Heals, Peter Jones and the like. The dining room, dim and shaded, contains an ornately carved chiffonier and a ponderously solid mahogany table with matching chairs upholstered in a Regency stripe. If Celia once rebelled about this inheritance she does so no longer – rather like the sun-consuming conifer she has grown used to it – and, in truth, she rather likes the old-fashioned stuff nowadays. She did manage to lose the postwar G-plan items; no amount of goodwill could make her live with those. In the large living area at the back of the house and off which the kitchen leads, there is more of a jumble: a buffeted pair of Edwardian chaise-longues; another even bigger heavy carved table whose surface shows a history of children painting, hot coffee cups and Ribena; and a long hide covered pre-war Heals settee, much scuffed. To these they have added their collection of Tate Gallery prints – Hockney, Jim Dine, Allen Jones – and some contemporary teak and pine cabinets. Celia likes the effect of such a mixture and feels that her home has a bit more style about it than those of some of her more interior-design-conscious friends. Mrs Green, on the other hand, cannot understand why these people, who will spend a fortune on electrical items and second bathrooms, will not bother to get in some nice new furniture. In Mrs Green's opinion that hide settee is ready for the dump, and she no longer bothers to polish the table top. It is this kind of attitude which Mrs Green cannot make head nor tail of. Two sets of cutlery and a scuffed old settee: it doesn't make sense.

The only room that Mrs Green approves of is the front room, which is all light and bright and Swedish wood and fabrics, with a rug on its polished floor that comes up to your ankles. If Mrs Green only knew what had taken place upon that rug from time to time then she need make her prurient bedroom investigations no more. As a fly on the wall (heaven preserve Celia and Alex) she would, undoubtedly, have been so sated that their cutlery drawers could overflow with the best-quality Sheffield and it would no longer matter. For this room is the parental sanctuary. This room contains the adult's television, the video, the hi-fi, the John Makepeace occasional table, the precious things, and it is out of bounds to the children. This is where sometimes, after the guests have gone and the French carriage clock strikes one a.m., Celia and Alex might put aside their brandy glasses, slide on to the rug and make love in the lamplight with the dark silence of Bedford Park streets shut out by the Swedish cotton curtains.

There has been some altercation between them about this, since the last time that Alex put aside his brandy glass, threw off his Jaegar jacket and slid his eager body to the floor, Celia declined to follow suit, on the grounds that Dirty Harry had rubbed a sore spot on her labia – what they call between them her honeypot – and she did not feel up to it. Alex clearly did and had gone very noisily to fill the dishwasher after that and was not only seen to be but, if the cracked crystal glass and the sound of dropping cutlery was anything to go by, was heard to be extremely put out about this. A very strongly sexed man, Alex, and growing even keener in his forties. And he liked Celia to be keen too – though not, of course, as keen as he. Before they were married he welcomed her overt responses which matched (and, unless she was careful, surpassed) his. After marriage and children he expected her to settle down sexually, which she did, finding the idea of wild romps far too energetic, especially with the wakeful Rebecca around. Sex became for her a way of relaxing, a healing piece of therapy through love – to be savoured gently and slowly – and sometimes it happened that way spontaneously. But in the main Alex was a gutsy lover, a hurdling humper, and it would have done his ego no good at all if Celia told him that she found the best sex was when it sent her peacefully off to sleep. He enjoyed the idea of being sexually tireless and privately thought that it was this that gave him his edge in professional matters. Supremely confident in the bedroom, Alex is also supremely confident everywhere else. Torn between the desire for his wife to be sexually rampant and yet seemly, he has opted for the latter as desirable. The mother of his children should need to be encouraged towards excess. Celia understands this and she lets him encourage her. Her relaxed and passive approach to their coitus is both irritating and proper. He treats her like some half-shy flower, with the rider that she should make the first move occasionally. Inside it makes her giggle as she goes through this performance for him and watches the pleased look of the master light up his face as she smiles at him provocatively. There is no doubt in Celia's mind that their sex life is quite satisfactory, though in the years immediately after *his* fortieth birthday Alex's requirement seemed to increase: almost, Celia thinks, as if he had something to prove. It was during this phase that the condom thing was introduced. But this has settled down again just recently, which is not surprising. Alex works very, very hard nowadays. This is the time in a man's life when his career is peaking (there are

22

enough role-models around in Bedford Park for her to recognise this) and she is not unduly worried about the change in his conjugal habits. With a little provocation she can soon turn him on again. And she will.

Well, anyway – none of this signifies tonight. Dirty Harry is tucked well to the back of her knickers and Tampax drawer, out of sight and memory of Alex, she hopes, and – though Celia knows nothing of it – much to Mrs Green's chagrin. Her honeypot is in good order and there is absolutely no danger of her period suddenly arriving. Not like recently when they took a naughty Easter weekend in Boulogne and the little beast manifested itself as soon as their feet touched foreign soil. The cramps had been so acute that she actually snarled at Alex when he suggested that despite her little problem they might circumvent penetration and go for external delights.

No, no. Tonight would be a good one in all the departments of her life. She scoops a little of the mayonnaise on to her finger and tastes it: absolutely perfect – she knew it would be. It might take effort but it is worth it. Celia could never give in to Isabel's trick of using shop-bought stuff. Well may Isabel perch her plump bottom on Celia's table and wag her finger at her and say that nobody could really tell the difference, and if they could, well, so what? Life was about more important things, wasn't it, like *job satisfaction?* (With that penetrating look that always attended Isabel's broaching the subject . . .) Celia forbore – again – to say, 'exactly – and this is my job,' as it did not seem diplomatic. Anyway, *her* guests on *her* birthday would be served the genuine article. Besides, no one in Bedford Park serves even the best-quality manufactured mayonnaise. But of course Isabel lives in Surbiton, which might be less than half an hour's drive away but is light years away in style. They certainly do things differently there.

The last time she and Alex had gone to Isabel's for dinner, they had been strolling around the garden with their beer or wine (the only drinks on offer) and dodging in and out of climbing frames, swings and other boyish detritus (Surbiton gardens, having been constructed without the benign precision of Bedford Park, were large enough both for strolling and for providing space for such child-orientated equipment) when Celia's brother-in-law, Dave, came bounding through the french doors of what was both the dining room and his office, in hot pursuit of their dog. Looking both agonised and amused at the same time he declared that Brillo, their mongrel bitch, had removed (chuckle, chuckle) a chunk of pâté from one of the plates. An anxious Isabel had rushed back indoors to deal with the disaster while Celia had felt helpless and sorry for her. The other pair of Surbitonites strolling with them had just found the whole thing funny and said that their dog did that sort of thing all the time.

'Don't worry,' said Isabel, returning much restored and apparently quite unflustered. 'I had a spare tin anyway. And I've washed the plates. Naughty Brillo. Down girl, down!'

And as if pâté out of a tin was not bad enough, the next course contained shop-bought mayonnaise with the potato salad. Celia saw that Alex had also noticed this by the very faint wrinkling of his nose. Later his full-blown compliments to the cook were edged with an irony that only she could perceive. Her sister simply took the compliments as her due. She was, Celia had to say it, a remarkably insensitive woman.

Isabel was five years older than Celia. Dark also, and pretty, but with a lot of grey in her hair now which she neither disguised with a simple tint, nor with blonde streaks such as Celia thought would look best. Certainly she would never play around with peacock-blue highlights. Once Celia had bought her sister a surprise birthday treat of a trip to Adrian's salon for a cut 'n' colour. Isabel came back looking much the same, having refused more than a trim, and to Celia's mild reproof that she should have entered into the spirit of the thing, had said that, frankly, she found the present a bit of an imposition, which put Celia firmly back into the silly younger sister state all over again. Adrian said that the criticism was pretty thick since Isabel had insisted he turned his music down while she was there. He had not done so, of course. One of the few who had ever stood up to Isabel and won. Isabel's husband never did, but he was a happy-go-lucky soul – a sociology student from Essex turned plumber – and one who did help his neighbours out professionally without charging them. He also voted Labour – a hangover from his Essex days when he had been in the forefront of the sit-ins and the walk-outs – and was the nearest thing to a liberated male that Celia came close to. She liked him and felt in sympathy with his subordinate marital role. Isabel was more than a match for both of them, so neither of them took her on. Alex found Dave's simple integrity annoying, feeling that no one with any brains could really still vote Labour in this day and age. Dave just smiled if Alex attempted to provoke him, and sipped his beer and said 'each to his own' or similar. Isabel had never been interested in politics, though she voted Liberal and spoke sardonically about supporters of any other party. She deprecated herself for reading the *Daily Mail*, but continued to read it, and told Celia in no uncertain terms that she, too, should read a newspaper of some sort if she was not going to stagnate as a housewife.

'I'm a mother,' Celia had, for the umpteenth time, risked replying. 'I didn't stop work to be a housewife.'

'Well – you spend enough time being one,' her sister countered, curling her lip.

It was only afterwards that Celia thought she should have said that you couldn't, really, consider the *Daily Mail* a newspaper.

So often in exchanges with her sister she found it was only after the event that she found the words to hit back. They were forever locked into the superior/inferior sibling game. Isabel would have to be peeled off the ceiling if Celia tried to criticise her. Life was easier if she conformed to what the past forty years had made law between them. Fleetingly she wondered why on earth she had invited them tonight, but the answer was simple. They were family, bonded deeper than any despite such things. How could Celia celebrate this special birthday without her sister at her side?

She would place Dave next to Hazel to whom all politics were irrelevant and have him well away from Alex, who always found it difficult not to bait him. Isabel could also sit next to Alex: he would be prepared to resist mentioning the *Daily Mail*, just as he had resisted refusing the tinned pâté, because Isabel did, at least, vote Liberal, which showed some degree of good sense. Also, since Isabel was a deputy headmistress (state secondary) Alex held her in some esteem intellectually. That was something solved anyway.

Popping a sprig of tarragon into the bowl, Celia covers it with cling-film and puts it in the refrigerator. No one, she thinks, will guess what the subtle flavour permeating the mayonnaise is, and I will have to tell them. It is my own invention and I am proud of the idea. So says Celia to herself, letting the happily satisfactory thought remove the somewhat sour mental taste left to her after considering the best way to deal with the vagaries of personality she would surround herself with tonight. And then a sniff at her shoulder, coupled with the chink of two empty mugs at her elbow, brings her back to the present and the duty of the coffee break with Mrs Green.

A curious ritual this, in which her cleaner seats herself at the heavy carved table within view of the kitchen while Celia prepares the drinks and carries them in. Quite how this role reversal came about is a mystery but it serves to satisfy Mrs Green's honour in some obscure way and to salve any wisps of conscience that Celia might feel at employing someone old enough to be her mother to do her dirty work.

Sighing, since she would have loved to start on the veal, she begins the ceremony – filling the Bedford Park mug for herself, and the thin china with pink roses for Mrs Green. She makes instant coffee. Personally she hates the stuff but Mrs Green cannot abide 'that ground muck' so Celia buys Nescafé especially for these occasions. Normally she only uses coffee beans and – fairly unusual even by Bedford Park standards – she will not tolerate tea bags either. This, like the individualism of her furniture, gives Celia an extra-special style. She likes that. So does Alex. Whenever, for any reason, he finds the jar of instant in the kitchen cupboard, he picks it up as squeamishly as if it were a live toad and sets it down, pursing his lips as if to say it lowers the tone. Celia doesn't mind this. We all have our quirks, she thinks. Hers, she knows, is lavatory paper. There is nothing so vulgar as the coloured variety – except perhaps the coloured *and* patterned type. Celia always buys white. Mrs Green considers that this lacks imagination.

She is just about to turn off the radio when she recognises a record by Manfred Mann – a hit when she first went out with Alex. Manfred Mann. Such a distinguished, *university* kind of group it had been after all those raw Liverpudlians. Who had said that? Alex or her? She couldn't remember now. But she could remember red lightbulbs and a room full of students swaying in the smoky atmosphere. His fellow students, that enviable breed on grants while she was already a working girl. She has that fleeting sense of loss that always comes when nostalgia prods. Where has all that hope and zest and innocence gone? Innocence? She smirks as she stirs in the milk. Innocence? Hardly. And yet it had been in a way. She had walked through her teens, full-bloodedly open to sex, an apple-fancier abroad in an orchard, a happy scrumper. Privately she always thought this was why she found monogamy so easy now, for she had certainly eaten her fill in those few years pre-Alex. Not that she ever told him that – she wasn't ashamed of it but she thought he would probably be ashamed of it on her behalf. He was very moral, really, was Alex. It hadn't been long before he had guided her out of that heedless world of the young Labour movement (which pinched wholesale from the Young Communist League so far as free love was concerned) and into the more thinking realms of his own beliefs. First had come the Proms, to take the place of pop music. She had loved that. Beethoven's Seventh in the Albert Hall had taken her breath away: he said that it would. And later, their first holiday together had been in the Soviet Union, which trip compounded all his views on the errors inherent in communism and had left her without a leg to stand on so far as her own commitment to socialism was concerned. To her weak suggestion that the British Road to Socialism, courtesy of Palme Dutt, was what she upheld and was altogether of a different kidney, he had merely come out with a string of loving ridicule in that monstrously chandeliered hotel room in Leningrad, and squeezed her breasts, and called her his little red. And that, in the end, was that.

'Doo Wha Diddy Diddy Dum Diddy Doo –' (could it really have been considered more arcane than Freddy and the Dreamers?) she hums, and takes the coffee to the waiting Mrs Green whose nasal excitement increases alarmingly as she draws near. Oh well, she thinks, I have the whole day ahead in which to do my cookery, I can spare these few minutes with her now.

'Thanks,' says Mrs Green with a nod of her head which would not disgrace a duchess.

She takes a box of matches and a packet of cigarettes out of her cardigan pocket and, having shaken them like a conjuror might, sets them down on the table. Celia steels herself. She gave up two weeks ago, much against her will since she only smoked one or two in a day, or perhaps more than that at parties. She never smoked in front of the children and it always caused her endless agony if Rebecca suddenly came into the room at eleven o'clock at night just as she was taking a light from someone at the table. Once she had actually burnt someone's knee in her effort to hide the offending item. On the whole it is easier to have done with the thing, though it seems unfair to give up such a sporadic and adult pleasure. Mrs Green knows all about this so she savours every single suck after lighting up, prolonging the procedure and letting the smoke out with excessive rapture: she'd give her two full sets of cutlery all right.

She blows smoke around ecstatically before saying, 'Get any nice presents?' Such a question is like rubbing salt into a raw wound.

'I got a new car from Alex,' says Celia, watching the smoke curl upwards, more interested in this than the subject.

'Another one?'

'He traded in the Renault. It *was* six years old . . .'

Mrs Green takes an enormous gulp of smoke and puffs it around as if trying to exterminate Celia.

'Course *we've* never had a car. Never been able to afford one. Not that I can drive anyway –' Her tone implies that the next stop for women who can is whoredom.

'But of course you could learn. It is such a liberation. A real freedom. Go where you please. Leave when you like . . .' Too late, Celia realises the fatuity of this. Liberation never got anywhere near the Mrs Greens of this world. Nor ever would, it seemed. They didn't want it and it wasn't being offered. The perfect stalemate of immovable objects. 'Perhaps a bicycle?' says Celia faintly, hating herself for even further stupidity.

'Not with my legs, dear,' says Mrs Green with satisfaction.

At least she has her legs, thinks Celia, for these are a great solace to the lady who uses them as a decisive factor in any losing argument.

'Of course not . . .'

There is a pause as Mrs Green smokes on.

Suddenly Celia begins, 'Mrs Green – would you mind if I asked you for a –' Her eyes are already on the cigarette packet, her mouth dry with longing. Mrs Green knows this and triumph lights her pale eyes. And then – like a miracle – the telephone rings. Celia experiences a religious moment of gratitude as she leaps up to answer it. Mrs Green experiences quite the reverse. Twice blessed, Celia considers herself, for she has not only avoided temptation but she has also got a reason for leaving the table and her cleaner's mordant conversation with honour.

'Celia?'

'Susie! Oh, I'm so glad you've rung.' This is perhaps just a little too fervent, if perfectly truthful.

'Are you all right?' Susannah sounds understandably surprised at this dramatic warmth. After all, the two of them spoke on the telephone only a few days ago.

'Yes, of course.' Celia's voice resumes normalcy. 'You are coming tonight? We've got your bedroom ready . . .'

Mrs Green sniffs. 'We' indeed. Puff, puff.

'Of course we're coming – but the thing is we don't need to stay. I've been telling Tom for ages that he ought to get a base in London and now he has – he's joined a Club – so we'll put up there . . . You don't mind? It'll save you all the bother what with seeing to the children and everything . . . All right?'

Celia understands perfectly. The last time they came up from Wiltshire and stayed had been something of a revelation to Celia. As if both the audience and the cast, she had seen her own household at its early-morning activity through somebody else's eyes. And while Tom hadn't seemed to mind the slopped corn-flakes and the decibels and the hysterical searching for Henry's recorder bag, Susannah, exquisite in her un-motherhood, had looked like an agonised Botticelli Venus among the discord and debris.

'Yes, perfectly,' says Celia. 'You can nurse your hangover somewhere nice and peaceful and grown-up –' She giggles, quite forgetting Mrs Green's proximity. 'What a sexy idea to wake up in a London club. Even more grown-up than staying in an hotel. What fun – hangover or not!'

'I don't get hangovers,' said Susannah. 'I've given up drink – remember?'

Celia did remember. Celia remembers very well now. Susannah went to very great lengths to explain the deleterious effects that alcohol had on ageing skin last time they met.

'Of course,' said Celia. 'What will-power.'

'How's the not smoking going?'

'Terrific,' says Celia brightly. '*Pas de problème.*'

'Good. So – we'll see you around eight. Have a nice day.'

'Well – *I'd* better get on.' Mrs Green stands up and shuffles off on her ninety-denier legs. Celia had seen those same legs whipping in and out of the crowds at the school jumble sale a few weeks ago. Stick-like, sure-footed, if somewhat lumpy; replicas of

30

Nureyev on a good night. She goes back to the kitchen and the veal and the raspberries vaguely wondering why she had bothered to invite Susannah to come tonight. They were worlds – no, planets – apart: worlds, lifetimes, eons and eons … she begins hulling the fruit. Susie has stayed so sophisticated, so untouched by the trammels of life …

Almost at once the telephone rings. Pink-fingered, she picks it up.

'It's me again. *Dear* Celia – I forgot to say the most important thing. Happy Birthday, my dear old friend. Blessings upon you and I hope you have a lovely, lovely day because you *deserve* it. Happy, happy birthday.'

Celia resumes the raspberries. That is why she invited Susie. Because, however different they were, in the end she was Celia's oldest friend – seldom seen but enduring always. Like that golden (or was it silver? Celia's brain is not what it was) thread in Father Brown, she has only to twitch it from time to time – a little kindness out of the blue, a piece of genuine affection down the phone – to reaffirm the bond between them. No Bedford Park friend, not even Hazel, has a link so fine and yet so strong as that.

Susannah and Celia grew up together in that unremarkable Wimbledon suburb, antithesis of Norman Shaw, called Raynes Park. Raynes Park (like Surbiton, with which it shares a geographic as well as anthrographic similarity) is as far removed from Bedford Park as school dinners are from *nouvelle cuisine* and neither woman referred to the place at all except in terms of amused disparagement. High spots in Raynes Park society were the opening of a Chinese take-away and the day that the Co-op converted to self-service. In Susie and Celia's girlhood the local menfolk were clerks and bought the *News Chronicle* for their journeys to town, and the womenfolk wore clean aprons and made the Sunday roast last through until Tuesday. They played in car-less roads, unseduced from their street games by television, and were brought up on the patriotic mysteries of the

Royal House of Windsor and Sunday school. When somebody's big brother in the road next to Celia's went to university there were general mutterings about youngsters getting too big for their boots. And when somebody else's unmarried sister got pregnant she was sent down to a home for the fallen in Godalming. Raynes Park was a place in which to Know Your Place and rejoice in tinned peaches and evaporated milk on Sundays. If it had not been for that brief aberration, the sixties, Celia would probably have embraced these tenets throughout life. Her sister Isabel, though one step removed from it, more or less had – the period came just a little too late for her to really shake it off. But whether the sixties came or not, it was a dead certainty that Susie would never embrace the life-style of her upbringing. Susie was a cuckoo in the nest so far as Raynes Park was concerned. For Susie, unlike her peers, had real ambition.

When they finished school Celia's secretarial skills were average. Susannah's were astonishingly good, she had also taken, and passed, maths 'O' level and showed a flair for accountancy. Celia went into a series of dullish offices before finding her niche in the Bond Street Art Gallery which, like so many of its rivals, had begun to employ ordinaries among the Hons (best of all was an ordinary with a northern accent, but Celia's unpretentious Raynes Park-ese had to do). The secretarial skills remained average to poor, but she was good-natured, intelligent, not bad to look at, and she got on. When she first got the job she was so thrilled with the *élan* of being in the art world that she had rung up Susie and told her straightaway. All Susie asked was what the salary was. Celia had to confess that it was not very high – you couldn't expect such a glamorous job to pay well also. Susie worked for a merchant bank – a fairly glamorous job that did. And though Susie said all the right things to Celia after the initial enquiry about money, she most certainly never envied her friend her apparently stylish coup.

Celia became involved with the Labour Party along with the Hons who found Conservatives and conservatism unfashionable: the difference was that Celia really began to believe in it passionately. The idea of socialism opened doors in her mind and was like a lot of fresh air blowing through, getting rid of the suburban fustiness. Not only did she refuse to eke out a Sunday roast – she quite often did not have one at all, a thing which always shocked her mother if she ever came to visit. She had a thoroughly enjoyable time forging her new lifestyle in the sixties and into the early seventies: shoulder to shoulder in demos (when she was not abroad arranging Art Fairs); seat to seat in the Royal Court enraptured by Brecht; and flesh to flesh in bed afterwards. A Wonderful Life – not at all unique for its time. Then she met Alex and, predictably and acceptably, began to settle down.

But not Susannah. Oh, no. None of that sort of thing had been for her. She went from job to job climbing all the way. She and Celia shared a flat for a time and Celia used to gasp privately at the effort Susie put into her career. 'Why do you do it?' Celia asked her once. 'Because I want to be rich,' Susannah had replied with widening eyes, as if nothing could be more obvious. And then, a few weeks short of her twenty-first birthday, Susie had gone to America – just when it looked as if she had fallen in love. In exasperation, because she rather liked the chap, Celia asked her why – just at that very moment – she had decided to up sticks.

'Because I've got to escape before I – you know – well – *you* know . . .'

'Know what?' Celia said, baffled.

'You know – give in to him. Do it . . .'

Incredulous, Celia had nearly expired. 'You mean you haven't yet, and you want to, so you're going away before you do?'

Susie had nodded.

'But isn't that the object of the exercise? I mean – boy meets girl – girl meets boy – they fancy each other – and . . .'

'Absolutely not,' said Susie firmly. 'Love is a hindrance. And anyway – I might get pregnant.'

'Not if you take the pill.'

'The pill makes you fat.'

33

'Eating makes you fat, Susie.'

'So does pregnancy. Anyway – I'm not going to risk it.'

Jokingly, Celia had said, 'What – you mean not ever?'

'I've managed up until now. I don't see it as a problem.'

Celia's knobs of disbelief grew knobblier. 'You don't mean that you've never – that you're still . . . Oh my word – Susie!'

Celia's amazement made Susannah cross.

'What's so extraordinary about that?' she asked huffily. 'It's only a function. I really don't see what all the fuss is about sex. . .'

'Well, I jolly well hope you'll find out one day,' said Celia. For the first time she felt superior to her elegant friend. It also happened, though she did not know it then, to be the last time.

So Susie vanished across the Atlantic in a welter of beautiful new clothes and smart luggage. Celia picked up where her friend had left off and went out with the discarded beau for a while. They had a thundering good time in bed – Susie was right not to get enmeshed there – but he wasn't really Celia's type, and she wouldn't marry him either.

Susie and she lost touch for a year or so until Celia began making occasional trips to New York and they met again. But by then there was no mistaking their roles. Susie was well on her way. Celia found her coldish and a bit distant and thought, perhaps, that their friendship was dead. Any mention of Raynes Park between them brought instant distaste to Susie's impeccable face and Celia learned not to say, 'Remember when . . .' over the fashionable tablecloths of Greenwich Village. But the Father Brown thread surfaced when Celia's mother, by now her only surviving parent, died suddenly, and Celia, distraught and forgetting constraint, rang her friend for comfort.

Sister Isabel had just given birth to her first son and was lording it over Celia as usual.

'I simply haven't the time,' she said crisply. 'You'll have to deal with it. You have no responsibilities, being single . . .'

True as this was, it made no difference to the prospective pain of organising a burial and selling up the paltry family home.

Crying down the phone to Susannah, Celia had said as much, and was shaken momentarily from her grief to hear her reply, 'I'm flying back. I'll help.' Which she did.

Going through a dead parent's belongings is one of life's more unpleasant and agonising experiences. The regrets, the memories, the feelings of guilty remorse will break the strongest. Susie saw Celia through all this wonderfully, even to pacing the streets of Raynes Park with her when the sifting became too much – streets she had once said she would never return to (*her* parents had sensibly removed themselves to a Torquay retirement) – and at the funeral, when it seemed that the whole gathering wished only to coo sympathetically over Isabel and her baby, Susie had put her arm round Celia's waist (in all that sorrow she remembered thinking that this was the first occasion she could ever remember being physically touched by her friend) and told her to bear up, be strong, Susie was here. So twitch, twitch, twitch, on that strong metallic thread, then as now. When she flew back to New York, brittle again at the airport, it did not matter. The bond had been renewed.

Of course, Mr Right had eventually come along for Susie, in the shape of an Englishman abroad called Tom. A rich young man, playing with ideas and the money he had made out of the sixties' property boom. Susie's letter, announcing her engagement, had ended characteristically by saying, 'Made it. In a couple of years I shall be coming home to England in triumph – just to show you.' Curiously enough, it had crossed with Celia's letter saying that she was getting married to a young business lawyer called Alex. Pipped again, she thought, as she read the transatlantic news.

The triumph incorporated Tom setting up a business in vintage cars. Not jalopies, of course, but fine old automobiles which his newly acquired plant in Wiltshire renovated and exported to those throughout the world who could afford them. It was three years before they returned to England to set up home in an Elizabethan manor house near Salisbury – where Susie remained as his rural business aide. He also opened a small Mayfair office to deal with the more boring end of things, like welcoming the buyers or their agents as they descended from Texas or Tokyo or Tenerife. By the time they had settled all this, and decided to have an English Blessing on their New York marriage (much publicised, thanks to Susie's flair for public relations), Celia had been pregnant with Rebecca and Henry had been a delightful, romping near-three-year-old. Fortunately, pregnancy sat well on Celia and at the Blessing she had felt well up to meeting her friend's husband for the first time. Alex had met Susie once or twice down the years and liked her tremendously – no nonsense about her and attractive too, was how he put it – so the occasion was very pleasant. Tom had beamed down at her from his dark handsome heights and Celia had felt unsuitably sexy when, after much champagne on his part, he had patted her swelling stomach and said how gorgeous it was. Her affection for him was compounded by his swinging Henry shoulder-high and feeding him the dregs of his glass, saying what a fine, fine boy he was. Alex never took to Tom entirely after that, for Henry was sick on the back seat of the Volvo going home, but Celia, in her bovine state, didn't mind at all.

'We'll ask Tom to be his godfather,' she said. 'If you still insist that he should be christened . . . We'll have Henry and this new one done at the same time.' And Alex, relieved that Celia had agreed to the ceremony at last, since it was very much the form and his mother had been pushing for it, did not argue.

It was a year later, at the christening party, that Tom had locked himself and Celia in the new second bathroom and said he would throw away the key (metaphorically speaking since the door had a brass bolt) unless she allowed him to make love to her. He said he coveted her as soon as he saw her and that he had a small flat in Belgravia about which Susie knew nothing – they could do it in that. She still did not know why she felt so flattered at this confidence for she could easily have been the sort of woman to stomp downstairs and declare all to her old schoolfriend. Either he was clever, or carried away – she decided it was the latter and on the crest of that flattery very nearly did give in, there among the toiletries. He was far too handsome, with his perfect Greek profile and fleshy lips, for her not to give it serious consideration. But in the end, rearranging the toothbrushes and fiddling with the flannels, she had made a magnificent resistance and fled. He had rung her the next day – not to apologise but to insist. She had fluttered for the following week before coming to her senses. It was out of the question. She loved Alex and that was that. Besides, she had dark rings around her eyes when she wasn't wearing make-up (Rebecca was a wakeful child from the word go) and the thought of the morning after a rampant night of love was not a pretty one.

Since then, on the rare occasions that they met, she always experienced a delicious unease when she saw him. She also took extra special care with how she looked.

Clearly from this phone call Tom has still not told Susie about the flat in Belgravia – if, indeed, he still has it. Celia's stomach gives a little contraction as she wonders (looking away from the shuffling Mrs Green) whom he has installed there in her place. If anybody. Anyway, dodging Tom has become quite a harmless and pleasant game over the years and she is quite sure that neither Susie nor Alex have any idea of it. Tom occasionally rolls his eyes and breathes hard in her direction, or holds her hand a little too long, and sometimes – usually after well-oiled dinners – squeezes her thigh under the table. He has never made the slightest difficulty when the children are around and will merely gaze at her fondly from a distance when she is with them. She smiles and hums as she pushes the raspberries through the sieve with great attack. After all, it is a very harmless little game.

It is not until the raspberries and the veal are dealt with and the results in the cold store primly awaiting presentation that Mrs Green is ready to leave.

'I've polished the cutlery,' she says. 'Every piece.'

'You needn't have bothered, Mrs Green,' says Celia, taking out the extra coins for the extra half-hour. 'There'll only be eight of us – not the full canteen. Ha Ha . . .' Her laugh tinkles and falls flat. Mrs Green merely looks dour. Celia feels that more is required of her and goes on with false gaiety. 'Rebecca said this morning that it couldn't be a party with only eight of us because there won't be enough to play games. I told her ...' She begins leading Mrs Green towards the front door. Another piece of the ritual – she always sees her cleaner out as if she were quitting a social call. '... that it was quite enough for the sort of games grown-ups play.'

Mrs Green adjusts her pink transparent headscarf as if it is Arctic winter and says from the pathway, 'I'm sure.'

Something in her tone makes Celia realise she must retract a little. 'Oh – I *don't* mean ...' she begins '... that is – well – not *that* sort –' She tries to think of a word which will convey, across their differing worlds and generations, the harmlessness of what she *does* mean. Blinking once or twice to dispel her inner eye's shocking snap into action following Mrs Green's understanding (a picture that would hit the headlines in any of the Sunday tabloids since – before she blinks it away – it shows all her proposed dinner guests in various attitudes of naked debauchery) she continued, 'By adult games (Christ! that's even *worse*) I meant – you know – parlour games – that sort of thing. That's all – really – just a few parlour games ...'

Mrs Green pauses to click the gate shut. Looking up she sniffs, once, and then moves off. Behind her she pulls her brown plastic shopping trolley like a tumbril. Over her shoulder, Sibylline in her chiffon pink, she says, 'Well, then. Happy birthday. I'll be in on Monday morning ...' Her tone implies that she is unlikely to live so long. 'Have a nice weekend ...' And she trundles off.

On the other side of the street the semi-retired judge (he who was so roughly awoken from his claret slumbers by alerted policemen some months before) looks upon this exodus with pleasant thoughts. A Bedford Park wife saying goodbye to her cleaner. What could be more fittingly composed than that? He has seen so much in his life that such things are necessary antidotes. He strolls off towards the delicatessen, for a few jolly words with the coloured folk who run it, and he feels at one with the world.

'And goodbye to you,' says Celia, closing the door in delight at being alone at last. The muddled thought that she need not have Mrs Green as a cleaner – a thought that quite often beats its feeble wings but gets nowhere – is quickly buried. People in Bedford Park have help – *ergo* – Celia has help. It is simply the way of the world.

Twelve o'clock. Six more hours of absolute freedom before the children return. She gives a little crow and then passing the hall mirror she drags her mouth downwards, screws up her face and ties a tea-towel around her head. '*I'm* sure . . .' she says to the reflection. 'Adult Games . . . Dirty Devils . . . Of course I *can't* with my legs . . . Parlour Games indeed! I know just what *you* mean by *Parlour Games*.'

Despite laughing, Celia feels rather aroused at the thought – and the sheer wicked sexiness makes her long, suddenly, for Alex to be there. She has to go and beat up the egg whites to work it off, and while they are coming into nice airy peaks (perfect for the mousse) she thinks that perhaps it would be nice to play some games tonight. She hasn't done it for ages – Alex finds them childish, which they are, which is exactly what she likes about them. She was taught to play such things by a Bloomsbury-set lady at the art gallery and found, surprisingly, that she was rather good at them – The Dictionary Game, Botticelli, and the wild thing called Flannel Doughnut. Yes – really – it would be nice to play something like that again. Even if Alex finds them untenable. She hums another Golden Oldie that was popular long before she met her husband.

'It's my party . . .' sings a lost popular vocalist called Lesley Gore. And Celia sings it too. If I want to play games then I will, she says to herself. After all, it really *is* my party. *I'm sure* . . .

This, then, is Celia, within the house within the place where she lives. Forty years old today and on the threshold of the next forty years which, if she thinks about them at all, she expects will be just as pleasing and unremarkable as those gone by. And the closest she has got to wickedness is the rum that will lace her chocolate mousse and a desire to play a few Parlour Games. Her contentment abounds.

So – Happy Birthday Celia.

2

Alex was in the second bathroom and had just trodden on one of Henry's more intricate Lego submarines. He swore so loudly that it echoed around the second floor of the house and could be heard, perfectly plainly, above the roar of the shower. Even the children, now tucked up in the attic rooms, heard it. Henry, attempting a reef knot with his pyjama cord for his mother's delight the next morning, shouted to his sister in the adjacent room.

'Did you hear Dad say Fuck?' he called.

'Yes,' echoed Rebecca with relish. 'It's dirty, isn't it? Very dirty ... ?' she added with hope.

'It's the worst thing,' he shouted back. 'It means hard willies.'

'Great,' said Rebecca. 'What about bottoms? (Alas for the less specific female generic in vogue – boys have penises, girls have genital areas – Rebecca is vaguely aware of this lexical injustice already.)

'No,' says Henry with assurance. 'It doesn't mean them.'

Rebecca puts her hand comfortingly in the place where her penis is not. At least something exists in its own right down there. She can feel that it does.

'Will you go to sleep right now!' yells Celia up the stairs. 'It's nearly half past seven. I don't want to hear another word ...'

'Bloody,' says Henry under his sweaty duvet. (Poor Mrs Green – all her efforts undone.) 'Shit. Sod. Bugger. Bums.'

'Can't hear,' says Rebecca, still holding on to herself, more sleepy than she wants to be since Hazel took them to the park for a picnic and they ran around a lot. Rebecca wants to stay awake so that she can come down in the middle of the dinner party. She likes the attention. And Henry can't do it. He may have a penis but he can't will himself to stay awake like his sister.

'Go to sleep,' calls Celia threateningly. She pounds a bare heel on to the first stair below their rooms. 'Or I'll be up . . .'

This unusual aggression silences them. Celia has other ideas about how she wants to spend the next thirty-five minutes and these do not embrace her children. She has heard about the duckpond, listened to their complaints about the food (Hazel's idea of a picnic was rather bland apparently – even the crisps were plain), heard Henry play and Rebecca sing a song about dinosaurs, bathed them, read a story, tucked them up, untucked them because they forgot to clean their teeth, resettled them, had a short philosophical discussion about death (sparked off by her birthday), cooed in a motherly way – and that is now that. It is adult time now.

'Do you hear me?' she yells as a final threat.

'What?' calls Alex from the deluge in the bathroom. He emerges, dripping and only half showered, to see his wife, naked except for a pair of dazzling drop earrings of peacock blue (Adrian's friend makes them), with one foot on the stairs, fire in her eyes, and her perfectly made-up face contorted with unusually vigorous anger. She has some strange new colour in her hair too – he decides to ignore this. The whole makes a very odd picture. He stares for half a second. For some reason she instantly looks down at his genitals and then up to his face, before saying very sweetly, 'Not you. I was telling the children to be quiet.'

'Oh,' says Alex, surprised at the passionate tone of this simple activity. 'Well do keep it down a bit. I've had a heavy day . . .'

Celia takes another quick look at his flaccid genitals, smiles encouragingly at him as he goes back to his shower, and returns to the bedroom. To wait. Ever since all that business with Mrs Green and the Parlour Games Celia has been thinking about sex – specifically, she has been looking forward to having one last bash before she is officially forty. Not that prissy well-married activity called making love either – a real hump, a quickie, like they used to do. A silly notion, maybe, but as she adds more mascara to her already raffish eyes she says to herself,

Why not? Surely a woman is allowed to be a little foolish today of all days.

Anyway, Alex certainly won't refuse her so it won't be a difficult whim to satisfy. That is, if he gets on with his shower. She looks at the clock: they will have to do it, murmur the how-was-it-for-yous for at least two minutes afterwards, stroke each other kindly – and then get dressed before the first guests arrive. Alex, she pleads inwardly, relinquish the shower-gel and turn off those taps, or there won't be time for the *après*-sex. Which might have a terrible consequence on the whole dinner party.

She hears the shower stop, hears her husband humming as he dries himself, hears the lock being opened, and out he comes.

'Not dressed yet?' he says with good humour. He crosses to the wardrobe and begins removing clothes from hangers. 'We've got the Brandreth case by the way . . . It's official.'

He whistles the 'Ride of the Valkyries' which is not a promising start – the myth might have sexual connotations, the tune is pure music hall – Celia cannot see the state of his genitals because he has a towel draped around his waist. The prognosis, however, is not good, for there seems to be nothing rampant going on under the soft weave of the cotton. The clock says twenty-five to eight. Celia decides to go along with Alex's little game and make the first move, so she takes a deep breath and lies back on the Victorian brass bed with its welcomingly soft duvet. This taking the initiative has always been slightly fraught in case he is veering towards the more proper side of his nature. Sometimes Alex can be a little shocked if she comes on too strong. She has to judge it just right. She decides to meet the situation half-way and drops the idea of woggling her private parts at him invitingly. Instead she lies, draped on the lacy cover, in the 'Venus d'Urbino' position. Someone once told her, possibly Susannah's ex-beau, that the pose was a real turn on (this was in the days when you also tuned in and dropped out which seems to have gone from the vernacular nowadays): whoever it was said that Titian's masterstroke of tucking his model's hand into the recesses of her sex was half invitation, half protection and twice as erotic. Very well. With this in mind, and fingers tucked persuasively into crutch, she calls her husband softly.

'Alex?'

He has his back to her and is staring into the mirror examining a couple of spots on his chin. By now he has on his underpants and his socks – an unfortunate combination.

'Alex?' she calls again, not quite so softly.

He seems to refocus on the real world and begins arranging his thin, sandy-coloured hair very delicately with a brush.

'Yes,' he says to his reflection as he slips on his shirt, 'the whole of the Brandreth case. Of course we were right to insist. No point in having half a dozen different fingers in the pie. Mmm darling?'

Already, having buttoned the shirt, he is scrutinising the spots on his chin again and running the palm of his hand very lightly over his head as if checking the density of what grows there. He then runs his hand over his paunch. Celia is about to croon, 'Look at me ...' or something similar, when he continues, '*And* we ran rings round that female from the other chambers. It was last month's little conference that finally did it, I think. She had to back down on everything.' He pauses, flicking his fingertips through his sparse quiff. 'Well – almost everything – she congratulated me afterwards and –' he stops, catching sight of Celia's over his shoulder's reflection in the mirror, and he looks at his watch which he has been strapping to his wrist as he speaks. '... Shouldn't you be getting dressed or something?'

'Come and kiss me,' she says provocatively.

It is now eighteen minutes to eight. It will have to be a really quick one after all and they will just have to risk the lack of after-care. Alex approaches the bed, pulling his trousers from the hanger on the way. He then leans over, kisses Celia's forehead, and puts on his trousers.

'Buck up,' he says, and she hears the final flourish of his fly zip.

44

He is back at the mirror, peering at himself again. Perhaps, thinks Celia, puzzled, this is what life is going to be like now that she is forty. Perhaps life really does begin anew. Certainly Alex's behaviour is new – both his apparent lack of interest in her body and his apparent gain of interest in his own. Maybe this relates to her coming of age, maybe he feels time's wingless chariot all over again now that she has joined him in the middle ground? Whatever the reason Celia is not yet ready to cede the battle. She makes one more attempt, emboldened by a sudden deep desire that contracts her womb. She wants him, and she wants him to want her. She rolls off the bed and stands behind this fully-dressed husband of hers; she puts her hands on his shoulders and presses herself into his back. It is twelve minutes to eight but she no longer cares – the peal of the doorbell when it comes will never be as important as this urgent need for intimacy now. He makes a playful swing backwards with his hand and smacks her bare bottom. It makes quite a crack. It is certainly not a tender gesture – more jolly than anything else. It is also body language for 'let me go', which she does.

'Come on,' he says. 'Get dressed now. Let's see the birthday girl in all her finery.'

'I am in all my finery,' she says quietly.

If he notices the involuntary pathos of the remark he does not acknowledge it. He merely taps her bottom again, kisses her nose (that part which least needs it, she thinks, *en passant*) and leaves the room. He walks upstairs on tiptoe and she hears the floorboards creak first in Henry's room, then in Rebecca's. After a minute he reappears, popping his head round the bedroom door.

'All asleep, even Becky ... Christ Almighty Celia! Are you going to your birthday party in your birthday suit or what?' He laughs at the witticism and looks boyish, and this time the lurch of emotion is not in her womb but in her heart. She smiles at him, shakes her head and turns to the wardrobe. Alex wolf-whistles but is already beginning to descend the stairs.

'Hurry up,' he calls softly, 'and we can have a quiet drink together before anyone arrives. I want to tell you about the case.'

Wagner continues to float up from below. Celia plonks herself down on the bed, more like a doll with its strings cut than a Titian now, and begins to put on her tights. These are black and seamed, with little diamanté motifs at each ankle. They mock her with their tartiness since she now feels as vulnerable as a stripper who has removed everything as alluringly as possible only to find that no one has bothered to look. Not for the first time is Celia feeling vulnerable over sexual matters. It is this thing that Alex has got about her being both Madonna of his children and Overt Floozy at the same time. If only he would sort it out in his own mind she would know where she was. It gets increasingly confusing. Especially when he switches back from latter to former without telling Celia. Not so long ago she overdid it – well, how was she to know? – by breaking what turned out to be a post-coital fatherly reverie and grabbing his balls (she winces at the memory) and suggesting in the voice of one accustomed to the Reeperbahn that so far as she and her organs were concerned, the night was still young. But his horrified response had been as nothing to Celia's astonishment when she saw the look of fastidious recoil on his face. Could this be the same man who had introduced Dirty Harry into the proceedings some weeks previously? Apparently it could. Such was her embarrassment following that incident that she has been pretty circumspect since then. And much more modest, which seems to suit him. But it is a thin line to tread between giving off an aura of allure while remaining sleepily and delicately willing. Maybe Alex's lessening of interest during the past few weeks is not entirely due to the pressures of his job. Maybe it has also got something to do with her not – quite – getting the balance right. If only France had not been such a travesty, if only Dirty Harry hadn't been quite so rough – if only, if only ... but there we are. If she thinks back, which she does now, right from the very beginning, when they had the uncontrollable hots for each other, Alex had liked to be ringmaster – and so, like a new-born baby, Celia had unlearned what she already knew, and let Alex teach her all over again. Then it had been a harmless little deceit, a little game of which only she was privy to the rules. Now it seems entrenched. The 'Ride of the Valkyries' mocks her up the stairs. Her little desire should not, surely, have become so complicated? This is all rather like walking on eggshells and for the life of her she cannot understand why. Nevertheless she will tiptoe. It would be foolish to do anything else tonight. She will get him later. There is always the adult sanctuary and the brandy glass to see to that.

So, instead of pirouetting down the stairs and demanding satisfaction in as seductive a way as she can manage, Celia sits on her bed, straightening her tights and having a little cry as she does so. But only a little one. It will be a stiff-upper-Bedford-Park-lip and down the stairs to greet the guests in a moment. Like her sisters-in-wifedom everywhere, she is not one to rock the boat with her private griefs if she can possibly control them. And especially not on her birthday and with a houseful of guests. Anyway, she begins to smile through the dampness, and then to giggle again, for she recalls the picture of Alex in his socks and Y-fronts. You had to love him really, for all his foibles.

After this thought, and by the time she has popped on her lacy blouse with the daring *décolletage*, she feels better. And once the tight-waisted (slightly more than last time? Perhaps ...) aquamarine skirt is zipped up and the velvet band fastened around her neck, she is happily humming to herself. She gives her hair a final brush, is pleased with the effect of the peacock highlight and how it accentuates her earrings and her skirt, and by the time she descends the stairs she is chuckling at her silliness. She thinks it would be a poor princess who, transformed by her beautiful trappings, remained miserable. Even if the princess didn't quite manage to make her prince come across. The thought of Alex in the role of Frog Prince is so funny that she guffaws as she enters the conservatory. He, waiting, well-cooled bottle in hand, notices.

'You look lovely,' he says, popping the cork. 'What's so funny?'

She decides that on the whole she had better not mention the Frog Prince. His sense of humour is not what it used to be since the children arrived and his professional responsibilities burgeoned, and she has learned to go for tact rather than comedy. She once made the mistake of saying that it would be fun to make love to him in his wig – a passing remark that he took very ill indeed. She subsequently learned that this is a common fantasy among the wives of professionals hereabouts and is received with similar husbandly disapproval. Her friend who is married to a photographer often dreams of him advancing towards her wearing only a zoom lens, and the osteo's wife sometimes indulges in the thought of coupling in his consulting room with him wearing only his white coat. Hazel says, wryly, that John has no recognisable tools of the trade for her to fantasise about unless it were a set square – and as for her sister, well, it is somehow inconceivable that she would show enough levity to request Dave to come at her sporting a blow torch . . .

'Well?' he says, with just the faintest *frisson* of irritability, for she is still smiling broadly in a far-off land. 'What *is* so funny?'

'Me – at forty,' she says quickly, and mollified he hands her a bubbling glass and bends to kiss her ear lobe.

'What about you at forty?' he whispers. His breath is so seductive that she has to swallow almost her whole glass of champagne to keep in check. Drat that exchange with Mrs Green for the idea of those games keeps tickling away.

'Oh . . . um,' she searches for something convincing to say to replace what is on the tip of her tongue which is, broadly speaking, How About It? Instead she says, 'Me – now: so settled, so secure – so bloody bourgeois –' she laughs, genuinely amused, delighted at her skill in the change of theme. 'So very contented . . .'

Princess Celia, smoothing the folds of her Liberty skirt, feels this to be true.

They chink their glasses and look quite perfect together before separating to their individual seats. Alex fills her glass again and they subside into the rattan armchairs that fit so well among all the plants. Celia is very proud of the way she has done out this little adjunct to their house.

It is a hot, bright evening. At the open door of the conservatory a yellow, scented rose bobs in magnificent finery, sending a heady perfume into the already fertile air. The plants are doing well: busy lizzies in shocking pink and iceberg white flourish; hot red geraniums whose dusty antique scent vies with the bobbing rose cut their colour into the rampant fronds; head-high palms and thick-leaved succulents set their greenery against the variegations of assorted ivies and dieffenbachia. When the English climate permits, Celia may be congratulated on her tongue-in-cheek creation of a little bit of Lost Empire here in Bedford Park. All it needs is a rotating fan, someone to call for a *chota-peg*, and Willie Maugham to shuffle in. While this amuses Celia she looks across at Alex stretching out his long, casually trousered legs and wonders, not for the first time, if he doesn't actually take the whole thing seriously. She can imagine him in an Ex-Pat club somewhere clicking his fingers at an obsequious be-turbaned attendant and calling for the gin-wallah.

'*Now* what's so amusing?' he asks suddenly.

'I was thinking about the Raj,' she says, being truthful in the general and deceitful in the particular.

He looks all about him. Up at the ceiling with its cascades of tumbling foliage, around the walls with their splashes of leaf and colour, and down to the raffia rugs and festooned planters on the floor. Then he looks at her, smiles and says, 'It is a bit like that, isn't it?' There is a definite hint of satisfaction in his voice before he calls himself back to the Liberal order and says, 'What an arrogant nation we were once.'

'Still are,' she says, almost without thinking.

'Oh, I don't know ...' His voice is satisfied, certain. 'I think we've learned our lesson.'

Too quickly she says, 'I don't. I don't think you ever learn a lesson over something so seductive as national supremacy. We still go on churning them out of our public schools and they still go on wanting to put the Great back into Britain.'

'There's nothing wrong with that. As long as everybody gets the benefit.'

'Well – I'm not altogether sure . . .' She is feeling a little rusty in discussions such as this. 'The thing is we were called Great in the first place because we went out and exploited everybody. If we are going to be Great again I rather suspect it'll be for the same reasons . . . Look at South Africa . . .'

'I shouldn't worry your beautiful head about that, my darling . . . especially not tonight.' He comes over to her and strokes her hair. 'Because we never *are* going to be Great like that again. All we can do is to struggle on to make sure we don't end up like the pygmies of the market place in whatever way we can.'

'Isn't that what this Brandreth man was doing?'

'Sort of.'

'And he's being prosecuted?'

'He overstepped the mark – got a bit too greedy. Great pity really since he's a personable chap – brilliant, cultivated, well-educated . . .' Alex smiles at her with a boyish look of triumph. 'Not my old school though – which probably explains his downfall. Obviously the only really good men come from Hartonhouse.' This is an old joke between them. Alex's little bit of jingoism. Celia waits for the laugh which usually follows such a statement. Oddly enough it does not come. Instead he says, 'You know, I'm very glad Henry's going there.'

It is a reasonable statement for a parent to make so Celia wonders why she feels irritated. Probably, she thinks, because she doesn't feel the same about *her* old school. It was very State and very Secondary and brings not one jot of loyalty to her lips. Her irritation is not prepared to go without a push.

'Don't count your chickens,' she says. 'We don't know that he will.'

'Of course he will. And Becky will go to Green-Cloaks. You know my views on sexual equality.'

'What about equality in general?' She surprises herself.

'They will emerge as fulfilled members of the community – well-educated, cultured and able to lead – someone has to. And they will be liberally minded too. Because we are. You can't say better than that as a gift to the future, now can you?'

'You used to laugh at all that sort of thing. Remember?'

He smiles at her quite fondly. 'I used to laugh at a lot of things. I used to call men of my age fogeys. I even had a Who tee-shirt saying "Hope I Die Before I Get Old". Things change, we grow wiser – that's all. It wouldn't be fair not to give him the chance. My school has produced some exceptional men, exceptional...'

Celia takes a swig from her glass. She wants to ask Alex if he includes himself in this production line of excellence but decides it might be better not to. There is the very faintest pinkening at the top of his cheeks. All the same she wants to say something so she does.

She says, 'Ours might turn out just to be snobs.'

'Rubbish ...' He smiles. 'They will be honest, caring individuals. Just like me.' He taps his chest and gives her a sideways look which is supposed to say that he knows he is being immodest and he can laugh at himself. At the same time the gesture and the expression say that he believes what he says. It is an extremely complicated assortment of innuendo.

Celia, who knows her husband very well, as indeed she should after so long, reads them all. For the first time she finds his smugness irritating, which is probably to do with what did not take place earlier. She decides to be a little contentious.

'I wonder where this Brandreth man went to school?'

'Rowton, I think ...'

'Well – there you are then ...'

He laughs. 'I told you they were a depraved lot. And anyway, what do you know about it?' He pinches her cheek. 'Coming from Revolutionary Raynes Park?'

'I went to an ordinary school, Alex. And I'm all right. Aren't I?'

'Things were different then,' he says. 'And you, my darling, are perfect and unique.'

Oh Alex, she thinks, how easily that tripped off your tongue.

'We are moving into the twenty-first century, Celia. Times change. We are educating our citizens for a new era. If we can afford to give them the best then we are obliged to. The baton goes to them, after all. These are the facts.'

It only requires his wig to turn this into a real bit of Perry Mason. Celia feels obliged to become the defence.

'Won't it make our children a little – well –' she swaps snob for something more refined – 'elitist?'

'My dear girl,' says Alex, amused, 'around here it would be elitist *not* to afford . . .'

And still laughing he pours out more champagne.

Celia cedes defeat. Alex's arguments are always amusing and witty. She remembers Dave trying to suggest that the Law Society was the biggest closed shop of all and how swiftly Alex had put this down. 'Since we are an acknowledged nation of same – it is hardly surprising,' he had said. Which drew such laughter and applause that it had quite drowned her brother-in-law out. Celia, suddenly, knows how Dave felt. However, the children's education has always been Alex's province. That and issues like Nuclear Armament, the Irish Question, Lead-Free Petrol. She gets on with the day-to-day decisions. Which, in their own way, are more than enough.

So Celia accepts the champagne and looks at the bubbling glass. She goes back to easier ground. 'Those Empire days must have been wonderful: to be in charge, to be waited on, to drink stuff like this in foreign lands and to feel that you were so absolutely top-drawer and *right*. Very seductive. Too bloody seductive actually.'

They look at each other in surprise. Celia does not usually come out with such things any more.

She continues. 'I'm glad that *I* haven't been given the opportunity of being the White Oppressor. I might have taken them up on it. It's one thing to have principles. It's quite another to be called upon to make sacrifices because of them. It must have been hell giving up all that power . . . I don't think we ought to have it again.'

Alex, slightly disgruntled, says, 'It would be all right providing we used it properly.'

'Ah,' she says, wagging her head. 'But we wouldn't – would we?'

'Some of us would – some of us do . . .' His voice has risen very slightly.

'Ah,' she says, 'but that's the other seduction . . .'

'What is?'

'Being educated to feel superior so that what you call the common good is really a continuation of *your* good. Status quo. There, my dear Alex, is the rub of an elitist education, and there – in a more historically obvious form – is the Raj . . .'

She chooses to ignore the shadow that crosses her husband's face after this. The champagne has made her feel relaxed and easy and she has just remembered – pleasant thought – that she is the star of the show tonight: it is all in her honour, even if she did do all the organising and preparation – which was entirely her choice and she enjoyed it. So she can flutter her intellectual wings a little. Why not? She has begun to enjoy the part now. Certainly a fortieth birthday *is* a great female shibboleth – so far as she is aware she has never called her husband 'My dear Alex' before though he has quite often used the sobriquet for her. Quite clearly he is not impressed. And she knows why. For having used it she realises that it is a delightfully subtle way of putting someone down. My dear Alex, she savours mentally, but she decides not to risk it again.

Suddenly she begins to understand the language of being on top. If you go around My dear-ing people you gain a lot of ground. She is heartened by this. It goes some way towards atoning for Alex's Wagnerian whistling earlier. Her fortieth birthday rises up like a shield to protect her. Just for tonight she can say or do whatever she likes. Tomorrow it will be different, tomorrow it will be back to normal again – but just for tonight, just for tonight ... it reminds her of saying to Henry that he could have whatever he liked once he had submitted to having his verruca frozen out – three ice creams, circus tickets, the A-Team sweatshirt – anything. Similarly for the next few hours she can have whatever *she* wants. A pity she hadn't got to this pitch of understanding when they were both upstairs. Ho hum – oh well ...

Anyway, to dispel the slight gloom that descends at the thought of her new maturity being like a verruca, she smiles across at Alex and says, 'It's nice to talk so candidly about important things with you – it seems years since we had a serious talk. I mean – we don't agree on everything, do we, Alex? Nor should we. It sort of lifts us out of the mundane, puts us in touch with each other again. We used to discuss things all the time. I'd like to go on doing it, wouldn't you?' Her bright face is eager as it leans towards her husband. Celia is opening the wings of debate, and enjoying it.

Why should marriage mean like-thinking? There is no reason at all.

Once she would argue half the night away with her men and make love for the rest. Forgetting, for the moment, the ambush of children, she thinks she should rekindle this intellectual liveliness with Alex again. Take her children's education, for example, take the state of the world for another; she would like to unfurl those wings completely and flap them about a bit. She would like to, she would like to – she looks across at her husband and immediately tucks those wings safely back at her side.

Alex, clearly, would not.

He wriggles in his chair so that the canework creaks and groans in complaint. It echoes in his brain which can think of nothing except the Brandreth case. He is longing to launch into the subject again but Celia deflects him.

'Do you remember how we met?' she asks safely.

He thinks. 'Yes,' he says, letting the rattan settle again. 'Of course. We met in Trafalgar Square on that Anti-Apartheid rally. We did our bit.'

He is right, of course, their pasts will bear scrutiny.

'We did,' she agrees. 'You were a Young Liberal and I was a Young Socialist. Dear me – what has become of us, Alex?'

The chair resumes its annoyance.

'What has become of us, my darling . . .' he says lightly, getting up and pulling the bottle of champagne from its cooler and bending to replenish her glass, '. . . is that we have grown up, had children, careers.'

She acknowledges the filled glass with a movement of her head.

'You've had a career –' It sounds plaintive, which she doesn't mean.

'And you, my dear girl, have had the children. They have become *yours* . . .' Alex is defensive.

'But would you go back to Trafalgar Square with a banner now? I mean, apartheid seems to be in its last true death throes, thank God. Shouldn't we be out there putting the boot in?'

'We don't buy South African goods.' He resettles in the suffering chair. 'Do we?'

'But that's not the point, is it? What I'm saying is how we've changed. I think that's sad – that's all. We're so respectable. So untouched nowadays . . .'

'A minute ago –' Alex's voice is waspish – 'you were saying that you enjoyed being bourgeois.'

'That's the seduction. Like the Raj. It's so easy, isn't it? Especially living here. None of us does anything remotely radical nowadays. I enjoy cooking. You enjoy getting cases like the Brandreth one—'

'My dear girl – Brandreth is a city crook of the first order. My success will have immeasurable consequences—'

'Within the confines of your profession it will. And his profession. But it won't touch the oppressed black majority in South Africa – or the millions of unemployed here – business law is about finance protecting finance and the City policing itself, isn't it? I thought you once said it was the acceptable face of ... Alex! Be careful with that chair – you'll break it if you go twisting around like that ...'

He stands up. His face is rather pink. A bad sign, that. 'And what would you do if I went waving banners all around the town instead of turning up for my cases?' he says.

'What would you do if I went picketing the South African Embassy instead of shopping in Waitrose or collecting the children from school?'

'I should take it easy with the third glass,' he says acidly.

And she thinks, how the hell did we end up nearly having a row on my birthday? So she mutters into her glass, 'I just thought it was a pity that with all our adult wisdom and influence we've lost the passion – lost touch with all the zest—'

He says, 'Grow up, Celia,' and she thinks that's an odd statement considering the occasion.

His voice rises a little. 'You can't be radical all your life. Somebody has to take on the baton of reason. I can't think of anything worse than being an ageing piece of Agitprop. And if I may say so, this is a bloody odd time to be accusing me of being mediocre.'

'I wasn't accusing you of anything of the sort. I was just saying that we don't seem to have the fire for changing things any more ...'

Alex has gone from light pink to a tone more in keeping with the nodding geraniums.

'I've worked my balls off to get this case. I get confirmation today – it's your birthday which makes it even more special – we're all set for a cheery, celebratory evening and then you come out with all this crap about social conscience. Well, I've done my bit. I did it then and I'm doing it now – just in a different way.' His voice rises, anger, hostility abounds now. 'And you really ought to be careful setting me apart like this with all your holier-than-thou homespun philosophy. I'm not a middle-aged lump of stone, you know. I do live and breathe and exist as well as you – to the best of my ability I'm out there every day in that market place struggling to do what's right. It's no picnic, it's damned hard work. I do what I can. Somebody's got to be leader or we'd have anarchy ...' His voice has gone very loud and matches its timbre to the nodding flowers. 'I can hold my head up. I may not shove placards in policemen's faces any more but what I do I do for the Good.'

'I know,' she says, feeling slightly alarmed. Why does the phrase 'Methinks he doth protest too much' come to mind?

'My feelings are just as strong as yours, you know. And my needs. Needs that you never seem to ...'

She is just thinking, So are mine – when the doorbell rings.

Alex stops, bashes down his glass on the rattan table, which echoes its vacated sister, so lately suffering under his bottom, and goes to open the door. Celia takes a deep breath, soothed by the scent of the rose and assorted horticulture, and thinks again that she cannot understand why they have got to this pitch. Why can't she discuss education and South Africa with Alex any more? Why is he so waspish? And why, she wonders, does it unnerve her so? It is as if a dimension of understanding about something was only just out of her reach. To do with Alex. But what?

When he returns, with her sister and her brother-in-law, she has completely composed herself. She has told herself she must not spoil things and she gives Alex a particularly long, sweet smile. Even on her very own fortieth birthday, which is hers to spoil if she chooses, she remembers the lessons she has come to learn as wife and mother. This is the mark of reason now. She lifts her face to be kissed by Isabel and then Dave. Her sister stands looking down at her, head on one side, scrutinising Celia's hair.

'I see Adrian's been at you again. Very artistic. Talking of which ...' She heaves a heavy parcel onto Celia's lap. 'Here's your present.'

Celia looks down at the weighty article which is wrapped rather haphazardly in Snoopy paper. Well, she thinks, I suppose I always *will* be Little Sister. She begins opening the card while Alex gives Isabel and Dave their drinks.

Over the popping bubbles Alex says to Dave, 'I know you'd prefer something more proletarian. But there is beer later.'

Inwardly Celia winces but her brother-in-law is not at all put out.

'I might even stick to this,' he says easily. 'When in Rome ...' He helps himself to a tortilla chip. 'Posh crisps too,' he says, smiling at Alex.

So begins *their* little game.

The card says, 'With love to Celia from Izzie, Dave and the boys. Hope this will help you in your quest!'

Puzzled and interested by the cryptic nature of the message, Celia opens the parcel. But when she looks upon its contents she is still puzzled, for there, nestling among the peculiarly inappropriate Snoopy images, is the new two-volume definitive guide to twentieth-century British painting. No coffee-table books these. It is a publication long awaited by art historians and scholars. But not, so far as she is aware, by Celia.

'Remember?' says Isabel. 'You said it was coming out and that you'd like to have a look at it ...'

Celia does remember – just. She had said it rather as one might say it of the new *Who's Who* or the addenda to the Oxford dictionary. She also remembers when she was ten or eleven, standing at a wintry bus stop with Isabel as the rain bucketed down and saying that she could do with an umbrella. She got one the following June, for her birthday, when the sun was shining. 'With love from your big sister,' that one was tagged.

'Oh,' she says, fingering the pages, flicking at them so that they fall through names like Bacon, Bomberg, Freud. 'How clever of you to remember.' She stands up awkwardly, releasing the heavy volume on to her chair seat. Its weight has creased her skirt, she notices. 'But you shouldn't have ...'

'You're only forty once,' says Isabel, happily. And she winks at her.

'It must have cost a fortune,' says Celia, kissing her sister.

'Put it this way,' says Dave. 'It cost the same as an old-age pensioner gets to live on for a week – or even two –' he winks at

58

Celia too. 'But we couldn't have principles where your birthday was concerned.'

She smiles back at him. She likes Dave.

'More champagne anybody?' says Alex slightly too loudly. 'There's *plenty* more where this came from.' He also winks at Celia.

Celia is beginning to feel like a music-hall turn.

'Well,' she says, 'you two are very, very kind – and I shall treasure it. What a surprise. You don't tend to get many surprises when you're as grown-up as I am.' Determined to jolly everyone along she continues, 'I love surprises. They are the best kind of presents – by far the best kind. Oh, yes!' she chirrups. 'Surprises are fun!'

Instantly she regrets being quite so positive about this as she sees a frosty flicker on Alex's face.

'I'm sorry,' he says coolly, 'that I had to ask you in advance about your present – but I was spending just a little more than that ...' He slops champagne into his glass and holds it up, watching the bubbles subside. 'Shall we say enough to keep a hundred old-age pensioners for a week? At least.'

It is on the tip of her tongue to say, 'Don't be so silly and childish, Alex,' but instead she smiles at him and says, 'You know I was thrilled – I couldn't have asked for anything more –' Exciting? She thinks. No. Not exciting. But what then? 'Useful,' she adds quickly.

'And what did this enterprising husband get you?' asks her sister.

'I'll show you,' says Celia and, relieved to escape, she beckons Isabel to follow her.

Passing through the kitchen she feels instantly restored at the sight of her own organised domesticscape. Here at least she is quite secure. They pass the mirror in the hall, two sisters, five years between them but it looks more like ten. Celia takes a quick peep at herself and feels pleased with the image. Her tetchy conversation with Alex is forgotten. She likes looking frivolous. Isabel, in her tie-necked white blouse and her navy linen suit, makes the contrast between them even more marked.

'I like your outfit,' says Celia.

'Thanks,' says Isabel, pleased. 'It's British Home Stores – why pay more, I say.'

'Well – *quite*,' says Celia.

'I've seen the same in Jaeger for three times the price. You'd never know, would you?'

'No,' says Celia, thinking yes. She also thinks how like their mother Isabel looks. And how Raynes Park that smugness about lack of style is. And how she is glad, glad, glad not to be a part of all that any more.

'It's very you,' she says, with wicked irony, which is all right because this is her sister she is talking to and the family bond is deeper than any slight tampering of duplicity can damage.

They look at each other out of the mirror.

'Well – you look suitably dressed up for your birthday, Cee –' Her tone implies that this is an allowable piece of silliness but for one night only. 'Have you still got your cleaner?'

This *non-sequitur* throws Celia for a moment.

'Yes.'

'It's no wonder then.'

Celia understands. Isabel means that Mrs Green provides her with enough free time to indulge herself in getting partyfied. She doesn't bother to deny it.

'But you really ought to be thinking of using that time creatively . . .' (Have you seen the food? Celia thinks.) 'Now you're forty you should be getting to grips with your future – you'll want a job soon, you know.'

Celia holds open the front door on to the pretty front garden, the white railings and the tree-lined street. 'How's the deputy-headship?' she asks, as Isabel steps out.

'Hard work and very rewarding,' says her sister. 'Now what have you brought me out here to see?'

There is the sparkling white Mini-Metro, with this year's registration, nestling up to Alex's Volvo. As yet it has not taken on the patina of age in the form of crisp packets, toys and the smears of a thousand sticky little fingers.

'Well, well,' says Isabel. 'How wonderful. You must be doing well.'

'Alex is,' says Celia, without thinking.

'You're a kept woman all right.' Her sister laughs at the witticism. 'Very well kept. You don't look forty, you know.'

'I sometimes feel it,' Celia says, thinking that right at this minute she feels about twelve.

'Well – at least you've got a new car to rest your ageing body in ... think of my old banger.'

'Which one? The car or the body?' Celia laughs. So does Isabel.

As they go in, Isabel smacks Celia on the botton.

'Now, now,' she says. 'Get along with you.'

It is the second time she has been so chastised tonight and, if anything, Isabel's attack was the more intimate of the two. Odd, thinks Celia, very odd.

Back in the conservatory Isabel says to Alex, 'What a sensible present.' And Alex looks pleased.

Celia thinks that, on the whole, she *is* disappointed with the car. As she relies on one so much it was rather like receiving a new washing machine or refrigerator for her birthday. Years ago, when they had very little money, she was given a new iron. They chose it together – with the aid of *Which?* – and Alex put it away until the day. He then presented it to her in bed that morning, gaudily wrapped in blue paper with lots of silly ribbons and a tag card in the shape of a heart. She rolled on to her stomach to open it while he fucked her from behind. She must have been the first woman ever to have an orgasm over a Morphy Richards steam iron. And tucked into the guarantee card was a pair of earrings, tiny forget-me-nots, very cheap, very pretty – a total surprise and still somewhere in her dressing-table drawer. She had hunted through the interior of the new Metro for something similar but there had been nothing.

To counter the memory she goes up to Alex and kisses his cheek. Their eyes meet fleetingly. He looks affectionate again.

61

She feels better. He nuzzles her hair fleetingly and says that she is beautiful. She squeezes his hand and then moves on to kiss Dave.

'Thanks for the books,' she says. 'I shall have to find time to read them . . .'

'A pleasure,' he says.

'You must make time,' says Isabel.

'That's easy to say,' says Celia.

'You've got as much as you want,' says Alex.

The doorbell saves any further brushes with recrimination.

As he goes to answer it, Celia wonders what is wrong with her husband – something is. He is not usually so abrasive. Even her sister cocks an enquiring eyebrow first at his departing back and then back at her. Celia shrugs.

'Needs a holiday,' she says, aware as she says it that this is the universal Bedford Park panacea. 'Some woman gave him a hard time over this new case of his.'

'Ah ha!' says Dave with a mock leer. '*Cherchez le femme . . .*'

'*La*,' says Celia. '*Femme* is female.'

'Pardon me,' he says, unabashed. 'I hadn't realised that.'

Laughter echoes down the hallway. Tom and Susannah have arrived. Any residual atmosphere is immediately dispelled by Tom who enters bearing a huge bouquet of flowers that eclipses any of the blooms growing in the conservatory.

'Oh, oh, oh,' gasps Celia. 'How wonderful. Are they for me?'

'Give us a kiss first,' says the bearer. 'Hallo, you two.' He nods amid the profusion of pink carnations, white roses and sprigs of freesia towards Isabel and Dave before advancing, with puckered lips, in Celia's direction. She kisses him lightly, judging the embrace so that it is neither too short to offend Tom, nor too long to arouse anyone's suspicions that there is anything other than friendliness between them. Then Susannah puts her hand on Celia's shoulder and kisses her cheek. Both actions are light as gossamer, as if her friend were not really doing it at all. Which is quite, Celia smiles to herself, in character.

'Now I must go and put these in a vase,' she says, extricating herself from them both and gazing at the lovely flowers.

'Open this first,' says Susannah, handing her an exquisitely wrapped box.

'I can't,' laughs Celia.

Isabel comes to her aid and takes the bouquet so that her hands are free. She begins opening the paper carefully, taking the ribbon off just so, undoing the folds so that the wrapping is scarcely torn. Then she pauses to read the tag which says, in Susannah's stylish hand, 'With love from Susie and Tom. May it and the next forty years always be full.'

'I wonder what it can be.'

'Come on,' says Alex. 'Hurry up and open it. You'll know then.'

'That's my sister for you,' says Isabel. 'Taking her time. I don't think I ever remember Celia ripping the paper off anything – she always took hours. Buck up, Cee, we all want to know what's inside – not what's wrapped round it. Here ...' with her free hand she takes a corner of the deftly opened wrapping and tears it with a flourish. 'Off ye lendings,' she says in triumph. How can Celia tell her that she finds unwrapping presents a sensual process, like her cookery?

'Thanks,' she says automatically and holds up the now denuded box.

'Careful with it. It's breakable. Don't let those children of yours anywhere near it.'

Again Celia is forced to rely on noises, for she sees that the box is marked with the name Asprey. 'Oh, oh, oh,' she repeats.

'Oh, do come on,' says Isabel.

There is barely time for Celia to run her fingers over the gold lettering of the name before, out of fear that her sister will wrench the present from her, she opens the lid. There, beneath white tissue and winking with a thousand hues of pink, blue, yellow, is a crystal vase; its intricacies apparently cut out of fire – very, very expensive fire.

'Oh *Christ*!' she says. 'You really shouldn't have.'

'We got you a really solid one,' says Susie, 'so that it'd be safe from everything that goes on here. Except a direct hit, of course,' she adds drily.

Celia holds it up. It is truly an object of beauty and would dispel any dissenter's claim that cut glass is cut glass. It sits there, heavy and rich in her hands – and all hers. Just for a moment tears brim up – not unnaturally (three glasses of champagne nearly, and all the emotional upheaval) – and Tom is instantly at her side, kneeling on the floor and wiping under her eyes with a hankie. She shakes him off, not only because the act is too tender and intimate, though that is part of it, but because despite the kindness of the gesture he keeps poking her in the eye and, with all that extra mascara she has on, she is likely to end up looking like a prize-fighter. Tom takes the shaking-off as disdain and leaps to his feet.

'Susie wins the bet,' he says.

'What bet?' asks Isabel.

'Well *I* said we should get her something more personal. A piece of jewellery or something—'

'Earrings,' says Susie. 'He thought earrings. I said that from what I knew of Celia she scarcely wears jewellery – unless it's that punky stuff – do you, Cee?'

What can she say? The proof of Susie's remark is hanging in outrageous splendour from her ears.

'Ah yes,' says Tom. He touches one lightly so that it swings, and then tickles her ear lobe as if pollenating a flower. Then he pinches it – and none too gently either. 'Not the likes of diamonds for our little mother here – too wicked by half.'

'And they might come from South Africa,' says Alex, 'which would be worse.'

'Not at all,' says Celia, rising with dignity and ignoring her husband's well-received witticism. 'As a matter of fact I like little earrings very much – the wickeder the better.' She looks across at Alex who looks back at her quite nicely but also quite blankly. The forget-me-nots have clearly been forgotten.

'Drinks!' says Alex. 'Ready for a beer yet, Dave?'

Isabel is squeezing the flowers far too tightly. Celia grabs them and says lightly, 'I must go and put *these* lovely things into water in *this* lovely thing. That is –' she laughs 'unless you two have brought me a special pint of that as well?' She gives her head a little shake so that the outrageous enamels tinkle about, puts the flowers down carefully and well out of Isabel's way, and goes off to the kitchen with the vase. Behind her she hears Dave say, 'You can get a taste for this sort of thing, Alex. But then – I expect you have.'

She watches the water sloosh into the beautiful object and wonders why, as she watches, she feels sad. There is an odd encroaching sense of doom in her tonight. Forty, of course. That is what it is, she thinks, and quite understandable too. '*Après-moi la ménopause,*' she mutters. If Rebecca were not such a light sleeper she would nip up and give her a cuddle, two women together: what comfort that simple thing called mother-love can be. As she turns off the tap and puts both hands around the neck of the vase to lift its heaviness, so she feels two hands go simultaneously around her own waist, and squeeze her gently so that she gets goosepimples from their warmth.

'Oh, Alex,' she breathes, 'isn't it a lovely present?'

'Right comment, wrong person.' It is Tom's voice, a hot exhalation in her ear. She tenses, but only because not to tense would be to give in to the gooseflesh, which is lovely. He feels it – and drops his hands from her waist.

'Goody-goody,' he says. The remark is an accusation, not a celebration. She feels his body pressing against her and – Oh God – her sense of touch is hallucinating, for she can feel a hard protuberance from him to her somewhere in the region of her buttocks. Tom has an erection. She nearly drops the Asprey marvel back into the sink.

'Tom,' she says in her best Joyce Grenfell manner, 'don't do that.'

Still he remains pressing up against her, the hard bit very hard indeed. It surprises her with its hardness, she finds herself dwelling on the rock-like aspect of it. Truth to tell (which she would not do – not even to Hazel) she is flattered by its permanence. Guiltily she swivels round to face him and the hard bit is now biting into her left hip. Were she not holding a hundred pounds' worth of crystal in her hands she might well pass out with the erotic counterpoint.

'Please – Tom.' She drops her eyes to where the hard bit digs in, quite unable to focus on anything but that.

'Typical,' he says. 'I come out here bearing gifts—'

Not lifting her eyes she sees his hand move towards the offensive area and she thinks, Oh My God – he's going to take it out – here – and me with my hands full of Asprey vase. She is stuck, motionless. And there is no doubt that of all the emotions running through her, fear and excitement are twinned.

Oh God, no! she thinks. And anyway – what am I supposed to *do* with it when he does? I've got my hands full enough as it is. Am I supposed to go Ooh, Aah, what a lovely one? Nevertheless her eyes are riveted to his hand which moves ever-stealthily towards the bump. He looks nervously over his shoulder. The hand moves stealthily on. It does not, however, engage his flies at all, but passes them by and digs down into his jacket pocket from which, surreptitious as a watch-seller in a pub, he removes a rectangular box, gift-wrapped. About the size and shape of a large pen and pencil set.

'For you,' he says sweetly, *sotto voce*. 'To be opened when there is no one else around. It is a special gift, from me to you.'

She looks up at him. His face is rather flushed and one of his eyes is twitching dangerously.

'Oh Tom,' she says, thrilled and thankful but a mite disappointed. 'You shouldn't have.'

'Where shall I hide it?' he asks peremptorily.

She stares about the kitchen, caught up in the pleasure of the deceit, and extremely glad that he is not a mind-reader. It must be jewellery, she thinks. Now here *was* a game. A whole series of them – from pass the parcel and guess the object, to hunt the thimble ... where would such a thing be safe?

'I know,' she says. 'Put it in the washing machine.'

He gapes.

'Go on,' she says. 'No one ever looks in there except me.'

So in it goes and he closes the door and they both walk out into the conservatory as if life were no more than a vase full of water on a special birthday night.

Alex pops another cork and remarks that Hazel and John are late as usual.

Celia says she expects it is the children.

'Very probably,' says Alex, meandering around with the bottle. 'No doubt little Caspar has shat himself again.'

'Surely he was doing that months ago?' says Susie. 'When we were last here with them? How disgusting.'

'Some children take longer to train than others,' says Isabel, sniffing the rose and smiling above it at Celia. 'Don't they? Usually the more sensitive ones.'

Isabel and Dave's boys were in nappies at night until they were ten. This has always been put down to their sensitivity.

Susie grimaces. 'Hardly sensitive, I wouldn't have thought. Thick more like it. I mean – if I can train Vesta in a week, surely he can be trained in however many years it is ... He must be remedial.'

'Who's Vesta?' asks Celia, trying to diversify.

'My cat.'

There is a deafening silence after this remark, broken suddenly by an agonised Dave who has been desperately trying to think of something to say before his wife does. So he looks at Tom, grins awkwardly and shrugs, saying, 'Kids! Who'd have 'em?'

'Not us –' says Tom, not smiling back – 'if you remember ...'

Dave's seat creaks with his embarrassment. 'Ah yes,' he gasps, anxiously searching for something diplomatic to say. 'No wonder you're so successful at what you do.'

'Oh – and does the one necessarily negate the other?' asks Alex. It comes out rather thinly as he speaks through gritted teeth.

Celia snaps the stem of a long carnation and wonders, again, what on earth is wrong with him tonight. Playfully she says into her flowers. 'Alex is very successful. Alex has got a big important case today so he's going to be even more successful, even more renowned because of it.' She plonks the carnation into the centre of the display. '*And* he's got children.'

Alex, who has been advancing towards her empty glass with the second bottle, immediately swerves away without filling it. He is definitely offended. Celia considers this and decides that very possibly it did sound like a criticism. *She* is also, now, feeling sensitive again, but puts that down quite definitely to the occasion being what it is. In fact, she thinks, everyone is behaving in an over-sensitive way. As if they were all in an early Pinter. Queer, very queer, she wants to say.

Dave says, 'I'm glad I don't have the professional responsibilities of you two.' He means the men. 'I made my decision back at university that I wasn't going to get on the gravy train and I opted out. It's either exploit or be exploited when you're high-powered.'

'That's what makes it so enjoyable,' says Tom.

And Alex looks at Dave as if he had just crawled out from under a palm pot. 'I don't exploit anybody. I help – that's what my profession is all about – fair play – justice, if you like.'

Celia clamps her mouth closed. She is not going to get into all that again and there is a strong desire to say what Alex has so often said to *her* – that in his profession it is usually the Law which is upheld rather than Justice.

'Oh, we all exploit somebody,' says Isabel.

'I don't,' says Alex obstinately.

Oh God, thinks Celia.

'If I had to change a crappy nappy,' says Susie, 'I should say that was exploitation.' She laughs and crosses over to Celia and begins poking around at the flowers.

'All women are exploited. And wives in particular,' says Dave. 'They have to be. If they weren't the whole economy would seize up.'

'People have nannies for that sort of thing,' says Tom, disparagingly. He is looking at his wife.

68

'I didn't,' says Celia happily.

'You're different,' says Tom.

'That's not to say you couldn't have.' Alex's voice is very sharp.

'Oh, I know – I just didn't want one, that's all. I was quite happy being a Mum.'

'Don't you exploit – as you call it – Isabel, then?' Alex's jaw has gone out a fraction, which is not a good sign.

'I exploit as few people as possible. It's a decision I made a long time ago. And woman is the nigger of the world, you know – sexually, domestically, financially – I just don't want to be a part of all that. That's why I didn't finish my degree. So that I could get out of something that would force me to exploit, and into something that wouldn't. That's why I'm a plumber. I'm not chasing anybody else's arse or required to show that I know how to behave in public. *And* I don't have to stay away from home – which is, I reckon, where all those mid-life divorces start – I'm around for the kids, and Isabel can get on with her job too. I respect my wife. Politically, I have to.'

All eyes move to Isabel who looks down coyly and with deep satisfaction into the rose. Celia feels – quite suddenly – that she could smack her.

Alex picks up the bottle. 'Great,' he says. 'Let's all become plumbers and go and live in Moscow. Meanwhile more champagne, you running dogs of capitalism?'

Susannah gives a delicate little snort of amusement. She has always admired Alex's wit. It is one of the reasons he likes her.

Celia holds out her empty glass but the question was purely rhetorical.

Tom stares at Dave, genuinely incredulous. 'Are you saying you understood all that at twenty? That's amazing.'

'It's not particularly,' says Susie. 'I'd planned my life by then.'

'Had you indeed?' says her husband.

'It isn't that amazing,' says Dave deprecatingly. 'After all – I was a sociology student.'

'I don't like even having my cleaner, actually,' Celia says – just as a general statement.

'Ah,' says Dave, 'even an ex-Labour supporter has her principles – doesn't she?'

But it was not principles she had in mind.

She is still holding out her empty glass. Tom notices and leaps to his feet, rattan racketing. Dave gives her a wink, pleased with his little barb, as if to say, That'll set the cat among the pigeons, but instead of what she expects, which is that Alex will immediately start to have a go at Dave about socialism, her husband gives a faintly derisory grunt – or possibly a chuckle, the two are often similar with Alex – and slaps his brother-in-law on the arm. Then they both snort together. It is unfortunate that it is Tom's face into which she is looking as he pours out her champagne because he – who does not in the least deserve it – gets the full, sour, not to say acid, benefit of her expression. Quite reasonably, on receipt of this, his handsome, indulgent features lose their affectionate light and go quite hard. Without finishing filling her glass he plonks the bottle back down on the table and himself back down into the chair which – just as reasonably – groans and shrieks in protest.

'Careful of that chair, Tom,' she says automatically.

'Sorry,' he says. 'Wouldn't want to break up the happy home.'

She turns away, aware that there is a flush on her face, and finds herself looking straight into Susannah's eyes, which smile at her. Instantly she is reminded of that wicked package in the washing machine. But it is all right – she would never let Susie down. Not really. Still, it's a nice secret – and harmless. She looks back at Tom as sweetly as she can manage but he is draining his class ceilingwards and does not see.

Susie says, 'You're looking flustered, Celia. I knew we should have taken you out for a meal. It's unfair that you should have to cook for us on your birthday.'

'Oh, no. I like it. I really do. And I'm good at it.' She holds the dish of olives up. Susie runs her long pink nails through her smooth blonde hair and shakes her head looking faintly disgusted. She offers the dish to Isabel, who puts up her hand with sensible-length unpainted nails, and says, 'How anyone can actually *like* the taste of those things beats me.'

'*And* they're full of calories . . .' says Susie, giving Celia a look.

Celia pops one in her mouth defiantly. 'I love food,' she says, 'and I love cooking. It merges those two most dynamic forces – science and art. And it's something I'm good at.'

'Sometimes,' says Isabel, 'It's good to have a go at things you're *not* good at.'

Immediately Celia is twelve again, bringing home a book token for five pounds which she won for a composition prize at school. If it had been a prize for sums, her sister had said, she could see the point in being so proud – but since it was for something Celia excelled in anyway, well . . .

'I wasn't always good at it,' she says, 'I had to learn. The cookery I like best is as much about pleasing the soul as the stomach – and making it aesthetically pleasing as well as good to eat. Even at its lowest level cooking is about timing and co-ordination –' She is about to go on to say that you need only watch an inexperienced cook (she has Alex in mind but would diplomatically never say so) attempt to produce a hot meal comprising chops, mashed potato and cabbage to understand what she means, when her brother-in-law interrupts with the quip, 'And just what do you know about the lowest level nowadays?'

'Oh,' she says, 'children are very conservative on the whole. As long as it's well cooked they will eat very basic stuff – fish fingers and chips are the current favourites . . .'

Of course this is not what Dave was implying but she considers she has fenced it rather well. Perhaps an aspect of being forty is that your wits get sharper. It is a hopeful thought. She goes on swiftly. 'I do wish Hazel and John would get here.'

'Has she ever thought of smacking him when he shits himself?' asks Susie. Celia pictures Hazel's face if the suggestion were put to her. In Bedford Park residents tend not to inflict violence upon their offspring. They discuss, negotiate, find excuses, rather than let rip with the red weal of a handmark across the back of a leg. Uncontrolled passions are not a feature of the locality.

'He'll grow out of it,' says Celia. 'Once he discovers it doesn't create much excitement any more.'

'Perhaps that's what he needs,' says Susannah. 'A bit more excitement in the form of a smack or two.'

Alex stands up. 'We tend not to do that around here if we can help it. Henry never caused us any problems –' He looks at Celia for agreement. She gives him an uncomfortable smile.

'He was very good really,' she says.

Alex adds, 'And all without having to belt the living daylights out of him,' with a definite touch of pride.

And then, miraculously, everybody begins to discuss the way children should be brought up – even Susannah and Tom who, if they have no personal experience, were children once themselves and so can join in with impunity.

Celia takes the opportunity of slipping off into the kitchen, and wishes heartily that she still smoked. The last statement from Alex was not exactly true. There had been one unfortunate episode. A hot June day, rather like today now she comes to think of it, or even hotter. Rebecca had been a tiny babe in arms, as yet unseen by Alex's mother. Celia was due at the South Coast bungalow for lunch to show off the new offspring. (It had not occurred to Alex to arrange for his mother to come up and save his wife the effort of going down – all he foresaw was a lovely day by the sea for his family. Blessed are the peacemakers, he had said to Celia when she protested. Blessed are the dogsbodies, more like, she had replied.) All the same, there was no point in making an issue of it. Anyway, car journeys were one of the few things that helped keep newborn Rebecca asleep, and there were few enough of those. She prepared to set off in none too good humour. Her mother-in-law was not the most sympathetic of people and did not like (as well as blacks and supermarkets and policemen with beards) lateness, and there was a good couple of hours driving ahead in all that heat. Already Rebecca had sucked a few antirrhinum leaves, thoughtfully provided for her by Henry, and had dribbled pale-green goo all down the front of her best white frock. She had then protested loudly at the subsequent change into pink gingham. All this took so long to arrange that Celia's timetable (feed baby, drive off immediately after and therefore arrive with beaming infant because the next feed was not due yet) was all ruined. They would now, undoubtedly, arrive with a screaming Rebecca and mother-in-law would be able to consolidate her first impressions, birthed in Henry's babyhood, that Celia made a poor mother.

Well, she got them all into the car somehow – wound down all the windows, turned on the ignition – and was just pulling away from the kerb when the rich, ripe smell of crap pervaded the car. Shoes checked, she could only turn, in horror, to the carrycot in the back, but a quick motherly poke among the baby's Peau-Douce revealed just a pink talcum powdered bottom. And anyway, she sort of knew instinctively already that the smell came from something a bit more substantial than her own milk. Her eyes met Henry's – his alight with defiance, hers with disbelief – and she broke. She hauled him into the front seat and twisted his ear until even his screams penetrated her own red rage, kicked him out on to the pavement, slapped him all the way upstairs, and alternately showered the foulness from him while beating his bottom into a mass of red weals. And if you ever do it again, she said, I will kill you.

And when, fresh and settled back in the car, tears finished with, he had piped up that he would tell his father, she had braked hard, grabbed his hair and told him if he ever uttered a single word to anyone about it, she would kill him twice. Henry had never sullied his pants again, mother-in-law had been forced to compliment her on her well-behaved children (even Rebecca, perhaps because she had absorbed some of her brother's fear, arrived smiling milkily) and Alex never suspected that his perfectly potty-trained family owed its good grace to violence. Celia had never even told Hazel about the incident.

Not even when Hazel had bemoaned Caspar's inadequacies and asked her what the secret of her success had been. 'Just one of those things,' Celia had said and made up for it by saying what a sweet nature Caspar had. Untrue but it seemed to appease.

The sight of all the beautiful preparations in the kitchen makes her impatient. She wants to control the evening and not feel like an outsider which – peculiarly, unpleasantly – she does. She returns to the conservatory where everybody is chatting happily now and even Alex seems to have dropped whatever it was that made him tense. He and Dave and Tom are discussing pre-war Rileys as if they were desirable women: Isabel and Susie are talking about television soaps. It seems that they both prefer 'Dynasty' to 'Dallas'. In Bedford Park such programmes are not acknowledged as discussion points. Hereabouts 'Dynasty' and 'Dallas' are programmes that people catch when 'just by chance I was turning on for the news and caught the last few minutes.' Amazing how detailed the knowledge can be from just those last few minutes, Celia has always thought.

She goes over to the men.

Alex puts his arm around her shoulders and kisses her cheek and draws her in to the circle. 'Hallo, birthday girl,' he says. 'Happy?'

She nods and looks up at him. He is still intent on what Tom is saying about the Arab market for pre-nineteen-fifty models.

'I think we should ring Hazel and John,' she whispers.

'No point,' he says. 'They're either delayed or on their way. Telephoning isn't going to alter that.'

The very logic of this is annoying. As is so often the case with Alex's legal training, he goes straight to the dry imponderables and what he says cannot be faulted. That it would make Celia feel better to ring up is an emotional argument. 'I expect it's the way all that chrome winks in the sunlight over there ...'

'What?' she says, but then realises he is addressing Tom.

It is her birthday, so she asserts herself.

'You do it for me then,' she says. 'I'd like to know. That's all.'

Grudgingly Alex raises his pale eyebrows to the assembly, and then looks back at her. 'All right, all right – any whim of yours shall be satisfied tonight . . .'

'Ho Ho . . .' someone says, and there is laughter.

Alex goes off to telephone and Celia is left feeling like an idiot.

'Talking of which,' says Isabel, 'what had you planned tonight – apart from eating, I mean – anything?'

Determined to sound confident, Celia says, 'Yes. I thought we'd play some games. Like we used to in the old days.'

Somebody groans.

'Fair play,' says Isabel indulgently. 'It's her birthday. We'll all do whatever Celia wants – won't we?'

'I'm forty – not four,' snaps Celia.

Perhaps, she thinks, this is what happened to the *Marie Céleste*. They all got so niggled before the meal that none of them could stand it when they sat down to eat – so they left the table and committed a watery suicide *en masse*.

'I'll just go and put the meat in the oven,' she says.

'Good grief,' says her sister. 'It'll take hours, won't it?'

'We like it pink in the middle here,' she says. 'Not done to death.'

In the kitchen she finds Alex going through the telephone directory. 'I don't know their number,' he says.

She puts her arms round him. He, still clutching the directory, puts his arms round her.

'I love you,' she says, feeling immediately better.

He holds her closer, the spine of the *S-Z* digging into her back.

'Kiss me,' she adds, since he says nothing.

Behind them the telephone shrills making them both jump.

'That'll be them,' he says, disengaging himself.

'At last,' she says fervently.

She opens the oven which is already at top heat because she remembered to turn it on some time ago. At least, she thinks, some aspects of her domain still function normally whatever her age. She puts in the beautiful, symmetrical piece of veal. As she pushes the door closed she decides that any scratchiness tonight is probably due to her. And that if it isn't, it is still the easiest thing to think that it is. With this complicated piece of philosophy firmly tucked under the peacock-blue highlight she returns her attention to Alex and the telephone. On the way her attention wavers for a moment and fixes upon the washing machine. Any residual irritation, unease, ill-temper, is immediately overcome by peering through the concave glass door, mysterious and purple, wherein she is just able to distinguish the oblong of the gift. The prospect of opening the washing-machine door tomorrow is so tantalising that she smiles to herself quite involuntarily. It is a smile of such alluring proportions that Alex would, despite the Brandreth case and the hundred and one other things on his plate, find it hard to resist. As it is he has his eyes on the kitchen floor as he talks on the telephone and misses it entirely. It is Tom who gets the full beauty of its seductive mystery when he appears at the kitchen door – and it balances out the earlier one of sourness. For some reason, he too, looks at the washing machine with what appears to be just a twinge of remorse as well as conspiracy. Well, thinks Celia, remorse is a fitting emotion for a married man giving away presents to another woman.

'They're just setting off,' says Alex.

'Oh good – that means they'll be here any minute.'

Tom goes off to the lavatory, Celia and Alex return to the conservatory – her with her arm around his waist, he with his arm around her shoulders.

'You do look very beautiful tonight,' he whispers.

'Just a minute, you two,' says Isabel and she takes from her handbag her camera. 'Stay just as you are –' So they do, and she snaps them. 'One for the album,' she says.

Behind them comes Tom. 'What was all this about games, then, Celia?' he says, slipping his hand around her waist. Sandwiched and held between him and Alex she feels like a dancer from *Zorba the Greek*. 'Tell us what you've got in mind. You know me – I *love* games . . .'

76

Both men disentangle themselves from her body at the same time, as if choreographed. She feels rather relieved.

'I just thought it'd be fun. After all, we know each other so well we can be as silly as we like. It's a long time since I've done anything *really* silly. I feel like making an idiot of myself – I think it is kind of propitious for tonight. It may be the last time – I may never get the chance again.'

Isabel looks at Celia's colourful hair. 'I wouldn't say that.' She smiles quite nicely.

Celia doesn't.

Susie says, 'Games it is then.'

Tom says, 'I'm game,' and nudges Celia.

Alex looks heavenwards at the paucity of the wit. But he nods.

Dave says, 'That must be just about the height of bour-geoisiosty.' They look at him in wonder. 'If there is such a word.' He laughs.

'And John and Hazel will join in with anything,' says Celia. 'I'm sure they won't mind.'

Susie is dabbling her long pink nail in her champagne, no drop of which has passed her perfect pink lips. 'It doesn't matter. Nothing matters tonight except that you have a lovely time. Right everybody?'

Everybody agrees.

'They ought to be here by now,' says Celia, looking at her watch. 'After all, it's only a few streets away – it takes hardly any time to walk.'

'What a nice idea – to be able to walk to a night out instead of having to drive or get a train.'

'We do it quite a lot in our community,' says Alex.

'Proper little village, eh?' says Dave.

'More so than Surbiton I think.'

Dave and Isabel both open their mouths but Susie gets in first. 'More so than Wootton Deverill anyway,' she says tactfully.

'Have you still got a village school?' asks Isabel.

'No,' says Susie, 'thank God. It's bad enough having the youth club.'

'We're raising money for a computer at ours,' says Isabel.

'Oh, Tom's bought one already for them. Now they need software for it. We're always putting our hands in our pockets one way and another ... still – it's good publicity I suppose.'

'I keep telling Celia that. Computers are *so* important. We've bought the boys one since they showed such an interest in Dave's.'

'Have they taken it apart yet?' asks Celia.

Isabel gives her a look.

The telephone rings.

'I'll go,' says Alex. 'Open another bottle, will you, Dave? Or maybe Tom should. He's probably got more experience of popping corks than you.' And with a look of pleasure at the sharpness of his wit, he goes off to answer the call.

Dave takes the bottle from the cooler and opens it deftly. 'Plumbers happen to be good with their hands,' he says, and gives his wife a wink. 'Don't they Izzie?'

Celia is made supremely jealous by the blush that suffuses her sister's face. How she wishes she had been successful earlier in the bedroom. In a desire for some kind of appeasement she crosses the room to Tom and, not a little buoyed up by the washing-machine's secret and the champagne she has drunk, she says, 'And second-hand car salesmen?'

'Oh,' he says, 'they're *very* good with theirs, too ...'

So that she has to sit down and cross her legs very hard and remind herself that it is Parlour Games and not Adult Games they will be playing later. Surely Hazel and John must get here soon? Their presence would bring some kind of order, she feels sure. She squirms and the rattan shrieks. Alex, just returning, looks delighted as he says, 'Careful with that chair, Celia.' His mimicry of her earlier criticism is wickedly good.

Before she can reply he goes on, 'Enter stage left, a messenger, bearing tidings.' Like the good lawyer he is he waits for his timing to be right before continuing. 'That was John.'

'What!' Celia sits bolt upright; shriek, shriek from the chair. 'John! *Phoning?* Why?'

Alex looks pleased to have captured everyone's attention before dropping his expression to one of suitable commiseration.

'They've had a bit of a crash on the way over.' He holds up his hands at the oohs and the aahs. 'Nothing serious, but Hazel's got whiplash. She's a bit shaken up so John's taking her home. He may come on later. He said not to worry.' Alex pauses again for more oohs and aahs. 'He said it was the perfect example of the accolade "we nearly broke our necks to get there ..."' Everybody laughs, except Celia.

'Why on earth did they drive?' she wails.

'They were late because Caspar ...'

'Oh, don't bother,' she says tetchily. 'Why can't that dirty little tyke stop his tricks—'

'Now, now,' says Tom. 'That's not like you.'

'If you cry on your birthday,' says Isabel (as she used to say so regularly), 'you'll cry for the rest of the year.'

Two tears – one of rage, one of frustration – escape from Celia's eyes.

'That's done it,' says Dave.

Celia brushes them away and stands up.

'They aren't the first I've shed tonight,' she says.

Tom gives her a sad little look.

She ignores it, for its tenderness is too desirable.

'Let's get in to the dining room for Christ's *sake*,' she says. 'Or everything will be spoilt.'

3

The cool dimness of the dining room after the bright sunshine of the conservatory produces a calm and peaceful air among the guests. The sober glow of the furniture's old wood (nothing wrong with Mrs Green's ability to polish when the quality is worthy of it) and the simple precision of the table settings gives a quiet sense of harmony to the scene. Celia has chosen the soft whiteness of damask for the tablecloth and pale Italianate pink for the serviettes. The cutlery winks in the candlelight and a dainty arrangement of jasmine and honeysuckle from the garden sends out a delicate perfume. On the white plates the peachy-pink of the fish nestles against the sharp yellow of the lemon and the greeny-blackness of the watercress. She feels happy again: this is her domain; this is what she is good at. What has she been getting so het up about? She is a perfectly ordinary Bedford Park wife in her perfectly ordinary Bedford Park house within the bosom of her perfectly ordinary Bedford Park family – having a slightly special birthday. That is *all*, she tells herself, that is *all*.

She surveys the table, the guests, the setting and the players. Here is perfection, she decides, here is perfection that is mine; I could not have done all this when I was twenty; this is an art that comes only with age; like the furniture she has become polished. No more rough edges, no more risks. Which is as it should be. She sends a deeply satisfied smile in her husband's direction but finds that out of the corner of his eye he is scrutinising his reflection in the smoky gilded glass above the mantel. Odd, she thinks again, very odd. Perhaps her own middle ground *does* make him reappraise his. She looks at him with love. For all his shifts and foibles she loves him still. Passion recollected in tranquillity: a little sigh escapes her at this thought. It would have been so nice to recollect a more recent experience of passion than – when? – she thinks hard – when *did* they last make love? It must be over a week – she puts her fingers to her mouth to concentrate – no, more than that, more like two weeks – ever since the final intensity of the Brandreth case deepened and Alex has been either away from home or much too tired – it could even be three weeks … Guiltily and fleetingly she sneaks a quick look at Tom. Thank heavens he has no idea how often Celia is left alone for she is certain he would consolidate. (When thinking of Tom one does well to think in business terms since he is, by nature, a man of business.) Tom pursues Celia, so Celia thinks, as he would pursue a new market. She is not arrogant in feeling relieved that he is unaware of her spending nights on her own – she is right to do so – and as she does so another thought follows on which is, taking in the reckoning of her two, maybe three weeks' sexual hiatus, that she could have accommodated Tom very nicely if she had chosen to. Which, of course, she did not. This only goes to show what a good contented wife she is and what a good marriage they have. Alex is not the only one allowed to feel smug, she thinks. After all, she, too, has worked hard enough for it.

The correct approbation greets the scene. Little subdued noises from the throats of her guests that signal recognition of her prowess. Celia points them into their places. With the absence of Hazel and John there is more room for them to spread. She puts Tom to her left and Dave to her right. Then Alex at the head of the table, flanked by Isabel and Susie. In the glow of the candlelight everybody looks beautiful and the tensions at last seem to have evaporated. As they seat themselves they all look quite dignified and at ease. Even Susie, who is without the benefit of champagne, is relaxed enough to give the jasmine and honeysuckle only the most fleeting of arrangements with her lovely manicured hands. Celia notices that they do look better now. Damn. She shakes off the irritation. Ah well, she thinks, almost perfection. Susannah always did have the edge.

Alex wrests his gaze away from the mirror and takes one of the two bottles of wine from their silver coolers.

'First,' he says, 'a toast to my beautiful wife.'

They raise their filled glasses and drink to her. Affection and goodwill reflect out of the five pairs of eyes as they speak. She feels like a bride again and decides that this was the right thing to do after all. Gone are the hints of the *Marie Céleste*. She raises her glass to answer them, and gives a long, slow smile around the table, which ends on Tom. She is just about to sip her wine, having said 'To you all' in a suitably dainty way, when she feels his hand, very hot on her knee. The suitable daintiness gives way to a little shriek and some of her wine splashes on to the tablecloth. Tom is the only one not looking at her. She gives her knee a jerk, which does not dislodge the hand, and carries on gamely.

'Sorry,' she says to the startled assembly, and borrows the first phrase that comes to mind which is unfortunately one of Mrs Green's. 'One of my twinges ...' She shrugs. 'Rheumatism.' She embroiders the theme.

'You should go to a homeopath,' says Susie.

'There was an excellent programme on the radio this morning about diet and health,' says Isabel. 'I taped it for the staff. You can't begin too early getting the message across to children.' She looks at Celia pointedly. 'Did you hear it?'

'I had the radio on,' says Celia – rather cleverly, she fancies.

'Interesting, that bit about the RDA of Tricalcium Phosphate, wasn't it?'

'Very,' says Celia. 'Very, very interesting.'

What is RDA? she wonders.

What is Tricalcium Phosphate?

'So will you be taking it?'

'Will you?' Celia hazards.

'I already do,' says Isabel.

Tom's hand is creeping upwards.

'You look shocked,' says her sister.

'No, no,' says Celia, trying to adopt a nun-like expression. 'I'm quite unshockable nowadays.' And beneath the table she brings her knee up very sharply so that Tom's knuckles get a nasty squashing. He bites the bullet, in the shape of a great gulp of his drink, and says nothing. The hand remains just above the knee. As long as it stays approximately in that area Celia can deal with it.

To her relief Isabel and Susannah have begun to discuss alternative medicine.

'Let's eat,' says Celia. She gives her leg a hopeful shake. Tom removes the hand and gives a loud sighing exhalation.

'No need to blow on it,' says Dave. 'I think it's already gone cold.' He indicates the prettily arranged plates.

Tom looks meaningfully at Celia and says, with surprising vigour, 'I know, old man – I know.' He drains his glass.

Alex says, 'I'm not going to stand on ceremony tonight. You can all help yourselves.' He points at the bottles and adds another to the pair.

Tom reaches for it and refills his glass. Celia grabs a baguette, breaks a large chunk off and plonks it on to his plate. It destroys the harmony of the food but she thinks it might soak up the drink.

'Thank you, Mummy,' he says in a squeaky voice.

Alex, not one to be overwhelmed by others' conversations, steers a straight course between the virtues of evening primrose and charcoal tablets, and says to Dave, 'You should approve of this new case of mine. Bringing the City to book...'

Dave is peering suspiciously at his plate and poking about at the little pink fillet, breaking it up into pieces in his quest for a bone or two. He prefers his fish from the supermarket freezer where its shape bears no relation to its origins and where a machine (clever this technology) has succeeded in removing every trace of its skeleton. Celia leans towards him and whispers very gently that he need not worry, she has removed all but the finest hair bones. He dips a chunk of it into the mayonnaise and thinks it is a bit bland compared with the stuff they have at home. It has a strange taste, too. He carries on guardedly and says to Alex, 'Tell us about it,' knowing that he will anyway. And so Alex begins.

He begins with how many rival firms he has knocked out of the running and how all that their main rival has been left with is a piddling bit of consultancy – and this is to be done by a woman. He pays her the highest compliment that he can in the circumstances, which is that she has deserved her small success since throughout the preliminaries, and in all her dealings, she has behaved just like a man ... Celia would ordinarily have pointed out that this statement is in direct contrast to his earlier assertions about sexual equality but she does not. She is still walking on eggshells tonight and will go as lightly as she can. It is not worth risking the adult sanctuary later. So much for Lesley Gore, she thinks.

'What an odd taste this mayonnaise has,' says her sister, wrinkling her nose and sucking in her cheeks like an expert wine taster. 'What is it?'

Susie has dipped the very tip of a watercress frond into hers and tastes it. 'Tarragon,' she says.

And so much for Celia's little surprise.

Dave looks even more suspicious.

'Good for the digestion,' says Susie knowingly.

'Makes you burp a lot.' Celia giggles at her brother-in-law. Dave giggles back. Isabel raises her eyebrows, opens her mouth to speak, but is forestalled by Alex's determination to keep the subject of the Brandreth case and its social implications alive.

'On the whole,' he says, 'doing something like this is much more useful than waving banners about.'

He and Celia exchange looks. Hers defy his pointedness by assuming a greeny-blue innocence. Not an eggshell cracks. Celia's eyes remain empty of remark. Alex, if he ever did so, might be excused for thinking that, on the whole, his wife is not *au fait* with his career.

Very soon everyone, except Tom, is apparently listening hard. Tom is the only one to whom eating has not become secondary: this is because Celia, who is both trying to listen hard and also to deal with Tom at the same time (not too difficult for her since she quite often has this dual role to play when they eat with the children), keeps pushing bits of food around his plate to entice him. Susannah is eating the watercress and not much else and thinking to herself that Celia is looking decidedly mumsy and that if she is not careful she will end up looking exactly like Isabel who *is* entirely mumsy – always was, always will be. But Susie always had hopes for Celia. That aquamarine skirt may match her eyes, but it also seems to Susannah that there is more than just the material bunched up around her hips – Celia has definitely spread in the last couple of years. Two or three pounds at least. She catches Celia's eye and mouths the word 'delicious' as she crunches more of the dark green leaves. Celia guiltily removes her hands from the proximity of Tom's plate in case Susie has noticed, which she hasn't, and smiles back 'thanks'. Susie thinks, on the whole, Celia is looking strained.

'That's awful,' Isabel is saying to Alex.

'I quite often have to spend time away from home,' he says.

'Your poor family,' says Isabel.

Celia has been working quite hard at moving Tom's glass away from his reach. Like an illusionist she has managed to push it fractionally every so often when his attention was elsewhere so that now he must really stretch to get hold of it. She is enormously pleased with the achievement and finds her sister's comment – whatever its fount – annoying.

'Oh, I don't mind,' she says chirpily. 'It can't be very nice for Alex either. Anyway I've got used to him whizzing around the country in pursuit of financial felons.'

'Yes – but tomorrow . . .'

'What – tomorrow?' She moves the silver cooler and the bottle half an inch. Another two such moves and he will have to reach out like a prostrate monk to get both his glass and the bottle in hand.

'Alex going away . . .'

'Oh,' she says, still paying scant attention, much more involved with moving the wine, which she does successfully at last. 'He quite often does.'

'But tomorrow! It's the weekend. What about the children?'

Celia suddenly enters the conversation cognisantly. Tomorrow? 'Tomorrow is Saturday, Alex.'

He looks uncomfortable.

'You can't be going away tomorrow? You never have to go away at the weekend . . .'

'It's the Brandreth case, darling . . .'

She just manages to stop herself saying Bugger the Brandreth case, which might be considered grounds for divorce.

Isabel looks truly aghast. 'But you really shouldn't let business get in the way of the family's weekend. It's so important. Think of Rebecca and Henry . . .'

'Never mind them,' snaps Susannah, 'Think of Celia. Tomorrow's her real birthday – isn't it Cee? You'll just have to put it off, Alex.' She taps his arm with her long pink nails. 'Won't you?'

'I can't do that,' he says. 'It's all under my control.'

'Well,' says Susie. 'If it's all under your control then you can change it, can't you? If you can't then that means it must be all *out* of your control.'

Alex goes very pink.

Celia lets Susie get on with it – she is much better at this sort of thing – no wonder Susie got on in the world.

'Of course I can't . . .'

Susie is fighting for Celia and will not let go. This is the only sort of thing, really, that she likes to get her teeth into. 'If you've got a properly set-up organisation working for you then it should be able to function – for a short while at least – without its head. A true test of your capabilities is your ability to devolve.'

Alex is beginning to go off the lovely Susannah. Celia sees this and finds it quite amusing.

Dave says, 'T.A. would say that you only can't change it because you don't want to.'

'T.A.?' Alex says. 'The army?'

'Transactional Analysis,' says Isabel. 'Dave and I do it. It helps your relationship with yourself – and others,' she adds with pride.

'Very *Guardian* of you,' snarls Alex.

'No, seriously,' says Dave. 'It does wonders. Izzie and I . . .'

Susie still has the bit between her teeth. 'Never mind that. What about Celia? If you do control your concerns, Alex, then you should be able to leave them to their own devices – that's the way we did things in the States . . . didn't we Tom?'

Tom is gauging the distance of the bottle and the glass, more in puzzlement than desire. 'Personally,' he says, 'I wouldn't leave Celia all alone – she's far too desirable for that.'

Rancour dies in the smiles and nods that follow this – a silly statement for a grown-up to make but sentimental enough to amuse. And quite in keeping with a birthday – especially a woman's fortieth. Celia pushes the wine cooler back in Tom's direction. What the hell. He deserves it. He touches it lightly with his finger as if it might disappear which, given Celia's prestidigital activities, is not a surprising reaction.

'Well, everybody,' she says. 'As it's my birthday let me have the last word. I don't mind if Alex must go away tomorrow. I understand. And so will the children. We shall all do something lovely together, like have a picnic on the river, and I'll go and take poor old Hazel some grapes and take her children with me too.'

On the whole the prospect of spending a day with only the uncomplicated psyches of children to deal with is pleasant after this lot. Anyway, Celia feels happy to be able to show them all how good her relationship with Hazel is. They may be the folk who knew-her-when, but Hazel is as relevant as they are. More so, perhaps, since the *raison d'être* of this dinner party seems to have fallen flat. They may all know her of old, but it doesn't seem to bring with it that effusion of warmth and affection and security that Celia had envisaged. Nor do they seem to care – very much. She invokes Hazel again to make herself feel better. If Hazel were here she would, at least, have had someone whose eye she could catch with an understanding. True she has Susie, but there is the small question of shadowy guilt regarding the washing machine and – well – you only need look at Susie to see she exists in a different life zone.

'My poor friend Hazel,' she says, perhaps a little too loudly. 'Yes – I shall take the children off her hands tomorrow and after we've had a lovely day I shall sit with her in the evening, to keep her company.' This has a nice touch of Jane Austen about it. Bedford Park is a bit like Jane Austen land, she thinks, a kind of microcosm of life. All Human Life Is Here, she says to herself, and then, remembering that this is actually a quote from the *News of the World,* laughs out loud. Alex, in mid-sentence, gives her a quelling look and if he had ever thought he might rearrange his schedule so that he could spend Saturday at home in the bosom of his family, the thought dies. Celia, about to explain what was so funny, decided better not risk further interruption of Alex's monologue. She will save it to tell Hazel tomorrow. Hazel will see the humour of it.

And talking of Hazel, right in the middle of all this, John arrives.

Celia goes to the door, disappointed to find that he is alone, that Hazel is not with him.

'Happy birthday,' he says, rubbing his hands in bonhomie. He is wearing an extremely bright jade-green tracksuit and bounces around on his heels. 'Ran here,' he announces. John is very figure-conscious, very social, breezy on the surface with the trained good humour of an ex-public schoolboy. Anyway, in Bedford Park it is quite acceptable to turn up to an informal dinner party wearing a designer tracksuit. Indeed, round the corner, in another Norman Shaw, there is a host sitting down to table with his neighbours in exactly the same outfit though not – like John's – slightly damp from running. He is an accountant, this other tracksuit-owner, and feels that in some way he is shrugging off his calling for one night at least. Very probably the two will meet one day at the same dinner party, wearing their twin outfits, and feel embarrassed. But, for the time being, they both feel buzzy and unique . . .

To Celia's enquiries about her friend's well-being John at the front door is cheerily dismissive.

'Old girl's a bit shaken up,' he says. 'Left her in bed watching 'Dynasty'. Thought you wouldn't mind if I came along. Alex said I should. Happy birthday.' He puts his arms around her, kisses her cheek, and manoeuvres himself in, all in one move. The sort of social skill his parents paid their fees for.

'Of course – I'm glad you've come. Shall I ring Hazel up?'

'Shouldn't do that,' he says. 'Blake and Krystle are having a hell of an argument. Hazel loves it all really, you know, watches it all the time if we're in ... Got it on video too – all at the back of the drawer.' He rolls his eyes.

Celia feels that she has cheated Hazel of her pretence that she doesn't take television soap operas seriously. She will have to think of some private and secret way of making up for this. 'I'll have the children tomorrow,' she says.

'No need,' says John. 'We've been lent a nanny for the weekend – until the middle of the week, actually.'

Celia feels, oddly, slighted. 'Oh? Whose?'

'Josephine's. You know. Hazel's tennis partner. The crash was outside their house. They've been terrific. The kids are there now and they're coming back tomorrow with said nanny. Josephine's a brick.'

Celia is almost in tears. I want to be a brick, she thinks.

'Why didn't you ask me?'

'It's your birthday, honey-love,' he says. 'You don't want to be bothered. And Jo and Freddy ...'

Jo and Freddy? thinks Celia. They have always been Josephine and Frederick up until now.

'... are quite happy to link their kids and nanny up with ours. It's half-term or something so it all fits in quite nicely.' He raises his hands like a conjurer. 'Perfect. Everything solved.'

It is as if Celia has been pricked with a pin. Not only has Celia forgotten that it is the half-term holiday next week (which is bad enough since she has planned nothing to amuse her offspring and Bedford Park children expect to have amusements planned for them) but – and much worse than this – Josephine, rich, elegant, American Josephine, who has been making overtures in Hazel's direction for nearly six months – ever since they moved into Bedford Park – has made a direct hit. Hazel, the non-political Hazel, was unbothered by their strong connection with the Conservative Party and professed to be unconcerned with them at all, except that Josephine belongs to a tennis club and Hazel likes tennis. Celia, coming from Raynes Park and weaned on the big-brother shadow of Wimbledon, does not ... The few tennis sessions that Hazel and Josephine have undertaken did little damage to Celia and Hazel's united front but now, well, just when she should have been asserting her ascendancy as friend – the good deed has passed to another. Oh, she could weep, she could stamp her foot, she could wail, gnash her teeth, spit – in Raynes Park parlance – in John's eye.

She says, 'How nice. Come on in then.' And makes way for him. As he passes a whiff of something catches her. Before she can stop herself she says, 'John. You've been drinking ... Oh God – you weren't – um – well – when the crash happened ...'

He looks less-than-brightly public school for a moment – understandably – before putting back the mask. 'What a good legal wifey you are, fair Celia.' He laughs. 'As a matter of fact – no. But Freddy has a selection of Highland malts such as I have never seen – and a very generous chap he is too. He also told me ...' Very definitely he has been drinking because, once the excitement of coming through the front door has gone, he relapses a little and he is not, altogether, distinct. '... that your husband – revered chairman of our Neighbourhood Watch ...' He makes a little bow. It is on the tip of her tongue to really hurt him by saying that she can see his bald patch quite clearly – a topic, as Hazel has told her, that is as taboo as incest. '... has said we need no others on the committee. Freddy very put out about this – being in the City and everything.'

She is about to say that in the light of the Brandreth case this is hardly a recommendation. Why should she continue to be tactful Celia? After all, her one really good friend is now (champagne talking to her emotively, but talk it would) under the sway of another. And, what is more, she now realises, this other has one under sway whom she badly needs to be sitting with her at table tonight making her feel, what she has so far *not* felt – that she is a beloved birthday girl? But she stops herself. And further, to make up for the mean, private thought about his thinning hair, she puts her arms around him and gives him a big hug, slightly harder than she might under normal circumstances since, really, the hug contains a good deal of her pain. He sways, backs off a little, catches his trainer heel in the leg of the hall stand, and down he goes – quite well really – either his trips to the gym have paid off or it is the natural crumple of one who has been imbibing Highland malt. Celia, at a loss and still holding on, goes down with him in a flurry of aquamarine and petticoat.

'Bloody hell,' says a voice in the hallway. 'Who's that underneath you?' The owner of the voice kneels down and pulls at Celia's shoulders saying, as he lifts her upwards, in a passionate tone, 'And why couldn't it be me?'

'Tom!' she gasps.

'Hallo, Tom,' says John from the floor, still bright with bonhomie. 'I was hoping you'd be here, old man. How are things?'

They exchange a few pleasantries before Tom goes off to the lavatory.

In the dining room no one seems to have noticed her absence. Straightening her hair and her face she takes John in, makes room for him at the table and departs for the kitchen.

She puts the blade of her knife deep into the veal which spouts the perfect pink juice of a correctly cooked joint. Which restores her. She takes it out of the oven and sets it on the dish to rest a little before carrying it in for carving. Then, mopping her brow, she begins to muster the vegetables – which need little attention – and wonders, annoyed, what is happening to her life. While she is pondering this and checking that the Kenyan beans are exactly right, a hand creeps round her waist and up on to her breast. She is not going to get caught again. She takes the hand and pushes it away, saying easily, 'Oh Tom. Not again, please.'

Alex, jumping as if he has been bitten, says, 'I beg your pardon?'

We all like to think that we can think quickly under fire, Celia amazes herself by discovering this talent now.

'Joke, darling,' she says, turning.

He looks mollified, even smiles – then he produces a laugh, a gay laugh, one that Celia would usually recognise as heralding some kind of defeat or guilt on his part, but she is so immersed in her own that she does not recognise it for anything other than – a gay laugh.

'Darling,' he says, 'I wanted to make sure it was all right about my going away tomorrow. You know that if I could get out of it I would. Don't you?'

So that's it. He's feeling bad about all that. She looks at his anxious face. Like a naughty schoolboy's. Well – if she was feeling annoyed and hurt over him, she is feeling doubly so about Hazel. Perhaps there is a silver lining to be had here? If Alex is away, taking the bloody Brandreth case with him, she can concentrate on evening things up with her friend. She will wrest the children from the grasp of the munificent Jo's nanny and take them on the river. That's what she will do. One in the eye for Josephine and a Brownie point from Hazel for her.

'I don't care. Not really,' she says, and taking Alex's head in her hands (only slightly greasy from the meat, it was low-fat after all) she gives him a long, lingering kiss.

'Christ almighty,' says a voice from the doorway. 'Not another one. I can see I shall have to reassess my opinion of Pure Mother Earth if this goes on . . .'

Alex jumps.

Celia, determined to avoid explanation, and also determined to show Tom how much she enjoys being a happily married woman, attempts to continue the kiss, but Alex will have none of it. Not in public. Besides, he is not at all sure he likes the way Celia said she didn't care. So he moves away, twice affronted, rubbing at his cheek where the slightly greasy deposit still lingers. To Tom this looks as if he is wiping away the embrace.

He glares at Alex. 'You swine,' Celia distinctly hears him say.

'What?' says Alex, still wiping.

'More wine, I think,' says Celia.

'Of course,' says Alex, and he picks up the two breathing bottles and carries them in, calling over his shoulder, 'All right to move on to the red now, darling?'

'Fine,' she calls after him. 'Tom!' she says warningly, for he seems to be advancing. He pays no attention but continues onwards to the washing machine.

'I'm taking this out,' he says positively, pressing and pulling at the door. 'You – apparently – don't need it.' He laughs. And then the laughter turns to sourness, a true sign of inebriation. 'Apparently it's only me who doesn't turn you on. You're at it all over the place with everybody else . . .'

He is scrabbling at the concave door ineffectually.

'Why did you have to choose me to play the madonna with? Open this door at once. Such gifts are not for you.'

Celia is damned if she will. More than ever now, faced with a bleak weekend, she looks forward to opening it. After all, Alex will be away, Hazel does not need her, and she will be forty. She stands sentinel before the concave opening.

'You will not,' she says, and realises that she is still holding the sharp knife. Tom backs off, smiling fearfully.

'Jezebel . . .' he says, continuing the Biblical theme.

'Make up your mind.' She laughs. 'I can't be both.'

'I like it when you laugh,' he says. 'Susannah doesn't do it very often.'

Celia thinks this is a nice variation on the wifely lack of understanding theme.

'Oh, Tom,' she says. 'Get away with you!'

He leans against the wall and folds his arms and looks at her. It is a very exciting look. He is always going to be a very attractive man. He says huskily, 'The offer is still open, you know.'

With the wall behind him he almost looks sober. He certainly looks dangerous.

Celia says, 'Have you still got the flat in Belgravia?' The words are out before she has thought about it.

'Ah-ha!' he says. 'You *haven't* forgotten then ...? No, as a matter of fact –' his voice is low and full of the remembered pleasure of a satisfactory business deal – 'I sold it for a nice margin. I've got one in Shepherd Market now. Empty most of the time. Like to try it?'

She puts a Kenyan bean in her mouth and crunches it, just in case there is the remotest possibility of the word 'Yes' popping out. Suddenly he lunges at her and takes the disappearing other end of the bean in his own mouth. They stand there, very close, sucking maniacally, each determined not to let the other win.

'What on earth are you two doing?'

It is Isabel, on her way to the lavatory.

Celia is doubly amazed at her continuing proclivity for invention.

'Practising for Parlour Games,' she says, straight out.

'I didn't know you meant physical ones,' Isabel retorts. 'And anyway – in my day it used to be matchboxes for that particular one – not vegetables ...'

Since Tom has all the bean in his mouth now, Celia's is free. She pokes out her tongue at the disappearing back of her sister. She has longed to do that ever since she was born. It has taken her forty years to realise it.

Tom, galvanised at the sight of that seductively glistening article, attempts to treat it in similar manner to the Kenyan bean, but Celia will have none of it. She pushes him away and he returns to the dining room and the bottles. He is torn between respect and desire. It appears she is only bashful with him. Perhaps the gift in the washing machine was the right thing to do. Anyway, Celia will see the funny side – she has a good sense of humour after all. Not like Susannah. Give *her* one and she wouldn't know what to do with it.

Well, on the whole, the main course passes off beautifully. John, as latecomer, brings a fresh breeze into the proceedings which eases any prevailing atmosphere, and there is plenty of chatter and plenty of laughter so that anyone listening outside the door would think that lot in there are enjoying themselves.

By the time the puddings are trundled in on the trolley the table has rearranged itself. Dave is now sitting next to Alex and they are united in their views on the iniquities of City sharks. Beer is no longer mentioned and Dave enjoyed his meat course since Celia was thoughtful enough to give him all the outside bits of the joint. Susie and Isabel are side by side and deeply involved in discussions about New York, Susie for it, Isabel against it (though she has, of course, never been – which does not stop her having strong and certain opinions about the place). Tom and John are leaning quite close together, on Celia's left-hand side, and she can't quite hear what they are talking about, though it looks interesting for John is gazing with rapt and slightly flushed expression at Tom who is looking very committed. Since Celia gave up the unequal struggle with Tom and the wine hours ago they now have a bottle each. And why not? This is a party, after all, she reminds herself.

She judges that it is not quite the right time to invade all this happy companionship with the puddings so she pushes the trolley to one side and sits down, wondering who to talk to. If she selects Alex and Dave she will have to shout across her sister and Susie, and if she chooses her sister and Susie she will have to talk about New York which, on the whole, does not interest her since really they just seem to be scoring points off each other the whole time. And so for a minute or two she just sits, resting on her laurels, quite happy not to be doing anything and yet knowing that she could, if she chose, break into any of these twosomes and be welcomed as a third. At least, she hopes this is the case. She fiddles idly with an earring, traces the damask pattern on the tablecloth, sniffs to get the scent of the honey-suckle, puts a splash more wine into her glass, sips it, decides she'd prefer water and goes to get a bottle, sits down again and nobody notices the hiss of the cap as she undoes it, pours it into a glass, sips again, slips off a shoe and rubs her ankle, looks around the table at all those familiar faces and, finally, lets her muscles relax, her eyelids droop a little, and puts her head on one hand, lolling slightly in Tom's direction.

She has no thoughts of talking or listening for the moment – just to sit here for a five-minute reverie is lovely. She glances across at the puddings, those marvellous sweet creations of hers, crowning the repast. Celia, she says to herself, you've done really well tonight – she says this to herself because so far no one else has said it. But there is still time, she muses. She sits on in this calm, pleasant state for a while longer, rather wishing someone would break into it. It would be nice to be noticed again. But she disturbs no one. After the scratchiness earlier it is nice to see them happy and united. Even if the happy unity doesn't – quite – seem to include her. She keeps her mouth curved in a smile. It wouldn't do to look miserable on such an occasion. If only her daughter would sleep through a cuddle. *She* will have to go through this one day. It won't be the same for Henry. Men do seem to age better. She looks down the table at Alex. He is positively glowing. The Brandreth case certainly suits him. She sighs contentedly. Not a bad life, she thinks, not a bad life at all . . .

Upstairs Rebecca stirs, turns over, begins to twitch her toes in an effort to make the rest of her wake up since her inner clock tells her it is time to go downstairs and disturb the adults. In her sleep she conjures up the image of chocolate mousse, which she has seen awaiting the guests, but try as she will Hazel's efforts have been too good – she cannot, still, rouse herself. Gradually the toes cease to twitch, she finds a cool spot on the pillow and sinks back into a deep sleep devoid of even the hint of chocolate. She will not wake now until morning. Celia's reprieve has come at last. Just, it seems, when she does not particularly want it. Ah well. Ah well.

At the moment that Rebecca ceases to stir, Celia begins to galvanise herself and to think about serving out the final stage of the meal. What else is there to do? Her eyes alight on Tom for a moment. Never mind candlelight only being for women, she thinks, he looks pretty good in it too. In fact, Tom looks so handsome that Celia finds herself thinking that he is just as Elvis Presley *should* have looked if he'd cut out the drink and the drugs: the wine has given his eyes low lids which makes them catlike and dangerous and there is a definite little curl to his full lips that really should launch themselves into 'One Night With You'. I wonder what it *would* be like? she thinks. And shakes herself free of a little creeping desire to find out. Well, well – she pulls the trolley and the pudding towards her – she will never know; never *need* to know she corrects herself. And she opens her mouth to say, 'Pudding everybody,' when there is a long, penetrating ring on the doorbell. Her heart leaps – shock followed by the nice thought that it must be Hazel, come at last. Until that moment she has not realised how much she is missing her friend. She rises – but not quickly enough. Susie, who is usually so poised, so laconic, rises even faster and puts up a beautiful restraining hand. 'No,' she says, 'I'll go.'

How very odd, Celia thinks. Even odder that nobody seems at all surprised by an interruption at such a late hour.

Now everything is suspended. She is being gazed at in silence by everyone at the table. She gazes back, facing them as if they were some kind of tribunal. She hears Susie's voice – commanding, self-assured – at the front door, and a man's voice, growly and alien: what he says is indistinguishable. The front door closes with a bang. Followed by a short pause. Celia looks questioningly around the table. Blank eyes look back at her. She finds this irritating.

'What on earth is going on?' she says, rising.

'Sit down,' says Alex.

She does.

He turns off the small wall light, which has been the only illumination except for the candles.

Still they wait.

And then a faint warbling comes from the hall – the hitherto unknown noise of Susie singing, which hitherto unknown noise is taken up in its strains by the rest of the table, except Celia.

97

Gradually she realises they are singing 'Happy Birthday To Yew ...' John holds open the dining-room door and there is a sudden vision of beauty in light and shade, a Caravaggio madonna – Susie to be exact – holding an enormous cake, bedecked in scarlet and white with ribbons floating and candles blazing, scarlet, white, scarlet, white, all perfectly positioned – forty candles fluttering away as the breath of the singers catches on the air.

'Move that thing out of the way,' says Isabel to Celia, meaning the trolley. Celia pushes it and watches her beautiful puddings move off into the outer darkness. The delicate honeysuckle and jasmine is pushed away, the peachy pink of the napery is consumed in the scarlet and white brilliance of the cake. Susie puts it down dead centre of the table and commands Celia to blow but Celia has no air left – she tries, and fails.

'Come on,' says Tom, close at hand, encouraging her with a squeeze of her upper arm. 'Blow ...'

She calls up her fleeting control and fills her lungs. She is about to give an enormous puff, being an obedient sort of person, when Tom, who perhaps suddenly realises that his fingers are around her arm and very close to her bosom, straightens those fingers so that they press into the soft swell of it. How can Celia blow out her candles with a man-who-is-not-her-husband-and-who-looks-just-like-Elvis-should-have-looked feeling her up? She goes limp and makes a very weak exhalation which barely flutters the flames. Everybody groans derisively. You try, she wants to say, with a man at your boobs. But she doesn't. She just smiles ruefully, apologetically, and starts again. Too late. At her side she hears the intake of breath, sees her sister take aim, and feels her fire. Out go the candles.

'There you are,' says Isabel in triumph.

One little flame remains. Celia blows it out. In the handclapping and jollity that follows no one sees her rearrange her face into a smile. Susie holds up a large silver knife drifting with scarlet ribbon which Celia grabs and plunges into the blood and snow before her. Who is she slicing into? It feels as if it is herself.

Enough, she commands her inner self, enough of all this pathos.

Celia has been given a surprise on her birthday after all. Courtesy of Susie's Harrods' account.

'I never knew they did that sort of thing,' she says.

'You don't know everything,' says her sister.

She forbears saying, 'I never said that I did.'

She congratulates Susie – and everybody – on the cleverness of the secret. They eat the cake. The puddings sit mournfully, like wallflowers at a ball, and Celia consoles herself that they can, after all, be put into the freezer. Good job she made them all fresh today. More consolation in that she can give Mrs Green a piece of cake with her coffee when she comes on Monday. It might even sweeten her a little. There will certainly be plenty left over. Despite the children, despite a whole tea-party, there is enough cake to last for a week. Harrods is a generous emporium. Susie is a generous friend.

And Isabel is a generous sister.

'Now – what were you saying about playing some games, Cee?' she says. 'When I caught you practising in the kitchen with Tom?'

Celia's cake becomes like sawdust in her mouth, a piece of crunchy icing sugar hangs upon her tonsils. The deep breath that Isabel's remark calls up requires something to drink to dislodge it, or Celia will choke. She reaches for a glass and takes a huge drink. At best it will be her Perrier, at worst it will be her wine. But, as seems to be the case now that she has attained this age of wisdom, Celia is wrong. She has picked up Tom's brandy glass. Alex has said of the brandy and the port, as he said of the wine, that all should help themselves. Tom, still delighted with the erstwhile experience of Celia's left-hand breast, and past caution, alcoholically speaking anyway, has been generous with himself. Which may account for Celia's mistaking the brandy glass for one containing something other than the best Napoleon. Few people would pour such a big nip. Down it goes – healing in the first split second, firewater in the next and

99

perpetually thereafter. Naturally Celia makes a great deal of noise and what Isabel calls fuss and is unable to say it was a mistake.

Susie says, 'You'll simply *kill* yourself if you drink like that, Celia. Remember your liver is only half the size of Tom's.'

This is an unpleasant thought bringing as it does the image of their two bloody organs sharing a scale, and it sets Celia off again.

Dave, not entirely sober himself now, says, 'Perils of the bored middle-class housewife. Drink. Ha Ha . . .' Possibly he is joking but he has longed to get in a side-swipe somewhere and Alex has been so unusually interesting in a sound socially conscious way that he must do it to one other than he.

John, relieved that in the nick of time he has avoided buying one of Tom's cars (now that his is all crunched up Tom moved swiftly) says, 'Let her choke,' meaning they should ease off the criticism but, of course, it sounds as if he actually wants her to die.

Tom, torn between selling the car (which, since it is cheap in his range, has been hanging around for two years) and gallantry for Celia, makes do with looking daggers at John and rubbing Celia's back, noting, finally, what he surmised from previous explorations, that she is bra-less. Susie wears brassières all the time though there is little need. Celia is certainly an exciting woman.

Alex, because he is going away tomorrow, pushes down the irritation he feels at seeing his wife being foolish and does, for once, the right thing. He pours out a glass of mineral water which is passed down the line to Celia so that calm is at last restored. He does not like the look in Celia's eye as she returns to normalcy and so he also says, 'Games darling? What games would you like to play. We are all here at your command . . .' He sniggers as he indicates the table of friends (he, it must be said, is not entirely sober either). 'Aren't we, folks?'

'Folks?' Celia splutters; since when has Alex ever used such a proletarian endearment?

'Even I, dear Celia –' Dave reaches out a burly hand and clasps hers – 'am prepared to indulge in such bourgeois entertainment and have a go. What had you in mind?'

Isabel looks pleased with the way her husband has handled the tricky fusion of principles and conformity.

'I know,' she says, for Celia is still unable to articulate properly. (Let those who call good brandy smooth take note – it is an illusion.) 'Cee used to love that game called, – oh, something-or-other – where you have to say things like, if you were a dog what sort of dog would you be . . .'

'I don't like dogs,' says John, who finds that jogging on Bedford Park pavements produces certain substances on his trainers that he would rather not think about.

'All right,' says Isabel. 'It can be any category. Can't it, Celia?'

Celia nods. She would have preferred Flannel Doughnut but there we are.

'What then?' asks her sister.

Celia takes a deep breath to speak.

Isabel says, 'Make up your mind.'

Celia says, 'You choose.'

Isabel smiles around the table.

Susie says sharply, 'It's your birthday, Celia. *You* decide.'

'Flowers,' says Isabel quickly. 'OK, Cee?'

Celia is exhausted. She has also gone from being fairly sober (the food took care of the champagne imbibed earlier and, since she was so absorbed with Tom's intake, she scarcely touched wine during the meal) to being much brandified.

'I will accept any category you choose for me, dear sister of mine,' she says. 'And any game you see fit.'

Tom puts his hand back on her knee under the table and she scarcely reacts.

'Let's play that one, by all means.'

And Susie, always one, as we have seen, to put the one deserving of limelight *into* the limelight and also the only one there to recognise that Celia has, basically, had it, says, 'Better by far – since we are here to celebrate Celia – that we should make a variant (being sober she can say such words) of the game. We'll all go round the table saying what flower we think *Celia* represents to *us* – who know her so well. And Celia can just sit quietly and listen. She's done enough for one night.'

Celia looks across at the darkness surrounding her trolley with its untouched delectables. Curiously she feels she could join them and nestle between the raspberries and the chocolate. 'Does anyone want a bit of my puddings?' she asks.

Everyone but Tom declines but then, she thinks, he would probably have accepted toads in aspic given the state he is in. He makes yummy noises over the dish she sets before him but she can tell he isn't tasting it at all. He holds a cigar in one hand while he eats with the other – which at least means that she can have her knee and bosom back again.

In the years to come, if Celia thinks about that night, a wry smile curls around her lip as she remembers the various floral tributes on offer. Dave's sunflower would have been all right – would have been lovely really – if he had not added in high good humour and under his breath so that Celia alone could hear it, 'Or perhaps a scarlet runner would be more appropriate.'

Celia awaited Isabel's reason for choosing buddleia in trepidation, and she was not wrong to do so. 'Because it grows so effortlessly anywhere . . .' her sister said, and then appended, as an afterthought, '. . . and it's so pretty.'

Tom growled something about Alpines to which Celia, much strained by the whole thing, snapped back, 'They keep a low profile and have to make do with pretty rocky ground.' Tom looked rather hopeful after this and Alex looked annoyed.

John said apple blossom but when asked to explain the characteristic behind this choice it proved to be diplomatically pragmatic. He shrugged and said, 'Because everything Celia produces is delicious, of course.' It would have been nice to think of this as profound but she didn't, it was merely meaningless twaddle. She almost said as much.

If she had hoped for the rose without a thorn from Alex, she was disappointed. He was having to think very hard and once or twice coughed and said that he didn't know the names of many flowers. Then, quite suddenly, he said 'Pansy' which made Dave and John snigger across the table at each other. When asked why, Alex said, 'Because they've got such funny, innocent little faces and they look so shy.' Celia neither felt funny nor innocent. She was forty (or would be tomorrow), for God's sake, and she would like her husband to put her more in the full-blown floribunda class. Something told Alex that he had not quite scored maximum points with this explanation, so he added, 'And because I have always loved them.' Everybody said 'Aah' and Celia would have liked to bask a bit but, truth was, Alex could have been in a courtroom as he said this for it was delivered like some devilish masterstroke.

But Celia just smiled at him with her mouth. She was absolutely and completely beyond doing anything else.

And then, of course, there was Susannah. A fragment of hope fluttered into Celia's heart. Perhaps Susie would name the rose but she did not.

'There's no question,' she said. 'Celia is a daisy. A daisy is the first flower we recognise, children love it, it is homely but beautiful in its simplicity. Sophisticated gardens and natural countryside would both be the poorer without it. So –' she shrugged in a beautiful gesture – 'Celia is a daisy.'

'I used to pick daisies all the time,' says Tom, rather too loudly.

'What did you say?' asks Susannah, peering across at him.

'Celia,' says Isabel. 'You should tell us what flower *you* think you are – now that you've put the rest of us through it . . .'

Why say it wasn't her idea?

Why say anything?

She stands up. She leans upon her hands upon the table. She looks around at each of them in turn, very slowly. Then she says, 'Clematis. That's me. Tough and hardy. Thriving anywhere. But only –' She swallows to gain control. 'But only –' She swallows again to keep it. 'But only if I've got some support . . .'

And then, trundling her trolley in front of her, head held high, she marches out into the kitchen. Where she weeps. And weeps and weeps. To the distant sound of merriment as her guests continue to enjoy themselves. Ho, Ho. Such wit from their hostess.

She will never play Parlour Games again, she vows, and she weeps a little bit more. They may have been fun once but she knows now that you can never go back, only forwards. If a tear shed upon a birthday denotes tears all year, what Celia weeps will last for the next forty years. Unless, she comforts herself, that saying is just an Old Wives' Tale. And then she cries afresh. For that is what she is now. An Old Wife. She takes a big spoonful of the chocolate mousse and swallows it ruminatively. And then another, and then another. Poor Rebecca, stay with your sweet-toothed dreams, for your mother had greater need than you. Undoing the button on the back of her skirt, Celia returns to her happy guests. And she now feels so full that speech is impossible. She merely remains at the table, smiling fatly, and waiting for them all to go home.

Somewhere the accountant in the jade-green tracksuit is engaging his guests with tales of his exploits in the shipping world and, the situation in the Gulf being what it is, for once his guests are riveted. They stay as late at Celia's, which is why, despite the Neighbourhood Watch, three houses in the area are burgled successfully. There would have been a fourth but the flickering light of Hazel playing some of her old 'Dynasty' videos discourages the felon. There is always, as they say, a silver lining to be had somewhere.

PART TWO

1

The house is silent.

Celia roams it.

She punches one of the cushions in the front room, the adult space, which is perfectly clean and perfectly ordered – or was until Celia made the dent in the cushion. There is no hint that any sexual activity of the slipping down on to the carpet variety took place in this room last night. Nothing is ruffled into tantalising suggestiveness. Alas.

As she punches she says 'Pansy,' vehemently.

It is Saturday afternoon, Celia's real birthday as Susannah so correctly stated last night, and Celia is spending it quite alone. Neither Alex nor the children are here. She punches the cushion again and repeats 'Pansy' loudly, with a snarl of ill temper which is neither becoming to that half-shy floral tribute of her husband's nor the carefree pink-clad birthday girl of yesterday.

We must back-track to understand why.

Celia, who back-tracks with us, lets out one more, really defiant, yell of 'Pansy' to her distressed walls (distressed in the interior design sense – pearl on deeper pearl and done by a friend of hers – and now, perhaps, distressed in the emotional sense too, for the cry was of blood-curdling resonance) as she does so. It is just as well that her neighbours are green-wellie Bedford Park and have gone off for the weekend to Somerset for even they, who are blessed with total restraint in all response to matters of personal grief, might have been forced to rush to her aid. Let us leave Celia to compose herself after that outburst and make our back-track.

Last night, when the guests finally left, Alex stacked the dish-washer. He did this with the utmost care and precision saying to a hovering Celia that he saw no reason why his wife should have to do such a chore since she had already done enough and it was her birthday. So far, so good. This is a perfectly acceptable piece of Bedford Park male liberation. Rather like cooking at barbecues it is not viewed as emasculating. Dave and Isabel, were they still around, would be pleased to see it. It shows that Surbiton is not alone in having thoughtful husbands. If the husbands here would only *empty* these machines afterwards as well it might be a gesture of perfection.

So Celia, well used to the ritual, continued to hover by the dishwasher. But with no good reason that either her sister or an upfront woman's magazine would see, she became oddly irritated by Alex's absorption in the task. It seemed, to her, that it was taking an inordinately long time to complete. Being a good wife she did not do what she wanted to do which was to push him to one side and finish the job in half the time. Instead she went to the glasses cupboard (Mrs Green has spat in all the crystal before polishing it, to her great and dry-mouthed satisfaction – even greater satisfaction when Celia complimented her on the sparkle) and removed a brandy glass (Alex has already berthed his earlier one somewhere near the entrée plates) and a liqueur glass for herself. These she made ready with a nip in each, saying over her shoulder that she was going into the front room to wait. The word 'wait' had a sort of appealing ring of desire to it. Alex nodded and began humming the 'Ride of the Valkyries' again to himself.

And so Celia waited; chocolate mousse more or less digested, skirt still loosed, shoes kicked off, sitting on the white fur rug, head bent prettily to rest on the arm of the low settee. Very provocatively, she fancied. And she waited, and waited, and the little carriage clock went ping before Alex appeared. He picked up the brandy glass, drank it down in one, bent low over her – she, breathlessly waiting, raised her head, puckering up slightly, to receive what? The first kiss that would herald the beginning of some sumptuous sexual activity, of course. Which did not come. Instead from her husband's lips emerged first a little touch to her forehead and then a long, pleasant yawn and a, 'Come on, my little pansy, I'm tired. Let's get to bed.'

Problematical in this was the need for Celia to remove her make-up. A woman of forty must look after her skin (she could hear Susie's voice saying so) and so she did. By which time Alex was fast asleep. Pity overcame anger. He had had a hard day. She would catch him in the morning. And with that thought, snuggling up to her lovable if torpid husband, she slept her first sleep of her forty-first year.

In the morning she turned to put her arm around him and found only bare space. From the bathroom she heard the whoosh of the cistern, the beginnings of the shower. It was seven-thirty. Early but too late. At eight-fifteen she was standing on the doorstep waving goodbye to the Volvo and saying, 'See you Monday night.'

Hence the cushion punching and the cry to the wall of 'Pansy' now. Sheer frustration. A rose would have clutched him with its thorns. Stupid, mindless games, she thinks. Never again.

The Bedford Park Saturday street was deserted as Alex and his smart pigskin suitcase drove off. While he blew the last kiss she heard the telephone ring and she heard Rebecca answer it, but she waited until the car was out of sight before going back indoors. Which accounts for Celia being quite alone this afternoon, on her birthday. For the telephone call was from Hazel. Kind, well-meaning Hazel, who has arranged – apparently – for Henry and Rebecca to accompany her own children, with the munificent Jo's nanny, to a farm for the week. Hazel will go too – to recuperate.

So you see, Celia dear, you've got all that time to yourself.

Hazel, who knows nothing of Celia's sudden feeling of sadness and loss and fury with all pansies, still dwells within a relationship where taking the children off a friend's hands for a few days is as good as gold dust: Celia feels unable to say she would rather not have them go. If Celia had got to the telephone before Rebecca she would have vetoed the motion, feeling in need of her children as she will not have her husband – but Rebecca's radiant face at the news is insurmountable; Henry's excitement (already looking for his other gumboot in the understairs cupboard) is something Celia feels unable to take away. She thanks her friend, offers to deliver the children so that she can see her, but Hazel laughs. No need, Celia, no need, the nanny will drive by (such an Americanism – picked up from 'Dallas' or 'Dynasty', Celia wants to say, but stops herself). You are free, Celia, to really enjoy yourself.

'Break a leg, duckie,' exhorts Hazel, well pleased, certain that Celia – bright, lively, adorable Celia – will make the most of it – 'Break a leg, see you at the end of the week. Bye-ee . . .'

So now, roaming the silent house, punching cushions, yelling at designer walls, Celia avails herself of all this free time. A whole weekend of it without Alex, a whole week of it without the children. Not even Mrs Green will penetrate the self-indulgence until Monday – nor will the Bedford Park friends since it is weekend time, family time. Celia could be a speck of dust on a cloud-strewn hill for all her neighbourhood will think of her today and tomorrow. She punches the cushion yet again, and then she picks them all up and holds them fast in her arms before throwing them into the air. 'Oh shit,' she yells. 'Oh shit, shit, shit,' and – feeling better, kicking at them as she passes – she goes back towards the kitchen. On her way she must pass the big table – usually strewn with Plasticine and Lego by now. It is bare. And this stops her in her tracks. Little family, she thinks, I miss you. And she pauses to stroke the empty table with her finger.

The table is not quite empty. It supports the beautiful crystal vase and the flowers in all their finery. She thinks, briefly, of Tom and his face as he twitched with desire. That was cheering. But, just as if her sister were in the room with her and wagging a finger in her direction, she sees that next to the flowers is Isabel's present: both books sit heavily on the table top and she feels just like Alice. Read me, they say. She pauses, forgets that she was on her way to the kitchen and instead sits down at the table.

This should be a nice experience. A warm June afternoon with nothing to do except indulge herself. She has already done a bit of that – given herself a long, bubbly bath, a manicure, a pedicure, read *Good Housekeeping*, wandered down to the Indian delicatessen and bought some smoked salmon (enough for one) and amazed herself at how little time all that has taken out of the span allotted to her. Come on, Celia, she says, pull yourself together – make the most of it. She begins looking through the definitive *History of Art* and wills herself to become interested in what she sees but the text is too dry for her mood, the illustrations too much chosen for their historical importance than for their gutsiness. In any case, British Art may hold many epithets but gutsy is unlikely to be one of them. After that yell only something gutsy will suffice. She closes 'Book One' and turns her gaze upon the flowers. But the vase is cold today – the sunlight does not bring out the fire, and the blooms are too hothouse and have already begun to droop slightly, with faint browning around the edges of some of them. All this is suddenly too representative of how she feels herself just at this moment. Bugger Alex, she thinks, for she decides that all this low spiritedness is due to one thing and one thing only. Sexual frustration, frustrated need for intimacy. For something, anyway. Perhaps, she thinks, slightly amused, perhaps I *should* have learned to masturbate – a skill she has never really mastered. A skill, indeed, that she looks upon askance. The idea of it turns her off rather than on. And anyway, she argues, she has never had to. It might perplex her to know that her daughter can, and often does, which proves that some female skills are nothing to do with what is learnt at Mother's knee (or, indeed, under Mother's apron). Perhaps one day mother and daughter will talk of this but it seems unlikely – she hasn't even discussed it with Hazel, and the way she feels about *her* now, she probably never will.

Rebecca could tell her that it provides a very pleasant kind of condolence in times of frustration and stress, but she is not here – and, anyway, since when did parents ever seek counsel from their children? No – Celia must find some other way – but what?

She decides that perhaps the sound of a warm, friendly and totally loyal human voice will help. The telephone. She will ring up someone. Hazel, Best of Bedford Park Friends. Then, remembering Hazel's disloyalty with Josephine, she decides she will ring someone else. One in the eye for her BBPF. And then she remembers – more appositely – that Hazel is away. Which just about wraps up the disloyalty quite nicely. Worse, Hazel has taken away her children so if she *does* ring someone else locally what can she say?

'Let's go and have a picnic tea?' Without her children they would think she was mad. Give up all that lovely free time to sit on a river bank watching somebody else's children dribble ice cream and chase ducks.

Well then. She could say, 'Why don't you come over tonight and we'll get a takeaway?'

Without Alex this would look at the least odd, at the middle screwy, and at the worst as if there was something up with her marriage. Besides, while the female of the invited couple might just about be able to relax, the male would be pacing the floor feeling very nervous and wondering who to relate to without another man around.

Possibly, 'How about going to see a film tonight?'

No good either. If the nannies are in, it's because they have been booked to babysit well in advance as their employers are already going out. If the nannies are not in, and therefore their employers are not going out, they are either looking forward to a quiet evening with the telly, or are giving a dinner party, or – even if they did think the idea was marvellous – they'd be unable to get a babysitter at this kind of notice anyway.

So much for filling the vacuum. It has never been difficult before. Of course if Alex had behaved differently last night she could have been lying around feeling sated but his cavalier disregard has left her frustrated and uneasy. And no amount of telling herself off for being wet makes any difference. The only person she can be sure to find in and willing to talk to her on the telephone without wondering why she has rung is her mother-in-law, and perish the thought of that. She ought to ring her, of course. She ought to ring her because her card (pastel flowers with a simpering kitten behind them saying, 'For you dear daughter-in-law') and her present (the annual subscription to *Good Housekeeping* fought for over the years by Celia who felt that if she received one more National Trust teatowel or set of coasters she would crack – so would Mrs Green come to that) arrived yesterday and should be acknowledged. She sits at the table setting her teeth against making this telephone call. For it would be thus:

'And how is Alex?'

'Very well indeed, Joyce.'

'May I have a word with him dear ... ?'

'Well – he's not here at present.'

'Oh? Where is he?'

The temptation here would be to say 'just popped out' but such lies do us no good in the end. So she would say truthfully, 'He's away working this weekend.'

There would be a pause, a little sorrowful silence, before Joyce would say in that false quaver of hers, 'Poor boy – he does work so hard.' With its implication that Celia forces him to do so in order to fulfil her selfish whims. If the women of Bedford Park do not lie around on silken cushions sipping sherbet, their mothers-in-law certainly think that they do.

But ye gods, the house is silent. No dishwasher, no washing machine, no hoover – for in the circumstances none of this is necessary. Celia decides that she feels hungry. The smoked salmon, while being wonderfully self-indulgent, does not mean she feels well-fed. She remembers the left-overs from last night and is already fashioning in her mind a sandwich made up of cold veal, mayonnaise and watercress when she pats her stomach which wobbles slightly and she knows that she must not. The chocolate mousse is still in there somewhere and even before it that aquamarine skirt was a shade too tight last night. Susie's flickering glance at her waistline did not go unnoticed by Celia. Neither, as we know, did Isabel's plumpness. No sandwich for Celia after all. So then, she stands up, resigned, and goes towards the telephone in the hall, where they keep their address book. It is of small comfort to Celia that still, after all these years, she cannot exactly remember her mother-in-law's telephone number, which she proceeds to look up.

She begins to dial carefully so as not to spoil the new nail-varnish and then a piece of paper catches her eye. Still holding the receiver she reads the paper and an idea comes to her. The paper is one from the leather-bound notepad that Alex carries around with him – Celia bought it for his Christmas stocking: it has 'Phone Home' embossed on the leather cover. He had liked that. It made up for the fact that when he took the children to see Spielberg's *ET* (which he had loved) Henry had howled and had to be brought out of the cinema. Rebecca had then howled because she had wanted to stay in. Alex had come home extremely put out. The notepad was a little consolation prize.

The piece of paper says:

Queen's Brough Hotel
Lowndes Street
Salisbury

Alex always leaves his hotel address in case there is an emergency while he is away. Celia's idea is that she will ring him. After all, if he is there and busy he can say so, and if he is there and not busy, they can have a chat. Instantly she feels happy again. This beats Joyce's quavering mother-love any day. But there is no telephone number on the paper which is an unusual oversight. Alex is generally scrupulous in giving all the relevant information required on anything. She hums, amused to find she is humming the 'Ride of the Valkyries', with its irritating memories, and dials Directory Enquiries. This now being privatised she has to dial and re-dial as it is constantly engaged and when she finally does get through to the operator, he dies in a fizzling pop of electronics. She dials again, engaged again – and all this takes a good deal of time.

This drawn out activity is relevant because while it is going on, Susie is attempting to telephone Celia from the Club, just before she and Tom set off back home. Twitching on the thread again, Susie is aware that Alex is away and thinks she will make sure Cee is all right – and thank her for the previous night. She will also apologise for Tom's state, and as she dials Celia's number she is looking at her husband's somewhat drooping hungover outline as he takes the umpteenth Alka-Seltzer, and is feeling doubly glad that she never touches the stuff. Had Susie got through, of course, she would have learned that Celia was all alone and blue and would have instantly invited her down to Wiltshire with them. They are entertaining a motley selection of Americans and local dignitaries on Sunday and Celia would fit in very nicely. Ah well, and alas. Celia's phone is engaged. 'I'll try again in a minute,' says Susie.

Tom, who feels that all he wants to do is to get home and go to bed, is peremptory. Not only because of his hangover, it should be said, but because – well – things that we do on the spur of the moment can sometimes seem very silly and puerile on the morrow – and he feels that perhaps he would rather not connect with Celia for the time being. The sense of silliness and puerility stem not from his behaviour towards Celia last night, nor from the flowers and the vase, but from the package that was placed in the washing machine. It is this which makes him uneasy about Susie telephoning Celia. So he says, 'Just leave it and come on. I want to get home.' He does not know, of course, that because of their flowers and Isabel's books and the general convolutions of the morning, Celia stopped short of going into the kitchen and did not, therefore, remember that the washing machine houses a secret. Too many other things have crowded it out.

Never fear, the rediscovery of the package will come – but later.

Susie, quite versed in apparently capitulating while in reality not doing any such thing, says mildly, 'You get the things put into the car and see to the lunch bill and what not and when you've done all that we'll go.' She calculates that this will take a good ten minutes, by which time whoever it is engaging Celia's telephone will have disengaged themselves.

But Susannah has not taken into account the newly computerised British Telecom. As a shareholder she should have something to say about that.

For eight (rather than the ten she hoped for) minutes later she tries again and Celia's telephone is still engaged. So much, then, for Susie's little thread. How much Celia would have loved to be rung up by her friend just at that point and be invited away. *That* would have vindicated all this free time of hers perfectly. Gone would be the 'don't know what to do with myself' blues, gone would be the residual sexual frustration, and it would have been hallo to a real, big, fat, social justification for her husband and her children leaving her in the lurch. She would have come back and been able to say, 'Well – it was just too perfect – everything slotted into place nicely: the children at a farm, Alex working, and me in the country enjoying myself . . .' All her friends would have been suitably envious and life would have continued as before.

But it was not to be. While Celia finally got the telephone number of the Queen's Brough Hotel, Susie and Tom were driving homewards in the late afternoon sunshine – Susie already wondering if her Philippino housekeeper had remembered to get enough aspic made for the *oeufs en gelée* tomorrow – a favourite starter of Susie since it looks so pretty and has so few calories per portion . . . Her thoughts are no longer remotely to do with Celia: an engaged telephone means activity. Cee is all right.

Having finally got through to the Salisbury number, Susie's prognosis is more or less correct.

The hotel receptionist agreed that a Mr Alexander Crossland was staying at the hotel, and that Mr Crossland and his party had also availed themselves of the use of the Small Conference Facilities on the first floor. She said 'small' in a way that made Celia want to say something rude, but she did not. Instead she asked the receptionist to try Mr Crossland's room. This was done and there was no reply. She then asked the receptionist to try the Small Conference Facility but the receptionist said that this was impossible, the group was not to be disturbed. Messages could be left. It was on the tip of Celia's tongue to say, 'Here is my message. Have you got a pencil?' and to wait until the woman said she had before continuing, 'Please tell my husband that his wife called and that she fancies going to bed with him . . .'

It was only the thought of Alex's face, receiving the message, that stopped her.

She was about to leave a few words saying something more suitable but still, if he was willing, able to catch Alex's marital imagination ('joining him in congress later' was a possibility) when a thought came to her that was so nice, so amusing, that she forgave the receptionist everything. She, Celia, was free. Why should not she, Celia, go down to this hotel? The thought took her breath away with its audacity. No, no, she could not. The Brandreth lot would have their conference, dine together probably, with more of the same tomorrow and Monday – she would be an embarrassing appendage in all this. But why should she be? Alex would not need to entertain her during the daylight hours, not even for dinner if it was difficult. She could have a wonderful time getting to know Salisbury – she could drive out and about during the days and perhaps dine on her own in some local pub or something, or even in her room if he felt her presence in the restaurant would be off-putting. The only time they needed to get together would be at night, tucked up in bed – and the Brandreth people would hardly be there as well!

She was about to ask if Alex had booked a double or single room but decided that if she went on asking too many questions the receptionist might spill the beans to Alex which would spoil the surprise (and, to be fair, give Alex a chance to Phone Home indeed and put her off). So – with great bravado and a sense that now she was forty she was entitled to be a real grown-up – she booked a double room for herself, in her maiden name of Wilde.

She then rang the number of the farm at which Hazel, the wondrous nanny and the children were resident and to her relief (because she wanted no inroads on this adventure and the thought of Henry wailing down the phone that he wanted to come ho-o-me was too annoying to contemplate; not least because, as she knew from experience, once she'd brought him back from the party, the overnight stay with a schoolfriend, the cub camp, wherever it was, he invariably wanted to get back there again – it was only the sound of her voice that started him off) was told that they were all out with the horses. Hazel too. So that she just left the hotel telephone number in case there was a real emergency, winced a bit as the woman who ran the farm began saying in her Welsh lilt that she thought it was a Real Good Mother's concern to think to do such a thing. And rang off.

And then, where once she had yelled to the walls in crosspatch loneliness, now she whooped about the house, packing and prettifying herself, slipping into a cream linen culotte suit that really was Jaeger, fluffing up the peacock-blue highlight and drenching herself in Patou 'Joy' which Tom had once brought her back from a trip to the States. The most expensive perfume in the world, so they said, and it would have been if she had done what he whispered to her as he handed it over. It was out of a kind of loyalty to Alex that she never used it. But now, today, well, why not? It gave things a very nice edge to be desired by others yet to desire only her husband. And, what was more, free and self-assured enough to be doing something about it.

Anyway, she thought, as she buckled on her seat belt, let's be practical about this. My new car needs a good ride to run in the engine.

She would say that to Alex as well as all the other frivolous, loving things – when she finally crept into his arms. He would like that. And it would make up, in part, for her grudging feelings about being given a car for her birthday. After all, she would never have seriously contemplated making this journey in the old one. And as for the Pansy – she made two vows, one to exonerate herself from such a connection in her husband's mind, and the other to promise Alex, when she told him how she felt, that she would never try to play Parlour Games with him again. It was unfair to judge him by such yardsticks. After all, not everyone was good at such things.

I will be grown-up now, she says, releasing the handbrake. Perfectly in control of the rest of my life. And this little jaunt is going to be Fun!

2

Good things were destined to happen. Celia could feel it in her bones. As she drove along she sang with the radio turned right up so that her disposition to go out of tune was indistinguishable. Irrationally, for after all she was going to meet her husband, she felt wicked. Something to do with the surprise and something to do with the anonymity of an hotel – and also (she congratulated herself) something to do with her and Alex having got life right somehow. She thinks that her husband's face will be a picture when she arrives. It is a nice thought, for it is a picture of which she is extremely fond. Her marriage, her life. The social conformities with a touch of spice. Perfect. Here I am, she thinks, on the crest of a wave, as happy as any human being can be in a simple sort of a way. And despite the fact that she would most certainly have felt aggrieved if Isabel had said it, she does feel childlike. Like someone out for a treat. Which, of course, she is.

The early evening sun bathes the countryside in a primrose and golden light and all around her as she drives she sees fulsome greenery marching into the heart of summer. It is intensely beautiful. The countryside is burgeoning, and so is Celia. Joy is a funny thing. We never in the least know when to expect it. It can come out of the most haphazard of circumstances, the most unlikely of situations. The sight of a full washing line billowing in the breeze, lit by the sunshine of a summer's day can do it just as easily as the more predictable moments of a child's first smile or a lover's first touch. Sentimental Celia feels joy now as she drives towards Salisbury. Perhaps the Patou helps? She laughs. Out of nowhere she feels a sudden, wonderful spasm of pleasure. For one shard of time, a millisecond, she thinks that if she died at this precise moment it would be the perfect time to leave the world. She slows down.

There is no need for her to take that thought too literally. And she has no need to rush – she has no appointment to keep, she can savour these moments. From somewhere in the universe she has pinched two whole days. They are hers now and nobody else's. She smiles and hums even more out of tune and eases her foot off the accelerator a little. Why eat it up too fast . . . ?

On she goes quite happily, running in the engine in the inside lane, while the Porsches and the Lancias rush past her, their white-knuckled owners as far removed from joy as a mole from the sun. Milky cows munch lazily, foolish sheep stare blind, sparrowhawks lie on the air above her. She feels quite euphoric as she slips along, contemplating the stolen time ahead. Of course there is a light shadow thrown over all this by the fact that Alex will be working during the days and probably in the evenings, too, so she must spend a good deal of the time on her own. But she smiles at the thought. For she can easily fill those days with walking in such a beautiful landscape, or nosing around Salisbury which is bound to have all kinds of interesting shops – and there is the cathedral, of course, and old Sarum . . . she goes on smiling . . . Oh yes, and when she is not being active in an out-and-about sort of way there will be that lovely chunk of uninterrupted time left over for reading. And not Isabel's books either. She has got a really soggy novel underway, one that she can't wait to get down to. Yummy, yummy, yummy, she thinks smiling away at the prospect.

And then the smile dies. Damn, blast – nay – sod it, she has forgotten to pack her book. Suppose it rains? Suppose she doesn't feel like walking or shopping? Oh no, she pleads, not the Sunday papers! Please not that. Oh, how could she have forgotten? And just when she had started such a good one, too. That big, fat juicy novel is still sitting on her bedside table. Damn and blast and sod it again. And then the smile returns to her face. Silly Celia. There is a very simple solution. Buy another book. She frowns. This is not quite the answer. She has never been any good at running more than one novel at a time and she gets quite confused enough with all the names and characters without having to hold two completely different sets in her head. And then the frown eases, the smile returns. Such a simple solution that she starts to sing again. Buy a book of *short stories*! Perfect ... if only all of life's difficulties were so simple to overcome.

Celia's horizon, untarnished by struggle, unshadowed by suffering, unstained by any creeping fears, is free now even of this small cloud. A book of short stories. *Perfect* ...

After a while she indicates left and turns off the main road towards Stockbridge. There must be a bookshop in this place. And only after she has parked and begun to stroll along the deserted shopping street does that small cloud skiff back. It is ten past six. No shops are open, particularly no shops selling books. Nor, for that matter, shops selling magazines, newspapers, periodicals – anything that she could pass the time in reading. A vague hope comes to her that Alex might be able to lend her something – but Alex does not read novels. He reads law journals, political weeklies and – for real excitement when they are on holiday – travel books. Real travel books, as he points out, the last one being a perfect twinning for him of politics and travel – *Alaska: The Geopolitical Wastelands*. He read that when they were in the splendid heat of Corsica last year. When she said it was not to her taste (he would keep reading bits out of it) he laughed and said it was the only thing that was keeping him cool – all those icy wastes and the machinations of the Cold War. If he considered that to be holiday reading what would he have with him on a business trip? No, no – Alex will have nothing with him to see Celia through.

Feeling very cross and very frustrated she goes up to the door of the bookshop. It has a big Gothic-lettered sign saying 'We Are Closed' to which she mouths, irritated, I know that you twerps, and peers in. It is dim and silent and does not even contain a bespectacled, carbuncular assistant tidying up. And across the divide of the glass door sit rows and rows of lovely books set out and ready for the needy. She makes a noise of vexation which comes out as a perfect comic strip 'Grrr' and shakes her fist at the empty shop, then she 'Grrrs' again. After this she is prepared to admit that she is being silly and turns away. She is somewhat thrown to hear what she takes to be a wanton piece of mimicry behind her growling a 'Grrr' back. Some little runt being cheeky, she thinks, and with a suitably disgusted look on her face, she turns around. Behind her a woman is walking a dog. The woman is large-boned, tall and stately, the perfect picture of the English/Elderly/Well-bred Countrydweller. Good tweeds, good brogues on solid feet and a complexion ruddily free of cosmetics. The very type which keeps Celia firmly living in London. Her dog makes an absurd contrast: a high-necked, aloof Afghan hound – of the two it has the most grace and is probably even better-bred than its owner. Also Celia is not altogether sure that it was the dog and not the woman that went 'Grrr'.

The woman looks at Celia as if she would like to sniff her – whereas the dog looks at Celia and immediately looks away, knowing it has no wish to.

Celia gives a little fluttery motion with her hands, uncertain what to say: what does one say when one is caught growling at shop windows?

'Closed,' barks the woman.

'I know,' says Celia helplessly.

The woman eyes her peacock-blue highlight with concern. Suddenly Celia realises that she is no longer in Bedford Park but in the country.

'Bit of a mistake,' she says wanly, flicking at it. 'Hairdressers!' She shrugs.

The dog looks away, embarrassed. The woman unbends a little, her gaze going from the peacock-blue to the cream linen Jaeger. This mollifies her. She can recognise good taste when she sees it. The woman wearing it has quality, therefore, to her mind, she cannot be a lunatic and is merely distraught. Why else would she be peering so hopelessly into a bookshop?

'Hairdressers,' agrees the woman brightly.

'Oh well,' says Celia. 'No book for me after all. I shall just have to grin and bear it.' She gives a toss of her head as if to say she will be brave, and makes to move off.

Courage is something the woman with the dog likes in a girl. She has seen many a female crumble in India when their silly husbands succumbed to breaking the yard-arm rule. Her own husband died of alcohol poisoning but she saw him through that. And got the pension. You had to have courage in this day and age.

'If you want a book,' she says, 'I've got plenty. Have one of mine.' There is no doubt that the woman barks far more heartily than the dog, which remains arch-necked and silent.

Celia jumps.

'Oh, no – really,' she says. 'I couldn't.'

'I'm looking after boxes of them for the church jumble sale,' says the woman. 'You can take whatever you want and pay whatever you feel is right. Take a whole box if it'd make you feel better.' She cocks a head at the doorway and says heartily, 'They only have rubbish anyway.'

Celia begins to back off. The dog regains its nerve and growls.

'Steady, Rebecca,' says the woman.

'Rebecca?' says Celia without thinking. 'That's my daughter's name.'

'Well,' says the woman. 'That settles it then. Come on.'

And suddenly Celia is matching well-brogued stride with tottering high heel down Stockbridge High Street. And she is thinking, as they suddenly dive under the portico of a fine Georgian façade, that this is the kind of thing the White Slave Trade might be about. After all, its perpetrators would only have to drive her car off and tip it over a cliff somewhere, and Celia would no longer exist. They might at the very moment be lying in wait for her within this desirable brick and wisteria frontage; she might never come out; she might never see Alex again . . .

One of the reasons that she always did so well at composition was her vivid imagination. Mostly she has it under control nowadays but occasionally, like now, it will break out. Stockbridge at six-fifteen on a Saturday has the air of Pompeii about it. No one has noticed her, she thinks, and she might very well end up in the tent of a sheikh.

Continuing the notion she refuses tea, for it might be drugged.

The woman, wife of her deceased husband and sensitive to other needs, suggests gin. Celia, looking about her at the Indian artefacts, and in particular a large elephant's hoof upon which a blossoming African violet gives forth, toys with the idea of it being a nabob rather than a sheikh, dithers momentarily, and then accepts after all. 'Just a small one,' she says, 'as I am driving . . .'

'Excellent,' says the woman forcefully.

And Celia realises that she was never going to get out of here without having imbibed something. Logic tells her that this woman is probably rather lonely. Imagination tells her that she should not touch the proffered drink.

Ah well, she thinks, so what if it is tampered with? She decides to risk it and to go with Fate. One part of her continues to think that the fantasy might be real, one part of her says very sensibly that it is not. She was born under the sign of Gemini which might explain this duality . . . She is also feeling uncommonly reckless. No one knows where she is. She has not been so completely untraceable since she married. It is quite exciting. Considering she is now forty, she doesn't feel very old at all.

The gin is a large one. Celia is offered a seat next to a beautiful rosewood cabinet, the harmonious effect of which is completely spoiled by its contents – a collection of amazingly hideous exotic brasses.

'Very nice,' says Celia.

The dog woman relaxes. Her first impressions were not wrong. This is a woman of taste.

'Ursula Stone,' barks the woman.

Celia gives her name.

'And are you a native?'

Celia is thrown by this. The proximity of the elephant's foot and the brasses makes a kind of muddled link in her head.

'I don't *think* so,' she says cagily and takes a sip of her drink. It makes her eyes water – the Indian influence seems to have stopped short of tonic. If she could she would drink up and go but it is hard enough getting one sip of neat gin off her tonsils and down her gullet let alone throwing back the whole measure in one. She resigns herself to sitting it out.

The woman understandably finds Celia's caginess odd. Surely one is either from Hampshire or one is not?

'Where are you from?' she says loud and slow. It is a communicative art well learned from her Indian days.

Celia tells her.

'Well, surely you have plenty of bookshops there to choose from?'

'Oh yes,' says Celia. 'It's just that –' Is it the gin? Is it the elephant's foot? Is it her latent love of invention? Whatever it is, Celia suddenly finds herself launching into an amazingly untrue account of why she is bookhunting in Stockbridge.

And all delivered in a kind of breathless vernacular of an Agatha Christie heroine. Whence its fount and whence it will lead she does not know. But off she goes. She listens to herself with astonishment as she says: 'I am on my way to weekend with some very boring people,' (thinking of the Brandreth lot this is hardly a lie) 'and I couldn't get through without a decent book to read.' (Decent is the sort of word she thinks this woman will like so she slips it in.) 'And I forgot to pack one. Just the *thought* of being adrift in their country house without a book is absolutely *ghastly*.' She hoots – she enjoys that bit. 'They are such frightful Philistines. Utterly, utterly boring, I'm afraid.'

She stops as suddenly as she started. She is aware that the smoked salmon was a long time ago. The gin is very current. Enough is enough. Any more and she will explode. There is quite a lot of laughter trapped in her solar plexus and it is probably hysterical. Silence – or betrayal: she clamps her jaw shut.

The dog, overwhelmed by the iniquities of human deceit, curls up and sleeps. Celia basks in the exaggeration which she has thoroughly enjoyed. *Why* is she behaving so foolishly? Reaction against the eggshells of last night, perhaps? Pansy be blowed. Anyway – it harms no one; she will never meet her hostess again, so why not have this little piece of fun?

The woman, quite *au fait* with Celia's assumed vernacular, agrees that there is nothing worse than bores. She begins to talk about India and the jolly times before Partition. It is a long time since she has had such a good listener. 'Never a dull moment,' she says. 'Until after Mountbatten. Then it got very dreary. Very dreary indeed.'

Celia pictures Alex's Maugham-like stance in the conservatory last night and smiles – how amused he would be by all this. What witty ironies he could fashion out of the post-Partition débâcle being called dreary – what fun she will have describing it to him when they eventually meet up. To her companion the smile looks very sympathetic. The woman leans across, responding to it, and puts her hand on Celia's knee. Celia, brought out of her cogitations, gives a little yelp and it is now Rebecca's turn to feel affronted at being mimicked.

'This *is* nice,' says the woman. 'One gets terribly lonely in the country sometimes . . .'

And her hand lingers warmly.

First Tom and now a stranger: what is it about her knees?

Celia's interpretation of this gesture is a confused and rather unfortunate one. What with the notion of White Slavery and Agatha Christie she imagines there is something a little sinister in the intimate gesture. Possibly even, oh that fertile brain, *just* possibly something – well – not quite right . . .

She brings her culottes very tightly together, sits bolt upright, stamps a glassy smile on her face and does a sort of bottom shuffle along the settee, out of reach of the hand.

This odd behaviour, being quite uncalled for in her hostess's opinion, makes the woman wonder if her guest is, indeed, a lunatic after all – despite the Jaeger. And being a woman more used to the ways of dogs than people she immediately recognises a look of fear on Celia's face. Why it is there she does not know, but how to deal with it she certainly does. She moves a little further forward and reaches out to pat Celia's clamped knee again, for reassurance, at which Celia leaps up and says in a high-pitched voice that she must go. Whereupon she promptly backs into the elephant's foot which releases its African violet in a shower of compost and petals all over the Tabriz rug.

With a superbly stiff upper lip the woman assures Celia that this is nothing, nothing at all, and watches mesmerised as her guest tramples over the dirt, crushing it into several hundred pounds' worth of floor covering.

Celia says brightly, 'Oh I *am* so sorry. Oh dear. Well – I must go now. Thank you so much. Cheerio ...' Trample, trample, trample.

The woman gets up and advances, attempting to avoid as much of the pot plant as possible, which means that she executes a curious little foxtrot.

Celia thinks that this definitely shows a sinister behaviour pattern.

The woman says, 'But what about what you came for?'

Celia, backing away gingerly and playing for time, says, 'And – um – just what *was* that?'

The woman's view on Celia's mental stability is confirmed.

'Why – your *book* dear ...'

'Book? Book? Book?' says Celia, sounding like a frightened chicken.

'They are all upstairs,' says the woman, hurrying away.

I bet they are, thinks Celia.

'Would you like to choose?' shouts the woman from the landing.

'Oh no, thank you,' calls Celia.

'Well, what sort of a book did you want, dear?' returns her harassed hostess.

'Oh, anything, anything at all ...' Celia is moving rapidly across the hall.

The woman's head appears over the stair rail.

'Surely you have some idea? Do come up. I have so *many* boxes.' This sounds wistful. In fact it is the nearest the woman can come to sounding irritated.

'Short stories would be nice,' calls Celia. She moves slowly, crab-like, past the foot of the stairs, towards the front door.

Rebecca the dog finds this behaviour untenable. She appears at the entrance to the sitting room and lets out a long, low growl. Celia snarls back at her. The dog woman appears at the top of the banisters. She is holding an arbitrary handful of books. She sees Celia growling at her dog. She will never trust Jaeger again.

'I hope one of these will do.' She descends rapidly, glad that she has her hound to defend her if need be.

Celia – feeling the front-door latch secure in her hand – gives her hostess the benefit of a radiant smile and her hostess attributes these mood swings to a personality disorder. Dogs get it too. The woman stands a safe distance off holding out the books while Celia wrestles with the door, which will not open. In her desperate state she is entirely in keeping, visually, with a heroine who has got herself in a bit of a jam. She is also scarlet in the face and – for some strange reason – puffing.

The dog woman reaches across cautiously and releases the latch. Then stands back, holding out the selection of books – as offering or barrier? It is hard to say.

Now the door is open, Celia decides to brazen it out and reaches for one of the books. For some reason she finds herself saying, 'That'll do nicely,' and then giggles again as she stands back to let the dog woman pull wide the front door. Celia steps out into glorious freedom. 'Silly, these advertising jingles, aren't they?' she adds conversationally.

The dog woman, who has not caught up with credit-card life-styles, misinterprets this as Celia having heard bells. She will never, she decides, bring in anyone off the street again, no matter, even, if they sport Hartnell kilts and corgis.

Politeness and sanity return to Celia once she is back in the safety of the Georgian porch.

'Oh, but I must pay something for the book,' she says.

The woman demurs.

Celia insists.

She presses a pound coin into the woman's hand. 'Well, thank you so much,' she says brightly.

To the immense relief of both parties the front door is then closed, with Celia on the one side, safe in Stockbridge High Street, and the dog lady on the other. This latter is looking at the money in her palm and shaking her head. If it weren't for the fact that the woman who gave it to her was unbalanced she would feel insulted, not least because the sum – one bright new penny – is so paltry. Perhaps Fate wishes to deal out a little retribution for she feels something akin to what the natives of Poona once felt when she gave them baksheesh. If you are going to do that kind of thing, she thinks, you might at least be generous. (And so, though they were too wily to show it, thought they . . .) In cream linen Jaeger there is no excuse for meanness. She *must* be deranged.

Ah well. She strokes the dog's indignant head. Pity the poor souls with whom she is going to stay for the weekend – *if* she really is – no wonder she finds them boring, being so dotty herself.

Celia runs back to the car feeling that if she is not careful this simple trip is going to turn into something resembling the Pilgrim's Progress: if the Slough of Despond was Bedford Park then the dog lady might be the Valley of Humiliation. Certainly the incident has been an unnerving one and has destroyed some of her confidence in the venture: she feels quite akin to Bunyan's character as she makes her way back to the car. Well, anyway, if she has met with the Slough of Despond and the Valley of Humiliation, then that must make Alex the Celestial City. Which thought restores her good humour immediately. Best not tell Alex though. He has become, she dares to say to herself, just a little bit puffed up about the Brandreth case. Much as she loves him he can be slightly pompous nowadays. He might take the Celestial City idea a bit seriously. Ah well. One good night together should restore the balance. Maybe in the morning she will say to him, 'You are my Celestial city,' and they will have a laugh over it. What a relief *that* will be.

Safely back in the car and out of reach of the White Slave traffickers, she looks at the book she has procured. It proves to be not short stories but a selection of historical love letters, which, given her quest, seems highly appropriate. Almost fateful. Celia sits and flicks through it, remembering a kind of game she invented for herself in her teens. At moments of intense crisis or indecision or pleasure (which just about covered every moment of teenage life) she would open a book at random – and whatever she read on the page she would take as some kind of karma. Of course she was always careful to make sure the chosen book was fitting – Shakespeare's sonnets and John Donne could always be counted on in matters of love and the Bible was best for general subjects. She smiles. How strange that it should come back to her after all these years. She looks around her slyly. Stockbridge is still deserted. Would it be too silly to play it now? No one will see. No one will know. The book in her hand being one of love letters, it is a pity to waste the prospective fluence, really. So, with Alex and the stolen weekend in mind, and Just for Fun, she closes her eyes, wishes very hard, and lets the book fall open where it will.

She is entranced. It opens at a love letter written by Henry VIII to Anne Boleyn (a happy adolescent pleasure in historical romances has long made the Tudors a favourite of Celia's – so that's a good sign) and she reads something so beautiful, so moving, so completely heartfelt, that she is sure it echoes her happy destiny. She also forgets that a few years later he chopped his correspondent's head off.

She reads:

My Mistress and Friend,

Celia naturally changes this to 'My Master and Friend' which, sadly, does not have the same ring of loving equality to it at all. However, she is prepared to slide over this one.

It goes on:

> I and my heart put ourselves in your hands, begging you to recommend us to your good grace and not let absence lessen your affection, for it were great pity to increase their pain, seeing that absence does that sufficiently and more than I could ever have thought possible;

Celia, sitting in her new car, all belted up, holding the book, is quite delighted. This is a *very* good omen.

She reads on:

> reminding us of a point in astronomy, which is that the longer the days are the farther off is the sun and yet the hotter; so it is with our love, for although by absence we are parted it nevertheless keeps its fervency, at least in my case and hoping the like of yours;

The sun is indeed hot; and she is, indeed, separated from her love. Inside the car Celia is roasting – partly from summertime temperature, and partly, it must be acknowledged, from the sheer longing of the words. Very romantic, really, is Celia. It all seems to echo exactly what she is feeling. The dog woman might well be some kind of deity sent to kindle the flame of Celia's resolve.

She continues:

> assuring you that for myself the pang of absence is already too great, and when I think of the increase of what I must needs suffer it would be well nigh intolerable but for my firm hope of your unchangeable affection;

Oh, breathes Celia.

> and sometimes to put you in mind of this, and seeing that in person I cannot be with you, I send you now something most nearly pertaining thereto that is a present possible to send, that is to say, my picture set in a bracelet with the whole device which you already know;

Celia pats the car in which she sits and says to it that a bracelet was all right for the Tudors, but she'd rather have a car any day. Of course it would have been even nicer to have both – she thinks with fleeting regret of those little forget-me-not earrings – really, given all her other blessings, such thoughts seem downright churlish. Dear Alex, she thinks, I wonder what you are doing at this precise moment?

In a slight blur she reads the conclusion.

wishing myself in their place when it shall please you. This by the hand of your loyal servant and friend,

H. Rex.

In pleasurable anticipation Celia breaks down, and sobs. The sheer weight of the love and longing has overtaken her (coupled, perhaps, with the gin) and she gives herself up to a really good cry. Oh Alex, she thinks, I can't wait to be with you again. Sob, sob, sob. But at least these are tears of hope.

The dog woman is walking Rebecca back down the empty High Street for in all the excitement of meeting Celia she forgot the real reason for the stroll which was, of course, the dog's daily bowel movement.

'We have a busy day tomorrow,' she says to her hound. 'So we will just go as far as the church. And then *supper* – eh, Rebecca? Eh?'

As she passes she looks into the lone parked car, as does the dog. They both see the sobbing woman within. Rebecca snarls and her owner, seeing who it is sitting so distressed, immediately crosses to the other side of the road, where the well-bred dog crouches thankfully and fouls, looked upon affectionately by its well-bred owner.

This typically English scene goes unnoticed by Celia as she dries her eyes, closes the book, and drives off into the low sunlight of a seven o'clock June evening in a pleasurable anticipatory melancholy. Such is the power of the written word, albeit centuries old. She longs for her husband as that Golden Prince once longed for his witch-like Anne. So

133

this is love. From Ages Past to Ages Given, Always And Ever It Shall Be . . .

Just outside Salisbury, half an hour on, she stops and adjusts her hair and her make-up. The Brandreth conference proper must be over for the day by now. Alex will be contemplating dinner. She pictures him showering and getting ready to relax, and dispels any fears she may have about her arrival by telling herself over and over again that she will be a discreet wife. If he does not feel able to include her in tonight's socialising, she will accede graciously and wait for him in the night. I am your mistress and your friend, she says to herself as she drives into the hotel carpark. And she sits, looking across the town to where the cathedral spire sends its shaft up into the clear evening sky like a grey finger of hope to any pilgrim who might chance to come its way.

Her step light, Celia enters the Queen's Brough and makes her happy way towards the reception desk. It is a grand coincidence, not surprising, she thinks, given her tryst with Fate, that while she waits to be dealt with she sees in the distance, at the bar of that worthy establishment, her husband, fount of all this pleasurable projection, opening his arms in welcome, and bearing the unmistakable creases of a face lit up with loving desire. Not unnaturally she thinks it is to her that he gestures and her heart lifts. She turns, she almost calls his name, she prepares to run towards him. There is nothing between them save a few potted palms. The bar is empty apart from the attendant behind the counter who has his back turned and her husband who has his arms raised in that unmistakably loving gesture. A swift sprint and she could be held within them. But what is this? Even as the soles of her feet are set to spring Celia now notices a woman who walks, with indisputable assurance, towards him. And yes – Celia squints but she is not mistaken – not only walks towards him, but right on into those arms as well. And the arms are apparently bent upon enfolding this creature, for they begin

134

to move in the manner of arms that will do so. They envelop this fair, coiffured female who is wearing (Celia feels it is right that she should take in every detail) a horrible, floating chiffon frock of pastel pink and primrose, which wafts around her high-heeled ankles as she enters what should, by right (both emotionally and legally) be Celia's domain. The arms of Alex.

Fascinated, Celia watches, as those familiar arms cease to be extended and close around the shoulders of Pastel Frock. Celia blinks, makes a little 'Aah' of disbelief and continues to stare. Presumably the arms will suddenly recognise that they enfold the wrong person. Celia blinks again and waits for this realisation to take place. But it does not. Her husband's arms stay put, moving even more tightly around the floaty form. They seem to be fixed there quite comfortably. In her head she lets out a long agonised howl and the book, which she held as a talisman, falls to the floor – plop – on to the deep pile of the carpet.

Someone says something to Celia. It is the receptionist, very close to her, just across the desk top. She says that Celia has dropped something. Celia retrieves it, blood rushing to her head as she stoops. The floor looks very black and is speckled with stars.

'How careless of me,' she says as the blur of the book and the fuzziness of her hand fuse before her eyes. She picks it up. The carpet is lovat green again and the stars have gone. Celia straightens, turns and says, very, very brightly, 'I am Miss Wilde. I telephoned earlier. A double room with bath . . .' To which the receptionist says happily, 'Ah yes.'

How strangely fortuitous it was that she used her maiden name for the booking. Then it had merely been protection from his discovering her lovely surprise. Now it is protection from discovery at all.

Celia says she will not need a porter. She can take her small amount of baggage up to her room.

Celia takes the proffered key.

Celia stands there, key in hand, suitcase (the one which matches the pigskin that Alex has with him) at her feet.

Celia thinks things like, Perhaps Alex is just being friendly.

Celia watches.

The couple she watches kiss, very, very passionately. They spring apart as the barman, finished with the titivations of his Pimms, turns around. They now comport themselves as Celia would wish them to.

But Celia can tell.

Alex looks boyish.

This was no friendly exchange.

The woman, as she turns a little, shows a profile that is (here Celia takes a small breath of cheer) not young. In fact it is a profile quite as old, Celia feels sure, as her own. If not older. No – that is too hopeful. This is merely a woman of much the same age as Celia but without the benefit of Adrian and Top Shop. She looks like a female from 'Come Dancing': very loud eye-shadow, firmly controlled hair, and – now that she has turned and her profile is in Celia's full view – pretty, in a sharp *retroussé* sort of way. She laughs at Alex as he says something to do with the drinks he is ordering, and Celia, good wife, notices she has sharp little teeth to match the sharp little upturned nose. Celia feels sick. As the barman takes their money and turns away again they kiss in brief secrecy and Celia sees Alex's familiar hand accommodate a pastel breast. Someone has just thrust a red-hot dagger into Celia's. She gasps at the pain of it.

'Miss Wilde?' says the receptionist. 'Are you all right?'

Celia turns and gives her another big, bright smile.

'Just coming to,' she says, 'after the journey . . .'

'Of course,' says the receptionist. 'You just go on up to your room whenever you want to. Or perhaps –' She has noticed how hungrily Celia is staring at the bar. 'You'd prefer to go and have a drink first?'

'Oh no,' says Celia. 'I'm fine. Third floor and the lift is to my right, did you say?'

Gratefully the receptionist nods and goes back to her accounts. Celia still stands there, mesmerised.

Suddenly, brushing past her, bringing noise to the proceedings, comes a whole welter of besuited young men. They hail Alex and the woman.

'Alex,' they call, their hands upraised.

And 'Felicity,' they say in delight.

Felicity Fuck, says Celia under her breath.

'I'm sorry?' says the receptionist from the depths of her accounts. 'Did you say something?'

'No,' says Celia. 'Nothing at all.'

Felicity, she thinks, *Felicity*. How stupendously inappropriate.

She picks up her case. Vaguely she hopes that Alex will catch sight of her and come over to her and all will be well. But in her heart, that bruised commodity, she knows this will not happen. How she curses being a forty-year-old woman as she makes her way towards the lift and her room. When she was twenty, twenty-five even, she would have been in there fighting. At forty she has learned the art of self restraint. She has also – quite suddenly and out of nowhere – learnt that, despite what the writers of yearning love songs say, you cannot retrieve love that is lost to another by simply asking for it back. And Alex did look very loving when he held out his arms like that, and the woman looked sickeningly at home in them. No, says Celia, confrontation is not the way.

But what is?

Just before the lift engulfs her she calls to the receptionist. 'Excuse me,' she says, 'but would it be possible to have a bottle of champagne sent up to my room?'

The receptionist nods. 'Of course,' she says cheerfully.

'Oh – and while you're at it,' adds Celia, 'send up a packet of cigarettes as well – any brand will do.'

The receptionist says, 'Certainly. Will there be anything else?'

It is on the tip of Celia's tongue to say, Only my husband, but she doesn't. And as the lift doors close she has a last glimpse of the jolly Brandreth crowd by the bar and Alex's grinning face.

3

From the window of her third-floor room Celia looks down upon Salisbury. She has a nice view, the sort of view any tourist would love, for she overlooks the fine cathedral with its charming surroundings. At this time of evening it is almost deserted. The neatly manicured lawns, the quaint cobblestones, the warm brickwork of the eighteenth-century buildings that surround it complete a harmonious and tranquil scene: in the June sunlight, Celia thinks, they should create a sense of hope. The bright radiant blue of the sky, the early summer flowers of the gardens, the freshness of the light, all speak of being at the beginning of something. Celia shakes her head and turns away: she smiles ruefully. She certainly is at the beginning of something but it is not a something in which she wishes to participate. This beginning belongs to Alex and Pastel Frock downstairs. What Celia has experienced is an ending. But then, she thinks, all endings are beginnings. Close the door on one thing, you automatically open it to another – even if it leads to total darkness. Not a philosophical conundrum that she wishes to dwell upon at the moment.

There is a knock at the door. She calls out 'Enter' and is pleased to hear her voice sounding just the same as before: if anything stronger and more imperious. At any rate it has none of the whimpering uncertainty expected of a newly wronged wife.

In comes a small, rather plain young woman bearing a tray on which are perched the champagne in an ice-bucket, a glass and the packet of cigarettes. Celia is so grateful for these things arriving that she gives their bringer a five-pound note. She will never know that her largesse meant that the chambermaid who received it was thus able to spend her next night off at the Three

Brass Bells (a very fine Jacobean hostelry on the outskirts of Salisbury) where she got extremely merry, accepted the advances of the head of the local darts team, had twins nine months later and now runs a nice little hotel near Swanage with her husband. She is a very happy woman and it is all thanks to Celia's five-pound note. This merely continues to illustrate that there are silver linings to be had in everything leaden – even if we do not know what they are. Out there, somewhere, someone or something is always benefiting from the misfortunes of others. Look upon this as a positive situation, one to be encouraged: it would be tragic to think that no good at all comes out of what we suffer, for we all seem to suffer so much.

Celia is definitely not in the mood for considering silver linings at this moment. She feels – well – how *does* she feel? She puts her hand around the neck of the bottle and clutches it tightly for a moment. But it is cold and wet and not at all like living flesh so she just gets on with removing the cork. Feelings? Ah yes. What she feels is what she imagines she would feel if a sweet-faced nun came up to her in Chiswick High Road and smacked her around the face twice. Shocked and unsure how to retaliate. Yes, she thinks, it feels exactly like that.

Idly, lost in thought, or perhaps just lost, she opens the packet of cigarettes and begins to smoke. That goes part of the way to pouring balm on her shocked condition: it is something to do with her hands which, she notices suddenly, are shaking, and also something upon which to concentrate her mind. While she is smoking she thinks only of that act – well, that and sipping the drink – and sits thus for a long while, looking down from her window, not facing up to anything except the smoke from her nostrils and the gradual reduction in the quivering of her hand. It is a sad thing to have to admit, and she puts it off for as long as possible, but the plain fact is that the cigarettes do not taste very nice: she is not getting the pleasure from them that she thought, yearned even, to do. It is possible that this is the way things will be in future – hollow dreams, hollow dreams. She shakes her head, and sighs, and begins to talk to herself.

'Why has it happened?' is the first thing she asks.

'I don't know,' she replies, thinking hard. But she can come up with no reason.

'Just one of those things, then?'

She agrees with herself. It must be simply that.

'Do you still love him?'

She does not even pause to answer this one. 'Love,' she says, 'has nothing to do with this.'

'What has, then?'

'Revenge,' she says, quite surprised at first but realising that her subconscious has taken over and is correct.

'And how will this manifest itself?'

'Can't say,' says Celia, puff, puff, puffing. 'Not yet.' And she adds more darkly, 'But manifest itself it will.'

It is only after this exchange that she suddenly feels the return of the knife in her heart. The children, she thinks. Oh my God. My poor babies . . . And then a recognisable emotion, impressive in its intensity, takes hold of her entire body and shakes it from head to toe. It is the emotion called Hate. Right at that moment Celia hates Alex with a depth she would not have believed possible. Neither, it should be said, would he. How thin is the dividing line upon which our civilised emotions turn. An hour ago Celia was a woman in love. Now she is a woman racked by hate and seeking vengeance. These are not the usual feelings of a Bedford Park Wife: it takes her a little time to get used to them. No longer is she the foolish paper cutout character of an Agatha Christie thriller, nor is she the wide-eyed Pilgrim making for the Celestial City: now she is that deeper, more profound commodity, the aggrieved heroine – and quite Shakespearian in her intensity.

She smokes, she sips, she thinks dark thoughts, she assimilates until the bottle is empty: then she decides that the assimilation period is over; she must move on to that new territory called action. But nothing is growing there. She does not know what to do. She considers telephoning Hazel but realises – despite her fuzzy state – that this will do no good. Firstly (and arguably) because she is not there – and secondly, because even if she were there, Hazel has already let her down. She was not there for her party, she was not there for her lonely weekend, *and* she has taken Celia's children away. If Hazel had not done that, if Hazel had not gone sucking up to rich right-wing Americans, Celia would not be in this situation. She would have been washing up the picnic things now, Rebecca and Henry would be sitting contented and rosy in the bath and she would be planning a pleasant night of television crum. She would not be sitting here, filling herself with toxins and being cuckolded. No. She will confide none of this to Hazel. Certainly not. For even discounting Hazel's disloyal culpability in all this, if she does confide in Hazel, then her Bedford Park life will never be the same again. While she, Celia, keeps all this to herself then her outward Bedford Park life can continue unchanged. Does she want to continue unchanged? She nods at the smoke spiralling upwards. Yes, yes, she does. She would also like to see Alex at the bottom of a lake, but you can't have everything.

What she is not going to do is be rash. Or silly. Besides, as she cannot remember her mother-in-law's telephone number, she cannot do what is currently uppermost in her mind, to wit, call her so that when they get to the quavering, 'And where is Alex now, dear?' Celia can say, 'Downstairs feeling up another woman, Joyce. Shall I get him for you?' Delightful as this would be it would solve absolutely nothing. Celia has a battle to win, a private battle. The battle is for her self-esteem. Her attackers are regrouping, having dealt the initial blow, and they will be back. She must win the next round – but how?

An extremely painful question forces itself upon her. How long have they been at it? And another. How many times have they done it? 'Be gone, pointless ponderings!' she says loudly into the room. And she stands up.

It is at approximately this time, with confused ideas of battle plans, that she realises three things. The first is that she wants to talk to *someone*. The second is that she wants that someone to be Susannah. And the third is that Salisbury is not a million miles from where Susannah and Tom live (fourteen to be precise, funny she did not think of that before). It is as she attempts to walk (having stood up) that she realises a fourth thing: she is, in all respects save – she thinks fondly – her mental control, drunk. She knows she is physically drunk because she wobbles all over the place as she attempts a straight course towards the telephone. A passing thought occurs – that it might have been better, healthier, to go for a hearty walk while she assimilated this new dimension. Perhaps, she thinks, half of those lone female walkers striding around on country hills with dogs are really trying to come to terms with some emotional calamity in their lives. Perhaps that is why they always look so fierce. She remembers the Stockbridge woman and winces. There was all that gin, too. She must be very, very careful. She must keep control and be positive when she talks to Susie.

At least she is still mentally alert enough to remember Tom and Susannah's telephone number perfectly. She congratulates herself on this, and she dials. As the ringing tone begins, she sits down, rather abruptly it is true, on the floor, one hand holding the phone to her ear, one arm hugging her knees to her chest. Thus did Celia sit, many years ago, whenever she prepared to have a long telephonic session with Susie. The pose comes to her without thinking about it and she waits, devoid of sentiment, remembering her watchwords of control and positivism.

The ringing is answered and Susie's voice says crisply, 'Susannah Mason here.'

Celia, control and positivism abounding, opens her mouth to say, with smiling composure, 'And Celia Crossland here ...' but this does not come out. Instead, what does come out is a long, heart-wrung cry, followed by some deep, foundation-shaking moans, with somewhere kindled from the agony the words, 'Oh Susie, oh Susie, what am I going to do ...?'

Round two of the battle also goes, I am afraid, to the enemy forces.

There is no question that Celia cannot drive in her condition. Celia is the first to admit this, followed closely by Susie.

'I'll come and get you,' she says, and adds, 'Wait there,' which is quite funny really. Celia finds herself laughing wildly.

'Celia,' says Susie sharply. 'Stop that.'

Celia says huffily, 'Well, honestly, Susannah – what a stupid thing to say. Where do you think I might go, for Christ's sake? I can't even stand up – at least . . .' She makes an effort, rather like a newborn calf, to struggle to her feet, but it is not successful. It *could* be successful if she really wanted to make the effort but on the whole she'd rather not bother. 'Anyway,' she says, 'I've thought of something you haven't thought of . . .'

'What?' asks Susie, impatient to be off, already calling over her shoulder to Tom that Celia is in trouble and she's going out to her.

'I can't leave my car here in the hotel carpark.'

'Why ever not?'

'Because Alex will recognise it.'

'Well, you certainly can't drive it in your state.'

'Thank you,' says Celia with some dignity.

'Well, can you?'

'No,' agrees Celia. 'Well – what *am* I to do?'

To Celia's rapidly befuddling mind her friend's voice goes very masculine all of a sudden as it says, 'I'll drive it back here.'

Celia says, 'How can you if you're already driving your own?' And she adds, 'Your voice has gone very low.'

'That's not me, fathead,' says Susannah. 'It's Tom – on the extension.'

'Don't call me names,' moans Celia afresh.

'Oh my darling girl,' says the masculine voice.

'Tom?' says Susannah.

'He's only making up for your calling me fathead,' says Celia, and then she stops. Why should she help out anyone of the masculine variety after what she's been put through? 'He's very fond of me – aren't you, Tom?'

He coughs in a manner that could well be affirmative.

'We're coming over now,' says Susie.

'And to think,' moans Celia softly, 'that he was to be my Celestial City . . .'

143

Both Susannah and Tom are ungrounded in Bunyan and they take the reference as something far more dangerous.

'Don't for God's sake attempt anything,' says Susie. 'Don't even *move*.'

'I told you,' says Celia crossly. 'I can't.'

But the telephone is dead. They are now on their way.

Celia, mopping at bitter tears, decides to ignore the advice and finally manages the calf motion successfully. She replaces the receiver and congratulates herself for negotiating such a monumental act. She goes into the bathroom where she reconstitutes her face with fresh make-up. Aspects of her are still functioning. It would not do to let Tom see her looking anything less than perfect.

By the time the two of them enter Celia's hotel bedroom, Celia has been checked out of the Queen's Brough. The efficient Susannah has paid her bill, overcoming the confusion of Celia's maiden name with sterling aplomb by repeating her friend's room number over and over again until the night receptionist finally rallied and admitted to there being a Miss C. Wilde in that particular room, though still nursing a small grudge since there is a Crossland staying in a completely different set of digits with the initial A. on the floor below and it is not his fault that this creates such annoyance. Susie, ruffled by this exchange, sweeps into Celia's room and says, 'You might have told me you weren't using your married name.'

And Celia, swaying slightly, replies, 'I shall never, never use it again,' and falls into Tom's outstretched arms.

Tom, apprised of what is taking place, as much as his wife can apprise him given the rather garbled telephone conversation she has had with Celia, looks at the crumpled figure crushed to his chest and says, 'I'm going to go and put one on him.'

At which Celia has two thoughts. The first being, how nice it would be, as an alternative to the lake, to see Alex punched on the nose – the second, more sensibly, being that she doesn't want her husband hurt. Blessed, indeed, are the peacemakers. She pulls away from Tom's embrace and says, 'All I want to do is to get away from here and *think*. I don't want Alex to know I know.' And she adds, with genuine sorrow, 'Oh, my poor children, my poor children ...'

And while Susie is packing Celia's things away Tom whispers in slow, dreadful tones, 'This hasn't got anything to do with what was in the washing machine, has it?'

To which Celia, much confused, says, 'What?'

But Tom, about to repeat it, is curtailed by Susie's reappearance from the bathroom with Celia's make-up bag (the only thing unpacked). So he merely backs off, whistling.

Celia repeats, 'What?'

Tom moves his head fractionally in his wife's direction and hisses, 'Nothing,' but the subtlety of the gesture is lost on Celia.

Susannah says crisply, 'Don't start questioning her till we get home, Tom. Can't you see she's had enough? And this is hardly the time to be whistling ...'

In the lift Celia has a vague recollection regarding the significance of Tom's whispered remark and says in a surprised voice, 'I haven't opened the washing machine. I meant to but I forgot.'

Tom winces and puts his hand over her mouth under the pretext of soothing her. Susie says, 'You just forget all about that kind of thing for the time being ...'

'Yes,' says Tom, keeping his hand where it is. 'You don't want to be worrying about all that nonsense now, do you?'

She manages to shake off his hand and, looking up into his eyes, as much as she can focus, she says firmly, 'Yes I do. I want to think about it very much indeed – as a matter of fact I—'

Back goes his hand. It is all she can do to concentrate on breathing. But the thought of that dear little illicit package nestling away in the Hotpoint is about the only good thing on the horizon at the moment.

'I love surprises,' she says, having ducked Tom's grasp.

Susie puts her cool, elegant hand on her friend's forehead and says, 'Don't be bitter darling ... They simply are not worth it. It must have been awful.'

The illicit package floats out of her consciousness to be replaced by Alex's face smiling boyishly at that gruesome chiffoned female. Which makes Celia begin sobbing again, loud and hard. She makes no further mention of the washing machine.

Tom looks at her with mingled relief and desire. Perhaps his moment has come?

She is still sobbing as they walk through reception but fortunately the desk is unmanned and there is nobody to see. They make their way towards the hotel door, brushing past the plants and negotiating the chairs (Celia is trying very hard to stay upright and doing quite well with the aid of Susannah's supporting arm; Tom is bringing up the rear and the suitcase) when suddenly, from behind them and from some distance, they hear a voice say, 'Good Lord. What on earth are you doing here?'

It is a voice that is full of astonishment and, to a discerning ear, a voice that even as it says the words wishes it had remained silent. Alex's voice, calling from down near the bar, human in its guileless response to the shock of seeing Tom. Human in its secondary response of wishing it had not acknowledged this. Alex, riveted by Tom's familiar appearance, has not yet noticed his two female companions who are a little way ahead of him, half hidden by a fronding palm. For a moment the shuffling trio freezes, then, as Tom turns to face his questioner, Susie, quick-thinking Susie, pushes Celia behind the plant and down on to a small settee. Celia bounces into the cushions and remains there, motionless and quiet. Susie and Tom then glide together to provide a human screen.

Tom, very red in the face, calls, 'Never mind us. What are *you* doing here?' There is a pugilistic quality about the way he sticks out his jaw as he says this.

Susie, sensing at once that she must act, puts up her delicate hand, half restraining her husband, half saluting Alex, and says, 'Hi.'

Alex calls stoutly, 'Brandreth case.'

Celia, Pavlovian in her response, shouts, 'Bugger the Brandreth case,' so that Susie, diving behind the bushy leaves, says 'Shut up.' And then coming out again says *sotto voce* to Tom, 'Leave this to me.' She begins advancing towards Alex for what, later, she will describe to Celia as one of the longest walks of her life. Over her shoulder she says to her husband, 'Get Celia out of here while I distract him.'

There is scarcely any need for this since, to put it mildly, Alex seems distracted already. As Susie advances he appears to jump sideways and is half way out of his seat, well away from the female sitting next to him. Susannah stands in front of him, as beautiful and charming as an icicle, and says, smooth as the same commodity, 'Oh, please don't get up.' She taps him lightly on the shoulder so that he sinks unresisting back into his chair. 'We're collecting one of our weekenders. We must dash . . .' And turning her gaze upon the pastel-clad woman she says, 'You must introduce me, Alex.' She extends her hand. The woman extends hers back.

'Conference for two, is it?' asks Susie.

'Everybody else is dining out tonight. They'll be back soon,' he says defensively.

'Really?' breathes Susie, staring at him. Susannah has a stare when she chooses.

'This is Miss Lyall,' says Alex. He is twisting desperately in his seat so that it groans and complains. Susie smiles down at him. 'Good job Celia isn't here, Alex.'

'Why?' His pinkness deepens to a peony hue.

'Because she'd say the same thing she says in the conservatory at home –' She dwells on the last word and taps the chair, giving him a very straight Susie look. 'She'd say that you're breaking it, Alex . . .'

He manages a taut rictus which is supposed to resemble the smile of the clean-conscienced.

Susannah takes the female's proffered hand, touches it limply as if it were diseased, and says, 'How nice.'

Alex stands up, looking guilty.

'And Celia's birthday, too,' says Susannah. 'Poor Cee . . .'

She gives a quick look over her shoulder. Poor Cee and suitcase-Tom have gone. Only the slight motion of the hotel door indicate where.

'Such a lovely dinner party last night,' adds Susie. 'But a pity we didn't have a chance to see the children.' To this last she also brings a certain emphasis.

Alex is certain something is up – Susie has never shown the slightest interest in his offspring – but he cannot tell what. He decides to bluff it out.

'Yes,' he says. 'Wasn't it?'

'They're so delightful . . .' Susie gives the pastel-clad lady the benefit of a long, unpleasant stare.

'Have you got children, Miss Lyall?' She looks away from the expostulating Miss Lyall to her watch, which she scrutinises with devastating seriousness.

'Must go, Alex,' she says. And turning on her heel she sashays off, leaving Alex to make what he will of the exchange.

Susie is in no doubt that it has made some kind of mark on the proceedings and she is not wrong. Later, having tiptoed down the corridor into his lover's room, Alex is not – quite – the rampant lover he initially showed promise of being. Which gives Miss Lyall pause for thought. She is used to her affairs with high-flying professionals lasting at least six months and giving her a good run for her money. She hopes Alex is up to it for although it was his brain that attracted her initially she prefers her intellectuals to have good-sized thrusting coronas as well. What woman doesn't? Miss Lyall detects a certain abstraction in the grimacing features of the man beneath her. She gyrates harder. One of the reasons she has been kept on the Brandreth team is that she gets the best out of her men. Alex, being ground down into the mattress like a piece of obstinate corn, is discovering that this capacity does not only apply to business law.

But we, like Celia, must not dwell on such activities. We, hearts, souls, and sympathies, remain firmly in our heroine's camp, an Elizabethan manor house fourteen miles away, with

Celia tucked up, hot Slippery Elm Food in a bowl at her bedside (Susie's healthy eating cure-all), plotting vengeance and wishing she had never, ever set off on this crazy escapade. She wishes, as she sucks on the spoon, watched by Susannah, what we might all wish at such a time: that she had never broken away from her lovely Bedford Park life. For there, suck, suck, nothing like this ever, ever happens. Suck, suck, suck.

'Well,' says Susannah. 'What are you going to do about it?'

Celia, whose drunken vows to maintain Bedford-Park-life-as-she-knows-it seem to have waned a little, tries out the word 'divorce', but it does not ripple off the tongue easily.

Susannah shakes her head. 'Why?' she asks.

'Because Alex Is Having An Affair With Another Woman.'

'So you're going to give everything up because of that?'

'I didn't realise,' says Celia, somewhat ashamed, 'that you took the sanctity of marriage so seriously.'

Susannah gives an unusually gutsy laugh. 'Nor do I,' she says. 'One of my favourite radio moments was in "Desert Island Discs" when the castaway said that as her inanimate object of no practical use she would like to take her husband . . .'

They both howl with laughter before remembering that this is a serious occasion.

'No,' says Susie. 'By everything, I mean home, life-style, comfort – nice things – you know, the stuff that life is really made of, not that tenuous thing called Love, or that even more tenuous thing called sexual fidelity. If those really were the two things that make the world go round then we'd still be grunting at each other in caves . . .' She gives a little shrug. 'And we're not – are we?'

Certainly not, thinks Celia, staring around the panelled room. She touches the heavy tapestries that hang about the bed, looks through the leaded windows to the darkening paddock and pastures beyond, and finally brings her gaze back to the big gilt mirror in which they are both reflected. They look, in their nighties, like portraits in a seventeenth-century painting – or characters from a Webster play.

'You and Tom certainly don't live in a cave,' she says. 'But what would you do if you were me?' And then she adds hastily, 'I mean, if you were me and you had this house and the grounds and all the money and everything?' She knows perfectly well that Susie would feel absolutely no loyalty at all to the house in Bedford Park.

'I'd do what I'm doing already –' Susie takes the empty bowl and the spoon from Celia, for the sucking is irritating.

'Yes but . . .' Celia says. 'What would you do if you found out Tom was having an affair?'

Susie laughs again, if anything more gutsily. 'He is,' she says. 'All the time. He's like the British Secret Service, with safe houses all over the place.'

'No! Really?' says Celia, plucking away at the rough weave of the bedspread, not daring to engage her friend's eye.

'Yup,' says Susie. 'He doesn't know that I know, of course. I just let him get on with it. We don't have sex together any more, anyway. You'd be surprised how much nicer our marriage is since we gave that old stuff up. We haven't – you know – for years.'

'But don't you feel debased?' Celia looks at Susie's incredulous eyes and rapidly changes this to, 'Or at any rate – let down?'

'Not at all,' says Susie. 'As long as he doesn't try to set up a *ménage à trois* or anything *avant garde* like that, it's fine. I earn my keep,' she adds drily. 'Anyway – we aren't supposed to be discussing me and Tom, we're supposed to be thinking about you and Alex.'

Celia is still very interested in this revelation about her friend's relationship.

'I never guessed,' she says in amazement. 'Was it all his affairs that made you stop loving him?' She asks this with a certain vested interest. 'I mean when did you stop?'

'I'm not sure,' says Susie, 'that I ever started.'

Celia sees herself in the mirror. She is wide-eyed. 'Then why on earth did you marry him, Susie?'

It is Susie's turn to look amazed. 'Because he was rich, of course.' She shakes her head at the silliness of the question. 'And handsome and clever and amusing and – well – he came the closest I've ever known anyone to making me use the word Love. It seemed right.' She looks down at her nails. 'What I didn't realise was that he wanted lots and lots of children.' She wrinkles her nose. 'And that just wasn't on.'

'You could have had just one. You never know, you might have liked it . . .'

Susannah, pulling at the little diamond chip in her ear lobe, gives Celia a long, hard look. 'Come on, Celia – do you really think it's me?'

Celia gives her a long, hard look back. Remembering the broken nights and the shitty nappies and the dribbling nipples (things she has conveniently forgotten over the years) she shakes her head. 'No,' she says. 'But I think it's unfair on Tom . . .'

Susannah gets off the bed. She smiles and pulls at her other ear lobe.

'Why Tom? *He* wouldn't be the one to have to deal with everything. All he'd have to do would be to hoick it around in his arms, throw it up into the air, say, Look everybody at my fine son – or daughter – and then I'd be left with the puke to clear up . . .'

Celia, remembering Henry after their Blessing, feels guilty and agrees. She nods at Susie. 'You're quite right. It wouldn't have been you at all. But how did you stay married to him? God – if I'd disagreed with Alex on something as fundamental as that it would have been grounds for divorce.'

'You've got grounds for divorce anyway, Cee – despite being such an agreeable wife.'

If this is rather cruel, thinks Celia, it is also accurate.

'Well?' she says a little tersely. 'How did you get away with it?'

'I staged a mock miscarriage—'

Celia is right. They are in a play. Her mouth opens but no words come out.

'No need to look so shocked,' says Susannah. 'Surely it's better than the real thing.'

Celia tries again but only the faintest of squeals emerges.

'I didn't find out about Tom's ideas until our wedding night – and frankly that was bad enough without the prospect of pregnancy and birth – but when he told me that he hoped I got one in the bag straight away, well, I just had to do something.'

Celia's voice has returned enough for her to say, 'Susie! You weren't still a *virgin* when you married him?'

'Of course I was. Why not?'

There was really no answer to that. Except, perhaps, You poor thing, which didn't really seem to fit at all.

'Go on,' says Celia.

'Well – a couple of weeks later I said I felt sick. Then a few weeks after that I told Tom I was pregnant. And a few weeks after that he had to fly to London and I stayed behind. And a couple of days later I was found lying at the bottom of the stairs of the apartment. No baby any more.'

'Oh Susie.' Celia is near to tears.

'It wasn't true, fathead . . .'

'Even so . . . But he must have suggested that you try again?'

Susie goes over to the door, opens it and peers round the dark carved lintel into the passageway. Then she comes back to the bed, puts her finger to her mouth and says, 'You must never, never say anything of this to anybody – especially not Tom.'

'See this wet,' says Celia, holding up her finger, and nods.

'Well – I got an actor I knew to come to our apartment and pose as my gynaecologist and he told Tom that I'd damaged both my Fallopian tubes in the fall—'

'That doesn't sound right,' says Celia.

'It sounded right enough to a man like Tom – anyway – he told him that, and said I would never have children, and there we are . . .'

'Susie,' says Celia. 'You have taken my breath away with your deceit.'

'Oh, don't be so pious – look at Tom and Alex. We all deserve each other in one way or another.'

'I don't,' says Celia, bending the truth a little. After all, hers scarcely qualifies compared to all these other deceivers.

'Well – it's about time you started.'

Fancy her thinking that she knew this friend of hers well. Fancy her thinking she knew people well. Even those people at her birthday party! If Susie is like this then what black secrets might her own sister have? And Dave – with all his plumbing and in and out of everybody's houses? Celia feels that she has been tame by comparison. *Is* tame by comparison. Parlour Games indeed! Life back in Chiswick suddenly seems extremely prissy. Or does it? She remembers the package sitting in her washing machine. She smiles, a nice, slow smile, and feels much better. Good – she isn't entirely respectable after all. A little tame, perhaps, but not entirely trustworthy. She winces. Is she seriously suggesting to herself that this is a virtue? Well – apparently it is. Certainly where Alex is concerned.

We are, she thinks, exactly like icebergs, with the tiniest tips showing through and the rest well hidden. Why – just think – she didn't even know her own husband. How long has he been doing this sort of thing? Why has she not noticed his behaviour? What about AIDS? Things like this flit through her head. Absently she picks up the spoon again and sucks on it, thinking.

'Susie?'

'What?'

'Are you absolutely certain it doesn't bother you that Tom has affairs?'

'Absolutely sure. As long as it doesn't affect the relationship we've got now why should it bother me? I'm not the keeper of his genitals.' Susie laughs at this witticism.

So does Celia.

But she is also thinking hard.

Vengeance is mine may have been the initial prerogative of the Lord but really, she thinks, might not she be allowed to borrow it for a while?

4

It is a sad fact for womankind in general, and for Celia in particular, that her idea of Vengeance renders itself as that rather banal commodity, tit for tat. How nice it would have been if she had chosen a different path to remove the knife from her heart. How nice if she had eschewed this matching adultery for adultery and sought her solution in some other more constructive way. Like confronting Alex with his deceit, perhaps, and saying to his stricken and humbled countenance, 'Very well – you have done this. Now I am going to do something altogether higher and worthier ... I am going to, I am going to...'

Well – going to what?

What can Celia do to heal the wound?

Leave him?

And what good would that do?

It might hurt Alex to separate from his family and all his little comforts. It might bring a certain amount of shame upon his head, though not necessarily – there is still something honourable in a chap having a fling – but so far as doing Celia any good, it would not. Susannah in her somewhat devious reasoning has a point. All Celia would get if she rejected Alex would be a harder life, more responsibilities, less freedom. He would have the little flat up in town somewhere and the ease of mind following the monthly maintenance stipend. Plus being Father Christmas every other weekend and the joys of knocking off whomsoever he chose, whenever he chose it. This does not seem to Celia to be a very exacting kind of a Vengeance.

What else?

Can she go and get herself what her sister would call a proper job?

Certainly Alex would not like that. But then – neither would Celia. She has been happy living her pleasant Bedford Park life – happy bringing up her children, cooking, making the house nice, living a life-style that looked as good from the outside as it felt from within. Certainly taking a job would change all that, and make life extremely difficult for the professionally fulfilled Alex. But it would not fulfil her, nor be sweet Vengeance, for up until Saturday night in Salisbury, Celia was already fulfilled. Also, despite the shattering Hate, she still rather loves him. Or at any rate she likes him better than anyone else. Recoil if you will, but so it is.

And what of Rebecca and Henry? Celia is locked into their well-being like the stitches in a well-knitted jumper. Break one thread and the whole thing will unravel.

No, no. We come back, as Celia has done, to personal revenge. Tit for tat. An eye for an eye will go some way towards releasing the anger and humiliation she is trying hard not to feel. She does not even need to tell Alex that she knows about him and Pastel Frock – nor that she has dealt with it in this way. To Celia this seems a most proper and subtle solution – the solution which hurts all parties the least and which at the same time brings her maximum balm. The unpoetic phrase 'one in the eye for Alex' settles in her mind quite nicely and will not budge. That is all she can think of. Celia will take a lover and in the consummation of this she will look for her healing. No one in the world need ever know except her and the chosen one, who will be? Well – there is nothing surprising in the choice. It will be Tom, of course. Quite perfect for the role of lover. Rich, handsome, available and willing. And, perhaps more to the point, since Celia wishes no woman to suffer as she has suffered, she has been given, if obliquely, *carte blanche* by his wife. A peculiarly appealing piece of morality on her part: very sisterly.

So then – when she returns to Bedford Park tomorrow morning she will exhume the package in the washing machine, open it, be thrilled by its contents and telephone its giver to say, 'Yes, you have won. I love the gift and I love the idea of becoming your lover. I have a whole week free. When shall I come to Shepherd Market? When can we begin?' The *frisson* of nervous excitement she feels at the prospect of this conversation (let alone the physicalities which will follow) help a little to alleviate the hurt. Which proves she is doing the right thing. She does not know how long the Vengeance should last. Maybe one night, maybe many. At the moment she is in no mood to make decisions like that. First unleash the dogs of wrath – then decide for how long they should be allowed out of the kennel.

This is what Celia thinks about as she slips from the covers and goes over to the curtains which Susie so thoughtfully closed for her the night before. She opens them upon another perfect June day. It is just as well that it is perfect: any depression in the weather would certainly make room for Celia's to fatten. Hers is a fragile peace, an uncertain buoyancy. Here is the first whole day of being forty and it is not remotely as she imagined it would be. She stares out of the window and for a moment what she sees is blurred, as if by a light rainfall. She blinks and the rainfall vanishes. The rich green swelling of the Wiltshire landscape is bathed in sunlight once more. She wishes very much that she had never set eyes on it but, since she has, it might as well be looking as perfect as it is. Perhaps, she wonders, the old adage about tears on your birthday is a true one? Well then, she will un-true it. She rubs her hands beneath each eye and pats her cheeks. And that's the last of *you*, she says.

A discreet knock upon her door heralds the Philippino housekeeper bearing her breakfast tray. Celia's very bright smile is replaced by one which is quite genuine as she beholds the single rose which stands among the grapefruit, boiled egg and golden toast. It is nice to be cared for. She could do with a lot of this sort of thing right now.

The tray bears a note from her hostess.

Make the most of this quiet morning. Everyone will be arriving from about noon onwards. I am riding until eleven but we can have coffee together at eleven-thirty if you like. On the patio. Don't if you'd rather not. The lunch will be full of bores, I'm afraid, but we can giggle about it later. Tom is playing golf. You have the house to yourself. If you feel like having a good scream go into the library. No one will hear you from there. I often do. Love S. xxx

No wonder, thinks Celia as she digs into her grapefruit, that Susie is content. How many women can give lunch parties for forty people and go riding beforehand? Hazel may watch 'Dynasty' or 'Dallas', but Susannah actually lives it. Celia, appetite unimpaired, pours honey all over her grapefruit and decides that she is not going to let this episode in her life get the better of her. She bends her head to smell the pretty rose – which is scentless. Ah well, she thinks, that is the least of life's little disappointments. No matter; the honey, like Vengeance, will be sweet, sweet, sweet.

On the patio later Susie says, 'How are you feeling?'

Celia looks at her. She looks wonderful. Fair hair newly washed and flowing around her shoulders, face and eyes still bright from the horse-whipped air, sea-green dress that sits upon her frame as if it were glued in place.

'I was feeling fine. Now that I look at you I'm not so sure . . .'

Susie is an honest person. Many women would have said, 'You look wonderful,' and let it go at that. She does not. She says, 'Borrow something of mine if it will make you feel better . . .'

So Celia does. Susannah takes her into her dressing room and together they look along the rails. There is not a vast amount of stuff hanging here. She may buy the best for herself but she is not feckless. It is unlikely that even one of the garments was bought on the spur of the moment, and even less likely that any of them is a mistake.

'Now,' says Susie, 'do you feel in the mood for blue? Or a print? Tan perhaps? Or white is nice.' She is flicking through the hangers and pulls a full-skirted jersey dress out. It is very plain and probably very expensive. Celia feels a certain rebellion in her heart for the frock is just right – why must Susannah always get things just right?

'Black,' she says. 'I feel like black today.'

Susie riffles her fingers along and pulls out a short silky dress which would be fine except that its one piece of decoration is a large printed poppy, its redness splashing all over the heart area and its stalk and leaves weaving down towards the hem. It looks like a wound.

'Um, no,' says Celia. And then she spies a black-and-white striped dress made out of some kind of shiny stuff.

'What about this?' she says. 'It's got black for me and white for you.' And she holds it up.

It is loosely styled, which eases the problem of the difference in the two women's sizes, and is double-breasted, half dress, half coat. And it might have been dull were it not for the chicness of the cut and the most outrageous shoulders which, in their jutting opulence, would not disgrace an American footballer. The fabric is feminine but the style is dramatically aggressive. A Janus of a frock. You may touch me for the caress of the material, it says, but go too far and I shall shoulder you out of the way.

'This one,' says Celia positively. 'Can I borrow this one?'

Susie looks at her strangely for one-tenth of a second before giving an amused and acquiescent smile. 'Of course. It'll suit you.'

She does not tell Celia that this was her wedding dress, feeling that it might give the proceedings too much unnecessary fatality. She uses a phrase much vaunted in her erstwhile New York circles. 'You'll be able to make your own space wearing that, darling.'

Celia smiles at the giddy idea.

And it does suit Celia. Because she feels right in it. And when you feel right in something, positively, from within, the zen takes over and you *are* right. It is also the perfect foil to her peacock highlight – the note of discord that makes the whole effect sing.

So, dressed and ready and taking on with delight the persona of the frock, Celia goes out into the garden and stands on the patio looking across the sculptured lawn. Her back is to the house and the glass doors (somewhere around 1750 an architect wrinkled his nose at the Tudoresque style and created a little bit of Florence on this side of the building) and her hand is resting on an Italianate urn full of sapphire-blue lobelia. Her eyes, garden-wards, are shaded by a big straw hat, which echoes the stuff of the dress in the band around its crown. It is not a pretty hat, it is a statement hat. The New York designer who created it knew his client well. It was made for Susie as winged arms were for Isis. Celia, though in her heart still Celia, is dress and hat Susannah. And she is quite enjoying the feeling. So she stands there, alone, while her friend is checking over the last remaining items with her housekeeper so that the luncheon will be a success. The *oeufs en gelée* are a treat. Celia gives her shoulders a defiant little wriggle which feels very good. She can imagine charging at Pastel Frock in them, which makes her feel even better. Quite aggressive is our heroine's stance at the moment.

Tom, coming through the french windows, sees what he takes to be his wife. The dress is familiar, though he cannot say why – but he just knows it is a Susie dress. He dislikes it, it gives him a creepy feeling of *déjà vu*. He has been feeling disgruntled anyway. Here he is, with the object of his desire in a vulnerable state right under his roof, sleeping in a bed scarcely half a minute's tiptoe away, and he has been unable to do anything about it. And his hopes of making some kind of move this morning were dashed by his wife wagging a finger at him and saying that Celia must be left alone and, 'No – certainly not, Tom!' when he ventured to suggest he could take up her breakfast tray. 'Out you go to golf,' Susie had said. And out to golf he went. And played a damned bad game too. Little soft unhappy Celia, lying all warm and open in her bed, while he was bunkered. He is also much concerned about the as yet unopened package in the washing machine. What was supposed to be a bit of a joke is about to misfire on him horribly now that Celia is so vulnerable.

He needed to capitalise on Celia this morning if he was going to be able to put that right. Bloody Susannah keeping him away. It has not put him in the best of humour by any means.

'Well,' he says, giving vent a little, 'you look your usual sharp self. Where's our poor little pansy flower then? Still lying in bed wailing over that horrible husband of hers, I suppose? I don't imagine she's up to all this socialising. She's the homely type.'

The barbs, of course, were meant for his wife.

Now it is a curious fact that wronged women (and – who knows – wronged men too) while feeling absolutely happy about vilifying their wronging loved ones, do not take so kindly to others doing it for them. In any encounter with a cuckolded friend it is not advisable to criticise too strongly the malefactor. One's role is merely to listen, to sympathise: it is *not* to extemporise on the failings of the wrongdoer.

'Well?' he says, receiving no acknowledgement. 'Is she coming down? Where is the poor mite? What a bastard that Alex is . . .'

Celia winces beneath her hat.

In part she is annoyed at Tom calling Alex horrible and bastard. In the main she is absolutely furious at being likened to a pansy (yet again) and a homely soul, a poor mite. She jolly well isn't going to let this potential lover of hers think of her like that. Not for one minute. She is going to show him that she is just as upfront as anyone (Susie) else. So she flexes those shoulders, straightens her back, holds her stomach well in, and turns.

'She is here, Tom,' she says, in a voice which she, let alone Tom, never knew she was capable of. 'And she will be able to cope perfectly well – I assure you.'

Tom suddenly feels that he has knotted his tie too tight and that his trouser waistband has suddenly contracted. He feels strictured. He tries to take in enough air to revive himself and Celia, much pleased at what she takes to be the devastating effect of her new image, slips further into it like a hot knife into low-fat spread.

'Oh yes,' she says, 'I'm a big girl now.' She pats the shoulders of the frock searching for the right words. 'Finding my own space. Don't you like the effect?' She gives what is meant to be a skittish flex of her arm-muscles. It is a gesture reminiscent of Tom's wife.

He stares. What he sees is unpleasant to him.

'What about your children?' is all he can find to say once air is restored to his windpipe.

Celia, well into the part, shrugs those massive shoulders. 'Who needs to think about them?' she says. 'I'm putting myself first for once . . .'

It is a courageous if false statement, but enjoyable. She licks lascivious lips – a gesture which is not at all Susie and much more latent Celia but the two are as one in his eyes now. He does not like heartless women, and he most certainly does not like women who do not require cajoling. Tom likes cajoling. He is good at it. It takes all the pleasure out of the chase if you are not required to cajole.

The waistband of his trousers returns to its normal proportions and in that small atom of time Tom's affection for Celia wanes a little. He wants the old Celia back, please, the soft, doe-eyed creature, the one who can mop up milk, find a recorder bag and kiss her children goodbye without complaint. Where is that motherly, pneumatic, domesticated woman? This Celia is none of those things. In fact, as she moves away from the urn and its trailing lobelia, and comes over to stand at his side, he can feel those shoulders digging into his upper arm like the unbending armour of a warrior woman.

He moves away from her.

Further considerations such as this on Tom's part are abandoned for the time being. The first guests have arrived. The lunch party has commenced. Susannah arrives to whisk him away. She winks over her shoulder at Celia. 'I'll come back in a minute and start introducing you if you like,' she says.

'No need,' says Celia brightly. 'I'm quite up to doing it myself.' She catches Tom's glance and winks at him. 'See you later,' she calls, in a voice as un-pansylike as she can possibly make it, and she watches them go down the steps of the terrace together, arm-in-arm, a beautiful couple who look as perfectly matched as any ideal celluloid creation. And that, she thinks, only goes to show . . .

There will be no time for dalliance during the next few hours. Celia, quite unaware that she has done her cause with Tom no good at all, proceeds to enjoy this borrowed personality very much indeed. She mixes and mingles away, moving around the shrubs, in and out of groups of unknown people. Whenever she catches Tom's eye she gives him the benefit of a seductive look, a cross between lust and cruelty, which she feels goes with the part. He, if he returns it at all, begins to look hunted. Which, Celia congratulates herself, he has *every* right to do.

Occasionally she bumps into Susannah and they exchange wry looks, and once, just as she is biting into a little canapé, Susie says, 'See that woman over there? the one with the powder-blue mini-skirt?'

Celia nods.

'Well – that's the vicar's wife . . .' Susie lowers her voice for dramatic effect. 'I'm almost certain she's next in line for Tom.'

Which causes Celia to nearly choke on her mouthful. How wrong Susannah can be sometimes, she thinks happily, wiping her mouth.

'Do not go near her,' says Susannah, 'for she smells just like a Turkish brothel.'

Which causes Celia to explode again, this time on a moiety of caviar which she sends everywhere like little black gunshot pellets. Susannah, who dislikes to be associated with such Lucullan habits, walks off, cool, head high, as if the choking fit were nothing whatever to do with her.

Hence Celia, standing alone, meets the eyes of a woman a few yards off, who looks at her strangely. This is not only to do with the voluble spattering of caviar. It is also to do with the woman thinking that she recognises, vaguely, this lone choker in black-and-white stripes. And Celia – apparently glaring back, though in fact merely attempting to cease machine gunning everyone – thinks that she, too, has met this woman before. The woman moves off hurriedly: now she remembers. And Celia's contorted face and heaving (outrageously large) shoulders help her to do so. This is very definitely an unhinged female. And Celia remembers too, suddenly. It is the dog woman from Stockbridge. Celia hurries after her, for this is a face she knows, someone to talk to. Even if Henry VIII to Anne Boleyn was all cods.

But the woman has energy. Celia speeds up. The two women are positively whizzing in and out of the shrubs and the chattering groups. The Stockbridge lady determined to avoid this woman who (witness how she pursues so relentlessly) is undoubtedly quite mad, and Celia determined to catch her up. Lunch parties full of unknowns are tiring occasions. The old Celia would have made friends with all kinds of people by now. The new Celia, shoulders a-flail, is finding her own space and doesn't want to be bothered with all that sociability stuff. She hastens after her slight acquaintance, in continuing astonishment at the speed with which she moves, but determined to manage some kind of friendly exchange. It will be a relief to talk to someone, even to her, and there's no fear of her doing anything sinister here in broad daylight. Celia pursues with enthusiasm. The dog woman feels exactly the opposite and ducks inside the house, coming to rest against the french windows, panting a little from the exertion and peering out to see if she is safe. She is. Celia is standing some way off, scanning the heads dotted about, her quarry lost.

Tom, passing through the room, finds this guest of his cowering and peering and says, 'Mrs Stone! How nice. And have you decided to sell me those wonderful Daimlers of yours yet?'

Amongst her widow's possessions, shipped back in the days when the residue of the Empire still paid for such transportation, is a pair of pre-war cars which have lain, unused, in a garage near Stockbridge, for twenty-five years.

The dog woman regains enough composure to say, 'Mr Mason. What lovely weather.'

And Tom, his charm abounding, says, 'It certainly is. Shouldn't we be out there, you and I, enjoying it? And how is that lovely dog of yours?' Fortunately he does not know that the well-bred Rebecca, disappointed by the lean cuisine that has come her way, is making her feelings felt by crouching near the hollyhocks and leaving her own version of a calling card.

He offers Mrs Stone his arm. She peers again, sees that Celia has moved further off from the house, and accepts.

'You look as if,' says Tom, 'you were avoiding somebody.'

'As a matter of fact,' says the dog woman, 'I am.' And feeling the need to unburden herself, she goes on to explain, pointing out the object of her avoidance, who is now wandering away from the house towards the artificial lake and swaying her tightly swathed hips with delighted abandon. The frock has certainly gone to Celia's head. As she sways she flexes those shoulders. The effect from the back is that there is a rampant and dangerous woman on the loose. Tom finds that this continues to be an unpleasant observation.

It is unfortunate that Mrs Stone gets to the point of her story about Celia's need for a book by saying, 'She said she was going to weekend at the house of some very boring people and that she had forgotten to bring a book. *Very* boring people indeed,' she adds. 'I wonder who it is she is staying with down here?'

Tom stops listening.

He also forgets that Celia could not possibly have known, when she said this, that she would be coming to his home for the weekend.

All he knows is that what was begun earlier, when he saw Celia looking too much like Susannah, is now compounded. If sufferers in cuckoldry do not like their transgressing partners to be criticised, most certainly would-be lovers do not like to be thought of as bores. Even if Celia said it jokingly it is an unpardonable joke. Tom begins to realise that this is no longer a woman for whom he would lay down his Burberry across a muddy puddle, nor yet a woman he might yearn to hold protected in his arms. This is a woman who wears her shoulders

164

like a man, who thinks of him as a bore, and who – as he can see perfectly plainly – will make up to anything in trousers. (In her roving sway Celia has been accosted by two homesick New Englanders; good family men back in Concord but oh those English hips of hers. She is smiling up at them and has the stamp of seduction all over her. Tom can read that even from this distance.) Quite suddenly that is good enough for Tom. He remembers Celia prostrate on the floor with John. Him too? More than likely. No wonder Alex has broken and sought solace elsewhere. Celia is clearly wanton. Worse, Celia has always refused to be wanton with him. And the reason is now apparent. He has not been exciting enough. And apparently she doesn't mind to whom she tells this. Well – fine! So be it. He will have no further truck with Celia apart – he decides – from absolutely proper day-to-day acknowledgement when it is strictly necessary.

He strikes her from his list of desirable conquests, straightens his back and gives Mrs Stone the benefit of his most charming smile. He will have those Daimlers anyway. He is very good with elderly ladies. He wafts her back into the sunny outdoors with the most English of phrases, 'Perfect weather for the time of year . . . shall we take a little turn about the garden . . . ?'

And Celia, seeing them together, feels that she cannot summon up the energy to be two such different things to two such different people, and leaves them alone. She has escaped her admirers with relief feeling very glad indeed that she has Tom lined up for Vengeance. In her heart and despite the shoulders she feels a bit scared of venturing into the realities of a sexual hunt. By way of escape she spends the rest of the time eating fondant chicken with the vicar's wife, who does indeed smell like a Turkish brothel and who, Celia notices, follows Tom around with her eyes more than a lady connected with the church should.

Hard cheese, lady, she thinks grimly. That one is mine. And pulling her grandiose shoulders back she says, 'Fancy Tom needing a flat in Shepherd Market when he has all this . . .' She is immediately gratified when the powder-blue mini-skirt becomes suddenly splashed with fondant dressing as its owner starts, and colours, and does what so recently Celia did (but for a more honourable reason) which is to choke. Ha ha, thinks Celia, so Tom is having it off with the vicar's wife, is he? Well, well – we shall soon change that, shall we not? And she offers the vicar's wife a tissue by way of compensation.

True to her promise, when the last guest has gone and the staff have cleared up, Susie settles down for a giggle over the day's proceedings with Celia. They each have a tray on their knees in Celia's bedroom. Susie is wearing a richly embroidered Chinese lounging suit and looks as perfect as ever. She is delicately spooning consommé into her pale, de-lipsticked mouth and taking tiny bites of unbuttered rye. Celia is wearing her white towelling robe and is smudgy-eyed. She knows that the dress was one thing, the future another. She could never really be like Susannah if she tried. And she doesn't really want to be.

She holds a large sandwich between both hands and bites into it. The two of them, let loose on the kitchen, made their own suppers. Celia's sandwich contains bacon and egg. Were Tom to join them now he might change his mind again about Celia, for she looks totally herself again, cosy, womanly, even a little vulnerable in the way she has her legs tucked under her. But Tom is not there. He is not in Celia's bedroom, he is not in the house at all.

Something has come up – to do with those Daimlers, so he said – and he has to go to London for the night. He will be back again tomorrow.

'On a Sunday,' Celia said, when he announced this. 'You're as bad as Alex, Tom . . .'

She felt unpleasantly disturbed as he darted her a look for she could have sworn it contained less affection than loathing. It must have been a trick of the light. Quite definitely a trick of the light, she decides, when Tom says, 'When are you planning to leave tomorrow, Celia?' in a tone of the utmost interest.

Susie says, 'You'll stay for lunch?'

Celia agrees that she will.

To which Tom says, with obviously heartfelt relief, 'That's good. Make sure you do. And I'll be back before you go.'

He says it so keenly because Tom has a plan.

Celia merely reads his keenness as desire for her. Which is cheering.

She is also glad that he will be at home tomorrow night. Once she returns to Bedford Park she will open the package from the washing machine and make her telephone call to him straight away. Before the colly-wobbles set in. Of course Susannah will also be around when she telephones, which will make the lovey-dovey stuff a bit difficult, but nothing in life is easy. She gives Tom a brazen valedictory smile. At this stage she is still wearing the frock, though truth to tell it has become a bit tiresome by now – the shoulders make it impossible to relax and like Victorian stays they make its wearer remain very upright. Tom is glad to be going out. He has never seen Celia looking less sympathetic. Alas for their love affair, it was only after he had gone that she slipped into the more appealing deshabille of her towelling robe.

While Susie prattles Celia's mind wanders. First to that alien territory of how it will be with Tom – which creates something of a churning in her stomach that may or may not have something to do with the largesse of her sandwich following, as it does, quite an assortment of the comestibles on offer at lunch – and second, fleetingly, though she would prefer not, to what Alex is doing now. She is right not to dwell on this conjecture for – innocent of his wife's knowledgeable proximity – he is at that very moment, in his room at the Queen's Brough Hotel, engaging Miss Lyall from behind while they discuss Brandreth tactics, thus making the perfect combination of business and pleasure. Alex finds his head is quite clear during sex. So is Miss Lyall's. As they hump they are coming up with some very sharp future planning that will do much to bring about the success of the case. Well, well – certainly Celia would never have been able to engage with her husband in such combination activities. It is just as well that her mind has something else to occupy it. She gives not a fig for what her husband is doing – not a fig, she tells herself. And she smiles that slow smile, bestowing it upon the wife of her intended. Who, unknowing, smiles back.

The game of Vengeance is almost afoot.

Tom also has a plan.

Tom's plan also has to do with the package in the washing machine. Tom's plan is to remove it before Celia gets home.

It was purchased and given in the cloudy rapture of secret love mixed with a certain feeling that his affections were a lost cause. It contains a little joke, and a little tribute. Twin commodities, for twin feelings, which are now as ashes. He wishes to redress both. So – he has a plan.

He will spend the night in his surreptitious flat. With the vicar's wife, who is at this moment telling her husband that she is off to see an old parishioner of theirs in Highgate (a useful old parishioner, dead two years back, but the vicar, not being worldly and much bogged down in confirmation classes, has not taken the time to enquire). She has popped the bottle of scent in her handbag, snapped it shut, and prepares to depart for rapture. Tom's plan, when this night of love is over, is to drive home to Wiltshire, via Bedford Park, and remove the washing-machine package on the way. In time, it should be said, to replace Celia's house keys in her handbag. He is fiddling with these in his pocket as he speaks to Celia. She interprets this activity as an erotic circumnavigation of his private parts, which is just as it should be.

And so, after Tom set off, Celia and Susannah have brought their suppers up here and among the louder of their gigglings is a frank discussion about their views on the vicar's wife which has recalled Celia from her meditative wanderings. It is the kind of conversation that would seem most unpleasant to outsiders, which makes it all the more enjoyable for them. Eventually, as it must, the talk comes around to Celia and her troubles, but she does not wish to dwell on them.

'When is Alex due back?' asks Susannah.

'Tomorrow night.'

'What then?'

'Ah well,' says Celia darkly. 'We shall just have to wait and see . . .'

'But not divorce?'

'Oh no.' Celia is firm. 'Most certainly not divorce. Perhaps a little fun though . . .'

'You be careful with your little fun nowadays,' says Susannah.

As usual she has gone, with practical correctness, to the heart of the matter.

She gives Celia a goodnight kiss on the cheek – such intimacy they share now – and departs to deal with her hair and her skin and her nails and dictate a few letters into her machine while she does so. Celia settles down in the four poster and – because she feels that she is at some kind of beginning and because it is there and because, well, she just cannot resist the foolishness of it – she opens the book which that mad Stockbridge woman gave her just to see – just to see – what Fate has lined up in the random opening of a page. She finds two lines from Proust to Madame Straus, and she yawns as she reads them.

. . . you do not deign to countenance the sentiments which give me the rapture of being

> The most respectful servant
> Of your Sovereign Indifference
> Marcel Proust

She snaps the book shut.

Silly game.

That can have no relevance. Of all the emotions she has experienced from Tom, Sovereign Indifference is certainly not one.

Silly, *silly*, game.

The egg and bacon sandwich has its effect and Celia falls into a deep, untroubled sleep.

5

Mrs Green wants to get to work early this Monday morning. She hurries along the Bedford Park streets until she comes within sight of Celia's house. She then slows down and shuffles for the rest of the way. Once in a while she likes coming upon her employer a little earlier than usual. It makes Celia edgy. Also, Mrs Green is aware, Celia likes to have a quick tidy round before her cleaner arrives. It is worth setting out ten minutes earlier sometimes just to get there before this little tidy. It flusters Celia and a woman who owns as much stuff as she does deserves to be flustered *often*. It also gives Mrs Green a certain ascendancy – an attribute singularly lacking in the rest of her life. If she can catch her ladyship still in her night clothes and half made-up, with the breakfast dishes lying around and old underpants draped across the landing, it goes some way towards compensating for not even having *one* proper canteen to call her own.

She is looking forward to having a profoundly justified sniff when she gets there this morning. The circumstances are right for it because it's the half-term holiday. (Mrs Green is aware of this even if Celia was not. Mrs Green watches Celia's calendar as closely as if she were a pregnancy-fearing lover: envy and thrill mingle as she reads of her employer's full rich life.) When the children are home from school is a good time to catch her out. With no reason for getting up, nine times out of ten Mrs Green makes a direct hit. She can get through the door silently (she has a key), slide up the stairs and be in Celia's bedroom before she has time to open her eyes. Best of all was once when she found both Celia and Alex asleep. That was one of the high spots in her career. Spoiled a bit by them *thanking* her for waking them (Mr Crossland had an appointment or something), but a sweet memory all the same.

Her beige face takes on the grimace of a smile as she pushes open the gate and notices that the milk has not yet been taken in. This is a good sign. As she goes up the path she savours the moments of fluster that will accompany her untimely arrival. She'll give her a portable black-and-white for the kitchen as well as a colour in the front.

She is about to ring the bell when she notices there are keys in the lock and the front door is ajar. Her heart sinks. Celia must be up after all. Disappointment reduces the folds on her face to the more usual, and, truth to tell, more aesthetically pleasing tight-lipped mordancy. She enters. She shuffles through the hallway and into the back room. Apart from a couple of books and some dying flowers there is nothing on the breakfast table for her to sniff about. She prepares to call out but on hearing Celia in the kitchen she merely plonks her shopping bag down and shuffles across to the door. But it is not Celia she sees. There is no sign of Celia, either prepared or unprepared. Instead, mesmerised, she stands and looks upon the crouching, well-dressed figure of a man. He is very red in the face and grappling, unsuccessfully it appears, with the door of the washing machine. Something in the way he wears his dark-blue suit and white collar tells Mrs Green that he is not a washing-machine mechanic. This is borne out further by his looking up with eyes that are dark with guilt. And, still crouching, fixed in the pose, it seems, it is further borne out by his saying, 'Oh my God,' in a voice that denies he feels at home doing what he is doing.

Mrs Green, suddenly sprightly again, takes a step back, pulls her mackintosh tight around her chest and says, 'Where is Mrs Crossland?' The man leaps to his feet. He begins to say that she is away and that he is a friend of hers and he moves towards Mrs Green. That lady, quite understandably, feels terrified and she screams. She has not screamed for many years, not since her husband put on a gorilla mask to come home from a darts' match and she opened the door to him. It comes out, amazing in its strength, and the man at the washing machine is galvanised. He thrusts his hand into his inner jacket pocket and takes out his wallet (of what else, under stress, can a businessman think?) and he offers her money to be quiet.

'It is a little joke,' he says. 'I'm playing a little joke. Here – take five pounds . . .'

But Mrs Green is not the chambermaid at the Queen's Brough Hotel.

Whatever is happening she will make full occasion of it.

She runs out into the street, still screaming, followed closely by Tom.

Early morning in Bedford Park has never seen the like. Dormant households rise up. The Neighbourhood Watch is at hand (though not, as those who argue against such vigilante institutions will say, the police: why keep a dog and bark yourself?). Tom is brought down in a flying tackle by the man from next door who has just escaped the breakfast chaos of his house for the peace and quiet of a day in the City. He sits on Tom's chest, making any explanation impossible, and squashes Tom's nose with his briefcase very inventively. The judge, from over the road, looks out through his bedroom curtains on another day, and wonders, as he struggles into his trousers, if this is yet another mistake made by over-zealous Watchers. They are turning, he surmises, the whole of a decent neighbourhood into a burlesque: he will have no part in it. He decides it has to be a mistake and removes himself from the window while he does up his flies in case any alert Mrs Green should see him draw the wrong conclusion from that, too. Even the status of judge is no longer sacrosanct. In this day and age, it seems, you can only avoid serious prosecution if you are something to do with the Stock Exchange or the Royal Family and while he agrees wholeheartedly with the latter, with the former he is at odds: the whole tribe seems to him to be an unpleasant little group of opportunists. The law and his judgements are not what they were. Perhaps he ought to retire fully? He looks out of the window again and shakes his head at the mayhem.

Mrs Green, thrilled and defiant, stands quivering above the two struggling men on the pavement, and screams and screams and screams. If only the intruder had been felled on Celia's front path it would have really brought them Crosslands into disrepute. Ah well, you can't have everything. Mrs Green screams louder.

Susie is in the shower when the telephone rings. The Philippino housekeeper is in the garden cutting roses. Celia, ready for the day in the jeans and sweatshirt that were to have been her apparel as she strode the Wiltshire hills as a happily married woman, lets it ring a couple of times before putting *Country Life* down and answering it.

It is Tom.

'Darling Tom,' she says, trying out her new role as lover. Her voice is dark and rich as velvet and cream.

Tom's voice is higher than usual and irritated. 'Celia,' he says, 'will you please speak to this policeman and tell him that I am a friend of yours.'

'Of course,' she says huskily, before realising what he has said and squeaking, 'Pardon?'

'I am at the police station,' he says. 'And they want an explanation.'

'Why me?' she asks, not unreasonably.

'Because they think I am a burglar or some damn thing.'

'Why will my telling them we are friends help?'

'Don't be so fucking obtuse, woman!'

'Tom!' she says, hurt by his tone and still very much confused.

Realising that he must adopt a more conciliatory approach he says, 'Celia. Dear Celia . . .'

That *is* better. She can respond to that.

'The thing is . . .' Pause. How to couch it? 'The thing is that I went to your house to Look At The Washing Machine.'

(Here the two police officers exchange glances.)

'. . . And your fucking cleaner found me there.'

Oh God, thinks Celia.

Mrs Green, who has been enjoying the hot sweet tea and the kindly treatment of the officers, forgets her role as poor wronged

173

old woman (which, indeed, she is) and rises up off the bench, cup rattling, saying, 'Don't you swear about me, you bugger.'

Celia hears this.

Celia feels just about able to talk to a policeman but not, she shudders, not to her cleaner ... and certainly not in these circumstances ...

'Celia?' Tom pleads.

And then a wonderful thing happens.

Celia finds that all the pain and humiliation she has experienced during the past thirty-six hours rises to the surface and she is soothed by a sudden decision to take control of her life, to take control, at any rate, of her cleaner. She has seen her husband enfolding another woman in his arms, she has been lied to by the person with whom she thought she shared the most intimate truths. After all that it seems absurd to remain amenable to anyone. Why should she be conciliatory? Why should she try to make everybody else's life as smooth as possible? WHAT ABOUT ME? She thinks sternly. WHAT ABOUT ME? – What is the ire of that old sourpuss after a revelation like that? It is as *nothing* ...

'Let me speak to Mrs Green, please Tom,' she commands, her voice quite unrecognisable in its proximity to well-honed steel.

Even Tom, despite the vulnerability of his position, is impressed. Wordlessly he holds out the receiver to the bridling individual.

Mrs Green, preening herself as she comes to the telephone, takes it and says down the mouthpiece, quavering, complaining, 'Oh dear, oh dear, Mrs Crossland. I have had a shock.'

And Mrs Crossland says, 'Yes, yes,' very snappishly. 'Well, perhaps when you have recovered from all this silly muddle' (she says silly muddle so that it implies Mrs Green is entirely to blame) 'you will go back to the house and begin what you came for.'

Now she understands the Raj from within. To speak thus is indeed sweet satisfaction.

She hears her cleaner take a sharp breath. Mrs Green begins, 'Oh, I don't know about that – it has shook me dreadful ...' And she makes a noise as if she has been winded.

Momentarily she falters, but, conjuring up the image of Alex and the be-pastelled Her, Celia is soon back on course. 'My dear woman,' she says. 'Pull yourself together. There is really no need to make mountains out of molehills.' (Mrs Green's favourite pastime actually.) 'Hallo. Hallo. Are you there?'

Mrs Green, somewhat confounded, nods.

Celia takes the silence as acquiescence and continues. 'This is what I want you to do: give the children's rooms a thorough going over, while they are away – do the windows and the skirtings – all that kind of thing. You should have time to do them both if you go at it.'

It is a breathless feeling telling Mrs Green to Go At It – especially in her state. Nevertheless Celia feels she can. After what she has been through she can say anything to Mrs Green. Why not? The delicacies of their relationship are as relevant as a pimple on a gnat's behind to her now.

'You've got your key?'

Mrs Green may be down but she is not out.

'I have *not*.' She lies.

'Then how did you get into the house this morning?'

'That *man* had your keys.'

'Aah,' says Celia. 'Of course.'

Trying to unravel the reasons for Tom being in her house with her keys is beyond her. But it will undoubtedly be with romance in view.

'That's wonderful,' says Celia.

Wonderful is hardly the word Mrs Green feels appropriate.

'You can use those and hide them under the plant pot by the front door when you go. I'll be back tonight.' And then she adds roguishly, 'Remember – plenty of elbow grease, Mrs Green – plenty of elbow grease.'

Mrs Green has never felt more insulted in her life. Neither does she like the lightness of joy in Celia's voice. And she has been made to look a proper charlie. She will have a really good rummage in Celia's bedroom when she gets back there. Fortunately she is so taken up with this idea when she returns to

175

the house that she forgets all about the curiosity of the washing machine and the package continues to lie there, like some ancient wreck in the purple deeps, waiting for Celia to come and rescue it. Tom has no intention of going anywhere near it again. Why people should lock their washing-machine doors is quite beyond him. He does not know (and, indeed, why should he since soiled linen is not his department?) that such appliances have to be child-proof. Poor Tom will never need to know this. He admits defeat over regaining the birthday present. What will be will be. A useful homily under the circumstances.

Leaving the police station with dignity is not easy: Mrs Green shrinks away from him at the mere suggestion that he give her a lift back to the house and the two policemen look at him as if his thoughts were set in glass and they could read every one of them. He is thinking how little and dove-like and vulnerable the vicar's wife was last night (mother of three and dimpled in the right places) and how harsh and unyielding Celia has suddenly shown herself by comparison. Why – hasn't she even sent her own children away for the week in their holiday time – *precisely* when they ought to be with their mother? *Just* the sort of thing Susannah would have done if she'd been able to have any. He thinks along these lines as he drives back to Wiltshire. And under all this – as if it were not enough to shatter all his illusions – comes the unpleasant recollection that Celia thinks of him as boring. Than which there can be nothing better guaranteed to finish off his years of devotion.

Mrs Green, rummaging, finds nothing in the bedroom. By way of compensation she makes herself a fine lunch from the outrageously lavish leftovers in her employer's fridge and eats it off the best china. Alas, cold meat and cold potatoes taste just the same as they do eaten off her boxed set from Woollies. And that fancy salad cream stinks. There is a lesson for Mrs Green somewhere in this but she ignores it. She has a sherry from one of the many decanters, poured into one of the many crystal glasses, and she holds out her little finger as she sips it. But it is thin and pale and sour to her palate; try as she might it does her bruised spirit no good at all. Disappointedly she sets to work as Celia has directed. Elbow grease indeed! She'll give her elbow grease. All the same she works diligently. Her employer's voice had an edge to it. She'd best keep on the right side just in case . . .

Alex falls asleep as he chairs the final afternoon's meeting of the Brandreth committee.

Miss Lyall, seated next to him, nudges his knee with her own. He, still remembering the post-luncheon coitus and the amazing discovery that such things as crutchless tights are not merely verbal jokes, smiles without opening his eyes and puts his hand under her skirt, giving the smooth be-nyloned flesh there an opulent squeeze. He grunts as he does so, like a pig in clover. Miss Lyall pinches the flesh of his hand very hard and sits bolt upright, looking like a golden-haired dragon. She fires an unanswerable question down the table towards the junior clerk, whose spots deepen to purplish-black in his effort to come up with something to say. Absorbed by this phenomenon the rest of the committee does not notice Alex's little cry of pain as his tired eyes blink open and resume, as best they can, cognisance of the proceedings. Miss Lyall writes on his pad 'pull yourself together'. He looks at her; she is as fresh as a daisy. Her stamina is amazing. She truly is just like a man. On the other hand, he thinks, and here he feels the beginnings of something stirring in his groin, on the other hand she is nothing like a man whatso-ever. He would like to suppress the stirring. His sexual organs might be game but the rest of him desires nothing but peaceful intellectual calm. He would like to get back on top (swell, swell, throb, throb – his erogenous zone assumes he is thinking about Miss Lyall) of this committee, but fears that while he is riding two horses (he crosses his legs hurriedly) he is not quite in control of either. He muses on all this, while all around him the Brandreth aspirants debate and discuss, under the subtle guidance of Miss Lyall who realises that Alex is not up to it. She is clever because the assembled still think that *he* is the one in the chair: so does Alex. She will go far, this woman. In her female shape she is always underrated, in her lusty appetite she is more than a match for her male colleagues who burn themselves out to prove they have no less libido than she, and with her built-in female tact she knows exactly how far she can go before dropping her eyelids, pouting her lips and shutting up. And she has the *soupçon* of humility required to accede (if only to herself) that she can learn a lot from Alex. He is brilliant in the middle range. She wants to get as much out of him as she can, both in practical knowledge and physical satisfaction. She expects he will get a second wind after this weekend. Quite often, at first, her chosen partners find it hard to keep up (she allows herself a quick smile at the pun) but they usually rally. Alex will too. She is sure. And if he does not? Well – she has one or two little tricks at her disposal which have stood her in good stead in the past.

Susannah comes downstairs and finds Celia curled up, Vesta the cat on her lap, *Country Life* in her hands and a look of almost mystical pleasure on her face.

'You seem to have made a good recovery from the pangs of being a wronged wife,' she says, pleased. 'Who was that on the telephone?'

'Tom,' says Celia.

'Any message?' asks Susie.

'He's going to miss lunch.'

Susie crosses to the settee and strokes the cat, which makes no response.

'Why?' she asks.

'Do you know,' says Celia, 'I forgot to ask.'

'Oh well,' says Susie. 'It really doesn't matter if he's here or not. Does it?'

Celia shakes her head. She feels no guilt whatsoever now. Each to their own, she thinks, with good-natured pity.

Susannah, stroking the unresponsive Vesta's silky ears, says, 'Have you decided what to do? Are you going to confront Alex or what?'

Celia says that she is not.

'Take my advice,' says her friend, 'and extinguish the word divorce from your vocabulary. Find some other method of coming to terms with it.'

'I intend to.' Celia strokes Vesta's tail very gently. At these two assaults on her sensuous nerve-endings the cat very nearly submits and begins to purr. But she holds off. No good ever came of rolling over and revealing your soft underbelly to anyone. So thinks the cat.

'Any ideas?' asks Susannah.

'Lots,' says Celia.

'Tell,' says Susie.

'Shan't,' says Celia.

Susie smiles. 'Well – don't do anything I wouldn't do . . .'

And Celia, returning the smile, thinks, You must be joking.

She sets off for London mid-afternoon.

She needs to get home before Alex arrives so that she can open the gift in peace and make her telephone call to Tom to fix their first assignation. She and Tom pass each other on opposing sides of the motorway – though they, of course, do not realise that. Tom stops off at Stockbridge and has a cup of tea with the dog woman just to add authenticity to his tale when he reaches home. During this visit they, not unnaturally, mention Celia. Like a man who will roll on nails, Tom exhumes the conversation of weekender bores. Mrs Stone gives unshakeable evidence and adds the souring festoon of the one-penny piece.

'So *mean*,' she says.

'So *mean*,' Tom agrees.

And, as Good King Hal before him, he submits to the hearsay of others to damn his Queen finally. The vicar's wife, like pale Jane Seymour, waits willingly in the wings. So much for Celia.

And so much for the power of the book game of chance. Judge for yourselves its felicity.

Driving home Celia makes a little detour through Salisbury, just to see how she feels. She slows down as she passes the cathedral, quite beautiful in the afternoon sun, and smiles and waves on the tourist pedestrians who dart across her path. They will take back with them to Minneapolis, Tokyo, Rome, the impression that English women are the most courteous and friendly drivers in the world. At the Queen's Brough her foot presses the accelerator without her thinking about it, and she whizzes on, away from its smoothly respectable façade, towards the edge of the town. She passes that Monday fruit and cheese market and subdues the old Celia's response of stopping here to buy some local produce for future culinary delight. Be hanged to that, she thinks, look where goodwifery has got me.

And onwards she drives.

Behind her, draped across her suitcase, is the borrowed black-and-white dress. Now hers. Susie's gift. 'Because,' said her friend, 'I shan't wear it again. And you like it so much.'

Note that she does not say, 'Because it suits you so well.' Susie hopes she will never have cause to say that. Celia is Celia, just as Susie is Susie. She may try to change aspects of her approach to life, but never her character. That is, after all, what makes her her friend.

Celia is thrilled to own the frock. She will wear it for her first illicit meeting with Tom. Why not? He clearly likes women with style. She has forgotten the vicar's wife's powder-blue mini-skirt.

Bypassing Stockbridge she remembers the book. How silly. Nevertheless, it nestles in her luggage. She is still puzzled by that 'sovereign indifference' of Proust. Hardly fitting ... So very wrong. Ah, well. She will keep the book as a talisman anyway.

She drives happily towards Basingstoke and the road for home. She puts on the radio, tuned to Radio One, but every single song seems to be concerned with love – both false and true. She swivels the knob away from such claptrap and finds Radio Three. Here there are unaccompanied voices singing out a spine-chilling vibrance of notes. Could be modern, could be ancient, but they are suitably odd for the journey. She turns it up. It lasts almost to the end of her road when the announcer says: 'That ends our programme of music by Gesualdo (Prince of Venosa, 1560–1613) whose chromatic modulations and nervous restlessness are thought by some to reflect his inner agonies . . .'

'Oh really?' says Celia to the radio. 'Another Renaissance man of culture.' She is thinking of Henry VIII again.

'. . . The madrigals, particularly daring in their harmonics, may well owe their arresting qualities to Gesualdo's private sufferings.'

'Like what?' she asks.

Obligingly the announcer continues: 'He murdered both his wife and her lover, his first cousin, and his own child, whom he decided was fruit of their union rather than his own flesh . . . The works you have been listening to were all composed after this date.'

Terrific, thinks Celia. First Henry and now let's hear it for Gesualdo.

'There will be more works by this undervalued genius of the late Renaissance in our autumn schedule.'

She switches off.

Perhaps they will intersperse it with readings from *Mein Kampf*, she thinks. Time clearly exonerates and the thought rankles.

Indoors she drapes the frock over the banisters, puts down her case, looks at her watch which says five o'clock, and rushes with joyful expectancy into the kitchen and towards the washing machine. She is a little disappointed to see no additional offering which might explain poor Tom's surreptitious visit – but still, what is in the washing machine will more than do. She takes the package up and kisses it. At last!

Up in the bedroom, seated in front of her dressing-table mirror (where else?) Celia regards the package. Apart from the wrapping paper being slightly damp it is unscathed. Her heart is thumping – the combined curiosity of what it contains and the projected telephone call after finding out makes her palpitate visibly – she can see the little pulse in her neck. Suddenly another emotion shoves its way in. Guilt. St Paul knew a thing or two about women. Of course Celia feels guilty. Men do not seek out other women unless they are driven to it. She can even hear her sister – whose aura seems to be somewhere in the room, over by the curtains Celia surmises – telling her so. Trust you, says Isabel, to be able to shift the blame ... And two wrongs don't make a right ... Look at it from Alex's point of view ... There had to be something wrong for him to start it.

Oh Hazel, thinks Celia, why aren't you here to plead for me? But, of course, Hazel is in the enemy's camp. Celia has been betrayed on both fronts.

Look here, she mutters to her sister, and she gets up, strides to her knicker and Tampax drawer and pulls out Dirty Harry. She wobbles the obscene piece of rubber at her phantom sister and she says, 'Which would you prefer? This?' She wobbles it again. 'Or this?' She holds up the romantic little package.

She feels she has won. Disapproving Isabel subsides. Celia's conscience is clear. She puts Dirty Harry down on the dressing table and rips the paper from the package. Rip, rip, rip, she goes, for where has her erstwhile deftness got her?

And as she rip, rip, rips another thought occurs to her. One that is infinitely worse than guilt. What if all this keeping quiet is of no significance? What if Pastel Frock and Alex are in love? What if *they* should come to her – openly – to say – to say – well, whatever lovers *do* say to the deceived party... She shivers. Supposing *Alex* wants a divorce? She shivers again. She remembers how they looked locked into their embrace. Perhaps Good King Harry and his French executioner had a

182

point – perhaps even Gesualdo had a point. Perhaps she should even now be pointing a gun at Pastel Frock's gleaming head instead of sitting here so smugly thinking that a little revenge on the side will do. And then fortunately she hears her sister's voice again and this time it says what she wants to hear. It says, 'Oh, come off it, Celia. Don't make such a drama out of everything . . .'

And Celia's fears subside.

Alex would never leave her for another woman.

If not for her sake then for the children – and if not for them then for his profession: he values that far too much.

God bless the Brandreth case, she hears herself say.

And Amen to that.

And God bless Tom, too. Let us not forget him.

If ever she needed the fillip of *un cadeau d'amour* it is now. Battered, defiled, aching from her wounds, she looks to this gift to restore her. Dirty Harry, his potency gone, sags on the dressing table. She waves the now denuded box at him, as garlic to a demon, and feels a happy surge of triumph. If she cannot be a rose for her husband, she will be one for Tom. Full-blown, velvet-petalled, thornless and infinitely desirable. For his long-serving loyalty he shall have her. (The fleeting thought that it is, actually, because of Alex's disloyalty that he shall have her is quickly dismissed.) For his loyalty and for the flattery of his desire he has earned the reward.

She looks down at the box.

Her hands sweat as they close around it.

Celia is *very excited*.

A child on Christmas morning could not be more excited than she. She kisses it and wonders what it holds. The box is black and shiny, laminated cardboard, and bears the embossed gilt word PERSONELLE. There is black tissue paper within which she unfolds carefully, her breathing coming faster and faster, driven on with longing, with the pleasure of what is to come. and from the black tissue folds she takes out . . . She takes out . . . ?

What?

What *is* this?

Is it a sculpture?

Is it some covetable piece of ancient Egyptian art?

It is coloured like ivory, a long, smooth-sided cylinder, rounding into a smooth peak at the top, perhaps nine inches long.

She stares at it, puzzled for a moment, before understanding dawns.

What she is holding is a fine companion for Dirty Harry.

She can almost see him quiver as he recognises its lewd proclivities.

What she is holding is a sex aid.

Willing herself to disbelieve this she cannot.

She recognises its alien form (for no man of her acquaintance was ever thus endowed).

What she recognises, God help her, is a vibrator. A VIBRATOR?

No, no. Her eyes, radiant and yearning for revenge, are playing tricks. She blinks. She looks again.

Yes, yes. She cannot look away. The truth is in her hands. That is what she sees. A vibrator. And it has a little card tied round its neck (no – not its neck – around its *tip*) and the card says:

Perhaps this will warm you up since I could not.

She blinks twice. She blinks thrice. It does not change. This is not her fertile imagination. This thing, this smooth, coned thing, this travesty is really in her hands. Bad enough it would have been had she opened it excitedly on Saturday morning, still as the honourable wife of Alex. Then it would have been no more than a passing disappointment, to be shrugged off, to be acknowledged as a good joke and understandable given the frustration she has doled out to Tom over the years. No more – then – than a fleeting blow to her pride that could, so easily, be laughed away. Now it serves to cause her the deepest disappointment she can ever remember, followed by the deepest unhappiness, as witnessed by the tears which begin flowing, down and down, plop, plop, all over her lap.

No wonder Tom tried to get it back. It was hardly the best way to plight his troth given the altered circumstances. She has learned enough during these past couple of days to be sensibly cynical and to understand that. First Alex and his rubber goods and now Tom and his plastic penis. What is it about her vagina, she wonders, that attracts these ideas? Whatever happened to flesh on flesh?

Whatever it is – Hell hath no fury, etc., etc. – and certainly not a woman scorned *twice*.

Tom and Celia never do confront each other about this incident. Celia assumes that Tom is mortified by her lack of interest in him which has turned him so quiet. And Tom, much more straightforwardly, thinks that two-faced Celia has just pocketed the loot.

The loot?

Ah yes.

It was the loot which turned Tom into Mrs Green's robber.

For secreted amongst the black tissue paper of that wicked projectile was something else. Something costly, something alluring, something that Tom was damned if Celia deserved after all. What else could he have put there to win her heart? What else – of course – but a pair of pretty blue earrings.

Tom would have made Celia a good lover. He has the memory of an elephant where she is concerned. He once heard her tale of the iron and the forget-me-nots (though not, of course, all the personal details) and he saved it to make use of. Such a pity that the loving gesture (loving? Perhaps speculative might be more appropriate) should prove so useless now that his desire is cold as ash. Nevertheless two little sapphires remain to be found. Quite expensive little sapphires. Sapphires he could have recycled and given to the vicar's wife. But he never got the chance. Neither, come to that, did Celia.

Sitting by her dressing table she begins to get worried at the amount of salt water that sploshes from her eyes. This must cease, she tells herself sternly, enough is enough. And by way of punctuating the flow she hurls the vibrator to the furthest depths of the room, the bay of the window, and the strength of the gesture acts like a full stop. The tears cease. She blows her nose, once, twice, thrice – and the crying is over. She is cleansed of the disappointment, cleansed of the anger, and quite, quite cleansed of Tom. When they meet again she will be icily polite, no more than that, for there is now no more to be.

And as for the vibrator itself, it is forgotten. It rolls quietly to rest in a hidden nook where the floor meets the curtains and remains there undisturbed.

Later Celia takes the vibrator box out to the dustbin and shoves it under all the fishbones and the lemon peel and the general detritus of her birthday dinner party. So far as she is concerned she has dispensed with the whole episode. She will not think of it again. She must redraw the battle plans and is more determined than ever to find her Sweet Vengeance elsewhere. That is all she thinks about as she fixes the dustbin lid firmly in place and goes back into her respectable no-frills house that looks just like all the rest.

It would be nice to think that a silver lining could be found here as well. It would be nice to think that a Bedford Park dustman found the expensive contents of the box and took them home to his wife, but this is not so. Together the two little sapphires were cast underground, along with the rubbish of the age, and may well be found a hundred-thousand years hence by some avid post-bomb excavator who, scratching his two ear-less heads, will wonder what the relevance of such items could possibly ever have been.

PART THREE

1

It would probably never have happened if Alex had not rung Celia at seven o'clock that night to say that he was not, after all, coming home. His reason was perfectly genuine. Old Judge Watson, doyen of the Circuit, had Things To Say on the subject of the Brandreth case. Strictly off the record but strictly relevant to Alex and his team's approach. The judge lived near Winchester. He suggested that Alex should come to his home for a private dinner to hear about these Things. Alex could stay for the night and continue on to London in the morning. That would not put Alex out too much. Now would it?

Alex – his eyes pricking from the tiredness of unaccustomed debauchery, his balls aching from constant activity, and the muscles in his arms strained and sore from holding some of the more bizarre positions the knowledgeable Miss Lyall encouraged – had but one desire: to get home to his own domain, to his own bed, to his own undemanding, agreeable wife. But judges are not bred to be gainsaid. Warmly, down the telephone, Alex thanked this influential septuagenarian and said that he would, of course, be delighted to come to Winchester. He then, scarcely able to restrain his tired crossness, telephoned his wife.

In the furious disappointment of the aftermath Celia has been contemplating other ways of getting even with Alex. She has conjured visions of herself down at Greenham, living in a tent of plastic bags and deriding the men who guard that vile place so heartily that they have no recourse but to arrest her. This is a seductive vision until she realises that it would shame her to use the radical commitment of those base-women for her own domestic ends. One should come to disarmament with a pure heart or not at all. Reluctantly (for Alex would be outraged, which would be nice) she rejects the idea and toys with another.

The sublime to the ridiculous.

What about appearing on television in one of those game shows? One of those *particular* game shows where the participants have to leap about and scream with joy and kiss the presenter a dozen times. Alex would go mad. She could alert the whole of Bedford Park to watch (she has a quick vision of Alex down on his knees pleading with her Not To Go To The Television Centre but she casts him aside like a worn glove). Wonderful thought! Oh the sheer joy . . .

But she abandons this too. She is not sure that it wouldn't upset her even more than her errant husband – and it would probably take too long to organise. Besides, she might have a latent liking for such things. There is something of the show-woman buried within her after all.

She toys with a few other ideas which – since she enacts them in her mind – do much to reduce her hunger for Vengeance and life begins to calm down a little, to regain a degree of sanity, so that, by the time Alex rings her, it is in the balance, really, whether she will do anything at all. But the conversation reverses all *that*.

'Celia?'

'Alex?'

Alex allows some of his irritation to surface. He has been a lover all weekend which has been a great strain. This is, after all, his wife. He feels snappish and it shows.

'Celia – where have you been? I've been trying to ring you all afternoon. As a matter of fact I've tried to ring you damn near most of the weekend . . . I telephoned *especially* on Saturday evening because of your birthday – And You Were Out.' It is the bluster of a man who is being only marginally honest.

Alex blinks at the truth.

Alex quite often must blink at the truth.

Alex's profession calls for quite a lot of truth-blinking. (We should, after all, have no jurisprudence were our lawyers unable to do this and before we pour scorn we should, perhaps, pause to consider what other system we might usefully replace it with. Ducking stools and hot brands perhaps . . .?)

His blink is rather a long one, for his 'most of the weekend' was one quick attempt on Saturday night while Miss Lyall was in his shower. Embroiled as he was it came as a considerable relief to receive no reply though he now makes a passing-fair imitation of umbrage that Celia should have been out. But since then, during this afternoon, now that the weekend's orgy of love and business is over, he has made up for it. He has attempted several times to telephone her to let her know about the inter-fering old coot in Winchester; and there are few things more designed to increase irritability than an unanswered telephone, especially if various parts of your body are aching from over-strenuous coupling: Alex, on getting through to his wife at last, is extremely sharp.

Celia, despite being fully aware of her husband's perfidy, is nevertheless astonished to hear how easily the lies trip off his tongue. She had assumed that now her consciousness was raised she would isolate the duplicity, and she cannot isolate it at all. This is very wounding, for a wife may at least comfort herself that she *knows* her husband . . . Celia feels, as she hears Alex's lies drip so smoothly (or rather, drip so irascibly), that she does not . . . She could swear he is telling her the truth. Which, of course, he *is*; the judge's invitation exists; Alex's resentment that the invitation exists, exists; in this particular part of the conversation his conscience is absolutely clear. To Celia it just goes down the plughole of deceit like all the rest. It revitalises her thoughts of revenge.

So – Alex is not coming home? Celia grips the telephone tightly and urges control upon her vocal system which is in danger of running amok.

With Celia feeling emotionally fragile, and with Alex feeling corporeally fragile, the conversation, redolent of connubial misunderstanding, continues thus:

'Not coming home?' says Celia very faintly.

'That's right,' says Alex irritably. 'Not home tonight. Home tomorrow. Well – where were you when I rang?'

'Not coming home?' she says. She is only half concentrating now for if she is not careful she is going to say something very loud, very rude, and indicating that she knows more than he knows she knows.

Alex becomes more waspish. If Celia can keep repeating herself so can he.

'You were out,' he repeats, with the venom of one whose balls ache. 'Where?'

'Judge Pastel?' she says – still faint but quite distinguishable to Alex.

'Judge Watson,' he says, crisp in his real truth.

'Attractive, is he?' says Celia, unable to stop herself.

'What?' says Alex.

'A bit of a goer?'

'Celia? What on earth are you talking about? Judge Watson is seventy.'

'What colour is his hair, Alex?'

Alex looks at the phone in disbelief.

'Blonde, perhaps?' goes on Celia.

'Judge Watson is completely bald,' he finds himself saying, and he wonders why.

'Really?' says Celia gaily. 'With a welcoming pudenda?'

He has misheard, he must have, she must really have said agenda. Perhaps his ears have been affected along with everything else. 'I *beg* your pardon?' he says coldly.

'Don't beg,' she says sharply. 'Sell matches.'

There is a pause.

'Celia,' says Alex. 'Have I upset you?'

It occurs to him that since at this precise moment there is nothing in the world he would like more than to be in his own home with his own children and his own wife he is not displaying it very well. But he cannot help it. Miss Lyall does not lack clarity. He is quite sure that if he telephoned her right now she would be very direct. Unlike Celia she is a very direct woman. Which makes the whole thing very flattering and very exciting. She knows what she wants and – as his brain and body tells him – she certainly gets it. Celia is reticent by comparison. In keeping with being a wife this undoubtedly is – but at the same time, at the same time, it is much more fun not to have to be constantly in control. Nevertheless he needs rest, he needs the unspoken harmonies of his quiet marriage bed. He needs his little amenable Celia right now and he decides to cajole her with the truth of this.

He says, 'I would so much rather be coming home to you...'

It sounds so genuine. Celia has to bite her knuckles very hard to avoid saying what she wants to say which is, 'You double-dyed shit ... I know you are lying...'

Which conversational turn would most certainly give the game away.

She equivocates. She says, 'Oh, please don't bother on my account. I hope your judge comes across.'

'Why are you giving me such a hard time, darling?' he asks. The darling sounds as if someone had just rubbed his teeth with sandpaper.

'Because you've been giving someone else a Hard Time!' There – it is out – she has blown it. He must pick up on that blatancy.

'But that's my job...'

'On the job,' she corrects.

The pips go.

'Celia,' he says wearily. 'I'll ring you later from Judge Watson's.'

'I shall be out,' she says.

'Where?'

'Well, it won't be at the Women's Institute!'

'Celia?!'

But the line has gone dead and the conversation, ending where it started, leaves both of them feeling frayed.

Women! thinks Alex.

Men! thinks Celia.

Needles and Pins
Needles and Pins
When two folk marry
Their trouble begins.

In Spain they bait the bulls with red-hot pricks to make them run. These are as nothing to the goads experienced by Celia. Alex did not even ask about the children (that he had no time to is not the point): she plonks down the phone. Bald old Judge Watson indeed! She'll show him. What is sauce for the gander ... oh yes ... sauce for the gander ...

Which sounds very fine said out loud in her hallway but it does not, yet, produce an answer regarding the sauce for the goose.

Alex begins the drive towards his destination in an even more ruffled state. Bad enough that interfering old Judge Watson should have caused all this difficulty with Celia (rather unfair on OJP but there we are) but Alex has got a secondary reason for his distinctly ruffled state. One which he has not liked to remember, one which he was doing rather well at subjugating. But now – with the drive ahead of him and a bad phone call with Celia behind him – remembrance of it surfaces to add to his rufflement. Very clearly he recalls how Miss Lyall, though understanding itself about the lacklustre level of his last sexual performance with her, issued a smiling parting shot as she sailed away from the hotel in her Golf GTI. To the effect that he was not to worry in the *least* (smile, smile) if he could not keep up (smile, smile, smile) for *she* would do all the worrying on his behalf. Ways and Means, she had winked at him, Ways and Means. Which both mocked his masculine capabilities and made his weary flesh ache even further. He will show her next time. He certainly will. Celia has been no help at all in smoothing thoughts such as this away. She might have missed him a little bit, she might have *said* she missed him a little bit. After all, he missed *her*.

But gradually, as the miles unfold and the thought of OJP's rather good cellar encroaches on his bitterness, he begins to whistle. A good night's rest will restore him. And then home to his calm and pleasing household, to his nice children, his nice wife and his own, very comfortable and nice other life ... He taps the wheel as he drives along. He cannot help feeling rather pleased with himself – and who can blame him for is he not husband to his wife, father to his children, lover (a little rusty but it will all be oiled up eventually) to his *amoureuse*, and peaking in his career? Judge Watson does not summon inferiors to his table. Perhaps a quiet night at OJP's is just what he needs. Yes, yes, it probably is. Maybe this unwelcome intervention is a useful hiatus.

So does Alex, somewhat mistakenly, conjure up a silver lining for himself. And his whistling increases as the Volvo bowls smoothly along.

While Alex is tootling through the countryside and whistling Celia storms back into the bedroom. Dirty Harry is lying loosely in amongst her dressing-table toiletries. Disgusting object. She picks it up and thrusts it into her knicker and Tampax drawer with such furious strength that as she flings the drawer shut it hangs out limply at her, the bobbles and knobbles of its condom end-piece (so carefully created by its manufacturers to arouse delight in even the most unoptimistic of clitorises) caught tight in the closure. She sees the offensive article's twiddly bits flapping at her as a kind of tongue-poked-out and with a roar of shame and disgust she pushes the drawer even harder upon it. Once, twice, thrice, she slams the drawer upon it and Dirty Harry gives in. Punctured, his proud end-bit exhales a little air and hangs limp. With glee she sees her assailant reduced to a nonentity. She opens the drawer for the last time and pushes him away, back into the recesses. The game's afoot. Celia is on the loose. Nothing will stop her now.

While the wherewithal for being unfaithful is readily available to those who pursue their careers outside the home, it is less readily available to those who pursue it from within. Those whose spouses remain housewards are, in general, able to rest assured. It is not easy to pluck a lover from the daily domestic round. Desirable milkmen are the stuff of joke merchants. Mostly they are cheery souls whose object is to deliver their goods, comment on the weather and go on their way. If Celia is to find a partner for her Game of Vengeance, it is not among her tradesmen. Not Adrian, not the soft-voiced Mr Ramish and certainly not the burly and blood-spattered butcher of low-cholesterol fame. No – none of these. Celia must search for her playmate elsewhere.

But whom? And where? Bugger Tom for being so crass and heartless just when she could make use of him. Alex and Dirty Harry, Tom and a Personelle vibrator. Red-hot goads that go prick, prick, prick into her vitals. She savages her nails as she sits at her dressing table. She racks her brains for a man who will do.

Not the osteopath.

Not the photographer.

Not – though she pauses – the dear old judge opposite. She pauses because it would be sweetly poetic to match *her* judge for Alex's but – well – although he *is* a twinkly sort of a person he is *old*. Celia feels that she deserves something better. Something younger. Something stirs in her nether regions. After all, if one is out for sexual revenge, one may as well enjoy it ... something younger ... now *there's* a thought ...

Do not be out of patience with Celia. Do not reject her for the immorality of what she proposes. To say that her solution merely matches baseness for baseness is too righteous. Lob the first stone if you will but first seek out the inviolable purity of your own hearts ... in homeopathy you cure the ailment with a little dose of the same; for a hangover you try the hair of the dog; all vaccines are injections of the same ... so with Celia – a little adultery to ease a greater one. Better this, surely, than that she be left to indulge in masochistic martyrdom so that on her death bed, having been eaten by the worm for forty years, she tries to tell the truth to ears stopped up with the boredom of being still young and hale? No one will be listening in forty years from now so she might just as well get on with it.

And she does.

Youth, she decides. I will have a bit of youth. That will double the healing process, for Alex is not young. Pastel Frock is not young. Dash it, she thinks, a young man will more than compensate. You have to hand it to Celia. She is brave. And perhaps a little unhinged. Nonetheless she is adamant. For youth she will go. Her memory calls up a place from her past. A place where the racy young men of her art-gallery days would hie themselves after a hard day over the Hockneys – for drinks, for dalliance, for débutantes. Not a place that she ever frequented, not a place that she can be sure still exists, but she looks it up in the telephone directory anyway – the Side Saddle Bar of the Churchman Hotel in Mayfair, fount of so many lost hymens in those far-off days. Does it still exist? Her index finger shows that the hotel does. She rings the number. Her heart pounds as it is answered by a grand and awful male voice which says, 'The Churchman Hotel. May I help you?'

If ever a voice sounded as if the last thing it wanted to do was to help, this voice is it.

Celia swallows. And she hears some stranger's firm tones issue from her mouth.

'Yes,' says this self-assured stranger. 'Is the Side Saddle Bar open tonight?'

'Certainly, Madam,' says grand and awful. 'It is open every night between . . .'

Celia puts down the phone.

Her mouth is dry.

Her palms are sweaty.

Let not any of you think she is coasting. Like Salome before her, this thing looks easy but it isn't.

Now the astonishing thing is that she begins to feel rather excited at the prospect. Adrenaline pumps where once there was merely fear. As Celia begins to address herself to the task in hand – to wit – her preparation for the game ahead, she rallies, and she sees silver linings in everything. Caspar shits, John crashes, Hazel goes to Wales with the children and she, Celia, is left completely and gloriously free to pursue her course. The pieces are moving around upon the board very nicely and so far she has the upper hand. As she tones down her flushed face with a pale foundation she smiles to congratulate herself. And then quickly stops smiling. It reveals far too many little crinkles and lines around her eyes. If she is going for youth she must stay humourless tonight. Dab dab with the gentle artifice of the blusher, and stroke, stroke with the blackening mascara. It is all coming along nicely. Each little addition builds up a face for the world. At the end of the process she glows with seduction. It is the best she can do and it will have to suffice. She sits back, satisfied. She looks as good as she ever will, despite the recent tears – in any case these have only served to give her eyes a softer look, a sort of hue of the dew. If it were not for the little lines she would smile at herself. As it is she merely risks a wink, which is good enough. Surely whoever this youth is he will be unable to resist? Carefully she closes her eyes and gives herself up to some rapturous imaginings. Which are suddenly and dreadfully cut short. There is a blight on what she proposes.

Celia has forgotten AIDS.

All made-up, and quite naked, she plonks back down on the dressing-table stool and stares at herself.

'AIDS,' she says. 'AIDS,' she repeats. *That's* what Susie was trying to tell her. The thing to be careful about. The passport to modern morality. How can she go looking for Vengeance with that in the dice?

Well, if our heroine is down, she is not out. With cool pragmatism – born out of fiery determination – she thinks it through. Celia has seen the advertisements. She has also seen a programme about how to deal with it in which a female journalist and a male television presenter enacted the strange mummery of *her* slipping the condom ('make it part of the ritual of loving each other') over *his* raised fingers while they both chatted amiably to a live audience half their ages and twice their understanding. It had been amusing at the time. Now it is critically relevant. Well, well, thinks Celia, those who mock often stay to pray . . .

Using, broadly, the same liberated logic of the sixties she knows she cannot necessarily expect her Knight on a White Charger in the Side Saddle to provide his Damsel in Distress with such wherewithal. After all he, whoever he is, might just have slipped in for a quick half of lager on his way home. He could hardly be expected to sport condoms on the off-chance that in between the office, the lager and the tube he will be accosted by a rampant floozy from Bedford Park. No, no, just as twenty years ago – if one was to be absolutely sure, and one was not on the Pill – one jolly well took care of such an item oneself . . . but where does one *purchase* such an item at seven-thirty on a Monday night? Especially in this well-bred garden suburb? Rubber goods hereabouts were tap washers and garden hoses – and even if they weren't, Celia can hardly ring up a neighbour and ask to borrow one.

As she slips into the black-and-white dress she gives a millisecond's consideration to Dirty Harry – but then dismisses the idea. Apart from the Thing's connotations she can just imagine her Shining Knight's deflationary shock if she pulls *that* out of her handbag right at the juicy moment. She is aware that puritanical streaks live close beneath the skin of even the most zealously wishful libertine. Too much taking the initiative might render her conquest flaccid with insecurity. After all, the sight of it made her squeak when Alex showed it to her, and she's known him intimately for years. Anyway – it is her husband's fantasy, not hers. No – she won't take that.

She slips on the red satin shoes that she bought for a local Vicars and Tarts party a couple of years ago (how long ago all that innocent fun seems now) and wonders if there is any point in doing so. Without a condom Nemesis cannot go to the ball – unless she is prepared to commute her requirement to heavy petting. Which, frankly, she is not. She pumps on the expensive vapour of Tom's scent and, as she does so, the solution comes to her. Of *course* – how can she have forgotten? She the mother of two? Two children who have brought their night-time's share of croup and strange rashes and earache throughout the years? Where did she go then for her apothecary's charms? Where else? To the late-night chemist near the doctor's surgery. Almost a second home to her once and not even five minutes' drive away. This time as she checks her reflection she permits herself a smile – and another wink – and she is gratified to see that her reflection winks back at her quite amiably.

Something else winks back at her too – behind her reflection, on the bed, lies that sibylline book of love letters, face-down and open, just as it has lain since she flung it there so carelessly when she came home. She ignores it, tottering past the bed on her foolish spindle heels, looking straight ahead, determined, determined not to play such silly tricks with herself again. The phrase 'sovereign indifference' comes to mind and she tries to repel it but it comes on board anyway. What relevance did that have ...? None ... she is almost through the bedroom door when she weakens and flinging herself on to the bed she grabs the paperback, closes her eyes ever so tightly and yanks it open. There are two letters printed upon the page – one from Oliver Cromwell to his Elizabeth, the other from her to him. This is hardly the red meat required for Celia's night ahead. Still – once embarked on such silliness – she might as well *pretend* it has some relevance ...

Oliver writes from the field of battle:

Truly, if I love thee not too well, I think I err not on the other hand much. Thou art dearer to me than any creature; let that suffice ...

Elizabeth writes:

I and our son and daughter wait for thy safe return. Above all save God is this our greatest desire. All else lies buried but your good return ...

She slaps the book shut, rolls off the bed, shakes out her frock's massive shoulders and marches, or rather wobbles, her way down the stairs. Out she goes into the beautiful summer's night.

'Crap,' she says to the clear azure arc above her. 'Crap.'

Which is also the name of another unrefined kind of game.

She takes the car to the chemist. From there she will drive to the taxi rank and go on to her destination by cab. Since the evening ahead will call for something stronger than orange juice this seems a sensible precaution. She may have abandoned her honest wifedom and her good motherliness but she is still a responsible citizen. This piece of moral wisdom gives her courage as she enters the shop. Which is just as well, for she suddenly quails at the task before her. She has to take a series of very deep breaths (not easy given the racy underwear she has on – how loose women ever got to be called that beats her, what with the underwired brassière and suspenders she has never felt more restricted) before going in.

In the chemist's there are many people milling around, making purchases, waiting for prescriptions, and the woman behind the counter, from whom Celia has often purchased Junior Disprin and Actifed, is the only assistant. She finds herself as furtive in her quest as any anxious adolescent. She prowls about, teetering on her heels, building up the courage to state her request. Fortunately she does not look any more weird than the rest of the assembled. There is something Hogarthian about the customers in an after-hours chemist. Here a woman mumbles to herself, there an old man in plimsolls has a finger in his ear, a youth with a personal stereo stares vacantly ahead, sightlessly nodding time at an array of swimming caps, and a girl with pink hair (Celia touches her own peacock hue fleetingly) chews gum like a tuberculoid cow. Oh no, Celia does not feel out of place at all as she wobbles around, but all the same she is not yet ready to say what she wants. Maybe, she thinks, she can camouflage her real requirement in a selection of goods? She picks up a tub of something from the counter, clutches it to her half-cup underwired bosom, and staggers along towards the till – and it is here that the display of condoms is conspicuously placed. Rows and rows of them – all cheerily suggesting themselves as thoroughly tested, multi-coloured, strong yet sensitive, buy three packs get a fourth one free. It is very similar to buying breakfast cereal, she thinks, and not very titillating at all. The photographs that accompany the range show young men and women looking happily into each other's eyes – before or after? Celia finds herself wondering this. And whereas the bathing caps show encased heads and the paper panties show flat little abdomens snugly held, the condoms, rather sadly, do not follow suit. While she is thinking this the detached voice of the assistant says, 'Will that be all?' and looks at Celia enquiringly.

Oh God, thinks Celia, it's now or never.

She holds out the tub of something and with an extraordinary deftness that surprises even her she finds she has also picked out a little silvery packet from the display. It is marked, she notices, 'For Sparkling Nights', which seems fair enough. Then, thinking that they may provoke the same kind of reaction as Dirty Harry – for who knows what the sparkle content is – she also, just as smoothly, picks up a more subdued packet labelled 'Day Gear'. This done, she feels much better; quite on top again in fact, and with a certain aloof cachet, she prepares to hand her purchases over for wrapping. Prepares to – indeed, the muscles of her arm are already flexing to do so – when she retracts. For suddenly an oddly familiar shuffling noise engages her ears. It is a noise which makes her think, instantly, of her home. It is a very familiar noise. And it grows louder and louder, accompanied by another very familiar noise, the familiar – far too familiar noise – of sniffing. She turns around, still holding the items, and looks downwards, directly into the creased parchment face of Mrs Green. Who says, with shuddering triumph, 'I haven't been the same since this morning, Mrs Crossland. The shock of it has gone right to my legs . . .'

Celia feels faint. She whirls away, turning her back on the voice and the legs, and presents her immense shoulders to the

202

woman at the till, still clutching the items to her upraised breasts. She looks demented. The woman at the till sighs. It is almost closing time and it has been a hard day. She really does not have the time to indulge one more dithering customer.

'Will that be all?' she says, reaching out her hand for the purchases. It is very odd that at this perfectly straightforward gesture her customer takes on the shifty guise of one caught shoplifting. Celia stands mute and still, apparently frozen to the spot, pressing her purchases to her chest as if to pretend they did not exist.

The assistant peers askance. Yes, they are definitely there, tucked beneath the customer's spreadeagled hands. A jar of Vaseline, a packet of party condoms and a packet of ordinaries. Some people have all the fun, thinks the sales assistant bitterly. Her husband is an undertaker's assistant who takes his job very seriously. Party condoms are not for the likes of him. The only thing she can be sure of is a lovely laying out when the time comes. These thoughts make her peremptory.

'Madam,' she says, 'if you please . . .'

She reaches out.

Celia goes on hugging them to her chest. She can do nothing else.

Mrs Green feels badly done by, especially now that Celia has turned her back on her. The statement about her legs and her trials of this morning requires eye to eye contact. She moves round to Celia's front.

'Mrs Crossland . . .' She begins again.

Celia's heels wobble dangerously.

Anyone, anyone at all could have come into the shop and found her making her purchases – yes – even dressed like this – and she would have been able to dissimulate somehow. Another Vicars and Tarts party in Kingston would have done. They would have believed her. Bedford Park people are always attending such witty functions. But *Mrs Green*! Celia wobbles again, steps forward to right herself, steps back ditto, feels herself *sans* equilibrium and gives in to stagger frontwards again. And, most unfortunately, the red satin heel discovers, in a perfect bullseye, Mrs Green's slipperetted foot.

Mrs Green has used her lungs to full extent once today. Understandably, with her corns, she does so again.

She lets out a barely translatable cry of, 'My corns, my corns!'

Which is fair enough since she has them aplenty.

She recalls, as she yells, the endless line of shoes in Celia's wardrobe – soft kid things, the like of which Mrs Green has never, will never, possess.

She yells afresh. Even as the red satin heel is removed and the throbbing subsides a little she decides not to give up. A dozen pairs, she has counted, if not more. Why stop now?

Yell, yell, yell, she goes.

They collect quite a crowd.

Celia, taking advantage of the diversion, shoves her three items and a five-pound note at the assistant. The assistant, noting that there is now some urgency in her customer's mien, slows down.

We all play games. This is one of hers.

'Va-se-line,' she intones slowly, pushing the till buttons.

Celia, hunted by the yelling Mrs Green, implores the assistant to go quickly.

The assistant has few moments of power and slows down even further.

'Aaand Twooo Packeeetttsss of –' Long pause. 'Cccc—'

Oh God. Mrs Green has stopped yelling. she is looking with interest at what the assistant rings up. The very idea of Celia buying two of anything silences her towards interest. Celia is sweating again.

'ooonnn,' says the assistant slowly, rather enjoying it all.

'Cornplasters!' shrieks Celia.

And wresting the commodities from the assistant's grip she smacks Mrs Green's shoulders manically as if the woman were having a fit of convulsions. Diversionary tactics.

In the moment of change from till to hand, Celia drags Mrs Green away before the assistant can correct her customer's mistake. Try putting those on your tootsies, thinks the assistant, and she has her only laugh of the day. But she does not follow Celia and Mrs Green out on to the pavement to apprise them of the error, for the queue at the till is too long.

Mercifully Celia is left to deal with the situation in her own way but a serious malfunction in her brain area creates a useless void. Her mouth opens and closes but no sounds come out. Mrs Green's mouth also opens and closes but to better effect.

'Now I've lost me place in the queue,' she says.

She squints at the unbagged purchases which her employer clutches to her. If she can't get her embrocation she will at least have a packet of cornplasters.

'I can't go back in there,' she says defiantly. 'It'll take all night. You'll have to give me one of yours . . .'

If she cannot have Celia's cutlery, or her shoes, or even find some hint of sexual activity, she can certainly have one of these.

Celia's head is shaking from side to side and her bright-pink mouth is making a series of 'O's.

Mrs Green acts swiftly. She puts out her ancient shaking hand and rips the prettiest of the packets out of Celia's grasp, which produces a very satisfying squeal where once the random 'O's were.

'I will have them,' she says. And once they are in the deeps of her cardigan pocket she adds sweetly, 'You can deduct them from my wages.'

'Oh, now look here . . .' Celia manages.

Mrs Green sniffs long and joyfully. 'You won't be needing *all* them tonight, now, will you?' She looks down at the raffish red satin. 'Best thing you can do,' she says, 'is to put something decent on your feet instead . . .'

And with the sudden alacrity that is hers when she chooses she leaps off into the warm dusky night.

To laugh? Or to cry?

Celia is unsure which.

She takes the remaining package and the Vaseline and stuffs them into her handbag. A less doughty heroine might be stayed by such diversions but not ours. Ours has her resolution intact, perhaps strengthened, by such things. It is all uncharted anyway. What does one extra little loopline matter? She will get there in the end. She is committed to it. At least Mrs Green has left her with the daytime ordinaries. Oddly enough Celia makes no equation between the two purchases stuffed into her handbag. Well – naturally – to a woman such as Celia's maturity Vaseline and condoms are uncharted too. She can always find a household use for the former. It is very good, for instance, for slipping into one's finger-nails before gardening. As for the latter – she is perfectly well aware of the use she will have for them.

She puts out of her mind completely the residual drama of Mrs Green's corns and how they take to the application of Sparkling Nights. Celia feels that she has quite enough to contend with without dwelling on *that* . . .

(Mr Green, Arthur, to whom nothing more exciting has happened recently than a re-run of Eliot Ness in 'The Untouchables', is dragged abruptly from his evening's stupor by the extraordinary sight of his wife crouching over her bare feet and delicately unwrapping something he feels sure has no place in his home. Mr Green, Arthur, was in the Eighth Army with Monty and Desert Rats never forget the wartime debt they owe to the Dunlop Rubber Company. He recognises what she unwraps all right. And he does the only thing possible in the circumstances. He turns off the television. After which his laughter shakes their modest but cosy walls. It is several minutes before the truth can be imparted to his wife, during which time that good lady makes some remarkably inventive attempts to adapt the item footwise. Yes, on the whole, it is better that Celia does not dwell on such possibilities. She has quite enough to cope with ahead of her – *quite* enough –)

Things do go a little more smoothly for Celia after this. She makes a smooth entry into a parking space near the taxi rank, finds a cab instantly, gives the name of the hotel, and is on her way. And, just as she did at the beginning of this story, Celia is looking good. Very good. Only different. More wicked, certainly, but also – it has to be said – a good deal more mature. The peacock highlight sits very well on her now – and it matches much more than her eyes.

2

The Side Saddle is an alien place, so Celia thinks. Not at all like the bright and spacious bar at the Queen's Brough. She has to squint a little as she stands on its threshold to accustom herself to the low lighting. It is about the size of two Norman Shaw front rooms, no more than that, with ten or twelve round tables set about the panelled walls. To her right is the bar itself, horseshoe-shaped, mahogany-topped, with stools ranged around its curve: most of these are already occupied. To her left are the tables, full of knee-to-knee young men and women all wearing the kind of stylish outfits that make them look like leftovers from forties Hollywood. There are champagne bottles littered about, gin and tonic glasses held in hands whose wrists are weighted down by Rolex watches, and Filofaxes lie pulsing to be opened amid the wet rings on the tabletops. All around the walls are equestrian artefacts: saddles, crops, bridles, and photographs of nameless horses. Of long and dusty duration these. The only aspects of the bar, apart from its polished furnishings and the barman himself who is greying at the temples and as supercilious as only a Mayfair barman can be, to hint at continuity. For the rest it is all to do with Now. No past, no future: just Now.

As that insensitive brotherhood, the pre-Raphaelites, managed to wipe out the Renaissance by saying that you should see every leaf on every tree and paint soppy eye-upturned knights if you wanted *real* art – so Celia observes in wonder that these stylish chaps and chapesses before her have done the same with pop music. It is, apparently, a peculiar piece of young upwardly mobile conceit to like only pre-Beatles vintage. And as she stands there the ridiculous plink-plonk notes of Adam Faith's 'What Do You Want . . .' goes 'Wish Yew Want-ed My Luv Baybee.' And makes her, not surprisingly in her heightened and

nervous state, want to laugh. She feels like a granny. Which is, after all, as it should be and which does not, after all, help her to feel better about it. It is especially not the right kind of feeling when you are out to attract a lover. Celia, attempting to ooze desirability, is aware only of creeping incredulity: the eyes, which should be smouldering and slitted, are open wide. What she sees is all rather horrible.

A noisy group near to the door calls to a young man at the bar. His name is, unsurprisingly, Henry, and he is, apparently, in the chair and being somewhat tardy with the old champers. Celia realises that she stands at the edge of the heart of Yuppiedom – and its twin organ, Extreme Youth. Such Extreme Youth, she thinks, as she gazes about her, that they appear to be Extremely Silly. She watches intently as one young man – rather attractive in a fawn double-breasted jacket with highlights in his hair, removes the shoe from a squabbling girl in Ungaro white linen – who scarcely notices – pours champagne into it and prepares to drink. Celia may see them as Extremely Silly but they do not. As she in *her* youth did not. They see themselves, if they bother to look at all, as no more nor less than what they are. Enjoyers of Life without need to count the cost. Savaged livers and cholesterol-laden hearts do not, should not, cannot affect them. Celia finds this enviable and it makes her sad. She sees herself standing there as some kind of *memento mori* – well-preserved they might call her, attractive older woman, with a nudge and a wink and a she-could-teach-you-a-thing-or-two. But not a part of them. Never a part of them again. And the irony is, she thinks, that she *couldn't* teach them a thing or two. Physical maturity she has, emotional maturity she has not, nor its sister sexual maturity, come to that. Age brings only experience, she thinks, growing even sadder, not answers. Top Shop and Bedford Park permanent youth seem suddenly both gross and empty. Oh dear, Celia, she says to herself, what are you going to do?

She cannot participate in this. Yet she cannot go home. She has come on a crusade for Vengeance and unless she is careful it will end up as only another Humiliation. Two Humiliations will finish her. Her plain and daily condoms throb with unconcealed amusement in her handbag. She gazes more fixedly around the bar. Everyone is part of a group. Even the few lone drinkers perched on stools have an at-oneness about them. Whatever their sorrows they are youthful sufferers, in need of youthful comfort. They will certainly not welcome the overtures of a sex-seeking housewife from Chiswick. Or if they do it will be as an experiment. Despite everything Celia does not see why she should submit to the role of guinea pig. Whoever she selects must submit to her requirements and certainly not the other way around. And anyway, Celia does not see herself in the Mrs Robinson role at all. It might be all right in films and books but from where she stands it looks most unappetising. I may not be looking for love, she argues, but I am looking for some kind of equality in this exercise, a little sensitivity, a little understanding: there doesn't seem to be any chance of finding that here . . . And to support this view she brings her gaze back to the youth with the champagne-filled shoe just as he brings it to his lips. She sees him grimace, dash it to the ground and say, in penetrating nasal tones, 'My God, Camilla, your feet do stink . . .'

Celia looks away. She hears the girl giggle and whoop and shout laughingly that he has simply ruined her shoe. And that is all. No Humiliation for her. She is one of them. If the same thing had happened to Celia she would have died on the spot – or punched him on the nose – or perhaps both. Regretfully she decides that she must leave. There is nothing for her here. Only the barman suggests any potential but he has a cruel mouth, a mouth which is even now curled unpleasantly as he looks across to the group with the shoe. No, no. Not him. No one then. She shakes her head and begins to turn away and thinks to herself that she has been a fool. Much more of a fool than any of these glitzy youngsters whose confidence has just cut her to the bone. Her courage ebbs. As it pulls away from her it begins to reveal the stark truth: that she is not, now, going to be able to go through with this. She will just have to get in a cab and go home and nurse her wounds in secret. Never tell Alex, never feel that warm inner sense of Vengeance achieved. It will just have to be the death-bed memoirs after all. Gloom and despondency creep in to fill courage's gap. Perhaps the death bed is not so far off anyway ... she certainly feels that she has aged a decade in this five minutes. She watches as a piece of bread sails across the tables and lands – quite perfectly – in a glass. Another piece of bread sails back again to be met by cheers and shrieks of pleasure. A joyful battle has begun. Quite definitely this is no place for her. She turns to leave. The suspender belt pulls uncomfortably, reminding her of her folly. She is about to hitch at it, unliberated monstrosity, when she hears a soft, male, American voice behind her.

'Jee-Suss H. Christ! That is definitely not for me ...'

She turns fully around and is relieved to see that the comment was not directed at her but at the bar itself. For the eyes of the speaker, half closed with displeasure, are looking beyond her, and the head which houses the eyes is shaking slightly in solemn certainty.

'Will you look at those kids in there ...?' he says, as much to himself as to Celia. 'Pitching all the stuff around. *Definitely* not for me.'

'Nor me either,' she says, surprised at how easily the phrase trips out.

'These hotel bars,' he says, still staring beyond her, 'are the absolute pits.'

'I wouldn't know,' she says, preparing to move past him. 'But that one certainly is ...'

'Where in the world,' he says, quite sincerely, 'do you go for a quiet drink before dinner in this place?'

And Celia, without art or planning, says, 'That's just what I was wondering. Excuse me please.' And she moves on by, the shoulders of her dress making negotiations a little difficult.

'Sorry,' she says, and smiles apologetically with the same charm she would show on vacating a supermarket check-out.

When their eyes meet, as eyes will under such circumstances, Celia is genuinely astonished. There is a certain quality about the look in those eyes. A certain quality that leads her to suppose she might – *just might* – have found an answer ... Can it really be this easy? She stares at him as searchingly as she dares. Apparently it can for he is looking back at her, quite relaxed, out of nice blue eyes with crinkled corners. She is not sure if she finds him attractive simply because he is, like the mountains, just there – or whether it is because he is physically attractive anyway. It doesn't much matter. She is grateful for his existence and she intends, fail or win, to have a go. If those careless young bloods in there think they are Hollywood, this one is much more like the genuine article. Vintage, though. She has to admit that he is more vintage than she might have chosen for he certainly won't see fifty again. But then, given the backdrop of all that zestful bread-throwing, his mature years seem a positive plus. She takes in as much as she dares without actually stepping back and giving him the once over. He will do. That is the main thing. And as she absorbs a clearer picture of his physicalities she decides that he will more than do – he will do very nicely.

He exudes stability which, given Celia's difficulties with her high heels, makes him even more acceptable. And he looks as if he is someone with whom she could converse, at least – gulp – at first ... She moves a little nearer.

'Excuse me,' he says, stepping to let her pass.

He has neat grey hair and a slightly sun-tanned face which is still creased with dissatisfaction as he looks beyond Celia to the bar. He shakes his head again and turns away so that they both execute a little side-stepping pavane which brings them a few steps further forward but still, more or less, in the same proximity. They both smile and shrug.

'Excuse *me*. Again,' he says with that peculiarly Transatlantic *politesse*.

'Not at all,' says Celia, delighted.

Dear old Fate, she thinks, for Fate will see me through.

She allows intuition to take the place of planning and waits to hear what it will have her say. This proves to be the correct course.

212

'I wouldn't go in there if I was you.' She laughs. 'Even if the Yuppies don't get you that barman will ... He looks as if he bites.'

He peers beyond her again, this time smiling.

While he does so Celia notes as much about him as she can. Neither fat nor thin, unremarkable grey suit, plain white shirt with dark-blue tie, slightly taller than her even with her heels. She decides that the mountains have nothing to do with this. He *is* attractive. In masculine terms, she decides, he is infinitely more attractive than Pastel Frock. This is a wonderful bonus and does much to restore her courage. She looks up at him and smiles very boldly – she hopes not brassily – and affects an air of rapt attention.

'He certainly does,' he says positively, and then turns back to her. 'What did you call them?'

'Yuppies. It's an acronym. Like Wasp in the States—'

'Ah yes,' he says. 'We have those there too.'

They laugh. They are on each other's side.

'Perhaps there is more than one bar here?' she says, much heartened by intuition's offering.

'Perhaps there is ...' he says, sounding equally pleased. 'Shall we ask?'

A piece of bread flops near their feet.

'Why not?' says Celia. '*Why not?*'

To Romeo and Juliet is the Side Saddle Bar, to Anthony and Cleopatra is the Consort Room. It has Regency-striped wallpaper, gilt wall lights that are bright enough to read by but not bright enough to pick out every flaw in a customer's skin. And the barman, though supercilious, is at least discreet about his contempt. Celia could whoop and holler with satisfaction and joy as she sits herself down. Made it, she thinks, and the triumph wipes out any of the humiliation she felt earlier on. She scrutinises this saviour of hers and thinks that he is a wonderful, wonderful find. Perfect, if she can bring it off, for the Goodwife's Revenge. In this light she can study him further.

Nearer mid than early fifties, she decides. Not that it matters one jot.

He says, toying with the olive in his martini but looking right into her eyes, 'Fifty-seven last month.'

She gapes.

He sips at his drink and looks amused and satisfied.

'How did you know I was thinking that?'

'I'm a mind reader.'

She gapes anew.

'You're *not* . . .' The very thought of his being able to read even half of what is going on in there is frightening.

He laughs outright and shakes his head. 'Of course not.'

'Then how did you know?'

'When a woman studies a man like that there can be only two reasons. Either she is trying to make up her mind how old he is, or how rich he is. I'd like to think it was the former . . .'

'Are you rich?'

That comes out before she can stop and she curses intuition for getting it so wrong.

But he laughs again.

'Not rich. Not poor. Average.'

'Me too,' she says.

'We should be properly acquainted,' he says solemnly, holding out his hand to shake hers. 'My name is Walter Flack and I am a fundraiser for the World Health Organisation.'

'How interesting,' says Celia.

She offers her hand and says, 'My name is –' She hesitates. 'Celia.'

He looks at her expectantly. She looks back.

'Just Celia?' he says.

For the moment she decides that is all the information she dares to render.

'Some people call me Cee,' she says, dodging, she thinks, quite nicely.

'Hallo, Cee,' he says with humorous formality, giving her hand a shake before releasing it.

'Hallo – Walt,' she says with equal solemnity.

He toys with the olive again. 'And the answer to your next question is . . .' He looks up, those blue crinkly eyes studying her '. . . that I am also a widower . . .'

Celia blushes. Perhaps he can read minds after all.

Celia is about to deny that the thought ever entered her head, and she begins, 'Oh but I—'

He holds up his hand. 'I know that sounds phoney but it happens to be true. I just think we should set the record straight. After all –' He indicates the table, the bar, the two of them sitting there. 'We are sitting here – together – and –' he shrugs – 'who knows? It might be relevant . . . So – a widower I am.' He smiles at her. 'OK?' He looks as if he has just made a good move in a game of chess.

'I wasn't going to question it,' she says, more prissily than she means to because she wants to cover up the fact that his widowerhood is oddly pleasing. She wants it to be true so that there is no other Celia somewhere in the world cooking nice meals and trusting him.

'I was going to say that this is a very posh hotel for a fundraiser to be staying in.'

'Not when you raise as much money as I do,' he replies cheerfully. 'I wouldn't be able to keep up the pace if I had to go back to the YMCA every night.' There is a short silence and he says, 'Well. I've told you. You tell me.'

'My name is Celia,' she repeats. 'Do you mind if I don't tell you any more than that?'

'Candidly – yes.'

'Later?'

'Sure.' He shrugs and pops the olive into his mouth.

Celia finds this strangely alluring. Perhaps because it seems such a relaxed thing to do. She finds herself relaxing too – or as much as all that unyielding underwear will allow. She winces as she thinks of it.

'I think you look much less than fifty-seven,' she says, still intuitively.

'I try to be a good advertisement for my job. And flattery like that wins you a dinner. That is if you . . .?'

'Oh yes. I'm very hungry and I would.'

Knight to Queen's pawn being decided, they can now relax further. If she had known it could be this pleasant and easy she might have done this sort of thing a lot more. Just as well she didn't . . .

She thinks that he has the kind of face that can be read easily. He shows his thoughts. Which means he must be a nice person. And she is profoundly grateful that he has not pushed her for more information. The combined forces of intuition and planning have not given Celia any clues as to how to explain her being here tonight. Well, not yet anyway. Perhaps after another martini it will crystallise.

'Do you do this sort of thing often?' he says. 'I mean – come into hotel bars on your own?'

'Certainly not,' she says quite primly. 'Anyway, how do you know that I'm not a resident?'

He looks surprised. 'Um . . .' he says apologetically, 'are you staying here?'

'I don't know,' she says softly. And amazes herself for now and ever after by adding, 'It rather depends on you.'

Oh Alex, she thinks, Oh Alex, Alex, my darling Alex. What have you made me do?

It is much the best way to blame him completely.

It stops her from feeling so bad about enjoying the experience.

Enjoyment had not figured in the equation regarding the Revenge of a Bedford Park Wife.

But it does now.

She smiles to herself.

It is a nice smile, a very feminine smile, thinks her companion.

He smiles back.

It becomes rather like the eating scene in *Tom Jones*. They begin the meal calmly enough. But there is something in the way she removes the snails from their shells and the juice and butter bespatter her mouth that looks seductive. And there is something about the play of his hands on the artichoke leaves and the sucking of their ends that beguiles her also. He, she thinks, holds his wine glass attractively; has the habit of touching his ear lobe suggestively when he speaks; eats unfussily, savouring each mouthful. And she has a way of tilting her head slightly as she drinks displaying her throat which is very touchable; a way of putting her chin in one hand and looking levelly into his eyes; an enticing manner of biting with her small white teeth ... By the time the entrée is cleared away they have both begun to stumble over words, to twist a little in their chairs. She waves away the menu for dessert with the slightest hint of impatience and he, galvanised to look for such small signs, does likewise. The conversation, which was about autumn in Maine, where he lives, suddenly peters out and he says, 'Are you sure?'

But the question he speaks is not, of course, about dessert.

He is not looking at her, as he smooths his serviette.

'I'd like a brandy,' she says, much more positively than she feels. And then adds, 'How old do you think *I* am?'

'Oh ...' He traces some kind of pattern on the folded linen. 'About several thousand years or so ...'

Celia pulls herself together. This is not going the way she expected it to. It is like participating in a love story. She reminds herself that she is here for Vengeance. Nice as he is. Enjoyable – *very* enjoyable – as the dinner has been, that is why she is here. And that is all.

'We could,' he says, 'have the brandy somewhere else ...'

The image of Alex and his dalliance is before her. Into her mind floats reason's certainty: I don't think, it tells her, that you can go through with this after all ...

'... Couldn't we?' he adds hopefully.

'We could,' she agrees.

... And floats out again. Quite forgotten.

He gets up and comes round to her chair which he pulls out from the table. His hand is light on her arm as he helps her to stand. This makes her smile as she remembers the crassness of the boy with the champagne shoe. Perhaps there is something more pleasurable in being Cleopatra rather than Juliet.

'Why are you smiling?'

'Because,' she says simply, 'I really want to cry.'

He takes the neatly folded handkerchief from his breast pocket and puts it into her hand. It has the initial 'W' embroidered in one corner. She is pleased that he has been truthful about his name. Very pleased. And being a widower makes it all perfectly fine from his point of view. If I'd known it was this easy, she thinks again, I really might have done this sort of thing years ago ... And then she giggles, puts her hand to her mouth as the giggle is replaced by shock and thinks, My God – what *am* I saying?

He puts his hand somewhere near the base of her spine to guide her.

'Will you come up and see my etchings?'

Then she takes her hand away from her mouth and allows herself a really joyous laugh.

'I thought only Europeans went in for such nonsense ...'

'Oh, it's pretty universal I guess,' he says.

In the lift he moves away from her and does not touch her again. At his room he pushes the door open and lets it swing away in front of her. She waits for him to put his hand on some part of her to usher her in, for the intimacy of the touch was so nice, but he does not. He waits. She can feel his breath behind her. The room has a double bed with the covers turned down. On it is an open newspaper – the *New York Times* – and a pair of spectacles with a black towelling robe draped across one corner. She pushes this to one side and sits down very gingerly, looking about her, trying not to notice that the door has swung shut again and that he is locking it.

'Do you do this sort of thing very often?' she asks. She had hoped to sound like Zola's Nana but it comes out more like J.M. Barrie's. Or a maiden aunt's.

'Nope,' he says.

He crosses to the telephone by the bed, picks it up, orders two brandies and loosens his tie knot.

Replacing the receiver he turns, crosses his arms and looks down at her.

'Do you?'

She shakes her head.

'You are wearing a wedding ring.'

'So are you.'

'I told you. I'm a widower.'

'Couldn't you even be divorced?'

'Would that help?'

'It'd be . . .'

'What?'

'. . . wickeder,' she says.

'I don't think –' He uncrosses his arms and squats down in front of her putting a finger under her chin – 'that we could get much wickeder than this. Do you?'

The kiss makes all kinds of inroads on her senses but she does have the clear thought, very fleetingly, that if this is Vengeance then it is, indeed, sweet. Out in the hinterland there is a knocking. The kiss ends. The door is opened, the tray taken, the lock reset. He takes off his jacket, holds out a glass to her. She is still clutching the handkerchief. She gives it back to him, drains her glass, and sighs. It is a sigh of absolute certainty. No going back now.

'Better?' he asks politely. 'I have some Scotch whisky here if you would like some?'

'I don't like it,' she says.

'Then you don't have to have it.'

The innuendo gives her goose-bumps.

Their eyes meet and he slides (rather well for a beginner, she thinks) on to the bed beside her.

And immediately rises up again with a startled grunt.

He has sat on her little bag.

'What the hell have you got in there?' He looks down at it in surprise. She makes to grab it, he gets there first. 'Women and their handbags.' He chuckles.

'Give it back,' she commands.

He holds it just out of her reach.

She snatches, gains it briefly, before he pulls it free. The clasp, which has always been faulty, gives way and out on to the bed tumble her purse, her scent mini-spray, a comb, a few other small items and – naturally enough – the jar of Vaseline and the packet of condoms.

'My God!' he says, looking down in disbelief. 'You *are* a hooker.'

'I am *not*,' she says fiercely.

He turns the jar and the packet over in his hands. 'It doesn't look like it.' The sarcasm rasps unpleasantly.

So then, quite reasonably, using one of the few options open to a woman in such circumstances, she bursts into tears.

He gives her his brandy, his handkerchief again; and pours himself a rather large whisky. He sits far away from her on his hotel armchair and watches her tears but he does nothing at all to stop them. She knows that he feels conned because she has gone through quite a lot of that herself just recently. There is no other way forward but to tell him everything. She sniffs, blows her nose, sips the brandy, sits bolt upright and says, 'Walt. You are probably not going to believe this, but I'm going to tell you the whole story anyway . . .'

And she does.

While Alex sips a very fine port, stifles yawn upon yawn and agrees with everything Judge Watson decrees, his wife is sitting in an hotel bedroom recounting her most intimate (and, there-fore *his* most intimate) secrets to a stranger from Maine. And this same stranger, as Celia speaks, is drawn slowly back towards her, coming to rest very gently beside her on the bed, and making an unhurried, sensual exploration of her body which begins with his fingers stroking the nape of her neck. Celia has an advantage of which she has never been aware: she can cry and look appealing at the same time.

At least, so it would seem from the investigative interest he shows.

By the time she has finished the telling of it she is lying back on the bed, the newspaper crackling beneath her shoulders. His hand has moved from external preludes to the fugue itself. Slipped inside her dress, it has encountered her underwired breasts which rise gratefully to meet it, quite as stiff as their metallic supports. Celia is now past considering the rights and wrongs of this, it matters not at all, though he, whispering close to her ear, makes it clear that he thinks what she is doing is right, is right, is Oh So Right. He kisses her ear, her neck, her ear again and says, 'Forty is a wonderful age for a woman, a wonderful age ...' And Celia whispers back, dreamily and just as softly, 'And how old is your wife, Walt?' To which the hand that caresses her shows no sign of disturbance as its owner utters the fateful phrase, 'A little older than you ...'

And then, of course, the hand freezes. The voice in Celia's ear stops and, when it starts again, it says one small phrase.

It says, 'Oh *shit.*'

It can say nothing else for Celia subdues it with her mouth which is laughing and triumphant.

'That's better,' she says, smoothly rolling on top of him and looking down into those brilliant blue eyes which are, not unnaturally, sheepishly questioning. The suspender belt is really cutting into her flesh now, biting at skin which has had quite enough of it and cries out to be soothed by a lover's lips.

Frankly, Celia cannot wait to get it off. And it is not long before she does so.

PART FOUR

1

Our smallest action has consequences. Tread on a beetle and the world is diminished, changed, however slightly. Stub your toe in the morning and the pain will lead to ill-temper, the ill-temper to erratic driving, erratic driving to lack of control, lack of control to driving into a stationary bus. And the consequences will not end there. You may yell something obscene at the driver, or call him a pratt for parking there, and the next thing you know you are having a punch-up; you are late for an historically important meeting; the client, furious at being kept waiting, uses someone else; you lose your job and cannot get another (your case for assaulting a public servant comes up next week) . . . take to drink . . . drugs . . . prostitution – and all because of a stubbed toe. But feed it backwards. Why did you stub your toe in the first place? You stubbed it because just as you were leaving the house for the important meeting you noticed a nasty squashy mess on the side of your shoe, so you take it off to clean it and on the journey to the shoe-cleaning cupboard you – stub your bare toe. The nasty squashy mess on the side of your shoe was, of course, the beetle.

Metaphorically speaking, Celia trod on *her* beetle back in June, the outcome of which has been gathering momentum over the last few months. But in the whole extraordinary, mad scheme of things, her metaphorical squashing of the insect went unnoticed: it was the smallest, most fleeting of incidents compared with the magnitude of the other things taking place in her life at the time, but the world – her world, everybody else connected with her world – will never be the same again because of it. She will learn all about it later today but, just for the moment, she is busy in her kitchen being just like any other Bedford Park wife.

All over again.

✳

It is a Friday morning in early October. Out of her window Celia can see Henry and Rebecca in the garden. They have one of those odd things called 'occasional days' from school. And Celia – fully prepared for its arrival this time – has made plans.

Goodfriend Hazel is going to have Henry and Rebecca to her house for the day. They seem to have grown away from Verity and Caspar recently and it will be nice if they can re-establish their friendship. Since their trip to Wales Hazel's kids have been horse mad and take riding lessons locally as well as tennis coaching at Guess Who's club. If Celia had been feeling more perky this summer she might have done something about the widening gap; arranged a few energetic diversions of the kind she was once so good at – a day on the river, Windsor Safari Park, a trip to the *Mary Rose* – but her energy for filling the vacuum has mysteriously vanished. What with one thing and another she just let the children coast through this summer and oddly enough they raised no objections. Providing they could potter about with some of their other contemporaries they had been perfectly happy. Their high spot of pleasure seemed to be gaining permission to go to the local shops alone. Celia found this somewhat crushing. All those years of organising them and it seemed all they had ever wanted was to go independently to choose their own ice creams ... She closed her ears to news reports concerning the abduction of children and let them get on with it. You had to let go a little eventually, she argued with herself, despite the tiny and terrible percentage of malevolence in the world. Otherwise you would be blowing their noses for them on their honeymoon. She had said exactly this to Alex when he confronted her with what he took to be a lapse in her motherly duties – though of course he did not put it quite as pompously as that. Celia knew he would object. Indeed, her first impulse had been to swear the children to silence rather as she had done all those years ago over Henry's potty training – but something made her baulk at the deceit.

'If they need diversions,' he said, 'why not take them down to my mother for the day?'

'Because I don't want to,' she said, without knowing that she would.

'We all have to do things we don't like from time to time,' he retorted.

If it hadn't been the crystal vase in her hands she would have thrown it at him.

Anyway, Hazel's resurgence today is comforting in two ways: firstly, because Celia has to get on with the Big Thrust, which is far less exciting than it sounds. The Big Thrust is her household clean-up before winter. She has been psyching Mrs Green up for weeks and Mrs Green has been resisting being psyched up for weeks. It is the annual battle between them. Mrs Green says that you do this sort of thing in the spring. Celia likes to get it over with well before Christmas. The usual result is that Celia wins by half a neck, but Mrs Green's unwillingness makes the Big Thrust more of a Small Poke.

However, this year there has been no battle. What has, in the past, been rather an exciting period of psychological preparation has this year been no more than a quietly determined drift towards compliance. After the suitable period of psyching, Celia merely told her cleaner what was expected of her and went on to say that if Mrs Green was not up to it then she should perhaps retire. (Wonderful thought!) If this took Mrs Green's breath away (not difficult with her smoke-racked lungs) it is nothing to how the sudden arrival of such a statement amazed her employer. For despite all that has taken place, Mrs Green still likes to consider herself the Gorgon, and Celia still pretends towards Andromeda. Perseus has yet to appear. He may, however, be in the wings, for following on from the suggestion about retirement, Celia feels much strengthened. Indeed, she is building up to not making the coffee this morning and, more to the point, not drinking it with Mrs Green either. The very thought still makes her sweat. Can she go so far so swiftly? Perhaps she can. There is something about the autumnal scene beyond the kitchen window that is making Celia snappish. Like a hedgehog in reverse. For it makes her feel that she is coming to life, which is rather an unseasonal feeling given the prelude to winter's barren call. Autumn has never touched her emotions like this before. So it is a good job, in Celia's opinion, that Hazel will be here in a minute to collect the children, for the combination of the Big Thrust and her snappishness does not bode well for a day spent in their presence.

Come on, Haze, she thinks impatiently, for the urge to talk to her is strong. She is vague about what she wants to say but the strength of the urge is definitely there – and growing. Indeed – what with the Big Thrust and this sense of renewal with her friend it should be more like spring in her heart than the autumn that creeps beyond the window . . . perhaps it will be once she gets a few things off her chest. Hazel, she says to herself, surprised at the intensity of her need, hurry, hurry, hurry . . .

If the children have grown apart, Celia has also seen very little of her friend since her birthday. The munificent Jo has found favour over her. Not surprising, in fairness, Celia thinks, because she has been, well, preoccupied – not quite herself – and unable to confide the reason why to anyone. Even Hazel. Then there were the summer holidays which came in the middle of everything with Celia and Alex setting off on the Saturday that Hazel and John returned. So all in all it *is* comforting that she and Hazel are about to resume some kind of normality in their relationship. Despite Celia taking some of the blame for the coolness between them, she does feel that Hazel could have shown a little more *push* in her direction. There was a time, not so long ago, when Celia began to feel ready for the Confessional, a time when she felt that even the slightest overture from her friend would result in a soul-easing confidence, a lifting of the burden of the recent past – but Hazel was doing an orienteering course at the time (with Miss Grab-all Liberty Belle, naturally) and couldn't find the time. 'Why not join the course with us,' she had said brightly. But Celia refused. After all, the landscape she needed to steer a course through could hardly be negotiated with maps. And after that the munificent and tireless Jo went on producing all kinds of Hazel-bound plans and Celia, cutting off her nose to spite her face, refused even to attempt to compete. Not a little wounded, she let Hazel slip out of her fingers with scarcely a murmur of complaint.

'She's not the usual kind of Conservative Party lady,' Hazel said defensively. 'Once you get to know her she's very nice ... I think you're just prejudiced against Americans.'

If only you knew, thought Celia, but she let it go.

But today, with the smell of the bonfire in her nostrils, and the sound of rustling leaves being swept up in the garden, she feels the need to regain that lost intimacy. Mrs Green can drink her coffee on her own and Celia will take Hazel into the front room, the adult sanctuary, and perhaps – who knows – pour out her heart. She needs to do this with somebody. She needs this very badly indeed. Those burning leaves make her realise that now.

Perhaps after that, once Henry and Rebecca are out of the way, Celia will find the housewifely energy required to begin on the downstairs woodwork. She has neglected her home of late. For some reason, as she thinks this, her mother's words come into her head and she finds herself nodding at the Raynes Park-ism, 'Idle hands make mischief'. She agrees and, in consequence, from now on, she will keep busy, busy, busy. She ought really to do some cooking again – re-stock the freezer – and think about another dinner party; she has not even thought about giving one for months – not since, not since – well, months and months anyway. And then there is the question of Hazel's birthday cake – *that* event is coming up in a couple of weeks – all these things that she has neglected. She must, really must, put them right ... She can hear Mrs Green thumping away upstairs and a certain guilt descends, just as it used to. She should be making the coffee now – she looks at her watch – perhaps she *will* make that concession after all. What greater sign of her hard-won superiority than the waiving of it? She giggles. Shades of the old Celia. She recalls that memorable conversation with her cleaner at the beginning of the summer – a conversation in which they both stalked each other like players in a game of cat and mouse, each one thinking she was the cat. Mrs Green started it by handing Celia a little plastic bag and saying, 'Yours, I think, Mrs Crossland.'

And Celia, taking it, had swallowed very hard (to suppress mirth rather than fear) and said, 'A present, Mrs Green – how nice – thank you.'

Mrs Green's nasal passages had gone into overdrive. 'I think you should look at them closely,' she said, her eyes glittering.

Celia peered in fleetingly and recognised the wrappings of Sparkling Nights.

'How pretty,' she said. And fixing her cleaner with a gimlet eye, she added, 'What are they?'

'Well,' said the cleaner, folding her arms and flushing a little. 'I can tell you what they are *not*, Mrs Crossland.'

Celia nodded encouragingly.

Mrs Green shuffled a little but more or less stood her ground. 'I can tell you that they are not the sort of thing you'd want to put on your feet.'

'No?' Celia give a radiant and innocent smile.

'And they most certainly are *not* cornplasters!' But Mrs Green's sense of triumph was a little premature.

Celia said musingly, '*Not* for feet and not cornplasters. I give up. What are they?'

The flush deepened. The sniffing amplified. All her life Mrs Green had avoided calling a spade a spade – even normal bodily functions were reduced to numbers. Too old to change the habits of a lifetime, she was not going to put a name to the unspeakable if she could help it.

'Well?' said Celia brightly, for Mrs Green's discomfort was a joy to behold.

'I'd rather not say,' she said firmly. 'But they are what you gave me outside the chemist's.'

'Then they *are* cornplasters . . .'

'They are *not* . . .'

'Get along with you, Mrs Green,' Celia said playfully. 'We really can't spend all day standing around here playing games like this.'

Mrs Green's struggle with decorum and desire twitched in every feature.

Celia kept innocence upon her face.

A few moments of stalemate.

Then Mrs Green said, 'I suggest you look into the bag more closely.'

Obediently Celia did so. She very nearly wet herself when she saw that the packet had been opened.

She looked up. Mrs Green's eyes were slitted with expectancy.

Celia said, 'Balloons, Mrs Green. How nice.'

Mrs Green opened her mouth.

Celia said, 'I'll put them away for Christmas, shall I? How very kind of you.' Seeing that her companion was struggling and in danger of overcoming decency in the name of accuracy Celia went on swiftly, 'Oh – and by the way – I have had a word with the people next door and they were quite ready to forget all about your mistake with Mr Mason. So we'll do the same, shall we?'

'*My* mistake?' said Mrs Green, getting a second wind.

'Yes,' said Celia kindly. She put the little bag down on the bench and patted it, giving her cleaner a long hard look. 'Well, we all make them ... don't we?' Then she smiled. 'Now – there is a lot to do so shall we get on ...?'

From this small and apparently insignificant victory, Celia derived a good deal of comfort.

Mrs Green, on the other hand, had put the week's clean socks away, all twenty-four pairs, without folding them into each other. But it was cold comfort. In her bosom, that flat and dried-out place, she stored a deepened resentment that only some monumentally awful discovery could ever allay.

As Celia sets down the mugs and has her last chuckle at the memory she finds herself wondering if that was the last time anything funny happened in her life. There doesn't seem to have been much to laugh about since then – more than three months ago – she sighs. So this is being forty, is it? Well, well ...

She looks through the open door into the conservatory. She really must sort that out too. Half the plants need watering and the rose has greenfly on its dried-up husks. The children have made a camp in there out of the rattan furniture and the wind has blown in leaves and dried grass. It looks exactly as if a bomb has hit it. She should make the two of them clear it up, and she will – when she gets around to it – but it took enough energy getting them to clear up the leaves. The prospect of making them deal with the conservatory as well is too much today. Come on, Hazel, she thinks, hurry up, please ...

The bonfire is smoking sullenly. Henry looks up to see if they are being observed. If they are not he will pinch a bit of white spirit from the shed and get a good blaze going. Alas for his pyrotechnic dreams, his mother is gazing out of the window at them. But at least she is smiling. By way of compensation for the lack of blaze he says to his sister, 'Quick. Mum's smiling ... go in and ask if we can have a drink of coke before she stops ...'

But Rebecca is too late. By the time she has said, 'Why me?' and, 'Bloody Hell,' (the current favourite between them), put down her rake and walked through the conservatory the telephone has rung, Celia has answered it, and already her mood has changed.

The call is from Hazel. And her cheery tone is transparently tense. Celia already knows the gist of what she is going to say before she says it – and she is right. Jo has decided, on the spur of the moment because England is so beautiful in the fall, to go down to their Cotswold cottage for the weekend. Tinkle, tinkle, tinkle, goes Hazel's nervous laugh. And guess what? More tinkles – there are shards of guilty laughter all over the place – she has invited Hazel and the kids to accompany her. Sorry, Celia. Celia affects bonhomie and says not to worry. Relieved, Hazel prepares to ring off with the reminder that she will see her friend at her own fortieth birthday party soon anyway.

'Ah yes,' says Celia. 'I was going to ask. What kind of cake do you want?'

'Oh – Um – Er,' says Goodfriend Hazel.

'Come on, Haze,' she says, endeavouring to regain some of their old easiness. 'I can do anything within reason . . .'

'Er – Oh – Um,' continues the prospective birthday girl, and Celia suddenly knows what is coming.

'As a matter of fact, Cee—'

Celia stays silent. She is not going to help her on this one.

'As a matter of fact – well – Jo – has kind of volunteered to do something . . .' and there go the nervous tinklings again.

'Fine,' says Celia, wounded beyond measure. 'That's OK. Fine.'

'But I thought,' continues Hazel, apparently impersonating Joyce Grenfell, 'that you might organise some games for us. You're so *good* at that sort of thing, Cee –' Joyce Grenfell has become somewhat strangulated. Celia lets her founder. 'Celia?'

'Bye, Hazel,' she says. 'Enjoy the fall.' She puts the telephone back in its rest. 'Hope it breaks your neck.'

For some reason the word fall has added to the soreness. Somewhere along the line Celia decides she has lost a skin.

It is not, therefore, the most propitious moment for Rebecca to appear with her request. Not only has Celia lost a skin but a great, gaping wound seems to have opened. She rounds on her daughter and lets rip, hating herself as she does so . . . does she want her teeth to rot or what? Get back out there and finish sweeping those leaves up, and put away all those summer things of yours or they'll get thrown on the fire. Rebecca, spirited like her mother and as yet unbound by adult convention, does not take this lying down. She suggests sarcastically that it wouldn't matter because – given the stupid refusal of their request for some real ignition – nothing will burn anyway.

'Go!' yells Celia, pointing a long and quivering finger, 'before I put you on the bonfire instead.' Rebecca decides to cede defeat. Her mother is showing unusual forcefulness. 'Out, out and don't come back in until you've done it.' As she says this she sees the Russian Vine, quite dead now, no more than a welter of ash-grey sticks. It adds to her anger but the spurt of words does little to relieve her feelings.

Bloody Hazel, bloody autumn, bloody *everything*.

And – while she is at it – bloody California too.

Susannah is in California.

Susannah will be in California until Susannah decides to come home.

Susannah went off to California just after Celia returned from her summer holiday. Never had she felt the need for a heart to heart so acutely yet what could she say to her friend? Susie – all excited at getting back to America for a while – explained that what with the dollar exchange rate (Celia had made what she hoped was a suitably understanding 'Uh-huh' down the phone at this) and the terrifically good sale of the dog-woman's Daimlers, it made it much more sensible for them to pick up some real estate on the West Coast.

'Sure you're all right, Cee?'

(Another noncommital uh-huh.)

'Good. Poor old Tom isn't. He's been like a bear with a sore head. God knows (tee hee, how apt!) what it was that the vicar's wife had, but it must have been wonderful. It seems to have ended very quickly and it's left him showing all the symptoms of a man who has been deeply affected by *something*. Poor Tom – knocked sideways by the wife of a rural rector. Do you remember what she looked like, Celia? All that powder blue and matching eye shadow. You wouldn't credit the things men fall for, would you?'

A silent pause.

'Oops, sorry Cee – I forgot about Alex for a moment.'

'It's OK. How long will you be away?'

'Weeks. Why not come out and stay for a while? I've got Vesta with me. We could be three girls together . . .'

'What about quarantine?'

'Who for – you or the cat?'

'Oh, ha ha. I mean for bringing Vesta back in. She'll be stuck for six months, won't she?'

'Ways and means, my dear, ways and means. She will come back when I do. She always has done in the past.'

'Susannah!'

'Don't ask. Just call me Miss Fixit. Talking of which, if you need a bit of a boost, why don't you let Tom take you out now and again – while I'm away? He's always been fond of you . . .'

(Celia's heart jerks in her chest. Surely Susie is not now going to admit to having known all along? Oh please, please no. Celia's heart ceases jerking and freezes instead.)

'Only platonically, of course, you wouldn't have any worries there—'

(And settles down and unfreezes again.)

'He's forever getting tickets for this and that given to him. Shall I mention it?'

'No!'

'My God,' says Susie, 'I've never heard you be that positive about anything . . . Incidentally – how are you coping with Alex's little infidelity? Have you done anything about it yet or are you just going to let screwing dogs lie?'

Despite herself Celia has to laugh.

'The latter,' she says.

The Churchman Hotel incident was not something she cared to mention on the telephone. If Susie had not been going to California it might have been different. But you never knew who might be listening in and besides (at the time of this particular conversation Celia had not quite sorted things out in her own mind) it was early days – sometimes she wondered if the whole episode had ever really happened? On the whole, she often thought at this point, on the whole, if this is Vengeance, it is not quite so sweet and healing as she supposed . . .

'Well – if it all gets too awful just jump on a plane and come out. I'll be there waiting.'

'If it all gets too awful I might just do that . . .'

Typical of people without children. How on earth can Celia just jump on a plane whenever things get too much? What is she supposed to do? Stock up the freezer with fish fingers, give them their bus fares to school and just go? It is a heady thought – but of course she rejects it. Mothers simply cannot do that sort of thing.

But now – just at this moment – Celia wishes she had.

So – bloody California and bloody, bloody autumn, the fall too . . .

Rebecca returns to Henry and says with an acid sing-song of pleasure that he was wrong, wrong, wrong – their mother is not smiling, their mother is furious. Henry kicks his sister, which is fair enough given the dual irritations of being wrong and not getting Coca-Cola. Rebecca wails. Celia rushes to the window, looks out, and her face quells her sparring offspring. Oh God, she thinks, I can't stand a whole day of this. Let no one underestimate the sacrifice of house-husbands. Who would seek to give up the world beyond domestic walls for such moments? They are doughty, those men, and strong, and liberated. Such a pity that they tend to wear old cords and socks with their sandals, or they might be the Knights of New.

She thrust the coffee mugs back on the shelf, an action which soothes her slightly. And bloody Mrs Green can whistle too . . . she goes to the telephone. She dials Isabel's number. Why not? She has to do something. And her sister might be in. Perhaps she, too, is having an 'occasional day'?

A little good luck spills out into Celia's life.

Isabel *is*.

'Hallo stranger,' she says to Celia, with her unerring talent for creating instant guilt.

Celia ploughs on. 'Hi,' she says. 'How are you?'

'You sound tense, Celia,' says Isabel. 'Having trouble peeling the grapes or are the silken cushions uncomfortable?'

Celia digs her nails into her palm, grips the telephone until the fury passes, and laughs at the witticism. She says, 'Well, I am a bit fraught. The children are here and . . .'

It is as far as her sister allows her to go.

'Why on earth should that make you tense? Don't you *like* your children? Honestly Celia – you are odd . . .'

You don't know the half of it, Celia thinks, and she lets Isabel ramble on.

Which she does in much the same high-handed manner. It is only Celia's desperation that makes her keep the phone in her hand and not dashed beneath her heel. She suffers Isabel's veiled criticism for spending the whole summer without so much as a telephone call. ('You got our card from France?' Celia manages to get in, but this scarcely made a dent in Isabel's righteous armour.) 'And what have you and Dave been doing with yourselves this summer?'

Isabel goes into marked detail. What a jolly family time they have all had: following the Arthur Ransome trail, shinning up low Welsh mountains, camping – the usual finale – on the Isle of Wight.

'Lovely,' says Celia.

'*Yes*,' says Isabel. 'And now I'm working very hard with my marriage guidance stuff.'

'I didn't know you did that.'

'You don't know everything, little sister.'

This, Celia thinks, is very true.

'Well done you,' she says. She means it, too. Inadequacy has won. All she has to show for the summer is an emotional pickle.

'I thought it might be nice for the kids to get together sometime,' she says.

'I thought yours were always organised into infinity . . .'

'No,' says Celia, 'we are doing nothing.' And thoughtfully, she does not go on to expand. Isabel does not guess that she is second choice. Sod Hazel.

Several Isabelesque barbs follow before, in the end, Celia gets what she wants. She and the children are invited down for lunch.

Sisters certainly have their uses from time to time. If there is no way Celia could ever bring herself to confide in Isabel, at least she can spend some time with her and not stop here brooding. Jo is quite right. England in autumn is a beautiful place. It is also supposed to be a poetically melancholy time of year. And certainly, in this golden light, with the leaves rustling in the wind, the evocative smokiness that permeates the house and the trees sighing for their loss, the last thing she can contemplate suddenly is to spend the day indoors here doing a Big Thrust with Mrs Green while the children scamper about demanding coke and crisps. Come on, she shakes herself, snap out of it, whatever it is. Let's get going. The children whoop with joy, which is something – they certainly like visiting their cousins. More guilt for Celia. She ought to give them the opportunity more often. In future, she vows, I will do so. In future, she vows, I will be good. Only perhaps not yet, Lord, not yet . . .

Mrs Green is up a step-ladder at Celia's front-bedroom window as she watches the white Mini-Metro – now glazed with grime and speckled with bird droppings – set off. The car sends a flurry of russet leaves in its wake as Celia roars with unusual speed away from the kerb.

Despite the vinegary disapproval with which Mrs Green greeted Celia's sudden change of plan, she makes a contented grunt once the car is out of sight. She can relax. Once these summer curtains are down and the winter ones in place she can stick on the washing machine, have a nice quiet cup of coffee, and a really good rummage around. She has not been able, one way and another, to have a detailed snoop for a long time. Either Celia has been in or they have been on holiday, cleaning unrequired. And Mrs Green desperately needs to find something with the same tantalising allure that Dirty Harry held for her nearly a year ago. Ever since the incident with the cornplasters she has been building up to this. She'll give her balloons indeed. Mrs Green touches her need for a reckoning as if it were a bruise. It still hurts. She no longer has to revenge herself merely for excessive cutlery and consumer durables, but for something much more profound, for has she not been made

238

a laughing stock on the estate? Once Arthur Green whispered the tale wheezily to the barman in the Happy Wanderer when he was a few pints in it didn't take long for it to spread to the rest of the regulars. And from there, not unnaturally, given the mentality of the neighbours, there was no stopping it. Her hand shakes with mortification as she unhooks the curtain. She has suffered for that. Oh *how* she has. The very thought of it makes her wobble up those steps. I'll give her two sets of curtains all right, she thinks, pulling savagely at the light-weight Laura Ashley and letting one curtain drop.

Two sets *and* fully lined indeed. And not knowing her French letters from her elbow! Silly bitch.

Celia watches her sister prepare the lunch. She wants to cry out as Isabel pounds the rolling pin down on the pastry which Celia made for her. On the cooker a pan of steak and kidney is boiling its heart away, its odour penetrating every corner of the house. Isabel's boys will not eat onions so there is not even that overriding aroma to combat the pungency. She wonders if there is any smell quite so unappetising as boiling kidney meat. It could easily win over fresh shit, she thinks, wincing again at Isabel's crash, crash, crash.

'I thought I'd take a bit of trouble since you lot were coming,' says her sister happily, continuing at the pastry with righteous gusto.

'Lovely,' says Celia, eyeing the greens lying in their watery grave in the sink. They have yellowish edges. She goes over and starts trimming them.

'Careful you don't take too much off,' warns Isabel. 'Or there won't be enough to go round.'

Nearby a bunch of carrots which has certainly seen better days points its ends at her accusingly. You next, she promises silently. If carrots can look baleful, these certainly do.

'We could stir-fry the vegetables,' she says above the din of bumps and bangs that herald the final departure of any airy lightness out of the pastry. Isabel laughs and redoubles her

239

efforts. There is no hope now. It will be steak and kidney biscuit by the time it is cooked and Isabel will say, Well, Celia, you may be able to do all that fancy stuff – but you can't make straightforward pastry.

Isabel laughs. 'Honestly, Celia. Where do you get your ideas from? Fry the greens indeed. What a weird idea. You go and open the cider, there's a good thing. I'll see to all this . . .'

She gives a little shake of her head as if to say that this sister of hers is, indeed, a strange one. Celia notices this. If Isabel thinks that stir-fried vegetables show dangerous lunacy there is certainly no hope for heart-to-heart confidences between them. Celia will just have to keep it all to herself. Small Talk – that's all she can hope for – and she is very, very disappointed. For what she needs – and desperately – is Big Talk. Very Big Talk indeed.

She opens the cider and froths it into the two glasses set out by her sister – which have stamped upon them the proud message 'Milk is Good For You'. In her own way, she decides, Isabel has style. It takes a lot of style to be quite so unstylish. She gives one of the glasses to her sister and says, meaning it, that it is nice to be here, and cheers. Isabel, moulding the transparent skin that was once rich pastry around the dish of meat, and popping it in the oven which is set hopelessly low ('So that it will cook through,' she says placidly), looks up at Celia and smiles, somewhat mollified by the genuine statement.

'Now,' she says, 'come and sit down and tell me what you have been *doing*.'

They sit by the double-glazed french windows that overlook the garden and watch the children playing with Brillo. It is a pleasant scene of childish delight. The cider, unpleasantly sweet as it is, produces a soporific effect on Celia. She is glad, after all, that she came.

'Your card was very odd,' says Isabel.

'Which card?'

'The one from France.'

'Odd? How odd?'

Isabel gets up and goes over to the mantelpiece. She picks up a postcard and hands it to Celia, who reads:

Having a lovely time here in Brittany.
Whether absolutely foul.
Love Celia, Alex and the children.

'It was perfectly true,' she says lazily. 'The weather was dreadful and we had a wonderful holiday.'

'We had very good weather in the Isle of Wight,' says Isabel. 'Of course – we always do . . .'

But Celia is not listening.

She is remembering that savage beach, the windswept rocks, the little log fire in the rented house.

'Alex slept a lot,' she says. 'The children were out playing most of the time: they made a lot of friends.'

'Did they improve their French?' says Isabel.

Celia laughs. 'Good God no. The only families left on that coastline were British. All the rest very sensibly went home. You've never seen such weather, Izzie – it was like starring in *The Tempest.'*

'I thought you were a sun-worshipper? Corsica last year, wasn't it?'

Celia shrugs. 'We change as we get older. I enjoyed myself.'

This is true. While Alex slept (the combined efforts of the Brandreth case and the redoubtable Miss Lyall left him in much need of rest) Celia was either huddled over the little log fire wearing her thermal Benetton and writing postcards which were sent, and letters which were not, or walking the ferocious beach with the cold waves splashing over her bare toes. Sometimes she would perch on a rock, the wind whipping at her hair and brightening her eyes, and she would look across the bare Atlantic, her face set in reverie, like some heroine in a literary love story. It had been a memorable if mournful holiday. And enjoyable. That was the truth.

Still with the thought of it in her head she refocuses on her sister who has been saying something.

'. . . well?'

'Mmm?' asks Celia, still vaguely smelling the salt from the sea despite the prevalence of cooking kidneys.

'Well, what else have you been doing this summer? Apart from going on holiday?' She asks this in the tone of one expecting to be told that Celia has spent the whole time supping on lotus flowers. 'Have you read those books we bought you yet?'

Celia, suddenly galvanised and struck with a wonderful idea, sits up and says, 'No – not yet – but I will. It's just that – well . . .' She pinkens a little: can she get away with it? She is going to try . . .

'I have been busy as a matter of fact . . .'

'Oh – really – doing what?'

'Well –' Celia steels herself for what is, perhaps, the biggest lie she has ever told. And certainly the most dangerously discoverable. 'Well – the thing is – I've been writing a *book.*'

If ever she has yearned to discomfit her sister, she now discovers the way. Isabel sits bolt upright.

'You've *what*!'

'Been writing a book.'

Biscuit the pastry most certainly will be by the time this conversation is concluded.

'But that's *astonishing*! What about?'

And Celia, startled by the enormity of the invention, yet confident of having a good plot, tells her.

Everything.

Changing only the names, as they say, to aid anonymity.

They get through a quart of cider between them. They watch without apparently noticing as Brillo stops her game for a moment to relieve herself in a great pile of excrement right in the middle of the lawn. They observe but do not register that the four children come indoors, help themselves to crisps and a Tizer bottle and settle in front of the television in the next-door room. Still they sit, side by side at the window, until Celia, coming to the end of her narrative, with the heroine in question leaving the hotel at four in the morning and taking a taxi home, says, 'So she drives off, having found her Vengeance, and that is that.'

And Isabel says, 'Well – I've got to hand it to you for inventiveness but you can't leave your readers with something so unresolved. So up in the air . . .'

'Why not?' says Celia. 'The heroine is.'

'They wouldn't believe it. Women just don't behave like that.'

'I don't see why,' says Celia, not without feeling.

'What a cosseted life you lead in your Bedford Park enclave, Celia. Don't you know anything about women?'

'Of course I do. I am one.'

'Well then – put yourself in her place.'

This is getting too surreal for words.

'What do you mean?'

'Did I tell you I'm doing marriage guidance counselling?'

'You did as, a matter of fact,' says Celia wearily.

'Well – believe me, Celia – women may think they just want a little affair on the side – but actually – they always end up wanting more. I know. I've seen the results.'

'What about the men?'

'Oh – they are *much* better at infidelity. Most of them can go in and out of adultery without batting an eyelid. Ninety-nine per cent of women think they can and end up doing the reverse. Almost always they end up falling in love. Or at least wanting more than just a one-night stand. I can tell you . . .'

'Well – this heroine *doesn't*,' says Celia warmly. And she thinks, Please shut up.

'Then she's no better than a prostitute and your readers won't like her at all.'

'That's a terrible thing to say,' says Celia, matching her sister and sitting bolt upright. 'Anyway – she didn't charge him – so she can't be.'

Steady, she says to herself, steady now. For the urge to give her sister incontrovertible proof of this grows strong.

'It may be a terrible thing to say – but it's true. Take my word for it. If you're going to make this book convincing, you can't leave your heroine driving off like that. Nice women – no matter how misguided – just wouldn't do such a thing. Besides – it's not reader-friendly. You'll have to give her at least one more meeting with the fellow. Even if it's only to say a really drippy goodbye.'

As always, Isabel speaks as if she is the only person in the world who knows what's what.

'Rubbish,' says Celia passionately.

'Hoity-toity,' says Isabel.

Celia grits her teeth.

'By the way,' she says, finding a suitable diversion. 'Your dog's crapped right in the middle of the lawn.'

But such a statement is small recompense.

'Oh, she's always doing that. Don't worry about it. We've got a pooper-scooper. Dave'll do it when he comes home.'

'You've got a good marriage, Isabel.'

Celia looks at her.

Isabel looks back.

'True,' she says, with immense satisfaction.

Funnily enough, though, what with pooper-scoopers and shitty kidney meat, and despite everything, Celia would still rather be herself than her happily married sister.

How odd we are.

They go in to eat.

Alex decided long ago that if he never saw another marital aid it would be too soon for him.

It was partly the introduction of these items into the relationship with Miss Lyall that wrecked him for his holiday in Brittany. For the first few days in France he felt like an untrained novice who has been forced to wrestle a series of Turkish heavyweights. Miss Lyall proved to be the owner of quite an array of these accoutrements, being a modern sort of a girl, and the first time she produced her little attaché case containing them he felt a definite loss of *sang-froid*. Partly excited at the prospect, partly embarrassed, he had launched himself into this new dimension with notable results: sex takes longer, he found, and its delights

244

become more leisurely (or more arduous, depending on your stamina) when organly flesh is protected from direct contact by latex. In her sexual liaisons Miss Lyall usually has to introduce them sooner or later ... it was not criticism of Alex, as she pointed out – absolutely no criticism at all.

Many of her attaché case items took the form of condoms with attachments – small bobbles, big bobbles, warty bits, size-doublers (Alex found this latter rather insulting) and the like. Alex, usually of middling range in the duration between the desire and the spasm, has found himself, once kitted out in one of these, able to last astonishingly well. They also have other advantages: they not only provide tantalisation and inflamement, but they also double as birth control. Miss Lyall has an unfortunate inability to take the Pill and although modern science has done wonders with the cap and the sponge it is nice for her, sometimes, to let the man take responsibility. Since she takes so much responsibility in her life, one way and another, this is not surprising. She certainly is a liberated woman. Alex had to hand it to her for that. And he quite often did.

It was after that rather difficult weekend at the Queen's Brough that Miss Lyall first introduced Alex to the contents of her attaché case. And they certainly did imbue the proceedings with restorative zest. It was like having a teenager's capacity matched with a mature man's sexual thought pattern: while the body could go on and on and on, the brain kept saying things like, Good Lord old man – haven't you had enough? The brain had had enough quite frequently – but that little layer of latex said that his thrusty bit had not. It was all very strange. Pleasantly unpleasant. There being little he could do, without loss of honour, he yielded himself up to it all as enthusiastically as his hard-pushed body would allow. He even contributed an item of his own. A few weeks into all this he remembered that he had an item at home somewhere which they could try. The recollection pleased him since, in particular, he wanted to show his avid partner that she was not the only one who knew what was what, inventively speaking. So he hunted about the bedroom for the one he had bought to use with Celia and which she, far less game than Miss Lyall, complained made her sore. He found it in a drawer amongst his wife's underwear and sneaked it away with him on the next illicit *nuit d'amour*. Somewhere around the middle of July this was, and Miss Lyall was entranced. Such gestures of contributory thoughtfulness were not usual in her experience.

They, and Dirty Harry, were at it all night.

It was after that particular session, testing in the extreme, that Alex had another judge to see very early the following morning. And it was during that dawn drive, when he began hallucinating and seeing cows and sheep doing grotesque sex acts all over the inside lane of the motorway, that he began to think things were not quite so wonderful after all. He had hit a plateau of tiredness and it was affecting his brain. Why, one of the sheep appeared to be winking at him out of its curly eyelashes. A frightening experience. One that he ought to heed. When domesticated farm animals appear to be giving one the old come on across a hedge there is certainly room for reappraisal. Especially if the animal in question is a sheep – than which there can be no more stupidly grotesque creature alive in the English greensward. This is not to say that Alex might have been less worried by some other animal making suggestive faces at him, it is merely to say that – since it was a *sheep* – he was aware that the situation was very bad indeed ... but pride drove him on and it was, eventually, (much to Alex's relief) Miss Lyall who finally ended the affair.

She did so much earlier than she had intended, it is true, but then, for some reason, she had gone off sex with Alex – maybe it was because he had started to look peaky, or maybe it was because he had begun to bypass foreplay and go straight for intercourse. Quite a few of her chaps did this eventually, but none *quite* so early on. Miss Lyall had no illusions about affairs like these, but she was quite fond of foreplay, indeed, curiously, during those hot middle weeks of August she had found herself enjoying it better than she had ever done before. By then, for some reason, intercourse seemed less and less important: she could only blame Alex's loss of style for this. The more she wanted the prelude, the less he seemed inclined. (Alex's logic in this matter was the quicker he got it over with, the quicker he could get off to sleep, which seemed fair enough to him ...) And so she told him, point-blank, just before he was to leave for France, and just before she was to leave for Corfu, that it had been fun but – well – all good things, as they say, all good things ...

Alex shook hands with her over a Campari and soda, resolved never to get entangled with another woman again and went off to France an exhausted wreck. As we are already aware.

Celia's passivity and lack of demand throughout this whole episode has helped Alex to see what a good, modest, agreeable woman he has married. He is not going to risk losing all *that* again in a hurry. How good Celia was in France, despite the weather. She left him alone to sleep, amused herself and the children, and seemed quietly contented, whenever he surfaced, to perform the slightest of acts commensurate with his being her fleshly partner in life. A good wife, he came to see, the best kind of wife, he thought on the ferry home. Oh no, most certainly, he will never be unfaithful to her again.

And so restored was his affection for this paragon of his that when they returned to Bedford Park he even fashioned a placard out of some old crates, saying, 'Polaris Out. Free Nelson Mandela. Celia rules OK' and walked solemnly up and down their garden path with it – a joke which he enjoyed hugely, a joke which his neighbours enjoyed hugely, a joke which merely puzzled and slightly irritated Celia. She had by then completely forgotten their conversation in the conservatory on her birthday for she had other, more pressing, things on her mind. Still, it pleased Alex to have done something ridiculous like that – perhaps Celia was right, perhaps he had got a touch too staid. He looked across at his wife and saw that she was still a young woman – a surprisingly dewy-eyed one nowadays – beautiful to behold with her smile and that melancholy light in her eyes. She had the sort of unfocused quality of a virgin princess about her. He broke out into a sweat. Bloody hell (this is where the children first picked it up, of course), to think he might have lost her . . .

Alex dropped Dirty Harry into the water off Kew Bridge on his way home one September night and, as it floated away, he felt immense relief. He could now settle down into middle-age and really concentrate on work. Which he did and work had been getting more and more interesting ever since. As his life returned to normal the Brandreth case became increasingly convoluted and challenging and Alex's self-esteem (so bruised by Miss Lyall, he realised retrospectively) returned. This was far more enlivening than illicit sex. The more convoluted it got, the more Alex thrilled to it. He was back on form and really going places again . . .

So – on this particular October day (the same as the one in which we have left Celia) – another interesting aspect must have developed for Miss Lyall (now merely a business colleague like any other) has requested a meeting alone with him first thing in the morning. He has left his little family with regret for they looked particularly appealing as he said his goodbyes. The sight of Celia, sitting up in bed, flanked by Henry and Rebecca still in their pyjamas (they are having something mysteriously called an 'occasional day', an odd aberration peculiar to the state system of which he does not approve but cheers himself by saying that they will soon be in the private sector where such fecklessness will not occur), made him wish – just for a moment – that he did not have to leave them so early. Still, duty, the Brandreth case and Miss Lyall call and must win over mere familial sentiment. He set off in fine fettle. A man at one with the world. Respected member of the community, chairman of the Neighbourhood Watch, and one whose sense of humour is restored to the locale, following the witty incident with the placard.

Gaily, he had waved up at the judge in his bedroom window, bonhomie and community spirit exuding from him. He had lost touch with everyone during those few hectic months (and is therefore unaware of Tom's little contretemps with the law) but he feels back on form now. Part of it all again. He will chair the next Watch meeting with alacrity, he vows, as he drives off in the direction of Miss Lyall's office in Knightsbridge. The children wave to him from the bedroom window. How sweet and innocent they look. How he loves them. He turns the radio on to Radio Three. Someone called Gesualdo is 'This Week's Composer'. He bears with the strangled noises which he does not much care for. They sound like an animal in pain. They sound like madness.

At around the same time that Celia is roused from her bed to answer the door to a well-pleased Mrs Green, he gets to Knightsbridge.

And just at the very moment that Mrs Green is feeling cheered in Bedford Park by her lugubrious watching of Celia and the children at their late breakfast, he finds a parking space. As he arrives at Miss Lyall's building Celia is dishing out orders regarding the clearing up of leaves in the garden and while he waits to enter his erstwhile lover's office his wife, in her kitchen, is remembering that funny incident with Mrs Green and the condoms. When he finally enters the office and Miss Lyall suggests that he might like to sit down, Celia receives the telephone call from Hazel. And if she is upset by *her* news, it is as nothing to the upset Alex feels from *his*.

At the instant that his relaxed and enquiring buttocks meet the dove-grey hide of Miss Lyall's office chair, Celia is shouting at Rebecca. At the moment when Miss Lyall offers him a very large whisky (despite the early hour) Celia is telephoning Isabel. And as the reason for the whisky becomes more and more dreadfully clear to Alex, Celia is preparing to set off to Isabel's for the day. And Mrs Green, as we know, is up a step-ladder taking down the curtains, watching the car go, preparing for her soul-soothing rummage, her voyage of discovery.

Such simple domestic detail, one way and another.

Such a mundanity of events.

So where, you may ask, is that beetle?

It is coming. Assuredly, it is coming. Its ghostly little spectre is even now creeping out from the woodwork. A tiny, insignificant shadow that brings a whirlwind in its wake.

The meal is over. Rebecca and Henry have disgraced themselves in Celia's eyes by eating almost everything and asking for seconds. The 'almost' which they left was the pastry. At least her nephews ate theirs. Weaned on Isabel's cookery they go for quantity over quality every time. Their aunt makes a mental note to get them something really nice and complicatedly electronic for Christmas so that they can have endless pleasure taking it apart.

Isabel looks at the discarded pastry on her nephew's and niece's plates and shoots Celia a look of utter triumph.

'You may be writing a book,' she says, 'but you can't make pastry, can you?'

Celia says, 'Fuck the pastry,' and feels much better.

Isabel gives a little shriek to try to cover the words and says loudly, 'Boys – take Henry and Rebecca out to the kitchen and get the chocolate ice cream. You can eat it in front of the telly.'

Off they all rush, kitchenwards.

'Did you hear our mother say fuck,' says Henry with pride.

The elder of his two cousins shrugs. 'Now, where the fuck is the ice cream,' he says nonchalantly.

Henry is firmly back in the shade.

'Oh fuck,' says Rebecca. 'I don't like chocolate ice cream.'

'Oh yes you do,' says Henry. 'You only said that so you could say It.'

'I'll show you some of our dad's magazines,' says the younger of the two cousins, doling out lumps of melting brownness into dishes. 'He keeps them in the shed. They're all about fuck.'

'Going to eat it in the garden, Mum,' he calls. 'OK?'

'Fucking well better be,' says his brother, low-voiced but wondrously assured.

Henry and Rebecca gaze at him admiringly.

'Yes,' calls Isabel cheerily. 'But make sure Brillo doesn't lick out the bowls. She may have worms.'

An investigation of the turd on the lawn shows this, indeed, to be the case.

Henry says it looks like their ice cream, which puts him in the running again.

Hearing the childish laughter from the garden Isabel sighs happily.

'They get on so well,' she says knowingly. 'And you are obviously overwrought at the moment. Why not leave them here for the weekend? My boys will be a good influence on your two. You could finish your book or something . . .'

So Celia agrees. Isabel has spare toothbrushes, spare pyjamas, even spare knickers for Rebecca.

'Why on earth,' says Celia irritably, 'have you got girls' knickers when you've only got boys?'

'Because we do fostering sometimes.'

Celia passes a weary and defeated hand over her forehead. How good this sister of hers is, and what a strong, honest relationship she has with the well-adjusted Dave. Celia feels quite mortified by it.

'They'll have a lovely time,' Isabel continues, as she scrapes the gristle and rejected pastry off the plates. 'Lots of fresh air in the garden and they'll probably make a den in Dave's shed. They often do. Dave doesn't know they've discovered the key. Ha ha . . . let them get on with it, I say . . .'

She begins to carry the dishes out to the kitchen, stopping and turning in the doorway. 'Oh,' she says, 'and by the way, we don't use swearwords in this house. I know you're tense but it really isn't good for the children. They don't like that sort of thing.'

Celia apologises and helps her sister by drying up the dishes she has washed.

The children have to be called several times before they emerge from the shed at the end of the garden. In her heart Celia hopes they will want to come home with her, but they do not.

'Bye Mum,' they say happily, putting their ice-cream bowls down in the kitchen. Each bowl is shining clean, well-licked by the dog. Later, after Celia has gone, Isabel will absent-mindedly put them away unwashed in the cupboard and they will all have a slight tummy upset after Saturday lunch tomorrow. Which is not unknown in this household. Dave will blame his grumpiness, which lasts well into the week, on this, though its fount is somewhat more esoteric. One of his favourite centre-spreads seems to have spilled something unmentionable over herself right where it matters so that he can no longer see the fulsome pinkness of what she reveals. The shed roof must leak. He spends the whole of the following weekend reviewing its water-tightness while Isabel, pleased with her husband's handyman thoroughness, cooks a liver casserole and thinks she will pass on the recipe to Celia sometime. Perhaps she needs the iron.

So, at two-thirty, Celia wends her way homewards, relieved of her children and expecting to find nobody in and a house newly be-curtained and ready for the winter darkness. She looks forward to a few hours on her own. Somewhere along the day she has picked up a need to think about a few things. She almost begins to believe she is writing a book, so deeply involved has she suddenly become with the peregrinations of its heroine. Isabel's words have made a salutary impression. Sod her. But Celia is resolved. Her heroine has said her last goodbye to her hero in the hotel. Her heroine can settle down now. Her heroine is prepared for – nay, welcomes – the opportunity to slot back into normality. Whatever the future holds it cannot be worse than what has gone before. She sought her Vengeance and she gained it, just as she planned, and the chapter, the book, is closed. Of that much she is sure as she drives thoughtfully along her road.

If Alex hallucinated on copulating livestock while driving in the past, those visions were as nothing to the pictures he sees before him as he drives home now. He has gone straight from Miss Lyall's office to the nearest pub. True, he has paused momentarily to telephone his secretary and say that he will not, after all, be in today but that was more the action of a man conditioned to do such things, rather than the action of a man fully in control of himself. For Alex, an hour or so later and negotiating the Fulham Road, is feeling each hundred yards that takes him homewards like a station of the cross. Gesualdo is still playing away on Radio Three. To Alex the music is soothing now, very controlled, and completely and utterly sane. Whereas he is by no stretch of the imagination any of those things.

He is heedless of cutting up other vehicles. He is heedless of bus drivers' yearning hand signals that turn into 'V' signs as he overtakes and slides swiftly on. Alex is driving back to Bedford Park and his little family like a man in a dream, like a man in a very bad dream. He is also, quite out of character, three-parts drunk. Which may, in some wise, account for the hallucinations. But not entirely. For they are the visions of a man drowning in his past, of a man who would, if he could, go down for that third time and never resurface. What he sees mocks him. What he sees is infinitely worse, infinitely more terrible than a raunchy sheep giving him the eye. What he sees, he is sure, holds the key to his undoing. Alex mourns for himself as he drives on and he gives himself up to the floating sights that hurt his eyes and make his stomach contract. How could he have become this man? And what are these sights that unfold before him? What surrounds him so palpably that – were he to dare – he knows he could reach out and touch? They are his undoing, certainly. For they are visions of rubber goods which come, menacing, inexorable, across his windscreen, over the dashboard, and slip through the locks and tensions of his seat belt. He relives the torture of holding Miss Lyall's ankles up against a wall until his arms, let alone his latex-with-bobbles-shod penis, come near to breaking. He sees himself drinking wine from her orifice and crying exultantly that he is coming, he is coming . . .

And for what? For what?

For what, he asks himself.

For this shame. For this humiliation. For this, only this, and this is all.

Familiar sights, like the landscapes of de Chirico, become draped in unspeakable objects. Dali has let loose his art upon the Hammersmith Flyover and the steeple clock tower, which once soared grey and stony, is now bedecked in an Ann Summers special; waving in the breeze it no longer tells the time but makes suggestive, plastic movements that promise pleasure unlimited for Miss Lyall and her kind. Dirty Harry reigns again, risen from the Kew Bridge swamp and wobbling his bobbles as Alex passes by. He blinks, to no avail. The blink merely transforms Fullers Brewery into a structure of Japanese Delight. Alex wails. The noise makes perfect harmonies with Gesualdo. This is, without question, the worst journey of his life, made worse, unbearably worse, by his having no one to blame but himself. As Miss Lyall said to him, her last words as he left her in that dove-grey scene of tranquillity, 'You must accept liability, Alex. It is nobody's fault but your own . . .'

The spectre of the beetle quickens across the floor.

Alex drives on.

Bedford Park is at hand.

The neighbourhood judge, out for a stroll, gives Alex a little wave. Alex, focusing, shrinks from such encounters and bends his head down towards his driving wheel. The judge, somewhat surprised, says to himself that if he hadn't known old Crossland better he would say he was plastered. And a man of criminal tendencies. Perhaps, he thinks, as he continues his stroll, he should fully retire after all. His judgement is clearly not what it was.

Alex parks outside the house, and takes some small and bitter comfort from the absence of Celia's car. He looks at his watch. It is well after noon. She has probably taken the children (he gasps at the pain of the thought; my babies, my babies, he thinks, rather as his wife did once) out for the day. Well – thank Christ for that. He can have a few hours to gather himself. There is an urgent demand in his bladder. Whether the drink or whether the nervous agony, who can say? Whatever it is he must get to a lavatory swiftly. He runs up the path, he pushes his key into the front-door lock – the very sight of that piece of metal fitting so snugly into its counterpart sends waves of further agony through his vitals. Even his key has become sexually explicit. Is there no rest from these terrible conceits?

He tears headlong into the downstairs cloakroom, relieves himself (not looking at the fleshy item in his hands as he does so for he cannot bear to see it, that cheat, that dissembler, that betrayer of good), and feels very slightly better. Sleepy even. Not surprisingly since he is unaccustomed to morning drinking, and Celia was not up in time to see that he ate breakfast (you see, you see, how small things make for larger ones? Alex would have been far less intoxicated and more able to cope if his wife had put a plate of toast and poached eggs before him). So he drags his poor, worn body slowly up the stairs. He has not even paused to close the front door (the Neighbourhood Watch such superficial pleasure now), nor to flush the cistern. Niceties are things of the past. Alex can only dwell on his iniquities – lusting encounters fill his mind like whips, sex objects loom in his mind's eye castigating him with their lubricious charms, the snares of titillatory items will not cease their dancing in front of his eyes: many-faceted sheaths, crutchless knickers, glossy photographs of Caribbean mouths holding Anglo-Saxon organs flap at him shamelessly. He opens the door to the bedroom with a head bowed in humiliation, in fear of what to do next.

He shuffles in. There is only one safe thing to do next: one thing above all others that is desirable. He moves swiftly towards the marriage bed. His only thought is to plunge upon it and sleep, sleep, sleep, until (dreaded moment) the calls of his wife, and his dear, *dear* children, rouse him to face reality.

He is mid-plunge, unable to stop himself from falling into the soft, forgetful enticement of the duvet, when he notices the final vision: this then is Hell; this then is his Orwell room. It is the worst hallucination possible. It is Mrs Green, the oatmeal of her face aflush with scornful pleasure as she sits so upright, so statuesque for one so shrivelled, upon that spreading receptacle of connubial charm, the bed. And she is holding aloft, like some decayed Statue of Liberty, an ivory-white vibrator which whirrs and shakes in her hand.

He cannot contain the plunge and down he goes. And his head, unable to stop itself, meets the duvet which should have been so soft; he feels pain. He opens one eye, he does not want to but he does, and he sees, oh Torture, that he has landed on another recognisable accoutrement, another vision from his steamy past. He sees a jar of Vaseline. Is there any pain worse than the sharp edge of a Vaseline jar on the bridge of a nose? At that moment Alex does not think so. He focuses both eyes now and looks beyond the pain in his nose to a yet more familiar and dreadful sight – a packet of condoms, opened, used, nestling up to his cheek. They seem to speak to him, the crinkling Cellophane is real upon his skin, and he knows, much worse, that Mrs Green is also real. He rolls over on his back, spreads his legs and arms akimbo and gives vent. Why not? He has earned the right to cry out. And he does. The noise would curdle the blood of a vampire. Not surprisingly it also has its effect on Mrs Green who leaps to her feet and runs, in a demoniac splendour, out of the room. She had sought for something, she had needed vindication, she has it. In abundance. Two sets of cutlery and a change of curtains is as nothing to this. She can retire now. And she will.

Those lisle-clad, vein-coursed, Stiltonesque limbs become the legs of Sebastian Coe – she grabs her mackintosh, her plastic bags, crams her beret down on to her head, and rushes like the wind out of the front door. Down the road, through the carpet of russet leaves she goes, sending whirls and eddies of the fruits of autumn in her wake as she flees. She is holding on to her beret with a hand that still clutches the vibrator – the final trophy – the final trophy, whatever it is. She is, as yet, unsure ... And

Mr Crossland drunk and all over the bed like that! Well! Riches indeed! Perseus has finally arrived.

The judge, returning with his bottle of milk and his Crunchie bar, looks on, amazed. Can this be Bedford Park? he asks himself. He shakes his head and enters his own home. Why do other people always seem to have the fun? he wonders. Must he always only sit ponderous and in judgement upon them? Life is very unfair. He would much rather, really, be in amongst it all as a participant. He *will* retire, damn it. There must be more to life than *this*.

Late in the afternoon Celia enters the house nervously. She has found the front door on the latch, which is alarming. Silently she glides along the passageway to the back room which is orderly and empty. The kitchen is also empty, although she notices with annoyance that there is still washing in the washing machine – her summer curtains by the looks of it. Why hasn't Mrs Green hung them out? Perhaps it is a gesture of defiance because of the Big Thrust. Her irritation grows: to leave the curtains to crease like that; and not to latch the front door properly. If only she had the courage to dispense with the woman. She puts down her bag and goes to the lavatory where she finds the ultimate insult: Mrs Green has not even seen fit to flush it. That settles it. Celia has grown in stature and confidence during the past few months. Her troubles have made her considerably tougher. And her sister's sanctimonious counselling today has certainly not helped. She will no longer be anybody's football and she jolly well *won't* put up with her cleaner any more. An unflushed lavatory is the final insult. The sacking of Mrs Green will be the first pleasurable pebble in the avalanche and *après* her the deluge. She has yet to discover that this pleasure has been pre-empted. Later this evening a note in Mrs Green's unwholesome spidery scrawl will be pushed through the letterbox, stating that their arrangement is terminated and referring obliquely to 'Goings-On'. Its effect, when it arrives, will be like a wart on an elephant, for by then Celia will have other greater matters on hand.

Stomping up the stairs she feels a pleasant, righteous anger. Which is a much better emotion than she has been experiencing of late: powerlessness.

Right-ho then, she counsels, this is it. Mrs Green, you have had your chips. I don't suppose you've left the bedroom as you should have done either . . .

The grim delight is very swiftly wiped away when Celia opens her bedroom door to find her husband stretched across the bed. She blinks, once, twice, thrice, but the picture does not remove itself. Alex is there all right and in the dying mid-afternoon light she sees other things as well. She sees her guilty purchases from the chemist strewn about him so that the bed resembles a wicked Hockney still-life. And there, on the carpet, is the dog-lady's book, wherein she hid the plain and daily condoms (well – the one that was left) . . . And her husband is pillowed on the Vaseline jar which had been tucked behind it. Oh my God. Has she been discovered? It certainly looks like it.

'Alex,' she shrieks, quite loudly for she has a terrible feeling that he may be dead. Overcome, perhaps, by her perfidy. But no. His eyelids flutter, he breathes – he even moans.

'Alex! Alex! What on *earth* are you doing here?'

He rolls over and puts his hand to his head. Lunchtime drinking, a jar of Vaseline and deep sleep have taken their toll. At the very moment when his legal mind should have been as sharp as an onion on an open wound, he is fuddled. He sits up. For a moment he has forgotten the recent past. He smiles, he blinks, he puts out his hand in welcome to his wife. And then he remembers.

Without recourse to his training he eschews silence, and damns himself.

'Oh Celia,' he says. 'I'm going to be a father.'

Several things occur to Celia. Predominant among them, but only for a fleeting moment, is relief. She has not been discovered. But the relief is, necessarily, short lived. The other things that occur are these:

Alex is drunk.

Alex is mad.

Alex *is* drunk.

Alex is *not* mad.

And if Alex is not mad then he must know what he is saying.

If he knows what he is saying and Celia is not pregnant then somebody else must be.

It does not take an inordinate number of brain cells to work out who.

With dexterous cunning she gathers up the scattered articles from the bed and thrusts them out of sight. And only once she has done this does she give her feelings permission to be verbal.

'You rotten, stinking, double-dyed louse,' she snarls.

Alex holds his head and says nothing.

She sits down very hard on the bed and pokes Alex in the ribs. Each poke is expressively accompanied by a word. 'Rotten, rotten. Stinking, stinking. Louse, louse, louse . . .'

'I know,' mumbles Alex.

'Well?' says Celia, crossing her arms. The truth is she is rather enjoying herself.

'I only slept with her once,' tries Alex.

'Don't give me that,' she says, poking him again. 'I know all about it. I've even seen you . . .'

Alex finds this startling since he is still bound up in those terrible visions and can only assume his wife means *in flagrante delicto* – if he thought matters could get no worse this disproves it.

'My God,' he says. 'When . . .?'

Celia gets brisk. 'It doesn't matter. The point is you are lying, and I know you are lying, and please don't lie any more.'

So he tells it as it really was and Celia listens without interrupting.

When Alex has finished she says, 'Wasn't she on the Pill?'

He shakes his head.

'Well why on earth didn't you take precautions?' An odd response given the circumstances perhaps – but a valid one.

'But we did,' he says, and the mystification is genuine. 'My God – we did nothing but take bloody precautions – dozens and dozens of them. Do you know, Celia, I even –' He decides to come completely clean. 'I even took that one I bought for us and used that—'

'You mean Dirty Harry?'

He nods mournfully.

Celia remembers something.

She remembers the last time she saw that profligate item.

She remembers it hanging in deflated fashion from her knickers and Tampax drawer as she rammed the wood home on it, once, twice, thrice. And she remembers its punctured response to the harshness of the treatment. She had holed it.

'Oh bugger,' she says.

Alex's little pansyflower resurfaces. In the way of women everywhere Celia robes herself in guilt. Somehow she had always known things would turn out to be her fault.

And the beetle, of course, skips its happy way across the phantasmal plain.

What with maternity leave and nannies there is no reason for Miss Lyall to dispose of her child. Indeed, now that the morning sickness has gone, she is looking forward to motherhood. It will be a challenge. One at which she, unlike the rest of her sex, will be extremely successful. It is no good telling Miss Lyall that all expectant mothers secretly think this. She will discover, in due course, sometime next March, that the head cannot rule the heart where motherhood is concerned. She will flounder in that vale of tears and joy just like the rest, but without benefit (or otherwise) of a husband to share the shadows and the sunshine. For Alex is most certainly not going to marry her. Celia did offer, very nobly, to let him go but she received such a look of stricken terror for her pains that she made no attempt to be noble. All Alex could do at this fine gesture on his wife's part was to shake his head and say over and over again, 'I should have thought of you only, and my little ones . . .' Which made Celia think, quite suddenly, of Oliver Cromwell, with a creeping goose-fleshy notion that her cabalistic dabblings in that poxy book seemed to have more than a little validity. Henry VIII to Anne Boleyn indeed. Surely what Alex was putting her through was quite as good as having her head sliced neatly from the shoulders? Anne may have had a French swordsman for her little neck but Celia had a French letter. The corollaries were clear. She pushed the little book under the bed with her toe. She would have to deal with it at some point – a ritualistic burning perhaps? But not yet.

'If you are not going to marry the woman what do you intend to do?'

Celia is sitting next to her husband and massaging his neck. He looks, as he feels, quite ill. And his nose has swollen on one side which makes him squint. Oddly enough this makes Celia feel rather tender towards him.

'I shall support the child, of course.'

Celia's tenderness deepens. This is the old Alex talking, the fair-minded, socially conscious, liberal Alex.

'Good,' she says. 'So you should.'

'And probably Miss Lyall too.' He does not add that this is the only way to avoid scandal. Miss Lyall told him that. Very directly.

What she had said, incontestably, was, 'A man in your position, Alex – a high-flyer, a leader, peaking in your career – you can't afford scandal at this stage. Look at Brandreth. No, no – I am quite prepared to be discreet providing you do not neglect to provide . . .' And she had smiled, pleased at the rather witty use of words and pleased at their incontrovertability.

Alex winces, recalling the smile, and his voice is much weakened at the memory. 'So I'm afraid it will necessitate some financial changes.'

Celia's tenderness diminishes. Not for what he says, but for the pompously businesslike way he says it. She removes her hands from his neck.

'I know,' he says. 'It's bad. But it can't be helped.'

261

'Like what?' she asks, prepared for sweeping changes – selling the house, taking in washing, becoming a Kissagram. The radicalism of it all has a strange allure . . .

He turns and looks with his pale eyes into hers which are bright and searching and eager with life. 'Oh God, Celia,' he says. 'Brace yourself. I'm afraid we won't be able to educate the children privately.'

Alex will be moved to remark many times in the years to come that women are a mystery to him. He will cite in perplexed tones his wife's response at this moment by way of example. For Celia laughs and laughs and laughs. She holds her sides with the mirth of it. And she says, when she can, 'My dear Alex. Just look at you. If you are a product of it then I'm bound to say it may very well be for the best.'

She laughs again and pats his sagging cheek. 'I was never convinced about it anyway and the local comprehensive seems rather good . . .'

Something shrivels inside her husband. He balances the two scandals in his mind – the illegitimate swelling of Miss Lyall's belly and his legitimate Bedford Park children cast adrift in an institution of the state. Perhaps they should move? 'I will resign as chairman of the Watch,' he says. It is all he can think of to say.

And Celia, infuriatingly, laughs again. 'Do,' she says, thinking of the munificent Jo's husband. 'I'm sure they will find someone as good as you to step in. After all – there's no dearth of leaders hereabouts, is there?' She looks at her husband's sagging, greyish features and the tender bump on his nose.

And so much for the Celestial City, she thinks.

Endgame

During the next twenty-four hours Celia behaves almost immac-
ulately. Her only concession to the situation when speaking to
Alex is an occasional reference to 'Your Bastard' which has a
pleasantly deflationary effect. It is, she feels, not the sort of thing
a pansy, given the power of speech, would say.

When Mrs Green's note arrives Alex is apologetic. Celia is
delighted. Alex is even more confused by his wife's behaviour.

'I wonder what the "Goings On" were?' she muses.

Alex explains.

He says, seeking warmth and pity, that his behaviour was
unhinged due to circumstances. He thinks back and recalls the
terrible vision that confronted him as he dived duvet-wards. He
touches his nose. It is indeed still tender. He puzzles. He says,
'Celia?'

She says, 'Yes, Alex?'

He says, 'You've never thought that your cleaner was a little –
well – *odd* – have you?'

'No more than the rest of us, Alex,' she says pointedly. 'Why?'

'Well – it's the strangest thing – but I thought – when I
surprised her in our bedroom – that she was – well – holding
something – and that there were other – things – on the bed –'
He shakes his head. These last few hours have gone too fast
for him, the world has been too unkind. Others get away with
it – why couldn't he?

Celia blushes.

Celia says quickly, 'You had had a lot to drink, Alex. And you
had just learned about Your Bastard.'

He winces. 'All the same –' he rubs the back of his neck which
has grown tense again – 'All the same, I could have sworn the
woman was holding a vibrator . . .'

263

There is a rush of wind where his wife once stood. He hears her ascending the stairs with peculiar alacrity. He follows and finds his wife on her knees in the bay of the window scrabbling at the curtain hem which, in its winter weight and not surprisingly, conceals nothing.

'God Bless Tom,' she says triumphantly, sitting back on her haunches. No wonder she has lost her cleaner for good. Even his hurtful little game has produced some good after all . . .

Silver linings. Silver linings in everything. If only we have the wit to recognise them.

Alex is finding Celia's behaviour a little tiresome. And he is rather hurt by it.

Where is the sorrow?

Where is the pain?

Should she not show *some* emotion?

Surely what he has done is worthy of some kind of suffering response?

He says, 'You and I should talk it through, you know. If we are to rebuild our future together we should begin it now.'

And Celia, surprising both of them, says, 'Who says we have one, Alex?'

Which makes him regret his little foray into psychology very much indeed.

'Oh, now look here, Celia . . .' he says.

'No, you look here . . .' she replies.

'Don't be unreasonable . . .' he argues.

'I'm not being unreasonable . . .' she argues back with vigour.

And thus, for a few blissful moments, they are back to being a perfectly normal married couple again before Alex remembers that he has lost a lot of ground in the normal marriage stakes.

'I love you,' he says.

'Well,' she says, still sitting on the floor, 'you've got a very funny way of showing it.'

She looks up at him. He looks down at her like a naughty puppy.

'What would you say, Alex, if I said that I had done the same as you?'

'I wouldn't believe you and I should say you were being extremely silly.'

'Would you now?'

'I would.'

He puts out his hands to help her up. 'And I would also say that if you did think of doing such a thing, then the only person you would be hurting would be yourself.'

She shivers. In Raynes Park they would say that someone had walked over her grave. She refuses his outstretched hands and continues to sit on the floor. Beneath the bed, just visible, she sees the spine of the book of love letters.

'Alex,' she says meekly. 'I think I would like to go away for a little while.'

Celia shivers again. Not surprisingly, for it is colder in the bedroom now that the evening has drawn in. Faint upon the air is a vestigial whiff of bonfire. It is extraordinary to think that it is still out there smoking exiguously despite the length of time it has been untended. The harbinger of autumn, the transatlantic's fall. It should be damped down for safety before they turn in . . .

Alex, all tenderness at this clear indication of feminine sensitivity, says, 'Of course, my darling. But perhaps you will come over here first?'

And then, rather beautifully, they make love. Celia, distant, dreamy, moves like a serpent about his body. Alex, delighted to be free of artificial methods, responds to the serpent like a tiger unleashed. The love-making is long, hot, tender and perfect. At the end of it the light in the room is silvery. Alex runs his fingers along his wife's spine which is naked and damp and just as it should be. He bends and kisses it and as he does so he says, 'It's a long time since I've made love like that.' He smiles down at her. 'How about you?'

'Um,' she says.

Which he takes to mean Yes.

They continue to lie there. After a while Alex says, 'Where would you like us to go away to? Shall we take the children with us or what?'

And Celia, rolling over, says to the ceiling, 'No. And no. Where I am going away to neither you nor the children may come.'

There is the shortest of pauses, the merest hint of a change in his breathing pattern before he says, 'Of course.' And, 'Certainly.' For he has regained too much ground to risk the losing of it now. 'You need some time on your own. I can see that. So where would you like to go?' He is still plucking delicately at her back.

'America,' she says.

Alex has a spasm; the flesh between his finger and thumb, which belongs to her, is pinched very hard.

'Alex,' she says sharply. 'Don't do that.'

'But you don't know anyone in—'

And then he stops. Of course, *that*'s it. Susie is in California. He relaxes again.

'Fine,' he says. 'I'm sure you'll be well looked-after.'

'Why do you say that?'

Alex tenses. Celia is going peculiar again.

'Because that's what friends are for.'

Celia sits up and gives him a hunted look.

'You'll need your suncream,' he says, by way of making conversation.

Celia moves away from him.

Alex has gone peculiar again.

They both eye each other nervously. Alex breaks the silence.

'All the Californian sun,' he hazards.

And Celia laughs, annoyingly, as he has come to expect.

'I'm not going to stay with Susie,' she says.

'No?' He too sits bolt upright. 'Where then?'

She says, 'Maine.'

'Main what?'

'The place Maine. In America. I want to go there and see the fall.'

He takes another deep breath. After all, what is one more piece of madness in amongst so much?

'Fine . . .' he says. 'That's just fine. Yes, yes, Maine in America it is, then.' Another deep breath. 'When would you like to go?' He doesn't believe it will happen but he must go along with it. He must go along with anything just at this moment. 'I can get my secretary to fix that up. You just say when . . .'

She does.

'Sunday.'

'But my secretary won't be in until Monday!'

'Then you'll have to go to the travel agent's yourself.' Celia's voice is very sweet but Alex recognises that it is an unyielding sweetness.

'I'm afraid it's not on, you know,' he says firmly.

'Oh? Why?'

'Because,' he suppresses the satisfaction, 'you'll need a visa.'

A little voice – which turns out to be hers – says, 'No I won't.'

'My dear girl,' he says, 'you will. Everyone does.'

'They've stopped requiring visas, Alex.'

'And how do you know that?' he asks fondly.

'Because,' she says in a small but certain voice, 'because I've already found out . . .'

And twenty-four hours later he is in a travel agent's, telephoning his wife, with the news. She can fly to New York on Sunday night, stay over, and go on to her final destination on Monday morning. If she *really* means it. He waits for her to say she does not but there is only silence at the other end.

'Will that do?' he asks wearily.

'That's perfect, Alex,' she says happily. 'Book it.'

She puts down the phone.

She rings Isabel.

'We'll collect them first thing in the morning,' she says, 'because I'm going to America tomorrow night. I've got to do some research for my book. I think, after all, that you were right about the ending. It needs looking into.'

Isabel is torn apart. She wants to be right. She also wants Celia's selfishness to be wrong.

'They've had a little tummy upset,' is all she can think of to say.

'Not used to your cooking, I expect,' says Celia.

It is a suitably equivocal statement.

Before Alex returns from the travel agency Celia goes up to the bedroom, pulls out the drawer of her dressing table and fumbles beneath it. Sellotaped to the underside is a torn-off corner, very scrumpled, of an old *New York Times*, with an address and telephone number scribbled on it. Mrs Green may have found ecstasy when she removed Celia's curtains and discovered where the Personnelle vibrator had rolled all those months ago: she may have added to that ecstasy by finding the condom packet and jar of Vaseline; but she missed the most important hint of sexual activity it has ever been Celia's privilege to own – the name and address of that attractive, desirable, and manifestly satisfactory one night stand. Celia's hand shakes with the pleasure of the memory as she holds the newsprint tightly.

They collect the children from Isabel's on Sunday morning. They are pale, and hollow-eyed, sated on videos, computer games and midnight feasts.

'They have enjoyed themselves,' says Isabel. 'Bless them. We've got more room for them to run around and play in our neighbourhood. Put some colour in their cheeks. You ought to think about moving out here, Alex.'

'You never know,' he says, thinking about house values. 'We might have to.'

Dave, emerging from his shed dark-browed and unsmiling, says, 'Bit of a come-down after Bedford Park, wouldn't it be?'

For once Alex lets the shaft lie.

As they make their farewells and set off down the dull street, Isabel calls for them to stop. Alex, about to say something rude regarding Your Sister, remembers even the pleasures of justifiable sarcasm are forbidden to him now. He brakes sharply, the tyres squeal, he winds down his window and gives his sister-in-law an astonishingly kind smile. One that so amazes her in its complete uniqueness that she says to her husband later, 'He's changed, Alex. Mellowed somehow. He's obviously much, much happier nowadays . . .'

She has stopped them to hand over a photograph.

'Meant to give you this ages ago. It's the one I took at your birthday, Celia. For once everyone's in focus and looking really happy. Susie and Tom, you and Alex – pity Hazel didn't make it, still . . . It's a nice souvenir to have – isn't it?'

Alex retains his smile, stamped like the image on a coin, sideways and grinning as he waits for Celia to remark on the gift.

'I don't think,' she says to her sister, 'that I could ever be happier again . . .'

'Ah,' says Isabel, looking at Alex who is still staring bonnet-wards. '*Isn't* that nice?'

Just as they are leaving for the airport a car pulls up. A small grubby Fiat, a woman's car. A very familiar one to Celia. Out gets Hazel, looking most un-Bedford Park. She wears no make-up, her face looks crumpled and blotched with emotion.

By contrast Celia is looking in the pink. In Susie's dress she could take on the world.

What a long time coming this friend of hers has been. A moment later and she would have missed her altogether.

'Cee-ly-a,' she groans. 'God am I glad to see you. We must talk.' She pauses and looks at the pigskin suitcase on the pavement. 'Off again Alex?' she says. 'Don't worry – you just say your goodbyes and I'll put the kettle on.'

She moves to walk up the path.

'Um – Hazel,' says Celia. 'What's up? How was the weekend?'

'*Don't* ask,' says Hazel. 'I've just had the most terrible row with that stupid, insensitive woman—'

'Who? Jo?'

'*Her*. God, what a friend *she* turned out to be.'

'What was the row about?' Celia asks this but her second sense tells her that she already knows the answer.

'Poor old Caspar – in a strange place – what can you expect? I said that to her – I said What Can You Expect? Anyway—' She stops, looks at the group around Alex's car. 'Well we can talk about that in a minute. Bye Alex.'

'He's not going anywhere,' says Celia. 'I am.' She opens the car door and slides herself in. 'And if Caspar were mine,' she says, 'I'd smack him. Hard. Right where it comes out. That's what I did to Henry.'

Hazel gapes.

So, for that matter, does Alex.

Hazel runs to the window which Celia kindly winds down.

'But you'll be back for my party? You're not going to let me down?'

'I don't know yet,' says Celia, but she smiles. 'Possibly.'

'But I need you to be there.'

Celia softens. She looks into her friend's sorry face.

'A word of advice on fortieth birthday parties, Hazel my love.'

'Yes?' she asks eagerly.

'Heavy on the food.' She smiles. 'And easy on the games. For what it's worth . . .'

And she winds up the window, smiling still.

Henry and Rebecca are well content with the prospect of the very big present their mother has promised them on her return. The uniqueness of being left alone with their father heralds an interesting new chapter in their lives, a chapter which is not without possibilities. Alex will have his work cut out and will more than ever find himself valuing his wife in the days ahead. Celia has yet to remind him that Mrs Green will never return.

On the plane, comfortably settled with gin and tonic fizzing in a little plastic glass before her, Celia takes out her book to read. Anyone watching her will find her actions very odd. For before she opens the book she closes her eyes. It falls open randomly, this book of famous love letters, though whether it be in the section called 'Beginnings', or the section called 'Endings', or any of the sub sections in between, she has yet to open her eyes and find out.

Such a harmless little pastime, on the whole, she thinks, willing her lids to flick apart. Chance is as good as anything else in the determining of one's pattern of existence. Life is, after all, just a game like any other, save perhaps for one sorry difference: that the struggle is also the prize. So thinks forty-year-old Celia in her comfortable airline seat as she focuses, at last, on the open page before her . . .

A selected list of titles available from
Faber and Faber Ltd

In case of difficulty in purchasing any Faber title through normal channels, books can be purchased from:

Bookpost, PO BOX 29, Douglas, Isle of Man, IM99 1BQ

Credit cards accepted. Please telephone 01624 836000, fax 01624 837033
Internet www.bookpost.co.uk *or* email bookshop@enterprise.net for details.